DOMINOES

A Compelling Love Story

J. L. Harvey

LEIGH PUBLISHING
ISBN-13: 978-1-8380841-1-0

CONTENTS

ACKNOWLEDGEMENTS

Many thanks to my friends for insisting they read this story when my confidence had deserted me – Ali, Trish, Sue and Katie. To AB for her design ideas. Also to Christopher Walker from York St. John University for giving me the best advice when I began, which was *'Find your voice.'*

To my publishing team at Kindle Book Publishing for support and guidance.

And of course, to my family, for their tolerance during the many months it took me to write this novel.

AUTHOR'S NOTE

One look across an airport changes Jake's life. The girl in the red shoes. A stranger. He can't take his eyes off her. Or the man with the world-weary look on his face, who doesn't deserve her. He should have heard the warning bell. But it was too late already. He's in it for the ride... for better or worse.

That one chance encounter sets off a chain reaction with consequences that race out of control – just like a line of dominoes ready to fall. One touch and down they all go.

The story unfolds through the eyes of four characters, but it is Jake and Amy who are the ones we root for – Jake, a teacher, in a tired relationship with a colleague, Amy married to an unemotional older man (they have a child) who has left his first family for her. They form an instant attachment, a shared love of life, but the affair is fraught with setbacks and a fear of discovery. All the characters have obligations to others, and, as in life, we never know what lies ahead of us.

I hope the prospective reader will recognize some incident or meeting that could have changed the course of their life in a similar way. It is a story with all the complications and heartache that an illicit passion can evoke, but the compulsion to carry on outweighs reason. Inevitably, the affair doesn't just affect the two people involved, but also their families and friends and the social structure of their lives.

I have tried to write about characters we could meet in everyday life, characters that live and breathe, with recognizable voices and behaviour and who reflect the fact that living, after all, is many shades of light and dark.

'Our lives are made up of choices. Big ones, small ones, strung together…
a line of dominoes ready to fall.'

Abigail Haas, 'Dangerous Boys.'

Prologue

It was the shoes he noticed first. Red and pointed, with ridiculously high heels. All over the concourse were sturdy lace-ups, trainers, slip-ons. People were expecting something arduous, something to be endured.

Not the girl in the red shoes, though. She was ready for an adventure.

The passengers were shuffling towards the boarding gate in an orderly queue of sorts, clutching boarding passes and passports. She was in the line ahead of him, a slight figure in white shirt and jeans, dark blond hair woven into a thick plait down her back. She was standing beside an older man. Jake found himself trying to catch a glimpse of her face and as she looked across at the grey day beyond the windows, rain smattering the glass, it was her profile he saw first; small straight nose, high cheekbones, smiling mouth. Lovely.

From that moment, he kept her in his sights. Trying to be casual, turning his head to see round a father clutching a wriggling child, peering under the raised arm of a tall woman in a beret, looking over the shoulders of the couple in front of him. It was as though he couldn't bear to let her go. He couldn't explain it.

The line was four wide and he relaxed as it came to a stop, while the flight attendant made an announcement over the tannoy. *'Calling Mr. and Mrs. David Jackson. Could you please come to Gate Number 11 immediately?'* He could see her more clearly now. She was talking excitedly to the man next to her. No, not exactly - she wasn't talking *to* him, she was talking *at* him. He was tolerating the chatter as though she were an irritating child who had to be humoured, his head turned slightly away. But she kept looking up at him and smiling. The man was good–looking; even Jake could see that. Hair turning grey, lean, tanned face, tall and straight-shouldered. At ease with himself. He wore a navy polo shirt and well-cut trousers and over his shoulder, a soft leather satchel. Urbane. That was the word that came to mind. Ok, she was obviously with him.

Jake shrugged his shoulders – well that's life – and he pulled his battered hold-all closer to his foot. Not much to be taking with him, but how many pairs of trousers and t-shirts could you wear in seven days? He looked away and felt something like the old restlessness creeping over him. *Let it all go*, he told himself. *You're off on holiday. Can't you just be normal and enjoy yourself for once.*

He re-read the instructions on his ticket to relieve the monotony of queuing and to distract himself. Someone's headphones were leaking tinny sounds and Jake turned to find a young boy behind him, who seemed to be in another world, head down, nodding to the rhythm. He remembered the last time he'd been on a plane, sitting between a talkative archaeologist and a large man who'd sneezed all over him. The downside of travelling on your own.

He sighed and rubbed his chin with the back of his hand. His mind wasn't in the mood to be distracted, anyway. It was behaving like a heat-seeking missile. He was searching the queue ahead again for the man and the girl, and then watching as they moved slowly forward.

She was perhaps in her late twenties (he wasn't good at guessing ages) but maybe younger – she had a naïve, questioning air about her. Her movements were sudden and quick, edgy almost, and as she talked, she kept tilting her head. She seemed bright in every sense of the word – shining hair, eyes that lit up, gestures that took in everything around her. God, she's something else, he thought. Alive in every movement and turn of her body, more obvious because the man beside her was bored, aloof, answering her with one-word throw-aways or a nod. Dismissive. Stupid bugger.

Jake closed his eyes, annoyed with himself, that self-righteous voice in his head telling him off – *you're watching her like some voyeur. Or a teenager with a crush on someone he's never met, for heaven's sake. Get a grip.*

The steady move towards the gate had come to a full stop. Someone was fumbling for a lost boarding pass, holding everyone up, while the stewardess gazed into space; the culprit was a woman in a long cardigan which had huge pockets, and after diving into those and coming up with nothing, she searched through her bag, papers spilling out onto the floor. The more she panicked, the more she scrabbled and floundered, looking up every few seconds at the irritated faces of the other passengers, who watched her as though ready to find her guilty of some crime.

But the girl wasn't irritated. She turned to the man in amusement and put a hand on his jacket sleeve, an intimate touch – it looked loving to Jake, who felt a twinge of envy. But no response, no reciprocal gesture. The man just wasn't interested. Why did it so annoy him? What had it got to do with him? Nothing. He didn't even know her. But he was unable to take his eyes off her. Or the man. Here was this cynical bastard with that world-weary look on his face who didn't deserve her.

The crowd moved forward again and the man leaned down to pick up his carry-on case. Someone stepped in front of him and, for a brief moment, he was left behind. And in the odd way that lines slide you forward and sometimes give you an advantage, Jake found himself beside the girl. She met his eyes as he drew level and words came out of his mouth that he'd only been thinking: 'I'd leave granddad behind, if I were you.'

She hesitated, looking puzzled for a second and then a smile spread across her face and her eyes filled with amusement - and something else – appreciation, perhaps – that someone had seen how things were. Jake bowed his head slightly in an old-fashioned gesture, an acknowledgement of some tacit understanding.

And how was he to know that this singular tiny exchange would set in motion a sequence of events that would turn his life around? Or that the consequences that would follow, dire and uncontrollable? If he had, he'd have felt a sliver of ice go down his spine. He'd have heard a warning bell. It might have stopped him, later, from letting his heart rule his head.

But perhaps not.

Perhaps there was nothing he could have done to change any of it.

Chapter 1

The front wheel of his bike skewed sideways, throwing up grit and tar as Jake struggled for control. No chance. It had him again. Bloody terrier from the corner house, lying in wait every morning, ready to dart out on scampering little legs, barking, its one aim to nail him before he made it through the gates. The pedal scraped the road and the only way he saved himself was by stamping on the ground, coming to an undignified halt, half-off the saddle. And watching of course, in their unhurried trek to school, were the latecomers, with their sardonic faces, all amused eyes and smirks, and even at ten to nine too weary to shout any verbal witticisms.

He shoved the bike into the shed at the far end of the car park and ran along the path round the side of the hall, its large glass windows reflecting the sun, slowing down to a walk as he reached the front entrance. He straightened his shoulders and pulled down his jacket, hoping his trousers weren't splattered with dirt and oil. He had to pass the office staff, with Mrs. Partington as commander-in-chief, and after six years of mutual mistrust, he still felt she was giving him marks out of ten for his performance each day. Beginning with the morning arrival.

He pushed against the doors and into the reception lobby, nodding to her through the open hatch and imagined he could read what she was thinking - late again, dishevelled, red in the face and shoes not cleaned. Such a poor example to the students. He tried to look nonchalant, shifting his gaze upwards to the words etched in gold on the nameplate above the hatch: 'Welcome to Forest Green Academy'. He smiled at the irony of its transition from Forest Green Comprehensive School to Forest Green Community College to its new status as an Academy, when nothing had really changed at all. He sensed Mrs. Partington was watching him and half-lifted his hand in greeting. 'Morning.' Her response was a bit long in coming. 'Good morning, Mr. Harper. Everyone's gone up.'

'Yeah. Right.' He quickened his gait, his rubber soles squeaking on the polished lino as he speeded up. Only two weeks into the new term and he would have to run the gauntlet of the staff room again to get to his usual seat.

He climbed the stairs two at a time, saw the door was open and hearing the buzz in the room, realised with relief that the daily briefing hadn't yet started. He must be on time. He could walk in without any sarcastic remarks or frowns directed at him. Dropping his backpack to the floor beside a vacant chair, he settled into it. In the next seat, Andy put down the newspaper.

'All is well in the world. Jake has arrived.'

'Don't make it worse. I'm not at my best.'

Andy laughed. 'When are you ever?'

A door shut, some hurried positioning, and he knew Tim had arrived, a sheaf of papers in his hand, with the deputy, Mr. Madden - no one used his first name - hovering at his shoulder, ready with the reprimands and carping, as though they were all naughty children.

I've been at this too long, he thought and turned his body so it looked as though he was paying attention and taking note of all the minutiae of the school day. *Thirty-two years old and I'm bored. Bored to the point where I'm beginning to feel like a leopard in a cage, pacing the few feet behind the bars that's the full extent of my territory.*

The briefing was finished, but over the general chatter that was growing louder, he heard Tim shout his name.

'Jake. Can I see you in my room before the bell goes?'

So, as everyone else gathered their belongings and headed out along the corridors to the classrooms, Jake followed Tim into to his room next to the front office. There was a discreet knock at the door and Mrs. Partington came in with the post. She walked across the room, almost bowing as she handed over a batch of letters, pretending Jake wasn't there. With those gimlet eyes and straight line of her mouth, she'd have made a first class spy. Tim manoeuvred round to the other side of the desk and motioned Jake to sit down. For a headmaster, he was a good sort. A bit casual, a bit careless of people's feelings at times, but he was bright and he could act decisively when trouble loomed, as it obviously was doing now.

'We've had a complaint.'

'Oh. About what?' Jake could hear the defensive rise in his tone. Almost unconsciously, he squared his shoulders, ready for battle.

'You gave Year 12 a book to read over the summer which the Reverend Shackleton found most offensive.' Tim steepled his fingers together as he leaned forward. 'Mr. Madden said he was furious and wants to talk to you about it.'

Jake groaned. 'How did he get involved? This'll turn into a five-act drama, now.'

'Well, he took the phone call.'

Jake could hear the whirr of the photocopier in the corner of the room producing page after page of paper and a phone was left to ring and ring in the office. It all added to his annoyance.

'Anyway, the Reverend is coming in this lunchtime. D'you want to hear his concerns?'

'Go ahead, but I can guess.'

7

'He says there was a chapter in the book describing the sexual act in detail and the word "fuck" is written at least three or four times.'

'He was counting was he?' Jake sighed.

There was silence as Tim looked at him, waiting. Flippancy wasn't going to work. He could see he was going to have to justify himself. '*The Handmaid's Tale*. Yes. A modern classic. Famous author, been on the exam syllabus for years, the word is used to stress the act – the mechanical reproductive process, with no love or sentiment involved. The story of a Handmaid. Hasn't he read his bible? It's all in there.'

'It's no good getting aggressive, Jake. He's a concerned parent, and you might try a bit of diplomacy. If you cast your mind back, you didn't handle the business of the ghost story too well, when it upset Mrs. Delaney on religious grounds. Remember?'

Jake stood up, shaking his head. 'It's bloody fiction, Tim. Can't they see that? It isn't real. And it's only the modern stuff they object to. Chaucer can be as vulgar as you like, but no one challenges that. It's medieval so it must be all right. Give me strength.'

'Yes, you're going to need it.' Tim smiled and shrugged his shoulders. 'Twelve thirty in here and I'll leave you to it. Calm down, listen to him, and try to explain. He knows the Chair of Governors, so my advice is – be conciliatory.'

The lesson bell cut short any further discussion and Jake hurried off to teach the first lesson.

But the whole episode had left him with a sour taste in his mouth and ill-tempered at the thought of spending his lunch hour with Reverend Shackleton, arguing the toss. In the eleven o'clock break, he decided he needed fresh air and walked round the perimeter of the school playing field. He didn't have to talk to anyone there.

Except for Nathan.

Thirteen years old and earnest, Nathan loved English. He loved writing poetry. He loved having Jake read it. He came sprinting towards him over the rough grass at the edge of the football pitch. Catching his breath and eyes full of expectation, he held out his exercise book.

'Sir, I wrote this last night. Would you have time to look at it? It's the best thing I've done so far. I don't have English till tomorrow and I wanted to know if you think it's any good.' He had the sort of expression that belonged to a trusting otter. Moist and unwavering, always hoping for the best, but deep down, fearing the worst.

Jake found he was smiling. Not many of his students wrote for the sheer joy of it. He held out his hand and took the book. 'Well, if it's as good as that one on the lightning strike, then it might get into the magazine. What's this one, then?'

'It's about a soldier. I was watching the news last night and an army unit was manning a road block and I thought how scared I'd be – you don't know who's the enemy and who's a friend - so I'm the soldier - pretending to be - and I'm imagining what he's thinking.' Nathan blinked and suddenly turned away. A group of boys was passing and he understood the rules he had to live by.

Jake stared after him and thought how sad it was that when you were thirteen and a boy, you had to pretend to be a football-mad, couldn't-care-less member of the pack. Don't be different or you get picked on. Perhaps that didn't just go for thirteen-year-old boys. Perhaps that was how life made you conform.

God, what a misery he was becoming! The sun was shining and he wasn't in Beirut or Afghanistan. What did he have to moan about? To cheer himself up, he stopped by the school fence and looked out over the Cheshire countryside. Heads of barley in one of the nearby fields was swaying, golden under a slight heat haze, and two trees marked out the horizon, like cut-outs in a charcoal drawing. He'd often wished he could paint, like his father had when he was a young man – capture visual images – he was sure those stayed in your head longer than words did.

A football thumped against his trouser leg and he turned with an automatic, 'Watch it, lads!' and saw it was a girl who scurried forward to retrieve the ball. Sending it back into play, she grinned over her shoulder at him.

He walked further, knowing lessons would start any minute and he'd have to move at a bit of a pace over the field and use the back entrance, but he didn't want to go in. The sun was warm on his face and arms and as he reached the far corner, he could smell the grass, earthy and sweet.

The bell, sounding hollow and distant through the still air, summoned him and as he cut across the rounders pitch, he saw Catherine coming towards him. She was wearing a green cotton dress and sandals, her long hair blowing back off her face, and she was smiling at him before she came close enough to speak. He tried to put on a welcoming expression but at the same time, experienced a sinking heaviness in his chest. He had the worrying sensation of being drawn in, of submitting to something he only half-desired and he couldn't explain how or when it had come to feel like that.

'Jake,' she fell into step beside him. 'The bell's gone.'

'I heard it. I was just heading back.'

'I know there isn't much time, but I didn't get chance to see you before break. I thought you might be worried about the complaint.'

'Does everyone know about it?' He was angry now rather than just annoyed. Did everything have to be so bloody public?

Catherine flushed. 'No, no. I overheard some of the English department talking in the corridor, that's all. Passing the gym. They didn't seem worried. Anyway,' she lightened her tone, 'you get this sort of thing at least once a year, don't you?'

He grunted. He didn't want her concern. 'Doesn't make it any easier to deal with though. I've still got to explain literary merit to parents, who probably haven't read the whole book.'

Catherine tried to keep up, taking two strides to his one. 'But I suppose he has a point…'

'A point? Who?'

'The Reverend. I mean the language in some of the texts you choose is sometimes, well…'

'Well, what?'

'Oh, you know. ..a bit…strong...'

Jake was silent. *How could you spend a year of your life with someone, who had no sense of you, had no idea what made you tick or what was important to you? Someone whose mind you really couldn't fathom.*

It was easier to say nothing.

'Jake,' she began, looking across at him as they almost broke into a run.

'Come on,' he said, as though he were concentrating on good time-keeping. 'I've got year 11 – they'll be killing each other if I'm late.'

'See you tonight?' Catherine ran alongside him, turning her head to watch his expression, her gaze never leaving his face as they approached the building. 'I'll cook supper.'

'OK. Fine. I'll tell you how it goes then.'

And he ran through the swinging doors as though he were running from a fire.

Chapter 2

Amy tried to stay beside Robert but the guests pushed her on; men in dinner suits and bow ties and women wearing long frocks, sweeping like a migrating herd along the parquet floor into the long dining room. The hotel with its arched doorways, frescoed ceilings and chandeliers certainly lived up to its five star reputation. And, across the room, twenty round tables were set with crisp white tablecloths and silver wine buckets and purple flowers. Against the walls, the servers stood, like regimental soldiers, backs straight, chins up, a folded serviette over one arm.

Amy looked ahead, with what she hoped was an impassive expression on her face. Best behaviour now. Not the kind of place to drink the wine too quickly and start discussing the minimum wage.

People were peering at place names as they moved forward and she had to steer round a waiter and an elderly man who blocked the way as he concentrated on slowly pulling spectacles out of his top pocket. She looked round to see if Robert was still behind her and saw that he'd stopped to talk to a colleague, John Ross, from Galt Smithsons. They had their heads close together, talking earnestly, and it was obvious it wasn't a casual chat. Amy recognised the times when she mustn't interrupt. She looked round, hoping to see someone she knew. Then she could relax.

The noise in the room rose to a sharp, discordant babble as the guests greeted each other - 'Oh, John, good to see you here.' 'Pat, what *have* you been doing!' And so it went on, each recognising one of their own, a mark of being a member of the club. An exclusive club at that. Amy breathed in and fought her way through the chattering groups. She didn't hear any words meant for her. Just the clamour shutting her out. Funny how with all her own friends in the book club, the young mothers at the school, the people she knew at the *Mercury*, she was confident and unselfconscious. Here she was only too aware she was different. And for all the wrong reasons. Too young, too outspoken, too guilty of the ultimate crime. She didn't know which was the worst offence. Not much she could do about it. There would be no forgiveness.

The evening hadn't started well. She had been sitting in front of the antique mirror in the bedroom, applying purple mascara that had looked black in the shop, and deciding her nail varnish was too bright, when she heard Robert's voice from the hall. 'It's seven o'clock, Amy.' She tried to keep her hand steady, refusing to be rushed. What did ten minutes matter, really? Tucking a strand of hair back into place, she caught the defiant look in her reflection. It was all bravado. But like a counterweight, the voice of reason told her to quicken up, not to start the evening with an atmosphere. The night was important to him and she was being unfair.

She fixed the locket on its black ribbon round her neck and stood up, pulling a silk jacket over her dress. Pretty good. She headed for the stairs, hoping her contact lenses were in the right eyes so she'd be able to read the menu.

In the hall, the dog, woolly, slobbering and affectionate was lumbering towards her as she made for the front door as fast as her high heels would allow. 'No, Jasper, not now.' She managed to push his nose away from her skirt, avoiding meeting his sad eyes.

'Why isn't he in the kitchen?' Robert, exasperated, grabbed the dog's collar and led him back through the door, Jasper's feet scrabbling on the tiled floor.

'I suppose Jemma let him out. She's too soft with him.' Amy stepped out under the porch light. 'You haven't said how I look.'

Robert glanced at her. 'You always look wonderful.'

'Nice to be told, though.' She called back into the house, 'Bye, Jemma. Make sure Harry's in bed by 7.30.'

Robert blew out his cheeks. 'Honestly, it's like a Tom and Jerry cartoon getting out of this house. It's *your* dog, Amy. Why don't you take it to training class, or something? Or send it away to a school for wayward animals for a month?'

Amy smiled and steadied herself to get down the drive without tripping on the paving stones. There wasn't much she could say. She knew Jasper was hopeless but he needed defending.

'He's only two. He'll calm down.'

'When he's too arthritic to run,' muttered Robert, but she could see that his mind was already on the evening ahead. He opened the door of the BMW and climbed into the driving seat. When he'd fastened his seat belt, he turned to face her.

'Cecilia White, Amy. Are you concentrating?' He waited for her to look at him. 'She's the important one tonight, remember. She's not married to Paul, but they live together. And there's a child from her marriage to a lawyer...' He started the car and moved off down the drive.

'Yes, you told me. Yesterday.' Amy could hear the edge in her voice. 'I'm an old hand at this now, Robert, I'm not twenty-two any more. I've learned how to behave so I don't make you cringe.'

She caught the change of expression, the set of his jaw line and the way his eyes whipped away from her and she knew she'd end up regretting any facetious remark tonight. She put out her hand and touched his as he held the steering wheel and although he kept his eyes on the road ahead, he nodded to acknowledge the silent apology. It was a few moments before she realised he was struggling to say something.

'What?' She clutched her bag, its sequins cutting into her fingers.

It took too long for him to find the words and when he did, his voice sounded hard and flat. 'You do realise...' he cleared his throat. 'I know at times I expect a lot. Too much, probably. But it's just that...when it's to do with work, everything has to go well.' He glanced across at her and when he was again concentrating on the road ahead, he said, so quietly she could barely hear him, 'I love you very much, Amy. You do know that?' But it wasn't really a question. It certainly didn't sound like one. It was a statement, words spoken aloud to reassure himself. 'I wouldn't change anything, however difficult it is at times.'

'Robert, it's all right.' Amy stared into the fading evening light, silently reproaching herself for her impatience with him, for her unwillingness to compromise. After all he'd given up for her. She shouldn't forget that. From the start, he'd always seemed the one in charge, the decision maker. But she had an uneasy feeling that now, too much depended on her to keep them steady. Like in those circus acts, where all the acrobats stand on each other's shoulders and form a tower and they're relying on one poor devil at the bottom of the heap to keep their balance. 'You're just anxious about tonight. I wind you up sometimes, and I don't mean to.'

Robert changed gear and a silence fell over the car until he braked at the first road junction. 'Just do me a favour, will you? Stay away from human rights. Animal rights. Whatever. Try not to be controversial.'

He shook his head, as if he thought it a vain hope.

They headed down Parkside and the longer they didn't speak and the silence spread into minutes, the longer the atmosphere simmered with underlying tension. She found herself looking out at the pavements filled with Friday night shoppers and early theatre-goers, couples arm-in-arm, hurrying past store windows and restaurants. And the bars with doors opening onto the street, where she used to spend Saturday nights on the town. A long time ago.

She opened her bag and checked for the second time she had her mobile with her. Just in case Jemma needed her.

Robert glanced over. 'Is it on silent?'

She didn't answer. Instead she asked, 'Is Sophie going to be there?'

'They're at our table.'

'Good. She makes me feel less like a kid at a grown ups' party.'

Why did everything she said lately add fuel to the fire? Shut up for once, she told herself. Just shut up and smile.

The car glided to a halt in front of the Hilton. 'I'll drop you here and go and park. Just wait in the lobby till I come.'

And then she was out on the pavement and climbing the wide stone steps of the hotel, watching the car disappear round the corner. She stood still for a few minutes, smoothing out the creases in her skirt and wondering what she would be doing with the night if she was alone, if she could choose to go anywhere in a city that was just coming to life.

Other dinner guests began entering the hotel, moving round her as she stood, a look of confidence, the one created for strangers, fixed on her face. She waited, searching the street for Robert's familiar figure. After a few minutes, he came striding towards her, taller than most of the groups he passed. Elegant in his black tie and evening jacket, she saw him for a moment as others would see him for the first time, passing on the street. You would turn and look, no doubt about that. Handsome in an old-fashioned way. Walking with assurance, with a grace about him that made him instantly attractive.

Yet with a look of detachment, of a man not easy to know. What on earth had he seen in her?

When he came up the steps and put his arm round her to hurry her inside, she wanted, more than anything, to have his approval, for him to say something that had meaning only for them, intimate words that would carry her through the evening. But in the foyer, there was Jane and Paul Barrington, the Haywards, the Pattersons, others she scarcely knew, the world of business and money and politics she had no part in. Except as a wife. She had accepted that as part of the deal. Why should it bother her after all this time?

Now, as she threaded her way through the room to their table right in the centre, she nodded at people she vaguely recognised and consoled herself - at least the meal would be good.

A hand rested on her shoulder and she turned to see Mike, hair ruffled, fancy waistcoat a little askew, with Sophie beside him. He kissed her cheek and gave her a hug. 'How about that! You're on our table. I made a special request and it was granted.'

Amy laughed. The night was looking up. 'Well, it's nice to know someone wants to sit with us. It's set for eight though. There must be others.'

Mike was circling the table, examining the place names on the silver-edged cards. 'Ooh, perfect manners tonight, Amy. We're with the big hitters. No bad language.'

She gave him a knowing look. 'You've no need to worry. I've been primed.'

'And don't you start stirring,' Sophie told Mike, lowering her voice as others began to join them. 'Love the outfit, Amy. Very London.'

'Thank you, Sophie.' She wanted to say more. She wanted to say, thank heavens you're here, with your warm smile and kind eyes and easy manner. Thankful for a bit of approval in amongst the hostility, none of this judging business – someone who sees me as I am...

'The Grahams are on their way. They won't be long.' Robert was hurrying up to them to take charge and do the introductions. He was good at this, she thought. He always remembered names and partners, and family situations and hobbies so people responded to him, deferred to him, felt safe in his hands. 'Cecilia, I'd like you to meet my wife, Amy.' A tall woman in a long black dress and beaded jacket had been following him. She inclined her head in greeting, before Robert directed her to a seat beside him. So, Amy realised, the partner, Paul, was obviously in her care. Ok, she could handle small talk. What was he interested in – boats, rugby, fishing? Here we go.

Amy wasn't aware of Mary Aisgarth approaching their table, until she was standing behind Robert. She was a large woman, all cleavage and jangling bracelets and a certain stature that exuded entitlement and self-confidence. She looked around at the guests and paused, slightly, as her glance took in Amy. Leaning over Robert, she touched him lightly on the arm and he rose from his seat to shake her hand. She clasped his as though they were lifelong friends.

Then she said, quite distinctly, in a throaty voice and loud enough for the whole table to hear, 'And how is Paula? You must give her our love. We do miss her.'

Chapter 3

The music blasted out over the park, loud in the still air. Catherine made her way up the tree-lined path, circling the gardeners' hut and the duck pond, where a young couple were throwing bread into the murky water. September and the sun was low in the sky but still warm, as she walked quickly, knowing she was rather late. It was Wednesday night after the long summer holiday and the youth club was coming into its own again, making enough noise to shake up the whole neighbourhood. As though it was coming out of hibernation. *'Breaking into Heaven'* pounded in her ears as she drew closer to the squat, wooden building, the open door shedding light onto the shrubbery. They'd have to turn down the volume before the complaints started again. But she'd missed it all. Funny, but she was at home here. Tony couldn't run all the activities single-handed and it was good to feel needed.

But she could hear her father's voice in her head:

'You want your brains testing, wasting your time with that lot. Not even getting paid for it.'

He'd never understand why she put so much effort into the club. And it wasn't just her father. She knew some of the teachers thought the same - after a day at work, they'd had enough of teenagers. Had enough of playing a role. But Catherine didn't have to play a role here - she didn't have to work at being clever or efficient. She didn't have to pretend. She could be herself.

Earlier, she'd dressed in joggers and a t-shirt, pulled on trainers and a fluorescent bib, and tied her hair up in a pony-tail. A quick wash, no make-up and out on the street, the pavements dry and the air still warm. She set off running, glancing at her watch to time herself. A breeze was blowing and her spirits lifted to be in the open air, feet hitting the earth, finding a rhythm, enjoying the sense of freedom running gave her. She'd always felt like that, even as a child. She'd followed her two older brothers as they'd explored the fields near their house, trying to keep up as they raced, heedlessly, ahead of her. She learned to rely on her body, to enjoy the exhilaration of being physically fit. And after what had happened in that last year at university, when everything had gone wrong, it had saved her.

The five-mile run had left her with no time to go back home and change her clothes, so she'd headed for the park, only ten minutes late for the opening. The smell of onions cooking rose from behind the building, where the mobile van was selling burgers and chips. She manoeuvred round a pile of bikes, which were heaped across the entrance. She kept thinking back over her day – a frustrating one because she couldn't rid her mind of the same nagging thought – Jake's unwillingness to commit, his lack of interest in making their relationship more…well, permanent. She needed to speak to him but kept putting it off. She should have braved it at the weekend, but wasn't sure what his reaction would be. If he'd be angry. And suddenly, because she wasn't paying attention, she was thrown off-balance when two teenage girls charged out of the club, red–faced and arguing, shoving her backwards.

'Hey, be careful.'

They gave her a brief glance, as though *she'd* been at fault and strode off into the park, their voices loud and shrill and full of anger.

Catherine climbed the steps into the long, low-ceilinged room and looked around for Tony. The music seemed to be vibrating into the soles of her feet and thumping through the air. There must have been fifty voices shouting to be heard above it, a discordant chorus of talk and shouts and laughter. But although it was noisy, there was no sense there'd be trouble. Not with Tony in charge. She'd always imagined running a youth club would need a calm, patient organiser, and that wouldn't be how you'd describe Tony. He was often quick-tempered and hard-headed. But he was caring and sensitive to everyone's problems. He understood teenagers. And his dry sense of humour made them laugh. So somehow it worked. And they respected him. No one was going to push their luck here and in this neighbourhood, you needed that.

All she could see of him was his blond head at the far end, as he stood between two boys. It was the usual stand-off, both claiming the table-tennis bats. She pushed her way through the groups, hands reaching out to her as though they were all friends together. As though they were all the same age.

The two boys were glaring at each other, some sort of disagreement over who was next in the table tennis rota.

'Lads, if you can't sort yourselves out and take turns, then it's not on,' he was saying, looking from one to the other, his eyebrows raised. 'Shall I toss a coin, or are you going to work it out?'

He saw her and waved. When Catherine first met him, she found him intimidating, with his uneven features and pock-marked skin and the way his face seemed set in a scowl. But then he would engage with some kid and smile and she could see something good-natured in that face and, after a while, she came to like and trust him. He was prepared to put himself out. And he often did, taking the youth football team on trips, organising barbecues and discos and raising money for the ones who seemed to have little home life or were too poor to pay up. Yes, he could be unpredictable, blow his top about something that annoyed him, but he'd forgotten about it five minutes later. And he never bore a grudge. But as far as anything else about him…she knew little… she accepted he wanted to keep his private life private. If he didn't want to tell her anything personal, then ok, it was fine with her.

He was waiting for the boys, with their belligerent stance and glaring, to make up their minds. Eventually, one boy half turned and handed the bat to the other one.

'Here. Didn't want to play anyway.'

Tony smiled and patted him on the shoulder. 'That's the spirit. Real sportsmanship. Thanks, Kyle. Your turn in twenty minutes.'

Catherine was shaking her head as he came towards her. 'I don't know how you do it,' she said. 'If that'd been me, they'd have been at each other's throats by now.'

'It's called brinkmanship. And… I have a secret weapon.'

'Which is?'

'They know I'm a black belt.'

She was laughing. 'You're not.'

'No.' Tony was laughing too. 'But it's all about perception. They see me as invincible.'

They were heading for the small room, the office that was more like a cupboard, where the kettle and the Jaffa cakes were kept. The latest track on the CD player was Amy Winehouse, 'Back to Black', plaintive and haunting.

'They think it's the spinach I eat which keeps me so strong.'

'They're too young to remember Popeye, Tony. Even I only know because of my dad.' She rinsed two mugs in the tiny sink.

'Yes…well. Anyway, glad you're here. Enjoy the summer?'

She didn't know how to answer. 'Pretty quiet, really. A few weekends down South. Went to Loughborough on a sports course.

That was all right.'

'Thought you'd be going away. Somewhere warm. And exciting.'

'No.'

The pause lasted a moment too long.

They both began to speak at once. 'Well, it's been...' Tony began.

'I meant to be early, but needed a run. Sorry.' Catherine cut him short. 'Thought I'd got plenty of time. Hasn't been an easy day and running relaxes me...' She stopped herself. 'Well, gets my adrenalin going. You know? Anyway, I wanted to get organised and see how many acts for the show we've got already. I know there's plenty of time, but still...' she made the tea and leant against the wall so she could look out over the hall. 'I can see Ryan and Matt – they were keen to do something from One Direction. But they needed three more to make up the group. Which is a bit of a long shot.'

'Yeah.' Tony rubbed a weary hand over his face then narrowed his eyes. Catherine knew he was going to come up with objections. 'Don't know how good an idea this is of yours, Cath. We were lucky last year. Not so keen this time and you know why. We can't afford to have any trouble – either during the rehearsals or for the three nights of the show. It could all blow up in our faces if we have any more complaints.'

'I know.' Catherine knew he was right. 'I'm sorry. I keep thinking I shouldn't have suggested it again.' She put her tea and the Jaffa cakes down on the table. 'But I've told them now and a lot of them are so keen – I'm sure they won't ruin it for themselves. And, remember, even *you* couldn't get over them wanting to give half the money we raise for Help for Heroes. Shows they think more about what's happening in the world than you'd imagine.'

'Well, some of them have family in the army, so they probably know more about it all than we do. I suppose that makes it worthwhile.' He nodded his head. 'OK, we'll get helpers nearer the time to keep everyone in line. Some parents would opt in. Just try and keep tabs on the Harris twins. And Eddie. If you think there's anything brewing, tell me fast.'

Catherine was looking through the door and frowning.

'What?' Tony followed her gaze to where a tall boy, dressed in black sweatshirt and denims, slouched against the wall, arms folded, watching the mayhem in the room. Not with interest, but with a patient, calm expression on his face. He stood alone, but that wasn't the only thing that marked him out in a singular way. Catherine had never seen anyone with hair as white, or a complexion that was so pale he looked as though all the colour had been washed out of him. It gave him a wraith-like appearance. Even his eyelashes were white and his eyes, a light, faded grey.

Catherine sighed. 'Lucas on his own again.'

'Yeah. Nothing changes. Tried to get him interested in the football team, but he just gave me that tired smile of his and turned his back.' Tony's tone softened. 'He's not rude or anything, he's – well, impossible to work out. I know there's problems at home – the police were round there last week. Some sort of domestic row. Can't be easy to live with.'

'No. But he's older than most of the others. Doesn't he have any friends his own age?'

'Not that I've seen him with. But you'd think he'd be bored with this lot. It's odd that he keeps coming.'

'Perhaps he needs an escape. From home, I mean. He's fifteen and it's a funny age, I suppose. Anyway, Tony, it's not as though he does nothing. He's good with the younger ones – gets their equipment out and sometimes I've seen him going over their homework. He even tried to teach Noah the guitar last year.'

Tony looked across at her. 'True. He's much happier with them. And he seems to be really keen when *you* ask him to do anything.

Perhaps he's more at home with women. I'll bet he'd help you with the show – be, like, an assistant. I'm sure he'd do it.'

'That's a thought.' Catherine noticed how still Lucas had remained, surrounded by all the noise and scurry; how little he moved his body, how unchanged his passive expression. 'Perhaps giving him a job organising something'd give him a bit of status with the others as well.'

'Don't think he cares about that really. But go ahead. Make him stage manager.'

She wasn't sure that was a good idea, but perhaps it was what the boy needed. Something to be involved in.

They were standing close together in the small space and she suddenly caught a look of concern on his face before he lowered his eyes. Surely it wasn't concern for her? Had she made it obvious that things hadn't gone well over the summer? She felt embarrassed if he was thinking she needed looking after. Or if he was sorry for her. Her old feelings of inadequacy flooded back and she turned away from Tony's gaze which seemed a little too earnest. Why did she always need people to think well of her, to approve of her choices, to make her feel she was doing ok? Surely by now, she was old enough to have gained some self-esteem. But even telling herself this didn't help.

She put down her mug, wiped her mouth and moved towards the main room. She'd get down to business. 'Have you got the sheet handy with the list of acts? I put it in the drawer. I'll start going round and see who's still keen and who I can persuade. Need auditions though, don't we, if we don't want it to be a disaster. I'd like you to be in on those.'

'Sure.' He nodded. 'You do that. I'll help when I can.' He rummaged in the drawer, and produced a folded sheet, a little dog-eared and stained. 'Think twice about letting Shona do her thing. She could easily think a belly-dance'd be cool!'

Catherine took the sheet. 'OK. I get it. They need to be aware of their audience.'

'Exactly.' Tony lifted his mug in agreement, and she sensed he was watching her as she picked her way between the computers and the stage area. She decided it was nice that someone cared. It was comforting in a way.

At least, for once, he hadn't asked about Jake.

Chapter 4

Robert was conscious of staying quiet and very still, as though he was sitting in a doctor's waiting room. The rain pattered gently against the leaded windows and the sound seemed unnaturally loud. His hands circled the glass of apple juice in front of him but he didn't drink. He didn't eat the two ginger biscuits on the plate either. He just waited.

The phone call had come, as they always did from Paula, as a harsh reminder of his responsibilities. And his guilt. Sunday afternoon and he'd been in the lounge, reading the Observer supplement, while Harry sprawled on the carpet, trying to build a red car from Lego.

'Can you get it?' Amy had called, so he'd gone into the study just in time for the phone to stop ringing. But almost immediately, it rang again. Even before the caller ID lit up, he'd guessed it was Paula, a shrill summons, he knew, even before he'd heard her speak. This would be another situation he'd have to handle. It could be anything from the car's flat battery, to lifts for the children, to a blocked guttering. In Paula's eyes, any problem had the potential to develop into a crisis. She'd always been a worrier. And Robert had always been there to take charge of everything until he'd left her to fend for herself with three young children. Difficult to escape a betrayal like that.

Her voice was soft and anxious, as though she didn't want to be overheard. There was an urgency in her voice that chilled him. 'I think you need to come, Robert.'

So as soon as he'd put the phone down, he'd pulled on his coat and, hearing Amy coming down the stairs, he'd stopped with his car keys dangling from his hand.

'Is it Paula?' she'd asked. A simple query, no judgement in the tone.

'Yes' he said, grateful for her understanding. 'I shouldn't be long.'

He'd climbed into his car and driven through the country lanes back to the village, so familiar with the houses round the green and the old tree standing on the edge of the grass where the children always played out. His windscreen wipers beat out a steady rhythm as he drove up to the house. The damp day matched his mood, grey and dismal and, with a stab of nostalgia, he thought of his own childhood in his parents' house in Beaconsfield – where his mother still lived in solitary grandeur – how in his memory it had always seemed to be summer, heat waves shimmering off the lawns, stone flags hot as he walked barefoot, down to the stream, French windows open early in the morning and in the afternoons, lemonade cooling in an ice bucket. Selective memory, of course. But in this part of the country, whatever the time of year, it always seemed to be raining.

He pulled into the driveway and sat for a moment, listening to the dying whirr of the engine. He had no idea what he was going to say. He'd shied away from the emotional stuff all his life - yet now, he was forced to deal with something so difficult and awkward, he was at a loss. But Paula expected him to have the answers. And he owed it to her to try. No, not 'owed'; he didn't need reminding what his obligations were.

He entered the house through the back door into the kitchen as Paula was putting a casserole dish in the oven. She turned towards him, drying her hands on a tea towel. A moment of discomfort, an adjustment to the space that separated them now, filled the room. He had wondered many times, and with some dismay, how it was that someone you had spent so many intimate years with, someone you once knew so completely, could become such a stranger. In her case, the hurt he'd caused her – well – that he *could* understand, but what threw him was how the distance, the separateness didn't lessen as the years passed.

'She's in the dining room.' Paula pushed her hair back from her face. 'Don't say I rang you. She'll guess, but don't say.'

Now, he sat in the quiet and waited. He looked at his daughter across the table, her dark head bent over her work, thinking that she wasn't so different from him at seventeen. Clever, hard-working, conscientious. True, she did look thin and pale, but was there really anything to worry about? Was Paula making too much of this?

Holly had been scribbling away on a large A4 pad, constantly looking at the textbook propped up in front of her. She put down her pen for a few seconds, not raising her eyes. Then she frowned, flexed her fingers, and resumed her writing. Robert leant back in his chair and let his eyes wander round the room, so much the background to his life at one time, and so little altered. Except for the photographs round the walls and on the oak dresser. Faces smiling at him – the children in their school uniforms, looking careless and windswept in the Lake District, playing ball on the sands, an older couple at a dance, holding hands, focus slightly blurred.

Not one photo of him. He had been wiped clean from the family group.

He turned his head away and rubbed his chin with his fingers. He should have had a closer shave.

As he watched Holly writing with such urgency, his anxiety grew. It began to dawn on him that she wouldn't stop what she was doing until he spoke but he hesitated, not wanting to disturb her intense concentration. She seemed so absorbed, almost unaware of him.

'Holly,' he said gently. 'Can't you finish this later?'

She kept writing. 'Won't be a sec. Just need to do this page.'

Another minute passed. Finally, she put down her pen and looked up.

'Sorry. Didn't mean to spend so long on it.' She shrugged her shoulders in a half-hearted apology and Robert noticed how her shoulder blades stood out against the thin green fabric of her cardigan. She sat back and folded her arms, cupping her elbows and hugging her body, as though she was cold.

He didn't know where to start. Easy to solve problems with figures and broadsheets and deadlines - but this – how do you get inside a teenager's head? Perhaps he'd been too distracted lately to pay enough attention to the changes. The whole business of children growing up was fraught, with enough problems without parents separating. He'd let himself believe that Holly had dealt with him leaving remarkably well. They'd remained close, going on outings, on holidays, to the cinema. And surely all the difficulties were in the past? It was years ago now. Half the families he knew were split down the middle. It might not have been his experience as a child - his parents were rock solid - but nowadays, half the nation, well, one in three marriages anyway, fell apart. But he couldn't quite fool himself. He had to admit to himself how much thinner she'd become. Her cheek bones were more prominent than a month ago he was sure and her eyes too large. As a little girl, she'd had such a round, smiling face. Now, her fingers looked almost skeletal.

'I wanted to get it done before Mum made me eat,' she said. 'And before Ben came home. He plays his music really loud and then I can't concentrate.'

'That's ok,' Robert gave an awkward smile and moved his chair a little further round the table, so that he could be closer to her. So that even if he didn't have the right words, he could reach out his hand. If that was what she wanted. What did she want?

Holly took another quick glance at the text book lying open on the table and seemed to find something she'd missed. There was a moment of stillness again, the only sound, the flick of pages being turned as she searched through the index. She looked ready to start writing again. Robert reached out and put a hand on her arm. Stop, he wanted to say, stop it, for heaven's sake. But he knew that would make her defensive.

'So, you're applying to Newcastle?' he said. 'Good university.'

'Yes. That's my first choice. But they want high grades and I don't know whether I can do it.'

'Well, if the teachers think you can, go for it. I'm sure they wouldn't encourage you if they thought you were aiming too high.'

'There's just so much to remember. I'm keeping four subjects, so I have to do extra,' she looked at him as though she trusted him to understand, as though he was the only one who would.

'Holly, you're being too hard on yourself. ' He tried to make his tone patient and kindly, but even to him, it sounded like the heavy-handed father. He started again. 'Holly, you don't have to throw yourself into all this in the first few weeks back. You've got a whole academic year before the exams. You'll be burnt out if you go on like this.'

'Like what?' she turned her head away and he could see she was fighting tears.

'Pushing yourself until you're exhausted. You'll make yourself ill.'

She pretended to pick up something from the floor and when she straightened up, he could see she wasn't only upset, but annoyed. 'Has Mum been bothering you? Asking you to sort me out? Saying I never go out and have 'fun' like other girls? Well, I'm not like other girls, Dad,' and her voice broke. This wasn't rebellion, he realised, this was a plea. *Be on my side. Can't you see, I just want to do well?*

'Look,' he said, hoping she'd listen to a sound argument, to a less emotional voice than Paula's. 'You can't expect to keep your brain alert and stay focussed if you aren't eating enough and you're not getting enough sleep. And working at the sort of pace you're setting yourself, you'll burn out. You just won't be able to keep it up.' He shrugged. 'We've all done it. Stayed up all night before an important exam and your brain gets sluggish and you slow down. You do yourself no favours, believe me.' Holly's eyes, dark and intense, were fixed on his. He put his hand over her cold fingers. 'I've always thought you were the one with good common sense. Use it now and get this into perspective. Work out a schedule so you're organised, dividing up your time for each subject and I'll go over it with you. How's that for a start?'

She suddenly bent forward, leaning her forehead on his hand as it covered hers. 'Oh, Dad. I wish you were back here with us. I know it's never going to happen but…'

He closed his eyes and his chest tightened in pain for what he was responsible for. For what he couldn't alter. He'd affected so many lives with what he'd done. There was nothing he could say that would make any difference to how Holly was feeling at this moment, and he cursed himself.

'Darling.' He stroked her hair and breathed in. 'Listen. In the October half term, we'll have a week away. Just us two. We'll go to Malham – you love it there – and we'll walk and have pub lunches and…'

The door to the dining room burst open, and Ben bounced in, bright and lively and untroubled. 'Hi, Dad. I didn't know you were here. Are we going to a match? Did you forget to tell me?'

Startled, they both sat upright, complicit in a pact of secrecy. Robert turned to face him. 'No, son, I was just passing. Thought I'd pop in to help Holly with some maths, but she seems to have solved the problem.'

'She always solves the problem,' Ben said without sarcasm. 'She's clever.'

Robert laughed in relief. 'She certainly is. I'm leaving her to get on with her work now and so should you. And Ben, don't play your music so loud. I bought you those ear phones so you'd use them.'

He put his hand on his son's shoulder and led him out of the room. But not before he'd looked back at Holly and caught the soulful look in her eyes. Soulful and grateful and loving.

What a bastard he'd been. What a selfish, mindless bastard! The past never lets you go. It's as real as the present. It follows you around and catches you out at the most unexpected moments. You're so certain when you start something that it's all you want, never mind the consequences, you'll deal with them. But in the end, *they* deal with you. And you're left to clear up a mess of your own making.

Well, one thing's for certain, he thought, I deserve no better.

Chapter 5

The voice alarm woke him - the seven o'clock news with more depressing details about Syrian refugees, fighting in the Middle East, a shooting in South Carolina. Jake leaned across, clicked the off-switch and yawned. He stretched his whole body to its full length, fingertips touching the top of the headboard, and thought about getting up. Then it dawned on him it was Sunday - the alarm was still working to its weekday schedule. Damn! Too many beers, then a whiskey – he'd forgotten to switch it off. He rolled over. He liked waking up alone, having time to adjust to the day, savouring the peace before work, but today was Sunday. And he could hear the steady stream of water from the shower. On Saturday nights, Catherine sometimes stayed over. More often now. At first it had been on the occasional weekend, but lately, it had settled into more of a routine. Weekdays in their own houses, Saturday nights at Jake's. Like a steady couple. Jake often wondered how he'd drifted into this arrangement.

It hadn't felt like a choice. Not his, anyway.

He sat up too quickly for his thick head, making him slightly nauseous but then his mind cleared and he remembered. Of course. Today she was running a half-marathon and he'd promised to cheer her on. He let his body drop back onto the bed. It wasn't his idea of a good way to spend the day, watching dogged, fit-looking athletes pounding the roads round Bramhall. But he'd promised.

He swung his legs over the side of the bed. Catherine always woke up with such purpose in the morning, as though she was fired up to take on the day – whatever it threw at her. At first he'd found this quite endearing, but lately, he'd begun to realise the effort she had to put into it. *Take on the day* seemed to be how she motivated herself. He felt obliged to keep pace and it had worn thin.

Part of the trouble was, he was the opposite. He surfaced, slowly.

Catherine came out of the bathroom, rubbing her head with a large towel and looking anxiously at him through strands of wet hair.

'You're sorry you said you'd go now, aren't you?'

He was ready for that forlorn look on her face.

'Course not. Just need time to get my body together.' He gave her what he hoped was an encouraging smile. 'Good job it isn't me running. I'd need resuscitating after a mile.'

'Well, I'm really grateful,' she sat on the side of the bed and stroked his arm. 'It's good to see a familiar face in the crowd when you're getting tired. Spurs you on.'

He struggled up and put on his dressing gown. As he started down the stairs, he called back. 'Do you want a bacon sandwich?' The thought of even smelling a bacon sandwich after last night, never mind cooking it for her, made his stomach turn. But she needed something to give her energy.

'I'll just have fruit and muesli. And orange juice. That'd be great.'

Jake closed his eyes for a second. She was so appreciative of everything anyone did for her, so damned nice. Too nice. It made him conscious of his own shortcomings; he wanted to apologise, but hell, he couldn't change now. It was a bit too late for that.

He passed through the dining room into the kitchen, which was too small and an odd shape, converted at some time from an outbuilding. But a house that was two hundred years old was bound to have gone through several metamorphoses and he loved that about it. Rooms which had no straight lines, half-sized cubby holes that went under stairs and jutting stone, dipped ceilings and the remnants of fireplaces in all the rooms. It had walls so thick you might have been living in a castle for the quiet, solid space you felt wrapped in. Just the occasional tap of footsteps on the narrow lane outside or the bark of a dog from one of the gardens leading to the allotments. He'd made a real find when he'd bought this place. Seven years ago and with barely enough money to come up with the deposit, he'd made it into a home.

And he didn't want to share it. Not with anyone. Not even someone who was always so nice. How do you explain that without seeming like a heel? As always, he pushed it to one side. It'll sort itself out, he thought, but he knew how often in the past few months, he'd ducked the whole business – ducked what he knew would be a painful confrontation. Painful and embarrassing for them both. He thought about her awful father who he'd met a few times, with that irritable face and loud voice – and those brothers, shiftless bullies. She'd had a lousy deal all round. And she'd had some problem at university with a bloke – not that he knew anything like the full story, she barely talked about it, but it must have been bad – it brought her home pretty fast. God, this was difficult. He didn't want to add to all that by giving her any more knocks.

He took the orange juice and blueberries out of the fridge and put them on the table. He made coffee in the cafetiere and sat in his pyjamas, trying to loosen up his face, which felt scrunched and tight.

Catherine, already dressed in white t-shirt and shorts, slid onto a kitchen chair. She moved gracefully, like a dancer. Her hair was tied back with a red band and her face, without a scrap of make-up, was flushed and shiny from the shower. He watched as she bit into the fruit with perfectly white, even teeth, and thought how young she looked, fresh, scrubbed and hopeful. She could have been twenty instead of thirty.

She sensed his eyes on her and stopped eating, the spoon halfway to her mouth. 'What?'

'Nothing. It's nothing. I'm just waking up.' He didn't want to talk at all at this time of the morning. He shrugged and looked away. He knew he could never say anything close to what he was thinking – that without meaning to, she seemed to sap his energy, that he longed to be on his own. He was being a bloody grouch, but he couldn't control a feeling of restlessness. Of wanting more. Of missing something that was getting further and further from his grasp. He couldn't be ready for a mid-life crisis at thirty-two, could he?

She got up from the table and came to stand close beside him. 'Thank you for supporting me today. It means a lot.' Her voice sounded hesitant. 'I'll buy you a hot dog at the end of the race. That'll make you feel better.'

'Not with the way my stomach is.' He checked himself and turned, trying hard to show some kindness. He closed his eyes and put his arms around her waist. Perhaps he wanted too much. Perhaps this was how it was with most couples and you had to accept it - a compromise - no dizzy heights, but no awful lows either. Just steady. Like background music you barely noticed.

He didn't even know what he wanted any more.

The doorbell rang and Catherine kissed his cheek. Then she leant over the table, gulped the orange juice and ran to the door. He heard her calling, 'Hi Rosie. I'm ready. Just give me two seconds.' Then the house settled and rang with quiet, spreading relief through its empty rooms.

He showered, put on a grey shirt and jeans, drank a cup of coffee and began to feel more alive. Combing his hair in the hall mirror, he looked hard at his reflection, the tan from the summer fading and dark patches under his eyes not doing him any favours. He made a face of mock disapproval. *You know what you're doing? Burning the candle at both ends, wearing yourself out. God, if only.*

He drove down to the makeshift car park in the field off Manor Avenue, slowing down to thread his way through the stream of people making their way down each side of the road. He must make the effort to reach the start and see Catherine off. It wasn't what they'd arranged, but he wanted to make up for this morning. He hadn't shown much enthusiasm and he didn't like himself when he thought about it. So, when he'd been flagged into a parking spot, hoping he'd find the car again amongst all the identical-looking silver ones, he set off, sprinting over the grass.

It was 9.30 and the sun was coming out, weak rays touching the trees and drying up the grass that bordered the lane. Before he'd turned into the main road, he heard the sound of a crowd gathering, and rounding the corner, he joined the spectators who were already bunched up at the Start. He looked over the heads of all the runners, some gathering in groups, chatting away, some in bizarre costumes, some turning serious faces to the sky, concentrating their minds as though this was the Olympics. But he couldn't see Catherine. She wasn't tall enough to stand out and there seemed to be hundreds of bodies in numbered bibs packed into the cordoned space. Two officials with clipboards were standing by the roadside near four or five children who were holding flags and jumping up and down, almost knocking each other over.

And then, suddenly, he stood stock still.

He couldn't believe what he was seeing. He tried to move forward, but no-one was letting him through. So he stood, smiling and shaking his head, a totally misplaced sense of euphoria sweeping over him.

Even after all these months, well over a year, he'd have known her anywhere.

The girl from the airport. The girl in the red shoes. Dark blonde hair in a thick plait down her back, sunglasses perched on top of her head, shoulder bag swinging against her cords. Just the same - he couldn't take his eyes off her, the smile, the way she tilted her head, that lovely face. She looked so at ease with herself, so full of life, interested in everything around her. Just seeing her had the impact of a physical shock. He couldn't explain it. It was crazy.

She was absorbed in a conversation with one of the runners, a Homer Simpson look-alike, his face a bright yellow, a placard on his back over white tee-shirt and blue pants. She paused as he answered a question, then scribbled in a reporter's notebook, listening intently, nodding as she leaned towards him. And when she smiled and thanked him, shaking his hand and edging to the side of the road to let him join the other runners, Jake kept on staring. He couldn't move.

There was only her. In such sharp focus that everything around her lost definition.

Then a pistol cracked and the runners were off, jostling each other, determined to get a good start, the mass of pounding feet and bobbing heads seeming to go on and on as they passed by.

Jake pushed his way through the line of spectators, taking deep breaths to calm himself, but his chest was tight and his throat dry. This was just ridiculous. He'd seen her once, a year ago at an airport, with a man who was probably her husband. What on earth was he thinking about? Stupid. Irrational. But nothing could have stopped him now. He fought his way through the crowd, heading in her direction, although he'd lost sight of her in the crush.

Then, there she was, just in front of him, putting her notebook away in her bag and turning to leave. Her jacket sleeve brushed his arm and she looked up.

'Hello,' he said. He was so close he could smell her perfume.

'Hello!' She looked at him for a long moment. 'Have we met?'

Her gaze was curious and candid and slightly off-putting. What could he say?

'Well, a year ago, you were in Manchester airport going to Washington... as I was... and...' He was beginning to sound like a pervert.

But she saved him. Her expression changed, amused now, rather than puzzled.

'Of course. I remember.' She laughed, nodding, as though the whole incident had just flashed before her eyes.

'We spoke. Only very briefly.' Jake ran his fingers through his hair in embarrassment.

'Sir Galahad. That's what I called you at the time. Not out loud, you understand.'

He smiled. He knew where this was going.

'Coming to the aid of damsels in distress,' she explained.

'It's one of the tasks when you sit at the Round Table,' he said solemnly. 'But it's not all chivalry, you know. We have to perform dangerous feats, slaying dragons, fighting sorcerers. Not to mention searching for the Holy Grail.'

'Well, I'm glad you made the time to protect me,' she said. 'I was very touched.' Then her eyes became serious. 'But I wasn't in distress.'

He wanted her to stand this close to him for ever. 'I know. You look as though you can take care of yourself.'

'Believe me, I can.'

She made a movement as though she was going to leave – and Jake knew he had a few seconds to act – it was that moment, he thought, when you have one chance – one chance before it's too late and it's gone forever - to hold onto what you can't bear to let go. He had to ask something, say something that would give him a connection, however absurd it might sound.

'What are you doing here, anyway? Are you a reporter?'

'Well, part time. I do a bit of freelance work for the *Stockport Mercury*. Features and Special Events, human interest stories. I worked for them full time a few years ago, so I know the sort of thing they want. So this is my kind of story.'

'And what are you going to write about Homer Simpson?'

She laughed and pulled a wry face. 'That his yellow face paint was coming off on everyone he brushed up against. And his wife was running as Marge Simpson. At least they were raising money for Oxfam. So good luck to them.'

'I'll buy the paper this week, then. Read your piece.'

'Great. I must go. I'm late already.'

'I don't know your name,' he said as she hitched her bag higher on her shoulder and turned to leave. 'Or will you get a by-line?'

'Probably not. It's Amy Wilson.' She held out her hand and he tensed as his fingers touched her warm skin.

'Jake Harper,' he said.

They stood very still, holding each other's gaze. Something passed between them that neither would be able to put into words. Then she was gone, walking rapidly, swallowed up by the crowds.

Chapter 6

The door had swung to behind her, shutting out the noise and fumes of the traffic in the market square, the terminus for the buses coming in from Hazel Grove and Buxton. No parking space nearby, so Amy had left her car streets away, and walking as fast as she could had meant losing her usual composure. She straightened her jacket, and smoothed back her hair, which the wind had blown into a straggly mess. She should have plaited it but she'd been in too much of a hurry as always. Even more so, today – she'd wanted to check on her 'Marathon' story. She'd intended to pick up the latest edition of the paper on her way into town and look which page it was on and if it had been cut. Well, they'd either liked it or not. Nothing she could do about it now.

She paused to get her breath then ran up the stairs. Large glass panels lined the walls, displaying recent editions of the *Stockport Mercury* and she stopped to scan the front page of the current issue to see whether her story had made it. No, not on the front page, then, only on the strapline, advertising a 'pull out' with four pages of pictures and results inside. Good enough!

She had that feeling of expectation she'd had seven years ago when she'd worked here full-time and written a piece she was really proud of and couldn't wait to see it in print. Hoping the sub-editor hadn't changed the first paragraph or put a heading over it that was a dreadful cliché. God, in those days, she'd been arrogant enough to think she knew better than anyone else – even when they'd been doing the job for years.

It was publication day, but already a new week had begun and there were the familiar sounds of activity as she pushed open the doors of the newsroom – a phone ringing, indistinct conversations, the tapping of keys, chairs scraping on the wooden floor. The ceiling was low and pitched, with a skylight near the highest point, dust motes swirling in the shaft of light beneath it. Desks with computers were placed at odd angles round the room, and at the far end, the editor's office, a make-shift glass cubicle, cordoned off in one corner. Framed news photos, some faded and indistinct, hung on the walls of rough brick and the paintwork was dulled with smoke and age. The whole room was filled with an air of activity, a sense of purpose, which Amy loved.

The desks were occupied by five men and two women, and Amy knew what to expect next. As she walked between them, she heard the usual greeting. Sam, grey-bearded and hunched over his computer, didn't even look up, but began to sing quietly: *'Once in love with Amy'* and Peter at the next desk, eyes still on his work, carried the second line, *'always in love with Amy.'* Smiling, she shook her head and acknowledged the ritual with a wave and a small bow in their direction.

She headed towards the editor's office at the end of the room and knocked on the glass. Ellie Cattersall was a big woman, and she seemed to overflow the desk with her voluminous clothes and wild, unkempt head of hair. When she saw Amy, she put down the letter she'd been reading on top of a pile of papers and gestured with her e-cigarette for her to enter.

'Now, Amy, what's new?' Ellie always reminded Amy of a character out of a Dickens novel, an eccentric one. She could never quite imagine her as a young woman. Even then, she would probably have worn the same colourful hand-knitted cardigans, and chunky shoes, and looped scarves thrown round her neck. And given off the same lavender smell. It was as though she'd been sitting in that chair for the same length of time as the yellowing, dog-eared folders on the shelves behind her. Impossible to even guess at her age.

Amy sat down facing her, expecting some feedback on her article, some word of praise, perhaps. But Ellie didn't speak and the expression of amused indifference on her face didn't change. Surely she was going to say something, make some comment, criticise the piece, for Heaven's sake.

Amy waited. She stared at her and eventually had to say, 'Well?'

'Well, what?'

'Ellie,' she leaned forward. 'Did you like it? Was it any good?

She raised one eyebrow. 'Did *you* think it was any good?'

Amy found herself laughing. 'Not perhaps *Guardian* standard, but I was pleased with it. It had human interest, a bit of drama and I got in as many names as I could without boring the readers to death.'

'That about sums it up.' Ellie took a puff of her cigarette gadget and finally managed a smile. Well, almost, and Amy knew her well enough not to expect more. 'Yes, it was fine. I liked the Homer Simpson bit. Very amusing. And the photos came out well.'

'You didn't use my name.'

'It was a news story, not really a feature. And a joint effort. The pictures deserved as much credit, don't you think? And his name wasn't on it either.'

She nodded. Sometimes, it was better just to accept the house rules.

'Have you anything else for me? Covering a murder in America? Interviewing Kylie Minogue? Investigating the drug culture at a pop festival?'

Ellie pressed her full lips together. Lifting her coffee cup off the diary and opening it, she flicked over the pages with a brown-stained index finger. Amy crossed her legs, laced her fingers together and tried to be patient. She turned her head to look into the newsroom, and knew that Millie, who sat at the nearest desk, had been watching her through the glass. She gave a slight nod of her head, but Millie, pretending not to have seen, leant forward toward her computer screen.

Ellie suddenly looked up. 'We heard yesterday that the Fire Station on Cheadle Road's facing cuts. You could go and see what you can find out, that's if anyone'll talk to us.'

'Yes, ok. I'll get on to that.'

She turned back to the diary. 'There's the Amateur Dramatic lot doing 'The Mikado' in Gatley but not till the end of next week, Friday and Saturday nights, so it won't go in till the following Thursday. You'd need Joe along to take the pictures. Any good?'

Not *Gilbert and Sullivan* again! But there wasn't much she could say. She couldn't afford to be too fussy. You go freelance, you take what you're given. And even though Robert would create a fuss about an evening stint, she had to hang on to her bit of independence. Doing this job was more important to her than she'd realised and she'd had to fight her corner more than once.

The latest argument the week before was hard to ignore. Robert always seemed to assume right was on his side. She didn't have to work, he'd said not for the first time. Harry was still young. He needed his mother. Not his grandmother, or his aunt. And Amy knew, from all these comments, there was another agenda. So much was unspoken. She was sure she was being compared to Paula, who had never worked after Holly was born.

She'd stood her ground. *Just a minute*, she'd said that night. *Let's get this straight. Devoting yourself to a child until they're a teenager is being a good mother. Yet, being sent to boarding school from the age of seven, like you were,*

Robert, is the finest upbringing you can have.

'*Obviously,*' she'd muttered, '*I'm missing something here.*'

But sarcasm didn't work with Robert. It made him silent and distant. When he was displeased, he withdrew, stepped back into himself, treating her like a child who must be punished. Amy was always wary of the cold, unapproachable man he could become. It was like the sun suddenly obliterated by a dark cloud. Earlier in their relationship, she'd taken the easy way out by avoiding confrontation. But lately, she'd felt that giving in all the time smacked of cowardice.

Ellie was waiting. 'Can you do it, or should I give it to Helen?'

'No, I'll do it,' she said quickly. 'I'll get the times and all the other gen from the website. Thanks.'

'Good. There might be something else before then.' She waved the diary at her. 'I'll let you know if there is.'

'OK. Thanks. Ring me if you're stuck for cover, whatever it is. I can always say no.'

'As long as you can get the copy in on time.' Ellie was already reading through some newsprint, circling sections of type with a black pen.

'I know. Have I ever let you down?'

Ellie looked up and the expression in her eyes was almost affectionate. 'You've never let me down, Amy.' Then she waved her away. 'Come back to me with what you can get on the Fire Station story.'

Amy left, shutting the door behind her; she moved quickly past the desks, but Millie, with an anxious frown on her face, was gesturing to her. 'Amy, did she give you anything interesting?'

'Not exactly, Millie. Something to investigate that might come to nothing and 'The Mikado' – I think by now I could *be* one of the Three Little Maids from School. If only I could sing.'

'Oh, well. I was worried she'd let you do the food poisoning story and I really wanted that.'

'Don't worry. She thinks you're far more capable with the news stories. I'm just a fill-in.'

Millie smiled, relief flooding her round, pink face. 'You've been at it far longer than I have. But I'm learning.' She looked so young, Amy thought, just like me when I started. Dead keen.

She stopped at Sam's desk, arranged for the photographer and was nearly through the main door when he called after her, 'A man was asking after you.'

She stopped in her tracks and turned round.

'Who?'

'Rang yesterday. Didn't leave his name, so it can't have been important. Said he'd call back.'

'Ok,' Amy hesitated. She wanted to ask more, but what good would that do. Without a name there was no point. She ran quickly down the stairs, out of the building and into the fresh air.

Making her way back onto the square, she looked at her watch, knowing it was close to the time she had to pick up Harry. He'd started going for a full day since the beginning of September and she had to be at the school gates in plenty of time so he'd see her as soon as he stepped into the yard. She couldn't bear the thought that he'd be searching for her among the other mothers and not finding her there.

The afternoon had grown cool as she hurried along the streets to where her car was parked in a two-hour slot. Plenty of time. Stop rushing, she told herself.

Five past three and at the school gates with ten minutes to spare. Clouds were making the sky dark and some mothers were putting up hoods and pulling gabardine covers over pushchairs to keep out the cold flurries of wind. She saw Josie, whose daughter Carrie was in

Harry's class, threading her way towards her and was suddenly glad to be back in this part of her life. She loved the moment when Harry caught sight of her and his face lit up with such joy because she was there, waiting for him. *That's what children do for you*, she thought. *They ground you, give you a special place in their world. And you don't even have to try. You can be irritated and out of patience, and it doesn't change anything. Somehow, you're still their touchstone.*

She could hear the school bell sounding in the building and then Harry's class filed out in raincoats and in shoes that looked too big and heavy for them. The teacher kept them in single file, but he waved to her before he reached the gate, and ran the last few paces into her arms.

'You didn't bring Jasper,' he said, making it sound like an accusation.

'No. I had to go into the office. We'll be home in five minutes and we can take him for a walk.'

His hand felt hot in hers as he walked beside her, rattling on about paintings and rabbits and Jack, who'd wet himself at lunch time. He kept looking up at her as he talked, stumbling a little to keep his balance, watching her to be sure she was listening.

Chapter 7

Catherine struggled out of the supermarket carrying two carrier bags in each hand, the thin plastic handles cutting into her fingers. She'd only wanted a few things, milk and some ham and salad for tea, so she'd decided to walk the short distance from school. But as she was heading for the self-service tills, her father had rung her mobile – 'On your way home, pick up some shopping for me, will you? Only a few bits.' But, as always, the list was long – it seemed to cover his whole week's groceries.

Would it never end - these demands he made that she somehow wasn't able to refuse? She was thirty, not fifteen.

And still at his beck and call, she reminded herself, wearily.

She was usually uncomplaining, willing to help anyone. But lately… it had all become a trial. Perhaps it was the change of season that had affected her mood, leaving summer behind. Now, the mornings began under a misty haze and lights had to be turned on as early as seven o'clock in the evening. It meant doing her running as it was becoming dusk and, at school, having to persuade the girls, when they hated cross country, to go out in the cold and trying to form teams on the hockey pitch in a gale. Neil had the advantage in the Autumn term. The boys loved football in any weather.

At least there was one thing to cheer her up - the head had given the PE department permission to arrange a residential activity course in Wales next spring. She'd researched it thoroughly before she'd put the idea to him – found a four-day slot at half term, costed the whole thing - and he'd been keen from the start. Impressed with her initiative. Something different, he'd said, as he studied the web pages she'd printed out, showing an old country house with rope courses and climbing frames in the grounds, and kayaking on the lake; even a maze. Some of the pupils had never stayed away from home even for a night, so it'd be a real adventure for them. And it felt good to be organising something, to be in charge for once. It always seemed to be the men in the department who did the interesting stuff. Well, now it was her turn. She'd even suggested to Tim that they needed some fund-raising to supplement the cost for the kids who'd struggle to pay. And he'd agreed with that too.

As she walked slowly, weighed down by the bags of shopping, her mind was occupied with thoughts of school, things she had to arrange, lessons to plan. But then inevitably, she returned to the concern that had nagged away at her far too much in recent weeks. The fact that Jake was no nearer suggesting they move in together than he had been six months ago.

But it was more than that. She didn't like admitting it to herself, but he was drifting away. Had she missed something - one incident, one night that had caused a shift in their relationship? Had she annoyed him? There wasn't anything she could remember, only perhaps the time she'd bought a Tiffany lamp in a sale for his lounge and he'd told her to take it back. It didn't go with the room. But there hadn't been an argument. It was just that they didn't have the same tastes. Not a big deal.

But there was definitely something. She would catch him staring into space, and when she asked him what was on his mind, he always said, *Nothing.* Obvious, then, that whatever was on his mind, he couldn't talk about it. Or wasn't going to talk to *her* about it. He just seemed absent, that's the only way to describe it. Like last night after dinner. He'd recorded an episode of *The Wire*, and when she'd suggested finishing their glasses of wine in front of the TV to watch it after *The Voice,* he hadn't even answered. As though he hadn't heard her.

'Do you want to?' she'd asked.

He'd turned his head, slowly, yawned and ran his fingers through his hair, making it stand on end. 'I'm tired, Catherine. I think I'll go upstairs and read. Not in the mood for TV.'

And he'd left her, his tread sounding heavy on the stairs. She sat, with the remains of the meal in front of her on the table and a sinking feeling that made her shivery and weepy. And a feeling of rising panic which she found difficult to control, making breathing difficult.

She'd picked up her wine, finishing it in one swallow but it didn't make her feel any better. What hadn't she noticed? At first, she'd thought it was the complaint from the Reverend Somebody about the A level text, but he'd shrugged that off - said the meeting had gone well, that most parents were reasonable once things were explained. It wasn't a problem.

But something was.

Five o'clock, now and the streets were quiet. The bags seemed to be getting heavier. Only a few hundred yards to her downstairs flat and, dropping the shopping on the doorstep to find her key, she opened the door and picked up the post - mostly begging letters from charities, she noticed - and her mobile started ringing.

She looked at the caller ID and answered it. 'Yes, Dad.'

'Are you bringing it round now?' No preliminaries, his voice hoarse and loud.

'Just got in this minute. Going to have a cuppa, then I'll be with you.'

'Hurry then. I was going to have the chops for my tea. And Tom's here. He hasn't eaten either.'

And he rang off abruptly, as he always did, without any of the niceties that most people practised. Without even saying 'goodbye'.

Catherine sat down on one of the kitchen chairs and her eyes filled with tears. She wished now she hadn't come back from Sheffield. She'd thought she'd escaped when she'd made it to college. But she'd chosen to come home. Of course she had. It had seemed the safest place to be... after what happened. But it had been a mistake. Yes, she'd got over it, slowly. She'd found work and started running again, which helped her make friends with the same interests. But coming home meant... her father (and, if she was honest, her brothers were like him), tactless, narrow-minded, only thinking of himself. He'd made things more difficult, even though he'd not known everything - not all the details. But enough. Anyway, he didn't seem to care or want to understand. After the nightmare of it all, she felt he'd looked at her with contempt; in his eyes, she'd been a fool, only herself to blame.

And he'd always been demanding, that much hadn't changed. Here she was at thirty, still at his beck and call, trying so hard to look forward and have a life of her own. Not be somebody's housekeeper! Didn't he remember she had a job? It wasn't as though he was ill, or unable to get to the shops. All he wanted was a substitute for the wife who'd done everything for him, and she was it. A girl and the youngest. Welcome to the twenty-first century. Well, she was going to have that cup of tea!

Spread out on the table from this morning was the local newspaper and a certificate recording her time in the half marathon: 2 hours 15; she was quite proud of that. Not her best, but pretty good. She'd enjoyed the whole day, keeping pace with the other runners, laughing at the crazy costumes, spectators shouting encouragement as she passed. A real sense of achievement when she'd passed the finish line and there was Jake at the side of the road, cheering and nearly as breathless as she was.

And all seemed well for a short while – as long as they were among the crowd, chatting and bumping into a few people they knew from school and the local clubs. But when they were alone, he'd gone quiet. And stayed quiet, however much she'd tried to involve him in what she'd been doing.

She began to think back to when she'd first seen him. The new term was about to begin and the staff training session was scheduled for the whole morning. September, three years ago. Only her second job and she'd managed to get head of girls PE at 27.

She'd walked into the meeting and hesitated, not sure where she should sit. She'd been interviewed in this room in May, but today it had a very different atmosphere – full of noise and laughter, chattering groups catching up after the six weeks' holiday. There were two rows of soft-back chairs to the right of her, but most people were standing, and on the left, tables with leaflets on them. Finding an empty seat, she sat down, but with everyone else standing, she'd felt conspicuous and isolated. For a moment, then, she'd wondered why she'd been so keen on a promotion, why go into a new school to start all over again. It was always hard at the beginning, and her confidence was ebbing away.

But as everyone began to settle down, coffee cups on tables and bags on the floor beside them, ready for the session to start, she began to feel less nervous and made a determined effort to look composed. It was a large school, sixty-odd staff and eight-form entry, a far cry from the one in north Manchester she'd just left. Now, she was part of a team of six instead of two, leading half of it. She opened a folder and studied her new timetable and tried to keep her foot from tapping against the carpet.

When she looked up again, she began to take in some of the faces around her. Diagonally opposite her was Jake, not that she knew his name then. He was sitting with two men about the same age, passing comments, comfortable, part of the fabric of the place. He'd arrived late and just dropped into his leather chair, looking relaxed, stretching his long legs out in front of him. He had the sort of face that seemed amused, even when he wasn't smiling; brown curly hair and eyes so dark, they were almost black. But what Catherine first noticed was his air of diffidence, of not seeming to care what impression he made. He looked at ease with himself. What she wished she could be, instead of this nagging uncertainty, always trying to please, to fit in with others. She noticed, throughout the talks and the activities that morning, that he seemed to be part of a group, almost a clique, lots of banter and in-jokes, an inner circle which didn't invite newcomers. They certainly didn't notice her. And why should they, she thought.

She smiled to herself when she remembered how things changed. It was their double act in the second term when they'd started to get to know each other.

It was all over two boys from her tutor group, who were always in trouble. If it wasn't in PE, it was in Maths; if it wasn't in Maths, it was in English. Catherine had tried reasoning with them, but that was never going to work. She had cajoled, sanctioned, given detentions, in fact every method she could think of. But they courted trouble like a badge of honour. Brody was the leader. He was always wearing clothes that didn't even give the nod to school colours or uniform. At thirteen, he was watchful, belligerent and smart. And school wasn't for him. The other boy, Dylan followed him with disciple-like loyalty.

Catherine sat in the PE office, turning her chair round to face the two boys who were standing, making no eye contact.

'Ok. Let's see if we can get to the bottom of this.' They looked over her head, chins up, ready for a fight. 'I've had another complaint, this time from English. Scraping chairs, humming, flicking bits of rubber around, answering back when you were told to stop. Is that about it?'

No reply.

'You don't like English, is that what this is all about? You're bored?'

Silence. Catherine waited.

Brody decided he'd speak. 'We like English. Most of the time.'

'So, tell me, what went wrong here?'

Dylan's turn. 'We were doing a leaflet. Sport and how it gets you healthy.'

'Well, that sounds useful to me. What could be wrong with that?'

Brody sniffed and pushed his hands into his pockets. 'Nothin'. But then Sam started making some comments about ours... saying it was rubbish...'

'Oh, Brody. You're not coming up with the old excuse of blaming someone else.' She sighed. 'I'm just getting tired of this. Mr. Harper's coming along in a minute and we'll hear what he's got to say. I'd like to bet there's more to it than a remark from Sam.' She paused. 'This is getting serious now. The third time in two weeks you've been referred to me.'

Dylan rubbed his hand across his mouth. 'They pick on us. We always get the blame...'

The door opened and Jake walked in.

His expression gave away nothing as he went to stand next to Catherine. He towered above the two boys, but they barely looked up to acknowledge his presence. He sat on the edge of the desk and, ignoring them, turned towards her.

'Perhaps we need their parents in to work out what's going on. Have you got their numbers? I know Brody's mother works in the kitchens so she could be round here in ten minutes.'

Brody glowered and Dylan began to fidget.

Catherine played along. 'Do you really think that's best? Surely we can give them a chance to try and improve their behaviour. After all, it's Parents' Night at the end of term...'

'Too long to wait. We need to stop this silliness now. And unless their mums and dads know what's going on, they'll keep on ruining everyone else's chances of learning anything.' Jake crossed his arms, deliberately slowly and looked at the two boys.

Dylan gulped and shook his head. 'My dad'll kill me if he's called now. He's on nights and he'll be asleep...'

'Should've thought of that, Dylan. Was your brother ever in trouble like this?'

'No, sir.'

'Then what on earth are you doing? You're only in year 8. You going to be doing this when you're taking your GCSEs?'

Catherine looked as solemn as Jake. 'I think we could give them one more chance. See if they can stay out of trouble for a week. Then we'll review the situation.'

Brody sighed loudly, more annoyed than sorry. His eyes were on Catherine. Wary. Lids half shut.

Jake shrugged. 'Well, you're his tutor. I'll go with what you want to do. But it's probation. Any more trouble and there's no respite.'

'Respite?' Dylan pulled a face. 'What d'you mean, sir?'

'No second chances, Dylan. This is your final warning. Yellow card. Get it?'

Brody still hadn't spoken.

Catherine studied his face and spoke with deliberate slowness. 'Do you understand? Best behaviour in all your classes. No more messing about.'

Brody hesitated and then grudgingly gave her the briefest of smiles. As good a thank-you as she was going to get. 'Yes, miss.'

Catherine allowed herself to smile back. 'Go on. You're late for your next lesson. Come and see me straight away if you have any problems. Make sure I know about it before I hear it from someone else.'

The door closed behind the boys and Jake looked knowingly at Catherine.

'Well done, partner! Your Good Cop was pretty convincing.'

She laughed, embarrassed, and picked up some paperwork from her desk. 'Well, let's hope it's worked. Otherwise I've got a hard three years ahead.' She saw he was getting ready to leave. 'Thanks for the support.'

'Oh, they're young and daft.' He shrugged his shoulders. 'Just need sorting out early. They'll settle down.'

When he'd left, she sat for a few minutes, knowing she was late for her own lesson. She could hear doors banging and feet shuffling into the changing rooms. Time to organise the basketball...

She'd been sitting too long. The kitchen had taken on a chill and she wrapped her coat tightly across her chest. No good thinking back, that wasn't going to solve anything. She could hear the dripping of a tap and the faint ticking of the oven clock, the only sounds in the empty house. Until the ringing of her mobile made her jump. She got up from the kitchen table, threw her cold tea into the sink and waited for the urgent jingle to stop.

She wasn't going to answer it. She found herself gritting her teeth and put her fingers to her mouth to stop herself. She knew it'd be her father phoning again – there'd be a voicemail and she wouldn't listen. She wanted time to herself for a bit longer – not really a lot to ask.

But there wouldn't be any peace, she knew. Not until she'd behaved like the obedient daughter. Take the shopping round to his house. Do as she had always done – give in.

Chapter 8

The ball ricocheted off the side wall and skidded low. Robert lurched forward and caught it on the rise, slamming it into a corner with all the strength and follow-through he could muster. It would have taken a much more agile opponent than Nick to be able to return it.

'Good one.' Nick's white sports shirt was dark with sweat and his hair hung over his headband, in damp spikes. He was red-faced and panting. 'God, don't you ever get tired? This is meant to be a young man's game.'

'Ah, but it's not all about stamina, my friend,' said Robert, patting him on the shoulder, knowing perfectly well how Nick hated to be mocked. 'It's technique that wins the day. Squash is like a Board Meeting – you have to outwit, see what's coming and be ready to take advantage. You'll learn.'

The sounds from the other courts rang hollow with shouts and the crack of the hard rubber balls rebounding off walls. The air was filled with the smell of damp and wood and warm bodies. Robert let his racquet balance on his fingers, spinning it as he waited to start the next game. He looked across at Nick, who was bent over, with his hands on his knees, catching his breath.

'Is it ten five?'

Nick straightened and gave a hoarse laugh. 'You know damn well it is! Just put me out of my misery. Then we can go to the Otter and get a drink.'

They finished the game, showered and changed, and walked down the street to the pub. Nick's complexion was still an unhealthy brick red and Robert wondered just how fit he was these days. Their games were getting more and more uneven, when once they'd been fairly well-matched.

They settled on bar stools, two pints of Black Sheep in front of them. Robert was content for the moment to just sit and say nothing, let his body relax; his breathing had soon returned to a comfortable rhythm and he felt good about himself. Forty nine he may be, but he didn't even feel middle-aged. Perhaps it was having a young son. His own father had seemed an old man from the time Robert could remember him, always formerly dressed, slow-moving, his face gaunt and unsmiling.

The pub was filling up and bar meals were being carried out from the kitchen, the young waitress holding the baskets high in the air and calling out numbers. As the girl passed by, the smell of chips and burgers made Robert feel hungry. All he'd had time for at lunch was a sandwich, snatched between two meetings. It had been a hell of a day. He was glad he hadn't cancelled the game tonight - he'd needed the exercise, something physically demanding to take his mind off work.

Nick's colour began to return to normal; he took a swig of his pint and blew out his cheeks in a long, loud breath.

'So how's life in the city?' He grabbed a handful of nuts from the bowl on the bar top. 'Shouldn't be eating these, full of salt. But what the hell!'

Robert knew Nick wouldn't understand anything about 'life in the city' but he was used to remarks like this. He sometimes wondered lately whether they had anything in common any more. 'Things are fine as long as you pedal fast enough.' He shrugged, looking straight ahead as he spoke.

'And the lovely Amy?'

Robert didn't reply. Nick was always too familiar when he referred to Amy. He was his squash partner, for God's sake, nothing closer than that and he'd only met Amy two or three times. It was ill-mannered and it grated.

A queue was forming next to them, people waiting to order food and Nick put his elbows on the bar and hunched his shoulders. He shifted his stool closer to Robert to make room for a woman leaning over the counter.

'Are we eating?' he asked.

'No.' Robert knew he sounded sharp but his sense of well-being at the easy win was fading. And really, he was hungry. He'd like to eat but not with Nick, who he was finding more and more irritating. He made an effort to sound regretful. 'Amy's expecting me home. I like to say goodnight to Harry and if we stay for a bar meal, he'll be asleep.'

Nick shook his head and looked sideways at Robert, disappointment in the downward turn of his mouth. 'You're a lucky bastard. You know that?'

Robert looked puzzled. 'What's brought that on?'

'Oh, just... envy I suppose. Things aren't that good at the moment.' He blinked rapidly a few times as though he had grit in his eyes.

Robert stared at him, alarmed that he was going to be told something too intimate, a confession that he didn't want to hear. It wasn't like Nick to show any emotion – he always seemed ebullient and irrepressible. Thick-skinned, to be blunt, Robert thought. A typical salesman, whose main concern was Number One.

Nick took a gulp of his beer. 'Not like me, is it? To get down.' He gave a smile that wasn't convincing.

'Everyone gets tired, Nick. You put a lot of hours in travelling, the market's still depressed whatever they say, and you're feeling the brunt of it. There's one good thing. People are always going to need bathrooms...'

'Christ, if that was the only problem!' He clapped a hand on his knee. 'You've no idea how complicated things have got. Work? I can cope with work. It's my whole life that's going down the pan.'

Robert looked behind him, aware that there were too many people within earshot; he was certain someone must be listening. Nick wasn't talking quietly anymore and two of the customers standing at the counter were already pretending not to notice them, turning their heads away, but ready, he was sure, to hear some fascinating gossip.

'Look, Nick, let's move over by the door. That couple's just leaving. Grab their table and we can talk in peace.' *Before you tell the world your troubles, for God's sake*, he said to himself, heading to the back of the room, carrying both their pint glasses. Nick slumped against the wall, with a resigned sigh and Robert edged between two tables to join him, apologising as he knocked against someone's arm.

'I wasn't going to talk about it, Robert. I really wasn't. But I'll go mad if I don't tell someone. It's all my own fault, I know that. Can't blame anyone else, just me. Christ, what an idiot I've been.'

'Nick, you're not making any sense.' Robert knew he was going to get the whole story, whether he liked it or not. And he'd rather not. It was already seven o'clock and he wanted to go home, read to Harry and watch 'The Game'. He'd only seen three episodes and that would be a lot more interesting than hearing this confession, whatever it was about. But Nick was wrapped up in his own thoughts now, he could see, and he'd have to sit and make the right noises. He felt enough concern at the strained expression on Nick's face and the way he was struggling to find the words, to sit and wait. This wasn't anything like the man he'd played squash with every week. But then, Nick had changed recently – constantly making sarcastic remarks and innuendoes that Robert had found baffling.

'There's no one else I can tell. All our friends are Julie's as well and there isn't anyone at work I'd trust.'

'Just start at the beginning. What's happened?'

Nick took a swig of his beer, leaving a thin layer of froth on his upper lip. 'It was two months ago. A Tuesday, calling in on a good client on my way into Huddersfield. We'd done quite a bit of business with Penrose's and they know me there. Always share a bit of banter with the office staff. You know how it is. There's a girl I like – well, a woman – she's a buyer. We'd have a bit of a flirt and a chat, she'd get me a cup of coffee - sometimes we'd have lunch at the Costa across the road, and this day I went back at five. This Tuesday. No reason really, just… anyway, we went out for an Italian…'

'Hold it, Nick. If this is about an affair, I'm not the man to talk to…' Robert had put up his hands to ward him off and shifted in his seat. This was heading into uncomfortable territory and he really didn't want to hear any more.

'Oh, Christ, if that was all!' Nick rubbed his fingertips up and down on his forehead. 'We spent the rest of the evening at a hotel. One night stand. I've done it enough times to know the type who can handle it. But, boy, not this time… not this time. I started getting all these phone calls about wanting to see me, more and more phone calls, demanding, wouldn't be put off…'

'What? Threatening to tell Julie?'

'No. That would have been bloody difficult, but I could always deny that. Her word against mine. But this was something else.' He paused, closing his eyes, briefly, as though preparing himself. 'After a month, when she knew I wasn't going to play ball, she jumped on the sexual harassment bandwagon. She said she'd go to her employers, then mine, report me for touching her up, having sex in the bloody stationery cupboard. I'd 'coerced' her. That was the word she used. Sounds like a farce, doesn't it? Far from it. She'd got witnesses, she said, they'd say my behaviour was improper, always had been, that I'd taken advantage of my position...'

'And?'

'Well, it was like a bombshell. You think you're a pretty good judge of character... Christ, you don't ever know anybody...' He took a breath, trying to control himself. 'She said she'd drop it all if I gave her £5,000. Didn't want to be greedy, but she'd built up some debts and it'd get her off the hook. I'd got a good job, drove a nice car, it wasn't that much money... then she asked for eight. I don't need to go on.'

'No, you don't, Nick. Finish it. Go to the police. It's blackmail and she'll come back for more money, again and again.'

Nick laughed, a hoarse sound that was a long way from humorous. 'No, I don't think so. If I could pay her off, I think she'd shut up. But the whole point is, I haven't got £8,000. I couldn't find anything like that amount. I'm only just breaking even myself. Two teenage kids and a mortgage that's crippling me. I don't have it.'

'Well, there's one thing for certain - you mustn't pay.'

'But if I don't, my job's gone, they'll pay me off and it might even go to court. Julie'll never forgive me.'

'You're not thinking straight.' Robert could hear the irritation in his voice, and realised he was talking too loudly. He dropped to a fierce whisper. 'How do you know she's got witnesses? Who are they? Work colleagues aren't going to stick their necks out for something like this. Call her bluff. Tell her to try it on and see where it gets her. It was two consenting adults having sex and she's committing a criminal act by threatening you...'

Nick looked at him, eyes imploring. His voice was shaking when he spoke. 'I can't, Robert, I can't let any of this get out. Don't you see, even if the charges don't stick, I'm done.'

'It might never come to that. She won't go through with it…'

'She will. Those phone calls never stop. She's not going to give up. Believe me, she's going for the jugular.' Then his expression changed. Not sorry for himself, anymore, Robert thought, but something…a shift in his eyes, a look that could only be described as pleading. *What on earth was coming now?*

'Robert, help me. Please. If you could just lend me the eight thousand – a loan, you'd get it back. You're the only person I know who's got that sort of money. I know it's a lot to ask but you could save me. Lend me the eight thousand. I promise, if it takes me years, I'll pay you back.'

Robert stared at him in disbelief. 'You're not serious.'

'I've never been *more* serious. I'm on a cliff edge and I'm… begging you.'

'Don't. Please don't, Nick. I'm not lending you anything. Go to the police and tell her that's what you're doing…'

'I can't. I can't let any of this get out.'

'Well then, you're a fool. She's playing you…'

Nick pursed his lips together, and his eyes filled with tears.. 'Christ, you're a shit, Robert!' He was choking with anger, working his hands until the knuckles went white. 'That's what you are – a shit. It's not as though you can't help me, you just bloody well won't.'

Robert had got to his feet, so quickly he had to throw his arm out to regain his balance and grab at his chair to stop it falling. He looked down on Nick and managed to mutter through clenched teeth, 'You're right, I won't. You've got a hell of a nerve asking. Sort yourself out. And, by the way, you've just lost your squash partner.'

Just as Robert was turning towards the door, Nick half rose, leaned over and grabbed his sleeve. 'I just bloody well hope you never need help from a friend. I just hope your charmed life doesn't go arse over tit. Because I'll be watching...'

The last thing Robert felt as he wrenched his arm away and bolted through the pub door into the evening air, was Nick's spittle on his face.

*

Later, as he lay in the comforting darkness beside Amy, who was sleeping soundly, he reached out and circled his arm round her shoulders. He rested his head on her warm back, finding solace in the rhythm of her breathing, the closeness of another human being, someone he knew so well, who he could trust, who loved him. He closed his eyes, thinking about the dreadful evening. How quickly it had turned bitter and vicious. No way would he be able to sleep. Nick's furious reaction had come as a total shock, like being punched when you least expect it.

He didn't need anyone to tell him he had a 'charmed life' – he knew how fortunate he was to have had a second chance and make it work. His own actions nine years ago could have led to even more disastrous consequences than they did.

Amy made a soft noise in her sleep and rolled against his arm, her chin nudging his shoulder. He held her to him, his mouth brushing against her hair. *Don't you think I've enough sense to know how lucky I am? Don't you think I know?* He hadn't any idea who he was saying this to – himself, to Amy, to Nick.

But he was annoyed for letting the vengeful little man get under his skin. Jealous little toad, he thought. Good riddance!

Chapter 9

Jake sat at his desk, papers and folders and jotted notes covering its surface, and straightened the line of text books propped against the corner. Facing him on the wall was a poster of 'Much Ado About Nothing' from the last Stratford trip and beside it, a timetable held in place with a red pin. He'd shut the door to his office, something he rarely did at break time, but he needed privacy. And quiet. The noise from the tarmacked play area outside the window was muted, but someone had decided it was a good time to wheel the dustbins along the path to the front of the school, and they made an irritating rumble as they went by. He waited, balancing his cup of coffee, with 'Keep Calm' printed on it, on a stack of scripts, praying for five minutes without any interruptions. Please, don't bring me anyone today who's not done their homework or who's used their mobile in class. Or who's normally a really good student but is behaving oddly. *I'm* behaving oddly. Someone should sort *me* out.

He pulled the phone towards him and dialled the number, his palm slipping on the receiver. He'd planned every bit of the conversation in his head and had thought it all sounded plausible. But now, waiting for someone to pick up, he doubted he'd get the words out in any way that'd be understood. *Come on, pull yourself together.*

'*Stockport Mercury.* Can I help you?'

'Could you put me through to the news room, please? I've

information about an event you might be interested in covering.'

'Could you give me your name?'

'Jake Harper.'

Canned music played as he waited.

A gruff voice came on the line. 'Sam Green here, Mr. Harper. What can I do for you?'

'Well,' began Jake, 'I'm head of English at Forest Green Academy – I think we're in the area you cover – usually, we contact the *Echo* – but I met one of your reporters at the half marathon and it gave me the idea...' He was sounding like a drivelling idiot and he stopped himself from rambling on any further. 'The thing is, Mr. Green, we're having an evening of Creative Writing and Performance to welcome new pupils and their parents to the school. It's on Wednesday, just one evening, and it involves some of the older children reading out their English work, poems and stories. That sort of thing. A bit of music, some refreshments, starts at 6.30.'

'Sounds good. Were you thinking photographs as well?'

'Yes, that'd be great. I can send you details in an email and then on the night, give a list of the pupils who are performing to... whoever covers it, and they could chat to the kids and get their side of things.'

'Right. I'll just take your phone number and someone'll get back to you. Got enough though, here, so...'

'I think the reporter I met was called Amy something. I really liked the way she wrote about the race, the atmosphere and stuff. The human touch.' He groaned inwardly at how crass this sounded, but he had to keep going. 'Any chance of her doing it?'

'Ah, Amy.' There was a pause and Jake had the feeling that Sam Green was enjoying this. Seeing right through him. 'I'm sure she can be asked. Not promising she'll be free, but I'll put forward your request. Nice to know someone appreciates a job well done.'

'Great. I'll leave it with you.'

He replaced the receiver and tried to remember exactly what he'd said. He was sure of one thing - it hadn't sounded natural. Well, anyway, the evening was genuine, even if the conversation was as contrived as hell. Sometimes, you had to throw your hat into the ring. And he'd certainly done that.

There was a knock at the door and Emily Hodge, the department's newest recruit, pushed it open. Anxiety was written all over her face. 'Sorry to disturb you, Jake, but I've got a problem. I can't seem to put the attendance marks into the computer. Could you show me again?'

'Ok, but it'll take me longer than a few minutes to set the programme up. Could we do it at lunchtime?'

Another knock and Jenny, all corkscrew curls and dangling earrings, shoved her head into the room, to announce, 'Mr. Madden is on the prowl, looking for some poor unfortunate to seize and terrorise. You have been warned...'

'Thanks, Jenny. I'll get the flak jackets.'

Emily looked from one to the other, half puzzled, half laughing.

Jenny pretended panic. 'He's heading this way...' and with a strangled cry, she was gone. Slightly barmy was the staff's opinion of her. At breakfast briefing once, Andy had shaken his head at Jake and asked him how he managed to work with someone who was, as he put it, 'as crazy as a box of frogs'. Well, she was brilliant in the classroom. That was good enough.

Jake picked up his register and books and headed out into the corridor. It was a relief to slip back into the routine of the day, the fifty minute lessons, the bells, the questions answered, the paperwork completed, the quick exchanges along corridors – a world he was familiar with. One he could deal with. It was a time he'd think about later with some regret - that he hadn't been content enough to appreciate it.

At three o'clock, he headed through the library to the sixth form block with *The Great Gatsby* in his hand. The students were sitting round work tables when he entered, talking to each other, some with their copies in front of them, some looking at their mobile phones, some not even noticing his presence. More girls than boys, as always in a Literature class. He shut the door and slipped off his jacket, then sat on the teacher's desk, waiting, saying nothing until they'd settled, ready to begin. Two latecomers hurried through the door, mumbling an apology he could barely hear. At last, they were all looking at him, expectantly.

'Right. Now, I know you've all read to the end by now...' he paused deliberately and hoped those who hadn't would do some fast catch-up. A few weeks into their A level course and they didn't seem to realise how hard they'd have to work. 'But the chapter I asked you to look at last week was chapter three, Gatsby's party...'

Some nods, some eyes not meeting his.

'So, why does Fitzgerald spend so long on this scene? What did you think was important here?'

No response.

He tried again. 'Well, what does it tell us about Gatsby?'

He knew it would be Matthew who'd answer first. A good looking, dark-haired boy, who was full of confidence and opinions, often based on very little evidence. Jake liked him, but after only a short time, he'd realised he was making the others shrink from giving their point of view.

'He's a loser,' Matthew began, his arm slung over the back of the chair. 'Letting everyone take advantage of him. He hardly knows all those people and he's spending a fortune opening up his house and lets them all sponge off him. He even pays for an orchestra. And he doesn't even enjoy any of it...'

'But that's not the point, is it, sir?' Morgan was getting impatient, shifting in her chair. 'He doesn't do it for that and he doesn't care about the guests. He's throwing the parties, just hoping Daisy'll come to them. It's his way of getting her back.'

'Then it's pathetic,' said Matthew, shaking his head and leaning back – his attempt to appear nonchalant. Jake could imagine him at forty. 'He's trying too hard. And wasting his time. Why doesn't he just find someone else? He's rich, he could have anyone...'

'And he puts on all this flamboyant stuff for nothing,' said Sadie, twining a piece of pink hair round her finger. She was already in trouble for changing the colour nearly every week. 'Ok, Daisy's unhappy with Tom, but even though she knows Gatsby throws these parties, she still doesn't come.'

Jake interrupted. 'Hold on. You don't know that yet. She's only just learned from Nick that Gatsby's bought a place across the Sound.'

'I'm sure she knows earlier.' Sadie wasn't going to be wrong.

'The point is,' Morgan said, in an exasperated voice, 'he's throwing money around to, like, show her what she's missed. I've seen the film, the Baz Luhrmann one, where Leonardo DiCaprio has known her years before, but he was poor and Tom, the rich one, gets there first. So now he's made it, he's come back.'

'You're getting too far ahead,' said Jake. 'For the minute, concentrate on the text in front of you. What sort of party is it? Who comes? How do they behave?'

A quiet voice came from the back of the room. '"*According to the rules of behaviour associated with an amusement park*".'

Everyone turned round, and Jess, the girl who'd spoken, looked down at her book and flushed to the roots of her hair.

'Exactly.' Jake smiled and softened his tone to encourage her. 'Someone's actually read the book! What do you make of that, Jess?'

They were all watching her; she coughed and started flicking through the pages, too embarrassed to go on.

'Everyone's behaving badly, Jess. So what does that tell you about the kind of world Fitzgerald is trying to create?'

This time, the silence lasted long enough for Jake to think he'd have to ask someone else before she curled into a ball. Then she spoke up.

'Well, I think it shows the people have no morals and only care about enjoying themselves. They just drink too much and they're rowdy and there's "*vacuous*" laughter...'

Jake could hear someone muttering: 'What does vacuous mean?' but he left it alone. They could look it up. 'Go on.'

'Well...' her voice was becoming less hesitant, 'there's money and it's lavish but it's all for show. It's empty. And no-one's sure what's real and what isn't. They say Gatsby killed a man, then he's a German spy in the war. They don't even know who he is.'

'Yes, things are "*said to be*" rather than 'are'. Jake was enjoying this now. 'And what do we learn about Gatsby here? It's his party. Does he join in?'

They had all begun searching through the chapter, looking for answers.

Sadie raised her hand in an involuntary wave. 'No, not really. He's not, like, part of it. He's standing alone on some steps watching people. He's on the edge.'

'Yes,' said Jake. 'Remember you're seeing it through Nick's eyes. And it's important how he describes Gatsby...'

Morgan was pointing to the page she was reading. 'He likes him. He says he had a smile that "*understood you just so far as you wanted to be understood.*"'

'Yes, well done, Morgan. He likes him. There's something innocent about Gatsby and his dream, isn't there? He's the only decent human being in a materialistic, corrupt world. And Nick sees that. His viewpoint is vital to this novel and Fitzgerald is using this device for a reason. Nick guides us. So, what makes the reader trust him?'

'Because…' Sadie sounded triumphant and paused for effect, 'I remember this bit. It says on the opening page - his father gave him some advice. Don't judge people. So he takes it all in and makes up his own mind.'

The discussion gathered momentum and finally, Jake had to cut them off as time ran out. He finished the lesson and the students filed past him into the corridor, still arguing over whether Gatsby was a fool or just a hopeless romantic and Jake laughingly called after them, 'He's not a real person, you know.'

Jess, slowly gathering her notepad and books into her bag, was the last out of the room. She scuttled between the tables, face still flushed, head down, not looking up as she passed Jake's desk. He knew he had to say something.

'Jess, just a minute.'

She stopped, uncertain, hugging her bag to her body with both arms.

'I just wanted to tell you how important your contribution was today. You set us all off on the right track, did you realise that?' Jess blushed even redder but Jake went on. 'The points you made were really insightful. You'd obviously thought about it.'

She shuffled her feet and look down. 'I read a lot,' she muttered.

'Well, keep on reading,' Jake grinned and picked up his text. 'Just remember, it isn't always the ones with the loudest voices or the ones full of opinions that know everything. They might sound good but they aren't always the cleverest or the most hard-working.'

Jess said nothing but she looked at him at last and he saw a glimmer of pleasure in her round eyes.

'Off you go. And be sure to speak up in the next lesson. Keep us on track. I need all the support I can get. '

She nodded her head, slowly and moved past him, shutting the door quietly behind her. But before it closed, he could just hear her say 'Thank you, sir.'

At times, he thought, this is a brilliant job.

He walked back to his room, the school emptying around him until all he could hear was the sound of the cleaners, mopping floors and tipping out the bins, calling to each other as they worked. He sat down at his desk and thought about his phone call to the newspaper. What on earth did he think he was doing? Making a fool of himself, that's what. He was behaving like an idiot, heading down a path that was leading nowhere. What did he know about her, really, other than one important fact - she was married. That should have been enough to stop him in his tracks.

But reason didn't come into it. Something much stronger had him in its grip, and like a rip tide, it was propelling him forward, no way of stopping, no way of changing direction.

He suddenly saw the irony of reading about Gatsby's obsession with Daisy. He'd be throwing wild parties next!

He closed his eyes, suddenly tired. Over thirty and acting like a teenager with a crush. An unrequited, foolish crush. But somewhere in the recesses of his mind, he knew with absolute certainty, this was something different.

Chapter 10

Harry hung on tight to Jasper's lead as Amy herded them out of the front door. Shafts of sunlight filtered through the trees, making patterns on the driveway, the gravel slippery from the yellow leaves spiralling slowly to the ground. The dog snuffled at an overhanging bush and pulled towards the car.

'Careful, Harry. Move a bit faster to keep up or he'll have you over.' Amy grabbed Jasper's collar and pulled open the rear door of the car. 'Let go now, he'll jump in.' The dog leapt into the boot, banging his head against the roof, then pressing his nose against the grille which kept him off the back seats.

'Why isn't Daddy coming? It's Saturday.' Harry wriggled as Amy pulled the seat belt across his chest. 'Doesn't he want to see Grandma?'

'Of course he does, but he's working. He has to finish doing all sorts of sums so he can have tomorrow off.' Amy climbed behind the wheel. 'Then you'll have him all day.'

'Are we eating at Grandma's?'

'We are. And Aunty Sarah'll be there with Charlotte — we can all go to the park — and you can play football. You're going to have a great day.'

As the car picked up speed, Harry went quiet for a while. After a few minutes, Amy heard a small voice say, 'But Charlotte doesn't play football.' She smiled to herself. She liked the simple logic of his mind. His problems seemed such uncomplicated ones. Different as you got older, when there was always something at the back of your mind that muddied the waters. Not always anything you could nail down. But waking up in the morning, it hovered just beyond consciousness and, however much you busied yourself through the day, it lingered. Waiting to be recognised.

'*Stop it*,' she told herself, *'just enjoy the day.'*

She drove along, listening to 10cc on Smooth and began to sing along. After all, she always considered herself an optimist. The sky was brightening, the traffic was light, Harry was talking to himself in the back of the car and she was going to spend the day with her family. She hadn't seen Sarah in weeks and she'd missed her – short conversations on her mobile, that was all. Sometimes she called her while she was walking Jasper along the tow path. But then other dogs came into sight and she had to quickly pocket her phone to control his mad dash to meet a new 'friend'.

'Here we are, Harry. Didn't take long, did it?'

The door was on the latch, and Amy called a breezy, 'Hello!'

Her mother came down the hallway, giving her a hug and bending down to kiss Harry. 'You're early. Good. Sarah's here already and your father wants you to help him with something on the computer before we go out. He can't understand some message that keeps flashing up. I told him to leave it to you.'

'OK, I'll have a look.'

Charlotte, in a pale pink dress with hair ribbon and ankle socks to match, ran towards her. 'Oh, you've brought Jasper. Does he want to go for a walk round the garden?' and she grabbed his lead as the dog rubbed his jowls against her, heading for the back door, with Harry trotting after her.

Amy looked at her mother with an expression divided between laughter and despair. 'Well, nothing I could do about that...'

Her mother held up her hand, 'Amy, in every way, that dog's a disaster. He seems to love nothing better than digging to Australia every time he's here. That Lavatera has never recovered and the border plants...'

'We bring peace offerings.' She held up her bag, which made a chinking sound.

'Don't be clever,' but she was smiling and patting Amy's arm with one hand as she took the canvas bag with the other. 'I didn't realise you were going to bring him – he'll have to stay in the garage while we eat.'

'Will he?' asked Amy, already knowing the answer.

'Well, we're having lunch in the garden, while we still can. It's all laid out.' Her mother was leading the way into the kitchen. 'And you know it upsets your father when he sits near the table and stares at him all the time while he's eating. I've never known a dog that slavers so much.'

'He's a setter. They always slaver.'

Sarah was standing at the window with her back to them, watching Charlotte dragging Jasper round the lawn. She turned when she heard them and laughed, lifting her shoulders in a helpless shrug. 'She insisted on wearing that dress. I knew it was a mistake.'

'And pink, too,' Amy said. 'Brown would have been better.'

'Leave her, she's happy,' their mother was pulling two wine bottles out of the canvas bag. 'Amy, that's lovely. You've brought the Italian one your father was going on about. I'll be helping him with that. Didn't finish my rounds till seven o'clock last night. Some old boy had fallen and in the end, he had to go into hospital. Couldn't do much else for him. But it was upsetting...' and she went on as Amy always remembered she'd done, shaping the familiar, long-established background to their lives, settling them back into their allotted places. It was comforting, somehow. Sarah, the elder, dependable, deferred to; Amy, four years younger, impulsive, not to be taken too seriously.

Except when Robert had come into the fold. Marrying him had created a seismic shift.

The problem with the computer was easy to solve ('Now why couldn't I see that!' her father hitting the desk in frustration) and the trip to the park and the lunch outdoors went as easily as these family occasions usually did; Harry and Charlotte, both now red-faced and grubby, being indulged and played with and listened to; and Jasper, begrudgingly allowed to stay in the garden while they ate, as long as he obeyed Amy's repeated commands of 'Lie down' when he kept crawling on his belly towards the table.

It was when the meal was over that Amy found herself sitting with Sarah, for what she thought was a companionable, lazy few minutes, elbows propped on the wooden table, the debris of the meal still around them. They watched the children crouching on the grass under the willow tree, studying some insects with great concentration, and, through the open kitchen window came the clatter of pots and the introductory music to a quiz programme. But glancing over at her sister, she noticed that Sarah seemed distracted. Her usually calm expression had become thoughtful and she was frowning. Amy looked away, waiting for whatever it was that Sarah was going to tell her – it would be only when she was ready – and memories of the many good years they'd spent in this house, playing, arguing, sharing school secrets filled her mind. A time when they'd been sheltered, safe and life had been simple. Or was that what all adults did, create an illusion – look back and select the best parts A make-believe childhood.

She brushed bread crumbs off her lap onto the lawn. 'So, how does Dan like this new job?' For the moment, it was the best she could do.

Sarah attempted a smile, weak and unconvincing. 'Yes. It's worked out ok. Funny - months of applying for everything under the sun, as you well know, and not even getting an interview, then bingo. Not as much money, but, hey, he just wanted to be working again.'

'I'll bet.'

'It was getting pretty difficult. Dan likes to be doing things. He was losing heart.'

Amy waited for her to go on. But the pause was too long.

'Is it ok now?'

Sarah ran her fingers through her hair and looked down. 'We lost it a bit at one point a few months back. Never happened before. In all those years. You meet someone when you're that young and you don't really look very far ahead...' Her voice trailed off. 'But I suppose, in the end, you know you're just going through a bad time and things'll get better.'

'Incredible to think you've been together fifteen years...'

'Seventeen from when we met.'

'God, it's forever. And it's ok now?'

'Yes, with us. But when you get one thing sorted out, something else comes up and hits you. And I wasn't ready for this...'

'You're not ill, are you?' A wave of panic swept over her.

''No, not ill. Pregnant.' Sarah was studying her face for a reaction.

Amy breathed again. 'Why, that's good news, isn't it? Even if it's a shock.'

Sarah shook her head. 'Come on, Amy. Good news? Bradley's thirteen, Charlotte's coming up to secondary school, Dan hasn't worked in months, so we're over our limit – money's tight, to say the least. And what about my job? It isn't the sort of place that keeps you on through your maternity leave and lets you do part time afterwards.

And we need my salary.' She pulled a face. 'Dan's been really good about it, but, you know, only with an effort. Right now, it's the last thing we wanted.'

Amy put her arm round Sarah's shoulders and said nothing for a while. Not a lot she could come up with that wouldn't sound trite. She wasn't used to being the one who offered advice.

'Does Mum know?'

'Not yet. She said I was looking peaky... obviously her radar was working.'

Amy searched for something positive to say. 'Listen, you adore kids, Dan's a lovely man and sometimes, money isn't all that important...' and she stopped, immediately realising how crass that remark was, coming from her.

Sarah gave her a withering look. 'Fine when you've got plenty, Amy. Fine when you're married to someone who's not only come from money, but who makes a packet on top of that.'

'Oh, I didn't mean to be... what I meant was, you can have all the material comforts going, but it doesn't guarantee you'll be happy. There are other things that are more important. Christ, you know that.'

'Aren't you happy?' Sarah gave her a sharp look.

Amy hesitated. 'No one is all the time, are they? When Harry was two, I wanted another child. I know Mum thought it just didn't happen. But Robert was adamant.' She stopped and swallowed, remembering. 'He wouldn't consider it. He'd already got four children, he said. He certainly didn't want any more. And I couldn't talk about it, even to you, because everything was getting back to normal after my 'scandalous' behaviour. So,' she could feel the tears coming and shook her head to get rid of them, 'eventually, I solved the problem.' She gave an apologetic laugh. 'I bought a puppy...'

Sarah clutched Amy's hand and nodded furiously. 'Please don't cry. I'm a selfish cow and I'm sorry for moaning. But you shouldn't keep things like that to yourself. Talk to me, whatever it is, you idiot. If we can't look out for each other...' She trailed off, hearing her father calling from the house. 'Come on, Mum'll worry if we sit here looking serious for too long. Let's get the kids sorted and take that crazy dog of yours up the lane.'

The drive home was quiet. Amy had turned the radio off and Harry was asleep in the back, Jasper curled up on his blanket in his usual place. The only sound was the dull beat of the tyres on tarmac and, once, the two-note clarion call of a speeding ambulance, which made her pull sharply into the kerb out of its way. She sat for a few minutes after it had passed, listening to its urgent clamour fading as it weaved its way through the late afternoon. *You plan ahead and imagine exactly how things are going to be,* she thought. *Certain of the story you've made up for yourself. But you've got to be young and naïve to keep believing in it.*

She stared, unseeing through the windscreen, then turned and looked over her shoulder to check that Harry was still asleep in the back seat. His blond head had lolled sideways and his mouth was slightly open, puffing small, even breaths which barely made a sound.

She turned the engine back on, put the car into gear and headed for home.

Chapter 11

'There are three seats over here. Fourth row. See them?'

Six thirty. Nearly time for the start. Catherine directed a mother and father and a spiky-haired little boy to their places and looked round the hall. She was pleased to see how full it was. The latecomers would have to stand at the back. When she'd offered to help with front-of-house, Jake had seemed diffident; the turnout might not be particularly good, he'd said, and the other members of the English department could cope well enough. She knew she'd looked hurt. No good pretending - she *was* hurt. She'd wanted to show support for him as he'd done for her. Surely that was what a relationship was all about. And she'd been relieved when he'd changed his mind a few days ago.

'Come if you want,' he'd said. It was the end of the school day and he was sorting through his locker in the staffroom. 'It's difficult to know exactly what the numbers'll be, but you're right, an extra pair of hands would be useful. You could make sure the prefects are in the right places; we need two in the car park, three in the hall, two at the entrance handing out programmes, although Jenny's meant to be looking after that.' He didn't add that Jenny could be a bit dizzy, but Catherine got the message. 'I won't be able to see much from behind the stage, so let's hope everyone's remembered where they're meant to be.'

So she'd put on her blue dress with the panelled skirt, tied up her hair and made sure she was even earlier than the rest of the helpers, arriving at the school before the cleaners had finished their shift. An hour to go, and, in the hall, students were sitting on the edge of the stage, on the first row of seats, some wandering backwards and forwards with scripts in their hands, muttering to themselves, trying to memorise their pieces. Jake was standing with a red-haired boy, neatly dressed in grey trousers, white shirt and school tie, who appeared close to tears. Jake held a notebook in his hand.

'Look, Philip. You don't have to know it by heart. No one will care if you read it. As long as you look up so your voice carries to the back row. It's better than going blank in the middle.' He looked as though he was about to ruffle the boy's hair when he must have thought better of it. 'Go on before Matthew, then you won't have so long to wait.' Catherine smiled and gave a small wave as he moved further backstage. But he was too preoccupied to see her. She'd leave him to it, then. She knew she'd be no help here, but at least she could go and check the dining room, see that the refreshments were laid out for the interval, then check on the prefects.

Half an hour later, a rising air of expectation spread through the hall, a buzz of excitement ready to be hushed at the first sign of action on the stage. Catherine positioned herself against a side wall as the Head climbed up the steps from the auditorium floor to start the proceedings.

'Welcome to our evening of...' he began, but didn't get much further. The door in the back corner of the room was flung open, Jenny leading the way, followed by a blonde girl in a suede jacket and a man, with a large camera case looped over his shoulder. They pushed their way down the right-hand aisle, all eyes following them as they approached the stage.

Tim was watching their progress and smiling. 'Ah, the press, ladies and gentlemen. Could you give us just a minute?' He bent down to speak to them, gesturing to a suitable spot for the cameraman to stand, and offering a front row seat, with its reserved notice on it, to the girl. Well, thought Catherine, they could at least have arrived in plenty of time instead of holding up the start. Not exactly thoughtful, when the kids were already nervous, waiting to perform.

Tim began his welcome speech again - delighted so many could come, appreciating the support Forest Green parents always gave to every event, praising the English Department for all its hard work. Then a word for the new starters (how small they always looked in those first few months, Catherine thought, small and vulnerable).

'We want you to realise just what you can achieve when you've been with us for five years. Some of the students tonight will go on into our sixth form, and from there to university and take up apprenticeships, so the sky's the limit. But for now, let's hear from them, reading their own creative writing. I know you'll enjoy it. I was at the rehearsal yesterday and, I can promise you, you're in for a treat.'

Even though Catherine recognised all this as a bit of a publicity exercise, she admired Tim, not just for the way he captured an audience. He really cared about the pupils, not just the clever ones, the sporty ones, but all of them. And Catherine had a moment of pride at belonging to a school which put the children first, not one that was obsessed with league tables and county prizes. It made her think back to her own schooldays, and the teacher who'd been her life-saver – Miss Morris, who taught PE, young and enthusiastic, who'd recognised the only talent she seemed to have at 14, and had given her enough courage to apply to a sports college. About the only time her father had taken any interest in her education and, of course, it was to challenge 'this daft idea'. She could hear him now, after all this time, grumbling away, 'It's not going to happen. We don't have that sort of money to throw away. And it's not as if there aren't jobs here you could walk straight into.' He'd gone back to reading the newspaper with a final remark that seemed to close the cage door: 'Forget it, we need you at home.' But she wasn't going to be beaten.

No blazing rows or bad temper. Just quiet determination. Head down in the library, part-time jobs to earn some money, help at school with the entry forms. There were times when she thought she'd never make it; but there were other times when she knew that if she wanted it badly enough, she'd have to fight for it.

Tim climbed down from the platform to take his seat. There was a moment's pause, some muffled coughing and whispering, then the curtain parted, and a tall girl stepped forward, pushing back her hair from her face three or four times and looking into the wings, where Catherine knew Jake would be. Let it go well, she thought. For Jake's sake. She knew him better than anyone and he'd been really anxious about tonight. To others, he might seem too casual about his job, about everything, but he'd felt the pressure this last week. Not that he'd talked about it, but she'd seen how preoccupied he'd been. Even staying up way past midnight last Saturday, when usually at the weekend, he was able to leave school behind, and she'd come downstairs to find him on his iPad in the semi-darkness, totally unaware she'd entered the room. 'Do come to bed, Jake,' she'd said. 'It's one o'clock.'

Applause filled the room, and Catherine realised she hadn't really been listening. Concentrate, she told herself, or you won't be able to discuss any of this later. When the break came for the interval, she made sure the prefects were doing their job, ushering everyone towards the refreshments. As the audience settled down for the second half, she saw the photographer heading for the exit, but the girl reporter was still sitting in the front row. Jenny, breathless and full of importance, joined Catherine at the back of the room, whispering, 'I'm going to do my act as a traffic controller, now - arms up for 'more volume', arms down for 'slow down'. Not sure what I'll do for 'smile'. People'll think I've gone mad.' She giggled. 'Well, they think that anyway. Are you enjoying it?'

To be honest, Catherine didn't remember much about the first half. Only a few lines from a story about a wolf that had been separated from the pack and a poem that hadn't made sense called 'Time Out'. But she did remember the earnest faces of the readers and their relieved expressions when they'd finished. 'Very much,' she said. 'Good to see so many parents here when all that hard work has gone into it.'

'Yes,' Jenny's eyes were fixed on the stage, waiting for the curtains to open. 'Good to see the Stockport Mercury, too. The photographer had another job, so he's gone, but the girl's going to interview three or four of them at the end. Oops, here we go.'

At eight thirty, the hall was empty and some of the helpers were edging along the rows, picking up dropped programmes and sweet wrappers. Catherine couldn't decide whether she should go backstage to join Jake and the other members of the English department and listen to the interviews. Well, why not! She could stay in the background and disappear if she felt she was in the way.

Jake looked up briefly as she ducked under the backcloth onto the stage, but didn't beckon her over She went to stand by Jenny who didn't seem to have a job to do, unlike the others who seemed to be occupied in finding coats and tidying away scripts. The boy being interviewed was Gareth, who'd given such a confident performance earlier - even Catherine could recognise it was the best piece - and he sat facing the reporter, both of them sitting close together on hard-backed chairs, she leaning forward with a notebook on her lap.

'So,' she was saying, 'what gave you the idea? Had you read a story or a poem along the same lines?'

'Well, we'd read '*The Rain Horse*' in class,' said Gareth, looking across at Jake. 'It's by Ted Hughes and it's not easy to understand, because, at the end, you aren't sure whether the horse is real or whether it's an imaginary one, like, in the man's head. So I wanted to write something a bit mysterious, something a bit strange.'

As Catherine listened, it wasn't the first time she wished she taught a subject that took you someplace else, made you think and come to your own conclusions. One you could feel a passion for. She could see it now in Jake, bound up in the discussion, his eyes intense and dark, his lips pressed together.

Jenny shifted her weight from one foot to the other. She never seemed to be able to keep still for five minutes. 'I'd love to have a job like that,' she said, speaking out of the corner of her mouth., but still a bit too loudly for Catherine's comfort. 'Every day different. Even on a weekly.' She nodded her head towards the reporter. 'Tell you what, she's got a way of relaxing them. Name's Amy Wilson. She was saying she'd interviewed Tim once, a few years ago, and she covered that half marathon a few weeks back – you ran in that, didn't you?' Jenny pushed air through her teeth, making a soft hissing sound. 'Look at that watch she's got on, all white and gold numbers – must have cost a fortune.'

'Careful, she'll hear you.' Catherine wanted Jenny to shut up. She found her embarrassing at times, gabbling on non-stop, without waiting for an answer and totally unaware of who might hear her. She tried to move away slightly to stop any more confidences.

'And what I'd give for that jacket...' Jenny at least was whispering now. 'Christ, let's be honest – what I'd give for that face! She's like the girl in that hair advert where she's running along the beach on some tropical island...'

Jake was frowning, looking over at them with an expression that Catherine knew well. She wanted to tell Jenny to hush, but had an idea it wouldn't do any good. So she muttered a goodbye and stepped quietly backwards and off the stage area.

After the warm fug of the over-heated hall, it felt good to be out in the evening air. There was only a quarter moon in the sky and the few stars she could see looked like pin-pricks, tiny and pale. No visitors' cars in front of the building now, just those belonging to the staff. She was about to descend the steps, when she caught movement behind the spaces the cars had left, something just within her line of sight, but blurred, indecipherable.

She stood quite still, narrowing her eyes, until she was able to focus.

Circling, like vultures waiting to pick at carrion, were seven or eight dark shapes on bikes, wheeling round and round, slowly, no shouting or laughing. Just the slow circles getting closer and closer to the remaining cars, moving in what seemed like a weird choreographed routine.

For a brief second, her breathing quickened, her hands clenched, as she tried to reconcile irrational fear of the unknown with common sense. *Come on, slow down and think carefully before you panic again.*

When her eyes had adjusted fully to the dark, she felt the tense muscles in her neck relax. There was nothing to be alarmed about. These were only some boys, lanky teenagers, most dressed in dark hoodies and what looked like combat trousers, their uniform of sorts, messing around because they'd nothing better to do.

No one, of course, was guarding the cars. The prefects had gone home long ago. She waited alone, trying to decide whether to go over and ask them to leave, or ignore them. They weren't actually doing any harm, but there was something menacing in their deliberate actions – challenging authority, or so it seemed to Catherine. They had no right to be here. And she didn't want the night ruined by some mindless vandalism at the very end of it all. Then she heard a 'ping' as one of the bikes caught something on a car – a wing mirror perhaps – and a stifled 'Fuck!' and a mocking cheer.

Then a voice called out which she thought she recognised, but couldn't quite place.

'Sorry, miss. Didn't mean to.'

Then another: 'Wait till we do our show, miss. It'll be a bloody sight better than theirs.'

And the bikes swung slowly off towards the trees, heading for the broken fence and the cover of the park.

Chapter 12

Robert rubbed his temples and closed his eyes, certain a migraine was starting. He might as well give Amy the bad news early on so she could start the evening without him. The way things were going, he'd be lucky if he got home by nine o'clock; he might not even make it for the coffee. He picked up his mobile from the edge of the desk.

After the fourth ring she answered, sounding breathless. 'Hi.'

'Amy, I'm still in the office and things aren't looking good.'

There was a pause. 'Well, how long d'you think you're going to be?'

'Difficult to say. Still pulling the budget together and I need to get it to a decent point before I can leave… It's only Mike and Sophie. They'll understand.'

There was a pause. 'Ok. We'll start without you.' He could hear the radio in the background and then Amy saying. 'Don't touch that, Harry. I've told you once.'

Robert smiled to himself. 'I'll leave you to it. Soon as I set off, I'll ring you.'

He sat back in his chair and stared at the computer screen, waiting for the excel file to finish calculating. The budget submissions had come in late and he needed to consolidate the figures to present to the board tomorrow. Somewhere along the line, there'd been a major cock-up and time was running out. He clicked the mouse, trying to work backwards and see if he could spot the error. How was it that Chris hadn't seen this before it had got to *his* desk? Christ, another bloody mess that should have been picked up earlier.

After ten minutes, he shook his head in frustration and clicked the intercom. 'Can you come in? We've got a problem.'

The door to his office was pushed open by a plump, tired-looking man, carrying papers in one hand and a large manila folder tucked under his arm. He was shaking his head, not looking at Robert, muttering, 'It's the cost income ratio, isn't it?' He didn't wait for an answer. 'I'll bet it is. I gave it to Paul and I shouldn't have done. He's too busy thinking about his rally cross and planning how to get out of the door at five o'clock... Sorry, Robert, this is my bag. I'll sort it. Give me until the morning.'

'Sit down, Chris, for heaven's sake. We won't solve it with you wittering on. No, you shouldn't have left it to Paul, he's a liability these days. But we're short of time – can't leave this till the morning – so let's go through it together and see where he's slipped up.'

An hour and a half later, they switched off the computers and the lights and emerged into the outer office, now deserted and in shadow. They made their way into the corridor, nodding to the security man as they passed through the lobby. It had taken them a frustratingly long time to solve the problem - a problem, Robert thought, which shouldn't have been allowed to go undetected through the various checks. No good dismissing it as Human Error – it was negligence. Some of the recent office appointments had been disappointing – he wanted people who were not just bright, but thorough - and he needed to see HR in the morning to find out what could be done about Paul. Never mind written warnings, he didn't want him on his team.

Leave it behind, he told himself as he opened his front door to hear the sound of voices and plates clinking, coming from the dining room. Jasper came leaping towards him, front paws reaching his chest and for once, Robert wasn't annoyed. The dog shouldn't have been part of the dinner party, but Sophie loved him and always objected when he was locked away in the kitchen. 'Don't shut him away,' she'd say. 'He loves company and he's part of the family,' adding with a sly smile, 'much more fun than some people I know.'

As Robert entered the room, Mike stood up, pretending to leave. 'Just going, Robert. It's been a good evening.' Then he laughed as Sophie pulled a disapproving face. 'Come on, I'll get you a stiff drink so you can catch up? Whiskey?'

'No thanks, I need food inside me first. Just pour me a glass of red wine, that'll do to start with.'

Amy leaned over as he joined them at the table and gave him a brief kiss. 'We waited a bit, so we haven't had the chicken yet. Are you ready to eat now? Or do you want a minute?'

Sophie held out the glass of wine. 'Get that down you and relax. You look tired.'

'Really sorry to be late like this, but nothing I could do about it.'

Robert felt the tension drop away as he sank into his usual chair at the head of the table. He loved the way, after all those years of having to run everything, decide every issue, this home was a haven, a sort of peaceful chaos, because Amy didn't need him to make all the decisions, to cope with everyday hiccups. She somehow managed to ride through life, fixing things, juggling all the plates in the air without constantly having to ask for help. It had always amazed him how self-sufficient she was - so unlike Paula. And it was no good feeling guilty about comparing them in that respect. It was a fact.

He sat back and watched her now, so easy with people she liked. He knew how difficult the other evening had been at the Imperial.

Made worse, of course, by that bloody woman, Mary Aisgarth, who just had to make her point. Would it ever all die down?

By the time the meal was almost over and the coffee and brandy on the table, the conversation had developed from a general discussion into friendly argument about a news story; a gang of youths on an estate had beaten up a householder who was trying to protect his car, and Robert had pointed out, quite strongly, that putting yourself in harm's way when facing mindless violence wasn't worth the risk.

'You're not going to win. Call the police. Better than ending up in hospital.'

Mike was leaning across the table to cut some cheese. 'So you're saying – just stand by. What if you saw some old man being attacked in the street. You wouldn't go and help?'

'I'm not saying that,' Robert put down his glass. 'I just don't think your heart should rule your head. Let's take a different scenario. The middle of Manchester on a Saturday night - someone's taking a beating and you're going to wade in? It won't be me. You don't know who's got a knife these days or who's high on drugs. You'd be risking your *own* life.'

'Ok,' Sophie looked over at Amy for some encouragement. 'Consider another situation. It's a woman who's in trouble - a man is dragging her up the street. No-one else around to help. So you'd just stand and watch?'

Amy lifted her hands, impatiently and joined in. 'Of course he wouldn't. He'd go up to the man and give him a good talking to. Tell him how important good manners are, wouldn't you Robert?'

He suddenly felt besieged. 'There are circumstances, of course, where you'd have to interfere. Morally. If a child was at risk or a woman was under threat...'

'Or an animal was being mistreated,' put in Sophie. 'I'd see red then and wouldn't think about what would happen after. I'd have to do something.'

'I would, too,' Amy stood up. 'Just hold on a minute while I brew some more coffee. Don't carry on till I get back.'

Robert sighed and stretched his legs under the table. 'You're bleeding hearts, all three of you. Sometimes, you have to think before you wade in. Do you remember the time, Mike, when we were driving back late and we saw that couple having a row by the petrol station in Didsbury village? Pushing each other about. And you shouted at me to stop the car. 'For Christ's sake, he's killing her.' Your very words. Next minute, they were laughing like maniacs and hugging each other. Remember?'

Mike grinned and nodded. 'Yes, well, I got that wrong. Sometimes you don't read a situation quite right.' He shrugged. 'But after twenty years, Robert, I think I know you - on the surface, all common sense and civilised behaviour. Is cerebral the right word? Yes, I think it is. But underneath you're as hot-blooded and savage as the rest of us. If you were threatened you'd be brutal.'

'Ah, if *I* was threatened, or if it was Amy or Harry. For your family. That's very different.'

Sophie put a hand over Mike's. 'Just like you, darling. Look at the time you took a swing at Harriet's boyfriend. You didn't give him a chance to say what had happened. Just POW! Like something out of a comic strip. Very embarrassing.'

Amy came in with the coffee pot and set it down. 'Gosh, I remember that. Hadn't known you long and I thought I was going to be mixing with some very interesting people – thugs, perhaps, but interesting!'

Mike bowed his head slightly as though he'd been paid a compliment. 'I know what *I'm* like. I was just making the point that Robert's the same, underneath. If it mattered enough, if everything we cared about was in jeopardy, we'd jump in and sod the consequences.' Mike touched Sophie's chin in a feinted punch, smiling at her. 'Trust you to bring *that* up. Harriet forgave me long ago.' They smiled at one another. And not for the first time, Robert felt a stab of envy. You could see how compatible they were. Even remarks that could seem contentious, for them, were just part of the fabric that bound them together. 'And the boyfriend - James, was it? – turned out to be a toe-rag.'

'Bloody good job you missed, Mike,' Amy poured coffee into the cup he was holding out. 'You'd have ended up in the *Stockport Mercury*. Think what that would have done for business.'

'I meant to say how impressed I was with your article on the Bramhall run, Amy.' Sophie pulled out an After Eight from its box, bracelets jangling as she did so. 'Great that they're using your talents again. Such a waste if you don't get back into it.'

'I have to say I'm enjoying it.'

Robert could feel a tightening across his chest. He didn't want any more stress with old arguments resurfacing. They'd been through that enough times. 'Well, she's not doing a lot. Harry's only six and we've decided there has to be someone at home for him until he's older...'

Amy was looking straight at Sophie and answered as though Robert hadn't spoken. 'It's only odd assignments at the moment and some are a bit run-of-the-mill, but others...well, a school this week was putting on a creative writing evening – pupils reading their own stuff, not all great performers to be honest, but what they'd written was wonderful.'

Mike downed his brandy and pushed back his chair. 'Creative writing isn't going to do them much good, though, is it? Look at Harriet – what sort of jobs has that Arts degree fitted her for? All this expressing yourself doesn't add up to earning a decent living.'

'Philistine!' Sophie gave him a withering look. 'Not everything's about money.'

'But Mike's right,' Robert said. 'We're in a downturn and these days, you have to study with an awareness of the market. You can't live with your head in a book and forget the practicalities. We need a workforce that's numerate and literate and we're certainly not achieving that at the moment. So something's going wrong.'

Amy put her coffee cup down too hard and folded her arms. He could see how annoyed she was. This had been part of the challenge in the early days; then, he'd liked her quirkiness and questioning of his conventional views. A young, intelligent mind forcing him to justify his prejudices. But now, her reactions sometimes threw him off balance, as though the difference in their ages was widening the divide.

He raised his eyebrows at her. 'What?'

'You sound like a politician,' she said, as though this was the worst insult she could pay him. 'Tired stock phrases that get repeated again and again. *An awareness of the market? A workforce?* We are talking about people here, aren't we?' She bit off the words, shaking her head in frustration.

They all sat very still; the only sound was the knife Amy had accidentally knocked against her plate.

Robert forced himself to smile. Did he sound glib and superficial then? Christ, he hadn't meant to. He'd thought this was just after-dinner talk with friends, an exchange of opinions and he couldn't figure out why she'd soured the mood.

He was grateful for Sophie coming to the rescue. 'Always like a bit of controversy to liven up the evening. It's a good job we don't all think alike. Conversation would be dead.' She patted Mike on the arm. 'Come on, you're nearly falling asleep. Time we went home.' She pulled herself upright. 'Work for me tomorrow, anyway, and I need to be alert. Our turn next time but there's no way I can compete with that lovely meal.'

The door was closed and Amy had headed upstairs to bed, leaving the clearing-up till the morning. Robert let the dog out in the garden for a few minutes before shutting him in the kitchen. Then he took his half-finished glass of brandy into the lounge and picked up the Guardian from the low wooden table beside the sofa. He sat down to catch up with the day's news, and started to read, but soon found his thoughts turning to the evening and Amy's remarks. He'd been taken aback, not just by the words she'd used. It was the sound of them. It had felt like an attack. He stared into the fireplace, trying to make sense of it, trying to solve a puzzle he had no way of understanding.

Eventually, he got up and climbed the stairs, turning off the lights as he went. And after the strains of the day, the house slipped gradually into the calming oblivion of night.

Chapter 13

The train drew slowly out of the station and Jake sat back against the hard, upholstered seat, glad to be on the way home. Glad to be out of the meeting. Didn't they love to hear themselves talk, these exam chiefs, these government gofers, he thought, six hours of deliberations that could have been dealt with in two? And why change the syllabus again, anyway? There was plenty of cynicism from the start this morning, moderators muttering rebellious comments and asking questions that challenged the whole premise of the new exams. Every time another Education Minister was brought in, it was the same old story – they just had to put their stamp on their new domain. Never mind what was working - here's a much better idea. Yeah, right.

He put his brief case, stuffed full with notes and guide lines and specifications, onto the seat beside him, hoping no-one had booked it. He wanted half an hour to himself. The blackened arches of the terminal gave way to low grey buildings and concrete wastelands. It was some minutes before the fenced back gardens, dirt paths and small allotment squares began to line the track. He had often thought that living by a railway line must be a great way of keeping time. There goes the 9.30 into Piccadilly. That's the last train to Heaton Moor. The rattling wheels punctuating the day, creating a timetable to live by. Noisy but giving you a kick-start when you needed to stop dreaming and get a move on.

Well, that'd be good for me and make me shift myself. Stop my mind from going its own sweet way.

He stared out of the window, then suddenly delved into his case with a sense of purpose, pulling out the new exam guidelines and taking a pen from his breast pocket. But minutes passed and the papers slid down onto his lap. He'd had enough for one day and it was pointless re-reading it all again. A man in uniform pushed a trolley through the half-empty carriage, stopping at each row of seats to ask, in a cheery voice, who wanted coffee, tea, sandwiches. And the train rocked on through the fading afternoon.

He drifted, allowing his mind to go back to that night, and how he'd felt when he'd heard Tim say to the audience, 'The press, ladies and gentlemen.' God, if he hadn't been nervous before, he had been then. He knew it would be her. He didn't just remember it all in detail, like a film he'd already replayed over and over, the whole scene, the conversation, the way she looked at him, how she smiled. He could remember the way his pulse beat faster and his legs felt weak, the tension holding his body tight.

The days before, he'd weighed up the odds of whether she'd be the one they'd send. Then when he heard Tim's announcement, he hadn't dared look through the curtain. But he knew, he just knew. At the interval, the chair of governors called him over for a brief introduction to 'the lady from the press' – how odd to shake hands like strangers – and he was conscious of his face going through all the expressions of feigned surprise that wouldn't have convinced anyone if they'd been watching him closely. Someone called his name and he just had time to suggest she might want to interview some of the pupils after the performance before he had to go.

After the parents had left the hall and she'd been led backstage by Jenny, he'd spent some time watching her with the students - talking away to Lindsey and Gareth, as interested in them as she'd been in the runners at the half-marathon. She had a way of concentrating on whoever was speaking, her eyes only leaving their face briefly while she made quick notes. Jake was only vaguely aware of other teachers near the side of the stage, and didn't notice that Catherine was leaving until he heard Jenny whisper 'Bye' to her retreating back. It was when Amy was checking the names and ages of the pupils with him and he finally found himself alone with her that they really got talking.

'They so enjoyed writing all of it, didn't they? Look how keen Gareth was to tell me how he'd thought it all through. How he'd rewritten it over and over again until he was satisfied.' She looked at him, curiously. 'I've never got away with poetry. You love it, don't you?'

He smiled and shook his head. 'Not all of it. To be honest, a lot of it bores me. I'm not into flowers and nymphs. I like the gritty stuff. Eliot, Carol Ann Duffy, Simon Armitage. The poetry that's about the human condition... sorry if that sounds pretentious.'

'No, it doesn't. What you choose to teach them obviously works – it gets them going. Really makes them think for themselves. That one - by Rebecca, was it? – about the old man... it made me, well, shiver. It shook me that someone so young could find the words to express such pain. Without it being...'

'Maudlin? I know. I'm often surprised, too. They often get more out of it than I do.'

'So how do you get a response like that?' She put her hand out in a gesture he thought was meant to be encouraging, just short of touching the sleeve of his jacket. It was an effort for him to keep calm. She sat back quickly. 'I promise I'm not going to quote you. I'm just fascinated. How do you do it?'

'I don't always know. Some fourteen-year-olds who think they can't write at all, just need a way in - like getting them to think about a memory that's still vivid because it's had an emotional impact, write a paragraph describing it, cut out some words to create a rhythm, and – hey presto – a poem.'

'Oh, it can't be that easy.' She leant forward, her chin cupped in one hand and he thought he'd never met anyone so bloody perfect.

'Sometimes, really, it is. And sometimes the most unlikely ones write amazing stuff.' She was nodding for him to go on, but he hesitated. 'Are you sure I'm not boring you?'

'I'd tell you if you were,' she smiled. 'Sometimes…?

'Well, it's perhaps not common knowledge but we take in a few pupils from the Unit down the road – Cheadle House. They get sent there from all over the country for different reasons – parental neglect, runaways, some for criminal behaviour. They might attend our school for a few months, then they disappear back to their home towns, I suppose. Well this lad, he was 15, not much school left for him. And I knew from someone that he'd set fire to a number of buildings. God knows why and he never said a word about it. Anyway, he joined my English class and there was something about him that shouted 'Trouble'. I remember his face, guarded and surly, eyes that never seemed to blink and a shock of black hair. Always wore the same jumper. He sat there for weeks, saying nothing, taking no interest, just... well, brooding. That's what it seemed like to me.' Jake paused, trying to recreate the exact memory. 'This day, we'd been reading a poem about a fox being chased by hounds, and I asked them to write their own, as though they were the animal. In danger. Any animal, they could choose their own. Well, half the lesson had gone and he came up to my desk and shoved this piece of paper down in front of me. His poem, neatly written, not even a crossing out, 16 lines long.'

'And?'

'It was so good. No, it was more than that. It was brilliant. He wrote about a hare, terrified by the sound of a gun firing, its beating heart, its fur quivering, long back legs pounding across a stubble field. I'll never forget it. Probably because I thought at the time - he's been hounded himself and felt scared to death. He knows just what it's like.' He stopped, and looked down, unable to meet her gaze any longer. Every fibre of his body was tense, every nerve on edge at the nearness of her. He felt he'd said too much and gave a derisive smile. Apologetic.

Amy was studying his face. 'Go on.'

'Well, the best part of it was - he'd done something he was proud of. He stood over me as I read it and when I told him how good it was, how remarkable the images were, his whole face changed. All the surliness gone...'

'So what you're saying is...'

'Nothing very profound. It's just that poetry's more than reading someone else's lines on a page and learning it by rote. When you write down your own thoughts, even if it doesn't obey the rules – who made *those* up, anyway - it can come alive and express things in a way other forms can't.' He ran his fingers through his hair – that habitual gesture when he was trying to convey something difficult - and gave an embarrassed laugh. 'God, what do I sound like? I don't usually go on like that.'

'What happened to the boy?'

'He was there one week, gone the next. Never saw him again. So I don't have an uplifting ending for you.'

'It's uplifting enough. Just to know he felt good about himself...'

And Jake knew he didn't have to say anything else. He'd never realised before how completely you could be understood, how it went far beyond the words spoken. It was a revelation - this connection – an awesome dovetailing of minds.

But he had to be honest with himself, there was more to it than that. Of course it wasn't just finding someone who thought like he did, who shared his ideas, who listened. It was physical, an attraction so strong he couldn't quite believe it was happening. That had been his first reaction at the airport, hadn't it? He felt the same now. He longed to reach out and touch her - if he'd had the courage - put his hand over hers, let their fingers entwine, feel the warmth of her. He had no idea whether she sensed this, or whether his *yearning* – what other word could he give to it? – could possibly be felt without some reciprocal feeling on her part.

All he knew was that he wanted this moment to last forever.

'Tickets please.' The guard calling from further down the carriage brought him back to the present with a start. He steadied the papers on his lap that he was meant to be reading, fished his ticket out of his pocket and held it up to be clipped. The carriage felt airless. Another ten minutes and he'd be at the station and he could stretch his legs on the walk home. He'd enjoy the exercise, even though he could see the wind had picked up, blowing fragments of debris onto the train windows. But just as he was ready to get up and move towards the doors, his mobile rang. He'd thought it was on silent – it had been through the meeting – but then he remembered changing the setting as he'd headed for the station. There was no way he was going to answer it until he was on the platform – he hated those one-sided conversations you overheard so damned clearly as you sat, irritated, in your seat – so it wasn't until he was making his way onto the road that he looked hurriedly at the screen and saw someone had left him a message.

He went into voicemail and felt a stab of anxiety when he heard his brother saying his name. Oliver never contacted him in the day. He listened to the message twice: 'Jake, will you ring me tonight. Mum's in hospital having tests – collapsed in a shop this morning, not the first time, apparently. She blacked out for quite a while. Anyway, they're running tests.' A pause. 'Dad's panicking a bit. Ring me after seven. I'll be at the hospital till then and there's no reception.'

Never plan anything, Jake thought, because there's always something unexpected waiting to throw you sideways. Just to remind you you're not in control. Whoever's dealing the cards has them all face down and you don't know what's coming till the very last minute.

He began to run, already in his mind packing an overnight bag, filling the car up with petrol and thinking what lessons would need to be covered on the following day. He'd barely given his parents a thought in the last two months. Not really. They were just there. Yes, the Sunday night phone calls were a regular thing, but brief - like touching base, just a sketchy summing up of what had happened that week. He didn't always listen carefully enough to what his mother was telling him, although they always discussed what was happening in the news and talked about TV programmes they'd enjoyed. His father ran out of small talk once they'd gone over how Leeds United was doing. It was a ritual that didn't alter. He'd never thought about his parents getting older, that circumstances might change, that something might happen to one of them. He'd allowed himself to be lulled into a sense of complacency. He'd certainly not been ready for this wake-up call.

He hurried home, skirting pedestrians on the pavement and trying to catch his breath, bracing himself against the fear that he might be too late.

Chapter 14

Harry sat, elbows on the table, slowly munching his way through scrambled eggs and toast, stopping every so often to gulp down the orange juice from his blue mug. There was no hurrying him. Amy had already finished hers, swallowing the tea too quickly and burning her mouth, and she was now clearing the breakfast table. Finally she stood over him.

'Could you please speed up, Harry? I'm not getting the car out to go 500 yards when it's a lovely morning and we can walk it. Come on.'

Harry kept on chewing and didn't look at her. 'I'm going as fast as I can.'

'You're going like a snail.'

His blond hair fell over his eyes as he tried to spear the last square of toast, which skittered away from him and fell on the floor. Jasper was waiting in just the right spot, to the left of Harry's elbow. *Oh, well,* thought Amy, no point getting annoyed. *Too nice a day out there to be cross.*

'Ok,' she bent low over the table to match his eye-level. 'Perhaps the snail could keep chewing his breakfast as he moves towards the back door. They are clever things – they can do two things at once, I've heard.'

Harry tried his best to keep a straight face as he jumped down. 'Where's my bag?'

'Here. Now put your jacket on and I'll get Jasper's lead.'

Amy locked the door and held Harry's hand as they walked over the sunlit pavements towards the cut, which bypassed the main road. The noise of traffic faded, muffled by the tall trees and shrubbery that lined the path. Two children ran past them as they approached the school playing fields at the rear entrance.

'See,' Amy said, 'we're nearly late. Let's hope Mrs. Parr lets us in.' She remembered when she was a child and there were no security gates and warning signs about trespassers and unauthorised personnel. How sad that all that carefree trust in people had gone, she thought. Or were we just kidding ourselves back then because we didn't know about the dangers and we weren't being bombarded with terrible stories on the News and the Internet. The stories with so much graphic detail they frightened Amy to death?

She realised that Harry wasn't talking, just walking stolidly by her side, his hand loose in hers. She looked down at him, wondering whether there was time enough to ask. Something was obviously on his mind.

'What's the matter, Harry? Are you worried about school?'

'No. We're doing 'Birds' today. I told you, Mummy.'

'So… if it isn't school, what are you thinking about? You're very serious.'

He took a few strides without speaking.

'Does Daddy love me as much as his other children?'

The question threw her. What on earth had made him think such a thing? She was shocked to discover how little she really knew about how his mind worked – she'd thought she could always sense what his worries were. Obviously not.

'Of course he does. He loves you to bits, Harry. Why would you think he doesn't?'

He looked up at her with such an earnest expression it made her heart ache. 'Because... because... last night, he was on the phone to Holly, and he said...'

'Yes, what did he say?'

'He said he was going to take her away somewhere. Just them.'

'Yes, well, he is. He's taking her on a short holiday - only for a week. Then he's coming back to us. He's not going to leave us. Is that what you're thinking?'

They had reached the gate and Mrs. Parr was walking off towards the front of the school. They'd have to go round and press the buzzer at the main entrance to be admitted. Harry stood, head bent, looking at his shoes.

'We never see them. His other children. They never come and see us.'

Amy knelt down, vaguely aware that Jasper had wandered off towards the farmer's field, and thought to herself, how the hell do I explain this! 'No, that's true, we don't. Daddy has two separate families, we've talked about this before. Lots of people do, Harry. Your friend Taylor's the same, isn't he?' She gently lifted his chin so that he was looking at her. 'We don't see them because Holly's mum feels it's better for her three children to see Daddy in their own home and not come to us. And we have to accept that.'

'Why?'

'Harry, I can't honestly speak for how someone else feels. She was upset when he... left and made *us* his family. So he keeps them separate and then nobody's hurt.' It sounded lame. But Amy was wondering how much a child as young as Harry could take in.

He nodded, but he had a puzzled expression on his face.

'Come on, let's get you in before you're told off for being late. I'll explain it was all my fault. Or we'll blame Jasper! Say he lost himself...'

'That's telling a lie. Look, he's coming back.' Harry beamed when he saw the dog trotting up to them, and clasped him round his hairy neck. 'Good boy. You see, he didn't lose himself.'

Later, walking back towards home, Amy felt chilled in the shadowy lane and wished she'd put on warmer clothes. However bright the day had looked, it had been deceiving. Out here, the air was sharp and full of autumn and a faint morning mist still hovered over the fields. Jasper was trailing behind her, sniffing on every blade of grass, ignoring her calls and jangling of the lead. She slowed down, treading over the muddy ruts that furrowed the path, waiting for him. She was in no hurry.

Harry would be sitting in his classroom, now, still worrying away. She knew she hadn't handled it particularly well. She just wished she could ring Sarah, who always seemed to give good advice, but she'd be at work. And her mother would tell her to talk to Robert. But that would be difficult, cause more hurt. What she needed to reassure him was the time to have a good talk and explain it all. But it wasn't something that a six year old could easily understand. Adults led messy lives and anyone might have difficulties making sense of *this* set-up. Paula had laid down rules when Robert left – the children would not be meeting Amy, or staying overnight; if he wanted to see the children, then he'd have to see them in the 'family home'. And when Harry was born, she had been even more insistent - no sleep-overs or joint trips or joint anything. And Robert had agreed because he wasn't going to make matters any worse than they were.

Amy had determined to make nothing of it, but once, early on, she'd tried to talk it through with Sarah; she should have known her sister wouldn't mince her words.

'God, Amy,' she'd said, 'I can imagine how I'd react if Dan had gone off with someone. Especially someone, twenty years younger, bright as a button, looking like a cover girl. And not just leaving me, but leaving the children. I'd be so pissed off, I'd want to kill her. And him. I'm not surprised she wants nothing to do with you.'

But what seemed strange to Amy, after all this time, was nothing had changed. A barrier had been constructed that wasn't to be breached under any circumstances. However many years had passed. She had only seen Robert's children at a distance, once at the railway station and a few times, from her car. She'd spoken to them briefly when they'd rung the house before she'd handed the phone over to their father. But they could have been living on opposite sides of the world, like long-distance relatives you never saw and barely knew, except for snippets of information gleaned from passing remarks or overheard conversations.

Amy didn't know what she was going to say to Harry. She just hoped something would come to her throughout the day that would put his mind at rest.

She let herself into the house and sat down on the stairs to take off her shoes. She'd meant to have fifteen minutes in the kitchen, reading the newspaper before starting on the jobs she knew she had to do, but instead, she found herself trying to imagine what Harry made of it all. And how she could make it seem 'normal'? Christ, it wasn't normal. Robert's two families never met. Ever. Amy could understand Paula's feelings all those years ago when he'd left her — she'd been hurt, angry, of course she had - but now, after all this time? What on earth did those children think? They must have wanted to know something about it all as they got older.

She went through the morning like an automaton — washing up, vacuuming, changing the double bed, putting the clothes in the dryer. The doorbell rang and she signed for a parcel from Amazon. Then she took her cup of coffee up to the smallest bedroom, which wasn't a bedroom any more but a little office, the computer desk in one corner by the window, books and papers crammed on the shelves and the floor, photographs printed on A4 sheets stuck to the walls. Sitting at the computer, she checked her messages, deleted all the junk mail, then went into Documents and found her article on the school - half-written, in need of editing, and only 700 words so far. Come on, this had to be with Ellie by Saturday. Concentrate.

She stared at the screen, changing some of the sentences she'd felt happy with yesterday. The interviews with the students turned out to be easy – they almost wrote themselves – but more difficult was trying to convey the excitement of the night, how infectious that was, how it affected the audience. To call it a celebration of talent sounded too inflated- she'd have to phrase it another way -but that's what it had been. She'd meant it when she'd told Sophie how wonderful the writing was.

She clicked on the school's website to check the names of the teachers – one thing Ellie wouldn't forgive was getting those wrong – and then back to Documents to try and complete the rough draft. After an hour and a half, she'd almost finished and sat back in her chair. She read through it all again and knew there was something missing. Her article covered most of it – but...well, the whole evening hadn't just happened without a lot of hard work and planning. She wanted to acknowledge how much effort had gone into it, pay some sort of tribute to the teachers. Perhaps not all of them, to be fair. Really, to Jake Harper. He'd been the inspiration behind the whole thing.

She'd seen how both the boys and girls looked at him, with perhaps not admiration, that was too strong; it was more comfortable than that. They *liked* him, they wanted him to approve of what they'd done, they recognised he genuinely cared. Or was she just transferring what *she'd* felt. She'd found his enthusiasm contagious; it was hard to take her eyes off him as he talked, that alert expression on his face, half amused, questioning, hands gesturing as he explained something; a little unsure of himself, even when he was on home ground. He didn't want to take the glory off the children, and she'd liked that. There was none of the ego, often so obvious in the business people she was used to meeting these days, who competed with each other and weren't happy unless they were centre stage. Jake was different. There was no need for him to *tell* her he was doing a great job – he just was.

Well, she couldn't put all that in; she'd sound like a groupie. She could just imagine the red pencil striking out the lines. She began to type up a final paragraph. It took her three goes but at least it was objective. Then she read the whole piece through. Some more editing and it'd be fine. The photographs would add colour to it, give it extra life – images had their own impact. She always thought they stayed in your head, sometimes long after you wanted them gone.

Enough was enough. She'd spent more time on it than she'd meant to. In the afternoon, she'd send it off to the *Mercury* before she went back to school to pick up Harry. Find out if he was still worrying. And try to explain a situation that she found hard to understand herself. She was meant to be good with words, after all.

Chapter 15

The text from Jake hadn't contained many details, just that his mother was in Leeds General, where tests would be carried out the following day; she was conscious and had been given sedation. Not as alarming as he'd thought. So Catherine just had to wait. He'd promised to ring her tonight when he'd learned more. Surely then, after twenty four hours, they'd know how serious it was.

Catherine pulled off her body warmer as she entered the flat and picked up the post from the mat, flipping open her mobile to read his message from yesterday, again. She wished she could have gone with him to give him moral support, that was the least she could do, but the next day had been Friday and she couldn't just take the day off. It wasn't *her* emergency after all. Jake would ring, perhaps after visiting hours. And if he wanted her to, she'd drive down early Saturday morning. But what if it seemed like intruding? She didn't know the family well enough to be sure of doing the right thing.

She'd spent one Christmas with them all – just two days last year – and they'd been really kind in an unfussy way. Warm-hearted, making her feel welcome. Not just Jake's parents and the brother, Oliver and his wife and children. But neighbours and friends. The house had been noisy, people coming and going at all times of the day, drinks flowing, in-jokes, a familiarity between them all that was so different from her own family. It was like a whole community getting together, sharing lives - the opposite of what her father had ever wanted. Or allowed. He had kept *his* family tight, bound together, separated from the outside world. Not just his children, but his wife too when she'd been alive. You keep control that way, Catherine thought, sad for her mother. Sad that she, herself, had never fought against it. Not hard enough, anyway. But it always seemed to be three tough, demanding male figures against her, probably not just because she was the only girl, she thought now - she was also the youngest. In Jake's family, though, there was no-one pulling the strings, no-one with the final say. They shared the jobs, and it was good to hear them arguing and joking, no fear of speaking out. She wished Jake had let her really get to know them. She could have been a help now. But anyway, this was a crisis that perhaps only those closest to his mother should deal with. Fair enough.

She tried to imagine how it would be for Jake - arriving in Leeds to a house that would seem empty - no good-natured bantering now - rushing to the hospital, trying to deal with what he'd find there and trying to put on a good face for his father. Jake's mother had been the centre of things, the one who held it all together, and now…

Catherine sat down on her sofa in the narrow little sitting room. There'd been a biting wind that day after a spell of sunny, bright weather and she hadn't turned the heating up. The change of season to the winter months always depressed her - the short, darkening days bringing to mind another November all those years ago, the dampness, the shutting of doors and empty streets, the lonely evenings with nowhere to go. So tired, she felt so tired as she had been then and she drifted, sitting in the tiny room with the light fading, into a drowsy sleep; images from the past vivid in her mind – unbidden, unwanted –a long corridor, a girl's voice, low and musical, a door flung open into a cluttered room, two bodies locked together, his anger, palpable and frightening… and the scream that went on and on, tearing through the building.

How many times did I tell them? I hate violence. I would never hurt anyone. Why wouldn't they listen?

She jerked awake, shaking. How could it still haunt her like this? Horrible events you worked so hard to forget, repeating themselves over and over again. As though the pain and heartbreak she'd felt then had left behind a residue - an echo of something awful you thought had faded. And through the summer months she could almost forget, blot it all out – but as winter drew near, the darkening nights and the cold awakened a sense of foreboding. She was certain her heart was beating faster and even though she fought it, she was aware of that familiar panic lurking, waiting to rise into her throat and take away her breath.

She flicked on the television to calm herself. She watched the five o'clock news, doing her best to focus on the changing stories but only half-listening, trying to feel some concern for the latest tragic events unfolding elsewhere. It all seemed so distant – not part of the world she inhabited at all. She recognised the debilitating sense of apathy which she'd been keeping at bay these last few weeks and the sudden jarring sense of hopelessness that came from nowhere. You can't rely on someone else to make you happy, she thought. Surely you've worked that out by now.

But no, she hadn't. She'd been looking forward to Saturday with Jake, so looking forward to putting things back to how they once were, and now... if she didn't follow him to Leeds, here were three days stretching out in front of her, hours to fill without him. And she certainly wasn't going to make matters worse by paying a visit to her father, even though he would expect it if he knew she was on her own for the weekend.

Her mobile rang and she nearly dropped it, her fingers fumbling with the casing. Quickly, she swiped the screen.

'What time are we going tonight? Do you want me to drive?'

Rosie. The Athletics meeting. It had gone completely out of her head. She looked at her watch and saw that half an hour had passed. She must have dozed off while she'd been waiting hoping he'd call. But he hadn't.

'Um... I'm not sure I should go, Rosie. Jake's had to rush off to Leeds, a family emergency, and I'm waiting for a call. So perhaps I should hang on here...'

'What's the family emergency?'

'It sounds serious. His mother's collapsed and she's been taken to hospital. That's all I know. He should be there about now, but I haven't heard from him.'

'Well, don't be sitting on your own all night, worrying. I'll drive us to the meeting. You can put your phone on silent and take the call outside the committee room when it comes. Don't you think that's best?'

Catherine sighed and pulled at the frayed edge of the throw on the sofa. 'I suppose so. I haven't even been for a run tonight. Perhaps I'm better out of the house.'

'Absolutely,' Rosie's positive tone was what she needed. 'I'll ring Heather and we'll all go together. Can you be ready in half an hour?'

'OK, thanks. Yes, I'll be ready.'

But Catherine sat, undecided for another five minutes. Should she try ringing him? Or just wait?

She flicked off the television and went into the bedroom. Through the window she could barely see the houses opposite, as grey cloud spread low in the sky. She knew she should get moving – she barely had time to change her clothes - but something made her pull open the second drawer of the dressing table and feel for the oblong packet, tucked right at the back. She needed to be sure they were still there. Ridiculous, she told herself, she hadn't taken any for a long time now. She'd been steady. It had taken her a year, eighteen months, to come to terms with it all, but she'd faced it. It was silly to keep them. And it was long ago, now. There'd be no sliding back, she told herself. Surely all that was behind her. But the same uncertainty crept over her, just as it had then. And it made her head ache.

All she knew was - she mustn't make the same mistake again.

The tooting of a car horn from the street made her hurry. Pulling on a woollen jacket, she ran down the stairs, grabbed her bag and turned on the hall light so the place would be cheerful when she came home. She dashed back for her mobile, slammed the front door behind her and climbed into the car.

*

The phone call came just as she was leaving the meeting and heading for the pub across the road. The mobile vibrated in her pocket and she saw from the caller ID that it was Jake. 'You go on,' she called to the other two. 'I need to take this.'

'We'll get you a lemonade, Catherine. Ok?'

She gestured to say that was fine, and turned into a driveway, head down, one hand covering her ear to blot out the noise of passing cars.

'How's it going? How is she?'

'Well...' Jake's voice sounded distant, as though he wasn't holding the phone close enough. 'Nothing much to tell, really. She's not in pain, just frightened because no-one's telling her much. We managed to talk to the doctor, but he was non-committal. Just said tests were being carried out and the results would take a few days. They want to keep her in...' Catherine could hear voices in the background and Jake muttering 'Keep it down, could you?' and then back to her, 'Was it ok today? At school?'

'Yes, fine. You were missed – Jenny was asking about you.'

'I've just rung her...'

Before me? Catherine frowned in annoyance.

But Jake carried on talking: 'They seemed to be managing fine without me and Tim's been good. Says I can have as much time as I need.'

'Shall I come in the morning? I could be there by ten, if I set off early…'

'No. Don't come.' Catherine closed her eyes at the sharpness of his tone. This was what she'd been afraid of. 'I'll be back on Monday morning if nothing alters here and, really, there's nothing you can do.' Then she heard his voice soften, as though he realised he'd been abrupt. 'The house is heaving and they only let close relatives in at Visiting Hours, so you'd just be hanging around. And Dad's all at sixes and sevens. I'll probably be coming back next weekend and perhaps she'll be home by then.'

Catherine was silent. She didn't know what to say and when she found her voice, it faltered. 'All right.' She cleared her throat. 'I'll leave you to it then. Hope your mum improves.' It was as though they were strangers, unable to communicate in any other way than platitudes. She waited to see if he was going to say anything else. But he'd finished the call.

Well, that was… horrible, she said to herself. *It's clear he thinks I'd be in the way.*

She looked across at the pub, lit up and welcoming, but she had no desire now to make her way over the road and be sociable. She'd no choice though, she'd have to go, even if the last thing she wanted was company. They'd ask her questions and what could she say? Not the truth. She'd pretend a different conversation with Jake, say what they wanted to hear. What *she* would have given anything to hear.

She wished she'd eaten something earlier in the day because now her stomach felt hollow and her mouth was dry. She wanted to ring Jake back and hear his voice, be told everything was really all right —

that he was under pressure, worrying, that he hadn't meant to just *dismiss* her – but she didn't have the courage. Better not to have her worst fears confirmed. So she forced herself to cross the road and enter the pub, with a bright smile on her face.

Rosie waved to her from a corner table where she was sitting with three other women from the meeting. The pub was crowded and Catherine was glad she'd already been bought a drink and didn't have to fight her way to the bar. They all shifted round to give her room.

'Everything all right?' asked Rosie. 'You weren't long. Here's your drink…' and as Catherine dug in her pockets for her purse, she shook her head, 'My treat. For heaven's sake, a lemonade won't break me.'

A woman called Helen, her face flushed and her eyelids fluttering, turned to her. 'We're on vodka tonics. You should join us. It's Friday night, no getting up early tomorrow.'

Rosie butted in, 'Catherine will be. I told you, her boyfriend was ringing to give her an up-date on his mother. She'll be off to Leeds at the crack of dawn.'

Catherine smiled in what she hoped they'd take for agreement.

She took a sip of the warm lemonade, wishing they'd put ice in it. 'Well, perhaps not at the crack of dawn. Obviously, Jake's very worried but nothing seems certain - she could have just passed out for a few minutes and…'

'My mother fainted once and it was down to low blood pressure,' Helen said. 'And d'you know, they can't do a thing about that. High blood pressure, they give you tablets, but low blood pressure – they say, just put loads of salt on your food.'

'Well,' said Rosie, looking at Catherine, her face all sympathy and kindness. 'You'll know when you get there.'

Catherine nodded. 'Yes, I'll know when I get there.'

Later that night, walking home through the empty streets, no one about, just her neighbour's cat scurrying under a hedge, she gave in to the sense of utter disappointment she'd done so well to hide. Fatigue swept through her body. What sort of future would she have without Jake? She couldn't bear it.

You're over-reacting, she told herself. *If you make a scene about this, he'll leave, he'll leave... and then where will you be? He didn't mean to shut you out. He doesn't always think, that's all.*

She reached her front door, thankful to finally shut out every body and everything that might throw her even more off balance. She'd been hungry but couldn't face food now, so she took off her coat and headed for bed. And as she went to close the curtains, the sound of quick footsteps on the pavement outside caught her attention. Someone running towards the main road. Gone before she'd caught a glimpse of them. Someone in a hurry.

She put out the light and told herself she must sleep. She was so tired. But she kept waking, looking at the alarm clock at two and five and six, relieved when the time came to get up.

So began a bleak Saturday.

The start of a long day.

Chapter 16

Robert strode quickly along King Street and under the wrought-iron arches of Burlington arcade, the city centre's hallowed district. Lights from the shop windows, gleaming in the covered passageway, made it resemble an Aladdin's cave. This late in the afternoon there were only a few shoppers, lingering to gaze at the silverware, the furs, the jewellery. No price tags to be seen here, just a few selected items placed strategically on pale display boxes, daring you to go inside.

Wrapped up in his black woollen overcoat and grey scarf, Robert walked with a purpose, knowing exactly which shop he was heading for, halfway down the passage - Beaumont's, Goldsmiths, established 1895. The bell jingled discreetly as he pushed open the door and a slim woman in a tailored dress, hair swept high with a tortoiseshell comb, stood up from behind a display counter. She looked at him expectantly and smiled as he approached her.

'Yes, sir. What can we help you with today?'

'Well, I'd like to see some necklaces, pendants, something a bit unusual.' Robert took off his gloves and placed them on the glass surface in front of him.

'Of course.' She hesitated. 'You've purchased jewellery from us before, I think?'

A small, plump man scurried out of the rear of the shop and beamed when he saw Robert. 'It's Mr. Wilson. I'd recognise that voice anywhere. Good to see you again.' He turned to the girl. 'I'll look after Mr. Wilson, Abbie. Leave it to me.' He had already turned and was pulling out a drawer which held strands of gold necklaces lying on a cushion of white silk. 'Is it for a special occasion, Mr. Wilson? Not a Christmas present this early, I think?'

Robert leaned forward to get a closer look, slightly irritated by the man's obsequious behaviour. And even though he wasn't prepared to enter into a lengthy conversation with him, he'd learnt to trust his judgement. 'No,' he said. 'It's for my wife's birthday.'

'Ah! Now... she'll be pleased with this. See what you think.' The man placed an intricate gold pendant on his fleshy palm with the chain draped over his wrist. 'You won't find another of this quality and design anywhere else in Manchester. It's a replica of a Victorian piece, so delicate, see how the strands are woven closely together? Such craftsmanship and...' He wet his lips and looked up into Robert's face. 'Trust me, your wife will love it.'

'Yes, I can see it's... lovely.' Robert studied it for a minute. 'Yes, just right.' The price was written on a tiny looped tag – a smudge of an ink blot he couldn't hope to read. Well, it didn't matter. He could afford it. He tucked his hand into the inside of his jacket and pulled out his wallet. 'Fine, I'll take it. I don't need to see any others. Really appreciate your help.'

And in ten minutes, the jeweller's box, wrapped and tied with ribbon, was in his pocket and he was walking towards Deansgate to collect his car. There was something about choosing presents that made him nervous, especially when it was important to get it right. And he so wanted to get it right. The little man at Beaumont's might be embarrassingly sycophantic, but he had a good eye – Robert had relied on him before. And with Amy's birthday only two days away, he'd left himself short of time to pick out something special.

Now, as he made his way through the city streets, the memory of the first present he'd ever bought with his own money came into his mind. It was early in December and he was ten. (How was it that lately, he thought more and more about his childhood? Was it because he was nearing fifty?) He hadn't been looking for a present, but he'd seen what he was absolutely certain his mother would love. In one of the six village shops, quite close to his home, standing high on a shelf was a round plate, a heavy pottery one, the sort you could hang on the wall. And moulded in relief on the surface was a picture – a scene of a cosy farm kitchen with a fire burning in the grate, with a man and a woman sitting either side of it; but best of all, was the cat curled contentedly on the hearth rug. It was painted in warm colours, red and orange and brown, and was so life-like, he stared at it in fascination for some minutes, unable to walk away. But when he asked the price, he realised it would take him weeks to save up the five pounds from his pocket money. But he did – and amazingly, his luck held out and the plate, which he checked on every time he went to the village, hadn't been sold. So the week before Christmas, he bought the plate, smuggled it into the house, wrapped it up and put it carefully under the tree. He could hardly wait for breakfast to be over on Christmas morning, but eventually, he carried his present through into the sitting room and handed it to his mother. And as she slowly unwrapped it and the wonderful picture came into view, he was watching her face and saw her expressionless eyes and the downturn of her mouth, and he knew it wasn't her sort of thing at all. It was too brightly painted, the figures too badly drawn, the pottery not fine enough. Even at ten, he realised all that. When his mother recovered herself and gave a thin smile, kissing him lightly on the cheek, all the pleasure of saving up and buying the present had evaporated.

He never knew what happened to the plate.

He thought now how ridiculous it was that, even after all these years, he never enjoyed the anticipation of giving – just in case the reaction was as dire as that first time. The present might be hopelessly wrong.

Funny how childhood slights could last a lifetime.

He drove homewards, concentrating on navigating through the evening traffic, listening to a political argument on Radio 4, until he became frustrated with the two speakers trying to score points off one another and tuned to Classic FM. He couldn't identify the composer, but the symphony filled the car with a sense of order and peace. Better, he thought, much better. He'd had another day of stress, of demands on his time, questions that the IT department couldn't answer quickly enough (so much for a new system that was meant to be twice as fast as the old one) and colleagues who needed handling with kid gloves.

He had no idea why, but when he was fifteen minutes from home, he swung the car onto the country road to Lymm and drove faster than he should have, down the dark lanes to his old house. It was like driving on autopilot, the route programmed in his brain. He didn't even ask himself what he was doing, just let the car swallow up the miles as it swept along the familiar roads.

He pulled up at the kerb, not wanting to turn into the drive when he hadn't been invited, and switched off the engine.

Why he'd felt the need to check up on Paula and the children, on this particular evening, he couldn't say, but now he was here, he'd have to make up some reason to justify calling in. Final arrangements for his trip to the Yorkshire Dales with Holly, perhaps, but he hadn't yet booked a place for them to stay. He'd check whether she wanted to go back to The Boatman. Yes, he'd do that.

He opened the car door and stood in the gateway, looking at the light from the hall window. He knew he was behaving irrationally. Not like him at all. He'd always prided himself on a certain clarity of mind, a decisiveness and sense of purpose that had guided him well, certainly in business. Only once had it let him down, he thought, and then it had turned his life into a chaotic mess - that was when he'd met Amy and emotions he'd never experienced before had swept away all restraint, all the rules he'd lived by; when he'd followed his instincts rather than logic for the first time.

Well, here's the chaos you created, he thought grimly, walking up the driveway. *And you've come because you feel guilty. You've bought an absurdly expensive present for Amy and it's on your conscience. You're trying to balance things up.*

Was it that simple?

He rang the bell and it was Ben who finally wrenched open the door and peered out.

'Dad!' His eyebrows shot up in surprise and he broke into a wide smile. 'Great. Didn't know you were coming.'

Robert stepped inside. 'No, well, I wasn't. But there are a few last minute things I wanted to sort out with Holly for next week. Is she upstairs?'

'Extra Psychology at college on Wednesdays, so she's not in yet.'

'Oh, well...' Robert turned to go, just as Paula came out of the sitting room. She looked at him enquiringly and he thought he should apologise for not ringing and letting her know he was coming. He was always apologising. 'Sorry, I wanted to...'

'I heard,' Paula said. 'Shut the door, Ben. I'd like a word with your father. Go and finish your homework, would you?' She waved him upstairs.

'I've finished it. I didn't have much tonight.'

'Then go on your PlayStation or something, please. Tea won't be ready until Holly gets in. You've got another hour.'

Ben took the stairs two at a time, looking back once at his father as though he wanted him to contradict the order. But Robert shook his head at him and followed Paula into the lounge. What's this all about, he thought. Something serious, by the look on her face and he wished, now, he hadn't come if he was only going to hear another problem.

She sat down on the sofa, preparing herself, Robert could see. He felt he had to sit down too, so he perched on the end of the armchair.

The silence, heavy and awkward, had the effect of scaring him, making it difficult to stay silent. So he didn't wait for her to speak first. 'Is it Holly?' he asked, noticing how she was clasping her hands together and straightening her back. 'Look, we don't have to go next week if it's a problem for her. Or for you…'

'It's not Holly.' Paula shook her head. 'She's looking forward to going.'

'Then what? For heaven's sake, Paula, what?' He knew he sounded brusque but he didn't like drama. Why didn't she just come out with it?

She swallowed. 'I was going to tell you before you went on Sunday, but… I wanted you to know…' she was speaking slowly, blue eyes serious as she looked up at him. 'I'm seeing someone.'

'Seeing someone? How d'you mean?'

'How d'you think I mean?' She frowned. 'I've met someone and I've been out to dinner and to the theatre a few times. I didn't want you to hear it from someone else.'

'Ok.' He couldn't quite take it in. It wasn't something he'd ever considered and after all this time, he'd got so used to the situation being the same, year in and year out, he hadn't imagined it ever changing. Paula had always been so wrapped up in the house and the children – she'd seemed content enough with that – and she didn't really enjoy going out; she wasn't particularly comfortable with people, certainly not people she barely knew. She'd needed him to have any sort of social life, and although, now, she helped part-time in the library, where was she going to meet anyone?

He said the first thing that came into his head. 'Who is he?'

Paula lifted her chin and set her mouth in a straight line. 'It doesn't matter who he is, does it? Someone I like who's thoughtful and who's kind.' Had she meant that as a jibe at him? But she was looking across the room and seemed to be talking almost to herself. 'I enjoy being with him. Anyway, I just thought you should know.' Then, with a touch of spirit he hadn't often seen, she added. 'He certainly doesn't have to be approved of by you, Robert.'

He studied her face. He noticed now that she'd had her hair done differently, cut shorter with a sort of fringe, and wondered whether there'd been other things he'd missed. She'd always been slim, and at times, painfully thin, but today she looked... what? He stopped himself. 'Do the children know? Have they met him?'

There was look of obstinacy on her face now. 'No, they haven't. And I don't want to introduce him to them until I'm more sure of where this is going. They've had enough disruption in their lives, haven't they?' She bit her lip as though she'd said more than she intended. 'Look,' she smiled but without much warmth, 'All I can say is that it's nice to have company and we seem to like the same things...'

Robert stood up, hurriedly. He didn't like the feeling that he was the outsider in his own family and had no right to even offer an opinion on something as important as this to them all. Well, he'd forfeited that a long time ago, he thought later. You can't have your cake and eat it, his mother would have said. He moved towards the door. 'Thank you for telling me. Yes, well, I won't mention anything to Holly. Obviously.' He couldn't think of anything else to say. 'Tell her I'll be here at ten on Sunday.'

Ruth was coming down the stairs, talking on her mobile phone and as he called up to Ben that he was leaving, she gave him a laconic wave, mouthing 'Bye, Dad.' Then, the door closed behind him, the sound loud in the still evening. He walked down the path to his car, and as he did so, he felt in his coat pocket for his keys and his fingers touched the small square box. Amy's present. He looked back at the house. What had he given Paula for her last birthday? Money, of course, he always gave her money.

He almost wished now he hadn't bought Amy the pendant.

Somehow it didn't seem right.

Chapter 17

The three days of visiting the hospital had been exhausting, but he'd got some comfort from the routines already set in motion – the monitoring, the blood tests, the heart checks. It meant, as they kept telling him, his mother was 'in the best hands.' Still, no-one, as yet, had any answers.

Jake had arrived at the house on the Thursday evening to find everyone - family, close neighbours, old friends - sitting round the kitchen table, mulling over possible theories and diagnoses - what they'd heard, what they'd overheard and what they'd learned from the Internet. 'Anaemia, that causes fainting.' 'Does she have a slow heart beat? She might need a pace-maker.' Jake stood and listened, exchanging a knowing glance with Oliver and his younger brother, Nick, across the room, each of them aware from experience that this wasn't the time to say anything. They were all, in their own way doing the best they knew to show support for their dad, who'd rushed from work when he'd got the news. Now, sitting with a whiskey in front of him, hair standing on end and his tie askew, he looked bemused. At ten o'clock, when no one looked as if they had a home to go to, Jake made a pot of tea, cut some rounds of cheese and pickle sandwiches and put the biscuit tin on the table. Still they sat. The trouble was everything they came up with was guess work. No-one was prepared yet, to go to their own beds and just wait patiently for official results.

The following morning, he'd been allowed in to see her, even though it wasn't visiting hours. He'd gone up in the lift beside a porter wheeling an iron bed, where a tiny frail woman lay, making small animal sounds, her hands clawing the blankets. He stepped out at the third floor into a long corridor, airless and smelling of cleaning fluid, the walls painted a sickly pale green. He found he was walking slowly, senses on high alert, ready for some sight or sound he'd rather not face. He wanted to avoid it all - seeing illness, hearing pain, having to cope with whatever was behind the next door along the corridor. Cowardice, he knew. He thought back to his time with Hannah – she'd come back late from the hospital and tell him about her day, nursing dying patients - and he'd wondered at her ability to cope with it all, how she'd never seemed to crumble – unless, yes, once when it was a child – but he hadn't been keen to listen. It was all too depressing to think about.

He came to Ward 3C, walked through the doors and up to the fourth bed, where his mother lay. She looked so much better than he'd feared and he immediately felt reassured. And grateful, She'd smiled in a way that said, 'You shouldn't have come.' But she'd clasped his hand when he'd pulled over a chair to sit beside her and she'd looked steadily at him.

'Sorry, didn't have time to get you flowers,' Jake had said. 'How's things?'

'Pretty good. Feel much better this morning. They're all panicking and it's crazy.' She hitched herself higher in the bed, an apologetic look on her face. 'All out of my control.' She touched her hair. 'I feel a real mess, but they won't even let me out of bed in case I fall over.'

'Sound sensible to me. What have they done so far?'

'They've looked at my heart through this machine, which can see how it's working from every angle. They're coming back later today to tell me the results.'

'Sounds as though they're being thorough, then.'

'Well, I'd feel a lot better if they'd turn the heat down in here.' She'd smiled and suddenly her eyes filled with amusement. 'D'you know what? I think I look a lot better than you right now. Are you getting enough sleep?'

He laughed, glad she was up to teasing him. 'That's a nice thing to say, mother, after I've come all this way. Good to know you're still treating me like a teenager. Everything's normal then.'

And as they fell into their usual easy relationship, Jake felt a wave of relief that nothing had fundamentally changed. She was tough, always had been, she'd weather whatever this was. Nothing really serious.

He just hoped he wasn't kidding himself.

And when Sunday evening came, they were still none the wiser about her condition. All the tests had been inconclusive, the heart monitor had shown nothing unusual, the bloods would be analysed in the week. And his mother had insisted he go back to work, getting short with him when he didn't agree.

'Pointless just hanging around, Jake,' she'd told him. 'I could be sitting in this bed for days on end with nothing happening. And what would you do?'

'Keep you company,' he'd said.

'Look, I'll get Oliver to call you if there's any need. But I'm certain there won't be. And Nick's around. Please... go back to Manchester and, if you want, come back next weekend. But don't sit here like a spare part, just looking at me.'

His dad joined in, 'Yes, son. Go. We'll ring your mobile if we're worried. I think she's going to be fine – they're doing enough tests. She's probably in better shape than all of us.' And he patted Jake's arm, such an awkward gesture, which left both of them embarrassed.

Oliver had walked with him out of the hospital doors and taken off his glasses to wipe them with a handkerchief. 'It's like a sauna in there. A wonder anyone can breathe.'

Jake nodded, wanting to thank him, the elder brother who always took the brunt of things. The one who'd worked hard, who'd married a nice local girl and given what his parents most wanted - grandchildren. Jake couldn't help making comparisons whenever they were together now, acutely aware of his own drifting existence. Yes, he'd got a good job, he was bright enough, but he didn't have the drive, he didn't want to settle down. And, unlike Oliver, he'd never looked ahead or planned for the future.

'Sorry I didn't have time to see much of the kids. Next weekend, I'll bring them a present each to make up.'

'Don't be daft. No one's had time for anything but the hospital.' Oliver put his glasses back on and turned to look at Jake directly. 'Are you still going out with that girl you brought last Christmas... Catherine, wasn't it? Why don't you bring her? It'll cheer Mum up to think you're "going steady", well, that's how she'd put it.' He grinned. 'She wants you married before you get much older.'

'No chance,' Jake looked away. 'No, it isn't that sort of relationship. It'd make things difficult if she came and she's probably got a marathon or something, and anyway...'

'You're bumbling.' Oliver was laughing. 'Ok, I'll let you know if there's anything to report.'

'Ring me anyway. See you next weekend.'

*

It was Tuesday and getting late. Cars were parked all along the kerb but there was no one about. It was quiet except for the slight rustling of trees, dark except for a street lamp glowing yellow on the other side of the road. Jake sat on the wall outside the village hall, his heart thudding a hurried rhythm in his chest, sounding to him like a drum beat in the stillness.

He looked at his watch and stood up. Five to ten. Surely it couldn't be much longer.

He'd arrived early. Too early and this waiting was making him nervous. He hoped he'd find his voice when the moment came. He had no idea how he was going to start, but at least he'd found a good enough reason for being there. Well, a plausible one, anyway.

He'd turned his back on the door of the hall when he heard the sound of it closing and light footsteps hurrying down the steps to the shingle path. There'd been no applause to tell him the show was over, so someone must be leaving early. Even before he turned to see, he guessed it was her.

She stopped in her tracks when she saw him, and he could see an expression of surprise and uncertainty on her face. He almost put his hands up in a submissive gesture, but instead, conjured a look of confidence. Pure acting, of course.

'Well, now,' he said. 'Leaving before the end. How dangerous is that?'

'Dangerous?' Her expression gave nothing away, and suddenly he thought this was such a bad idea.

'What if Pooh-Bah falls off the stage at the curtain call and breaks his leg? You've missed a scoop and the rival paper will have it.'

He could see her shoulders relaxing and her mouth softening into a half-smile. 'Well, I'd get the sack. But is that likely?'

He shook his head. 'I heard of a critic in London leaving a play at half time, and missing a ceiling coming down on top of the audience in the second half. Hard to explain why that wasn't in his review.'

'That's not likely here, now is it? This is Cheshire. Life is orderly and nothing unusual happens...'

'Yes, boring isn't it?' He could hardly believe he'd said it. This was the second time he'd blurted out what he was only thinking, as though he couldn't stop himself, like a lemming hurtling headlong towards a cliff edge.

She didn't answer, just stood looking at him for what seemed to Jake an interminable length of time. She held his gaze without blinking.

'This isn't a coincidence, is it?' It wasn't a question.

'No, it isn't a coincidence.'

She looked down, pulling at the flap on her bag and caught hold of her car keys. At that moment, clapping and cheering from the hall filtered out into the night, as though at any minute the real world was going to sweep them away, back to their own separate lives, back to where they belonged.

He spoke quickly. 'I came because I have an idea that needs your help. And I wanted to talk to you about it face to face. I rang the paper, and they said you'd be covering this tonight, so I just took a chance...' He ran out of breath. 'I apologise if this seems... if this seems presumptuous...'

'What's this idea?' She tilted her head as though ready to listen and Jake prayed he could explain enough before she walked away.

'Well, I'd like to arrange a newspaper day in the school, with about thirty kids as reporters, photographers, picture editors, researchers. Produce, say, two or three pages to go into the *Mercury*, along with the real news stories – just for one week. They'd spend some time before anything was published, getting stuff together about school trips, sports wins, projects... It'd give them an idea of what it's like to be a real journalist...'

'Like me!' she smiled, and his heart warmed to her.

'Not quite. You're going to be the editor.'

'Oh, promotion.' She put on a grave expression. 'Well, I can't turn that down, can I?' It was as though she could read him, could have answered before he'd even spelled it out for her. He'd never met anyone like her - quick and funny and...just so alive. He could have hugged her.

All wrong, he knew. From the start, he knew it was all wrong.

'So you'd do it?'

'Well, I can go back to the paper and ask the editor - check it out.' She pushed back a strand of hair from her forehead. 'I would think she'd like it. It's not as though we'd be using up space in the news room, we'd be taking the copy and the photos in from the school, ready to print.'

The doors were opening behind them and people were coming out of the hall, filling the night with noise, streaming past them, breaking into the intimacy of the moment. *Our* moment, thought Jake, wishing they'd all just sod off and leave just the two of them standing there.

'We need to discuss the details, I know.' He felt he was holding on by his fingertips. 'It's half term next week, so if you've got any free time, I could fit in with you...'

She paused and stepped away to let a family get by. 'Ok. Let me work something out. My husband'll be away, so I'd have to get someone to look after our son...'

How odd he'd never thought of it – that there might be a child.

Amy went on, 'Give me your mobile number...' she was pulling out a diary and a pen, 'and I'll ring you on Monday.'

And suddenly, Jake couldn't bear it any longer. They were speaking and saying nothing, circling around what was really going on, it was all so bloody ridiculous. She had to be feeling this too, she had to. He nearly, so nearly said what was hammering in his brain, 'I can't get you out of my mind, Amy. I can't stop thinking about you.'

But she was scribbling down his number and when she looked up, he realised she must have seen something in his face, some expression in his eyes that gave him away, because she flushed and left him with a quick wave of her hand, without even saying goodbye.

Chapter 18

Amy pulled the beanie over her head and tucked in wisps of hair that kept escaping. She examined herself in the bedroom mirror and considered whether she looked casual enough. Short belted jacket, black trousers, high boots, barely any make-up – just as if she were going to the shops.

She'd spent too long getting herself ready and if she was fooling one half of herself, the other half was looking back at her with a cynical eye. She'd eaten hardly anything all day, a bowl of cereal first thing, a hurried sandwich at lunchtime and here she was at seven o'clock, with time running out, and she suddenly felt hungry. Well, too late now. She wasn't going to make it if she didn't leave in the next few minutes.

The house held none of the familiar sounds. Instead, an emptiness seemed to fill every room, so it wasn't a home any more, just bricks and mortar. This quiet was discomforting. She'd lived on her own before – but now, with Robert away and Harry at her mother's for the night, it seemed strange. Even Jasper was almost motionless – just his eyes following her every move as he lay on the carpet beside her, head between his paws, waiting to look mournful as soon as she headed for the front door. She turned off the bedroom light and herded him downstairs.

'Don't *you* start making me feel guilty,' she said to the dog. 'I'm only going out for an hour. You've been for a walk and had your dinner. What more do you want?'

A wind was picking up as she drove, not sure of her way to the Green Dragon. She'd heard of it, but Stockport had so many pubs. She didn't recognise the street name she'd been given, so instead of being ten minutes late, it was nearer twenty when she walked through the door of a solid stone-clad building, tucked away in the old part of town. She glanced round the room at all the tables in front of the bar and saw he was already on his feet, heading towards her.

Funny how you build up an expectation of what you're going to see, she thought. An imaginary picture that's nothing like the reality. This just seemed strange, not exciting at all. Wrong somehow. She stood for a moment, wondering what on earth she was doing here. She'd allowed herself to be persuaded to meet in a pub to discuss – what? A half-baked plan for a school news day. And with someone she hardly knew. It was stupidity.

But too late now. She was here.

As Jake drew nearer, she watched him closely. He looked thin, she thought, his dark eyes too large in his handsome face, his whole posture awkward and boyish. Serious and anxious. And then he smiled, the sort of infectious smile that took you in with its warmth, all uncertainty gone. He just looked delighted to see her.

So, there was nothing she could do but smile back.

'Thought you'd changed your mind,' he said, taking her gently by the arm and leading her to his table and pulling back a chair for her. The place was crowded and the smell of beer hung in the air. 'I'd ordered you a white wine and was beginning to debate whether I should drink it as a chaser.'

She pulled off the woollen hat and shook her hair loose. 'I'd have phoned you – I mean, if I'd got held up. I wouldn't have left you sitting here, waiting.'

Jake sat down opposite her and sipped his beer. 'It's good to see you, Amy.'

She nodded her head slowly, unable to answer, and looked round at the other tables, trying to work out what sort of place this was. A bit old-fashioned in a way - the drinkers all ages, from students to middle-aged couples to pensioners. And somewhere behind the buzz of conversation. she became aware of a saxophone playing, muted and melodious – some tune familiar from another era.

'Where's the music coming from?'

'Upstairs. Haven't you heard of this place? I thought it was quite famous – it puts on jazz – modern jazz – three times a week. Brilliant group on a Wednesday, a quartet that plays all the Stan Getz stuff, Dave Brubeck, some Miles Davis. If you close your eyes, you'd *almost* think you were listening to the real thing.'

'Great,' she laughed, awkwardly. She wasn't sure how to handle this at all – the atmosphere was hardly right for a business talk. 'Not quite what I expected...' she glanced round the room... 'Is the background music meant to help with our planning...?' She needed to get them back to why they were here. 'You *are* ready with all those ideas for the school newspaper, I hope.'

He pulled out a sheaf of rolled-up papers and a pen from his jacket pocket. 'Started already.' He raised his eyebrows, mocking her surprised expression. 'You didn't expect that, did you? If you pull your chair round a bit, you can look over what I've thought up so far. We can change anything if you feel it's too ambitious or not practical. You're the boss.'

She pulled her chair closer to his and looked down at his notes, struggling to read his handwriting, but determined to concentrate on a task that would give some legitimacy to the evening. But she was aware of the warmth of his arm against hers, the way his watch strap curved round his wrist, the smell of aftershave on his skin. All her senses seemed like taut wires, ready to snap unless she moved away from him. But she sat as still as she could, agreeing with some of his ideas, questioning others, posing technical problems.

Thirty minutes later, they'd come to an agreement of sorts on how to go ahead, number of pupils, division of jobs, variety of content material, deadlines for drafts and pictures, possible publication date. Now, at least, it was official, a programme that had legs. Amy finished her drink. From the floor above, the strains of a melody carried down through the ceiling, the music haunting and sad.

'Well that didn't take long. So...'she looked at him, ready to leave. *Get up, girl, for God's sake, just get out of your seat and go. What's stopping you?*

Jake leaned forward and started to speak, 'I was going to suggest...'

She waited. 'What?'

He seemed to be gathering his courage, hurrying his words, 'That — if you want - we could go and listen to the jazz. Upstairs. Just for an hour. It's only on till ten and you wouldn't be late...'

They were both silent.

Around them was a crowd of people, buying drinks, telling jokes and putting the world to rights. A pleasant evening spent with friends, quickly forgotten. But for Amy, she found that, later, the memory would always stay with her, recalled like a scene from a film, just as it was happening now – the bar, the faint sounds of the refrain from above, the look on Jake's face. And a feeling of such intensity that rendered her unable to speak.

It was the point of no return.

Jake shrugged his shoulders. 'You've no one waiting at home, have you?'

Amy paused. 'The dog,' she said.

And suddenly they were both laughing.

'He can tell the time, can he? Ok, so will he allow you out till eleven?'

'He might.'

'Come on, you'll enjoy it.'

By the time they'd climbed upstairs to the jazz room, the musicians were on a break before the second set, having a beer at the tiny corner bar at the back of the room. Jake headed for the far wall, where a couple were just climbing down off two high stools, and he helped Amy onto the precarious perch, before settling on his own.

'Now you're going to hear something special,' he said, shifting around to get comfortable. 'That's when the band's finished their pints.'

Amy watched him, wondering about all the things she didn't know about him. She was curious. 'When we saw you at the airport last year, you were going to Washington like us. You were on your own. Don't you have a partner?'

He looked taken aback, as though the conversation struck him as odd. 'Well, I have a girlfriend, Catherine. She teaches PE at the school.' He took a drink of his beer and shrugged. 'It's lukewarm to be honest. It's coming to the end, but she doesn't quite see it that way.'

Amy nodded and let it go. 'So, in Washington – what did you do there?'

'All the touristy things everyone does, I suppose. Surprised we didn't bump into each other at the Air and Space museum under the Wright brothers' plane. Bet you did all the same stuff – the White House, Vietnam War Memorial, Arlington Cemetery... In fact, you might have seen me sitting on the steps of the Lincoln Memorial, watching a girl who's just left me, saying to myself, 'If she looks back, it means she's interested...'

Amy looked puzzled. 'What am I missing here?'

'Clint Eastwood, *In the Line of Fire* - he's Special Services guarding the president, but past his best and he's sitting on the steps of the Lincoln Memorial watching Renee Russo walk away. And he says...'

'Yeh, I get it. My father liked that film. I remember.' She thought for a moment. 'Does she look back?'

'Of course she does. It's Clint Eastwood...'

'Ah, that explains everything,' she smirked. 'So he's still irresistible at 60!'

'It's Hollywood. All older men are attractive there.' She saw Jake look at her quickly as though he was on thin ice and when she realised why, she felt embarrassed – *Does he think Robert's that old?* It made her suddenly acutely conscious of the situation she'd let herself be drawn into. The danger of following her instincts when the brakes should have been on. She shifted her position on the stool and moved slightly away from him.

She could see he was annoyed, she couldn't work out whether with himself or her, but he was frowning, looking out over the room. When his gaze shifted back to her, he said, 'So what *did* you do over there? Visit the president, go for dinner at the Mandarin, lunch with the Rockefellers ...?'

She held up her hand to silence him. 'Now, come on.' She could hear the edge in her voice and she fixed her eyes on him in what she hoped was a steely look. 'You think we're rich, don't you?' If he was going to pick a quarrel, he'd get as good as he gave.

'Well, aren't you?

'Not in the way you're thinking. Anyway,' she shrugged her shoulders, 'money isn't as important as you think. It doesn't really change anything, make everything wonderful. That's a myth.' She looked away, trying to show her indifference, trying to keep herself apart from him. She was annoyed. 'You seem to be judging me, God knows what for, and you know nothing about me. I'm as ordinary as you like.'

He stared at her. He just kept looking, without blinking, his irises so dark they looked black. She thought he was still angry but when he spoke, there was a catch in his voice.

'Amy, you're not ordinary. Not in any sense of the word.'

They were distracted by the musicians shuffling onto the built-up wooden platform, the pianist taking his seat, the other three picking up their instruments. Glancing at one another, they started to play, notes gliding together in soft, intricate strains. Amy had never seen an audience listen with such intense concentration, no one uttered a word, or lifted a glass, they just clapped after each solo, and the bass player or the pianist nodded his thanks and the rhythm went on, unbroken. Even when one piece ended and there was a brief discussion on the stage about what was to be played next, there was a stillness through the room, a quiet anticipation. Some tunes she recognised, but then the familiar chords took off on a spiral and she lost the beat and direction, each instrument doing its own thing, until, without any sign or look between the musicians, it melded into harmony again. Like magic, she thought and whispered to Jake, 'How do they all know where they're up to?' And he grinned and didn't answer.

They began playing *These Foolish Things* – one she *did* recognise - and she leaned against the wall and closed her eyes, letting the music take her. It had been a long time since she'd felt this good, a long time since she'd enjoyed an evening so much. She realised how much she liked him, how relaxing it was to sit by his side and just let the time drift by.

When he caught hold of her hand in the semi-darkness, entwining his fingers with hers, she knew she should have pulled away, but she didn't. She let it stay. She was afraid to move. She felt heady, light, as though if she breathed too hard, the spell would be broken and the whole evening would blow away, turn into fantasy. Which, in a way, it was. Pure fantasy. Foolish and romantic and irresponsible.

When the last number had been played, the band offered gruff words of appreciation to the audience, reminding them about next week's session and people began picking up their empty glasses to return to the bar. Someone turned up the lights and Jake let go of Amy's hand, but didn't move.

'Do you know what that last number was?' his voice was so quiet she had to move closer to hear him.

'No, what was it?'

'It's called *The Way You Look Tonight.*' It was almost as though he couldn't go on, she thought. Couldn't say the words.

'And?' she prompted, not knowing what to expect.

'You only heard the tune tonight, but the lyrics are... they...'

She found she was holding her breath.

'I'll repeat them for you – they go... *You're lovely, never ever change... Won't you please arrange it, cos...*'

'Jake, don't do this.' She cut him off short but her eyes filled with tears and she bowed her head. This was going to end badly. She had to make a move. Jumping down from her stool, she jammed the beanie onto her head and turned to face him.

'Come on. It's time we both went home. It's been a great evening and I've really enjoyed it. But it's getting late...'

'Amy...'

'No, Jake. Stop now.'

This couldn't go on. Christ, she felt as though she was on the edge. 'Someone's going to get hurt here and I've done enough damage in my time to know there are always consequences, bloody unpleasant ones, that you don't even think about until it's too late. For my sake, if not for yours, leave this where it is.'

He blinked slowly. 'You're right,' he said. 'You're right. I'm behaving badly.' He placed his hands on the table top and seemed to be considering what to do next. 'I don't want to bring you trouble, believe me. I'm selfish but not that selfish.' He smiled at her. Such a sad, warm smile. 'Ok, let's go.'

As they followed the last of the stragglers heading out into the night, Jake turned. 'We still ok for the newspaper day? Or would it be difficult now?'

'No, it won't be difficult. It's far too good an idea to throw away. I'll be in touch. Promise.'

She didn't remember anything about the journey home. She pulled into the driveway, wondering where the last twenty minutes had gone and how on earth the car had managed to find its own way. There seemed to be nothing in her head, nothing except for that last tune of the night playing over and over, and Jake's tender, hesitant voice speaking the words.

Chapter 19

Catherine wasn't in the mood for auditions. She sat in the youth club's main area, on a rickety wooden chair facing the stage, clipboard in hand, surrounded by jostling teenagers anxious for her attention. Her mind was on the conversation she'd had with Jake the night before, a conversation that had been left unfinished; it had made her feel not just uneasy, but scared. She should never have pushed things when she'd seen the way he reacted, should never have asked too many questions. Ones he didn't answer. Or wouldn't.

Around her now, the noise was becoming deafening. She raised her voice to a shout. 'Right, I can't start this until everyone settles down and forms a line.' Someone knocked against her shoulder. 'Trish, did you hear that? A line, then I can take down names and we can start. Everyone'll have a chance, there's no need to push.'

She looked down at the clipboard, already divided into long columns under headings - names, type of act, duration, comment. There was far more interest in this show than she'd anticipated and it needed proper organisation and control if it was going to work successfully. As she sat waiting for the kids to realise they were just wasting time, she heard the door open and close behind her and felt someone's presence at her back. Not so much felt, she thought later – it was a smell, sweet, slightly musty, more obvious when she turned her head - and there was Lucas standing behind her. She was pleased to see that he'd followed up on his promise to help and she realised, now, it was going to be needed.

'Great, Lucas, you've come just at the right time.' She smiled up at him, wanting to make him feel welcome. 'I'm starting on the list of acts. If only they'd calm down, we can find out what they intend to do and create some sort of programme. Could you take a look behind the stage and see what needs clearing away and... we haven't done anything about the lighting yet. Could you rig up something temporary, say a couple of those spot lights we have in the back – just to get the right atmosphere...?'

'Is the big cupboard locked?' He spoke slowly and carefully, unzipping his black anorak, with hands that looked too big for his thin wrists. Although he was tall, he had a spareness about his frame, as though he could do with a good meal, Catherine thought; there was something insubstantial about him. Perhaps it was his colouring, eyes that seemed almost as pale as his face and hair. Or his air of detachment, of being on the edge of what was going on, in the shadows looking on. It'd often surprised her that the others didn't make fun of him. He was different, that would have been enough for them. Did they let him be because he was like a big brother to the younger ones, she wondered. Or was it that he didn't rise to the bait? Perhaps, he just wasn't worth hassling.

Anyway, that wasn't her worry now - he'd always been good with her, polite and helpful – on hand when she needed something doing or sorting out equipment for the juniors. Ok, he wasn't a joiner, he didn't try to fit in; but he still came, so he needed something useful to do. She could understand that.

She watched him as he walked, measured and slow, over to the stage, glad he was there to give her some backing. She'd expected Tony to come but he hadn't turned up; she'd rung him about the arrangements, but so far she was on her own.

'Ok, who's first? Peter, what are you going to do?'

A small boy with a buzz cut, head shaved above his ears, came to stand in front of her. 'Michael Jackson.'

'Right. Need a bit more detail.'

'Dancing to *Thriller*. My mum says I do it really well.'

Catherine hesitated. 'Yes, I've seen you practising. Will you be on your own?'

'Yeah. Although I might bring in some ghouls and ghosts to make it look good.' He wiggled his arms about, slid his feet along the floor, and laughed. 'I've got the whole thing on my mobile, so I'll show you.'

'Fine. You can go first. Next.'

'Ryan and Matt – you were going to mime to 'One Direction'. Right. Have you found another three to do it with you?'

'We've got two, Miss and we're trying to persuade Tommy. We can do it with just four of us tonight.'

'Right,' Catherine looked up from her notes. 'Next...'

By the time it got to half past seven, she had ten acts, but knew there were too many similar ideas. She'd have to think up some others to give the evening variety. At least there was one harmonica player, a rather ham-fisted magician and a dubious suggestion from Beth, who wanted to bring along the family dog to perform tricks. That, she could see, might have its own problems.

But, on the plus side, at least they were all keen. There was an air of excited anticipation among them all and she stopped worrying about the whole venture – at least she knew no-one here was going to spoil things. She didn't need Tony to warn her, though, about the ones who might cause trouble just for the fun of it. Perhaps only a few, but it didn't take many to disrupt everything.

After one run-through, scrappy and disjointed, she'd made up a provisional order for the programme and set a date for a practice in ten days' time. Some parents had wandered in to pick up their children, and the hall slowly cleared, voices and footsteps fading away into the park outside. Eventually, there was only Lucas left to help her tidy up, put away the props, draw the curtains and lock the inner doors. They worked in comfortable silence until, looking round, Catherine was satisfied it would do.

'We've done enough, Lucas. You've been brilliant. It looks cleaner now than on a club night.'

The boy nodded slightly and put his jacket back on.

She waited at the door as he switched off the lights. He'd barely spoken to her all night, but he'd kept order backstage, worked the CD player for the singers and shushed the noisy kids, waiting for their turn when they got too loud.

Catherine felt she needed to say more. Let him know how useful he'd been. 'I'm just so glad you were here. It made such a difference. Thank you for giving up the time,' she said, hoping she didn't sound patronising.

He didn't answer straight away, just looked steadily at her. 'No problem.' He waited for her to go out first.

'Well, I'm sure you'd rather have been doing something else…'

'No,' he turned and looked down at her, and smiled. 'No,' he repeated. 'This was what I wanted to do.'

Catherine watched him as he walked along the path heading out of the park. She hadn't been sure he'd turn up but thank heaven he had. He'd certainly been as much help as Tony would have been and it was a relief the evening passed without any incidents. Without any jokers intruding and trying to ruin it all. Something was going right, anyway.

She stood on the steps for a moment, the shapes of bushes and trees and railings barely visible in the darkness. And clear across the flat ground came the loud squawking from the lake that stood in the centre of the park - the Canada geese she'd seen earlier waddling over the flagstones, taking over the ducks' territory, as they did every year at this time.

She pulled her coat collar up against the night air and headed for home. The feeling of satisfaction at a job well done soon vanished and once again, she felt sick and troubled, the conversation from the previous night in the forefront of her mind.

It wasn't a conversation really. It had been the nearest thing they'd ever had to a row and from the start, the atmosphere was fraught. Perhaps it had been brewing for days. From when Jake had decided to go back to Leeds to see his mother on the second weekend, and his plans hadn't included her. Monday morning and she'd sat down next to him in the staff room at break time, and asked how things were at home. Was there any change? He'd not answered straight away and she sensed her timing was all wrong. This wasn't the place to discuss personal matters. The room was crowded and noisy. Half-term over, it was a typical hurried catch-up for everyone, twenty-five minutes for a quick cup of coffee, a chat about a pupil, a lesson, a change in the timetable, and then back along the corridors to the next lesson.

He looked tired, she thought, shadows under the eyes and his hair needed combing. Perhaps the weekend had taken its toll.

'Is the news bad then?' she'd asked.

'No,' Jake had shrugged his shoulders. 'There's not much to report, really. The results haven't shown anything. She's not doing a lot, just sitting around – the GP's keeping an eye on her. I think everyone's relieved, but... difficult to know. ' Then, he stood up, and gathering a set of exercise books, muttered, 'Must go,' and moved away. Quickly. As though she'd no right to care about his family...or him. He didn't want to discuss any of it with her, or include her. He certainly hadn't wanted to take her with him.

And Tuesday night had been even more upsetting. Throughout the day, she'd fretted over everything that had been eating away at her over the past couple of months – he'd grown more and more distant, barely talking, staying up late when they'd been together, so that she was usually asleep when he came to bed. Distracted, that's what he'd been. Cold, in fact, if she was honest. She just couldn't let it go on.

It had been hard to get through her lessons. She was nervous, trying to devise an excuse that would seem genuine for going round to his house. By the end of the school day, when she hadn't seen him or spoken to him, she'd made up her mind. Sometimes, she told herself, you have to take a chance. He owed her an explanation. He owed her some consideration.

At ten past seven, she rang the bell.

Jake had come to the door with a tea towel over his shoulder and she could hear jazz music coming from the kitchen. She thought he might smile when he saw who it was, but, at first, there was no expression on his face at all. A blankness which frightened her. Then he gave a tight smile and moved aside so she went ahead of him, stepping sideways to pass his bike in the narrow hallway.

She saw that he'd been cooking himself a meal, some sort of stir-fry, a glass of red wine next to the hob. He went over to the stove and turned the heat down low and the CD player off. Suddenly the kitchen was too quiet.

'Looks good,' she'd said, sitting down at the kitchen table. 'Didn't mean to interrupt your meal.'

'It'll keep.' He didn't sit down straight away, then must have seen she wouldn't speak until he'd taken the chair opposite her, so he sat. Stiff-backed and not quite meeting her gaze. 'What's up?'

She'd swallowed and clasped her hands together, trying to keep calm. She felt wretched now she was facing him, but she had to say something. So she'd begun. 'I want you to know how much I love you, Jake, and I don't know what I'd do if this all came to an end...'

He'd reached over to get his wine and took a drink. She could feel a pulse throbbing in her ears and had to grip her hands tightly together to stop them shaking. But she was determined to go on.

'These last few weeks, well since September really, I feel I'm being pushed out and I don't know what I've done to deserve it. Tell me what I'm doing wrong, what I can do to make this better. I don't understand why you won't talk to me about anything...' she was breathless.

He put his hand up to stop her. 'Don't, Catherine. Don't go beating yourself up. It isn't you, it's me. I'm...' He hesitated.

'What? Something's changed What is it?'

'Nothing. Certainly not you.' He rubbed his forehead. 'I'm not sure what I want any more. That's all I can say, really. I'm...'

Catherine found she was crying. Noisily, hot tears on her cheeks, throat tight. She could feel panic rising in her chest, control slipping away. 'Don't do this to me.'

'I'm not doing anything on purpose, Catherine. Relationships change - things don't always stay the same...'

She'd had enough. She hit the table with the flat of her hand, desperate, her words choking out of her. 'There must be something more than that. Is this what happened with Hannah? You got fed up — after you'd spent three years with her — you just got fed up and dumped her? Please don't tell me this is what's happening with us.'

'What on earth has Hannah got to do with this?' His voice was low, the words measured — a warning in the tone. 'You didn't even know her.'

She knew he was getting angry, she could see it in his face, but she couldn't stop. 'The whole staff room talked about it when I first got to Forest Green. She was a nurse and you were together for years; you were almost living together...'

She knew she'd said too much. Jake had stood up, his face flushed. She saw how dark his expression was, how shallow he was breathing. He was trying to contain himself and she was losing him. She knew she'd pushed him too far. All she could do was put her face in her hands and weep.

'I'm sorry. I'm sorry. I love you so. I don't know what I'd do if...' and she raised herself from her chair and, before he could move away or stop her, she threw her arms round his neck and clung to him, repeating the same words over and over again.

Eventually, he'd put his arms round her and held her until she grew calmer and stopped crying. *Things were still ok*, she thought to herself, *this is just a silly misunderstanding, and I've let it muddle my mind.* Once something dreadful's happened, however long ago, it stays with you and you have this awful fear it'll happen again.

'Come on, Catherine, you're working yourself up. It'll be sorted, but not now.' His voice was soothing, patient. At least, he wasn't angry any more. 'I've had a lot on my mind and you're tired out and not making any sense. Come on. Leave this now. We'll talk when you're calmer.' He got up and led her back through the kitchen into the hallway. At the door, he hugged her gently. 'Go home, get some sleep and we'll talk about things later in the week. Don't cry anymore.'

'No, I won't.' She gave him what she hoped was a cheerful smile and kissed his cheek. 'I'll be ok. Really. I'm upset right now, but I'll be OK. I needed to get it all off my chest. Sorry.' She lifted her hand to his face and touched his cheek, the stubble rough under her fingers. 'Enjoy your dinner.' And she'd walked out into the street, emotionally spent but relieved.

She'd thought about what he'd said, going over and over how he'd spoken, what he'd meant, every detail of it.

And now, as she left the park after the auditions, she wanted, for the umpteenth time, to reassure herself. But she daren't go round again when she wasn't expected. No. She told herself how foolish that would be. So she climbed into her car, did a three-point-turn and drove past the park gates, along Hunter Lane – in the opposite direction of home. She drove along a tree-lined street, deserted except for a few cars and vans parked along the roadside. Slowing down to a crawl, her eyes focussed on the windows of one house.

Nobody home, curtains not drawn.

So where was he?

And she began to wonder if perhaps there was something here that she was too blind to see.

Chapter 20

As he walked, Robert was thinking about his time spent with Holly at The Boatman. They'd spent the day before visiting Aysgarth Falls, following the path that took them up the three ledges, through the woods then tea at the little café. He could see how much happier she seemed, studying the map, leading the way, pointing out landmarks. 'Look,' she said. 'Holly House. They've named it after me.' and just above the road bridge, telling him, 'This was where they filmed scenes from Robin Hood. Did you see it – 'Prince of Thieves'. It was on TV the other week.' She was a different girl. And on their last morning, she insisted on writing something in the Visitors' Book in reception, 'because it's been great,' she said and turned to him. '*Everything's* been great. Thanks, Dad.'

'Hey,' Mike shouted. 'Stop daydreaming and get on with it.'

'Sorry. Need to concentrate here.'

The day was blustery, but the light was good as he putted his ball to a few inches off the pin. Mike, waiting to take his shot from the bunker, did a slow handclap and gave a short laugh before picking a club out of his bag.

'Aren't you glad now you came out with me?' he said and took a chip shot which sent a shower of sand into the air and the ball rolling past the hole. He was five up already, but always pretended that playing off a seven handicap didn't make him a formidable opponent. He plodded across the green. 'Christ, I'm meant to be the one who can play. I either need to give this game up, or get some glasses.'

Robert grinned and waved a hand in the air. 'I'll give you that putt.'

They squared the hole and walked on in companionable silence. The course was fairly empty as it was a Friday, which Robert preferred to the weekend as there was no waiting about while the pedants weighed up every shot as though it was the Masters. He hadn't played much this autumn - squash was easier to fit into his limited free time but that had gone by the board since the Nick business. He needed to find another partner and he didn't fancy turning up in the changing rooms and walking into an embarrassing situation. Not that *he'd* anything to be embarrassed about. Nick was the one who should be hanging his head.

Mike strode in front, pulling his trolley over the narrow earthen paths, then, coming to a dog-leg, he slowed down to let Robert catch up. 'You need to come out more often, not just when you can wangle a day off. You've paid your fees, you should get your money's worth.'

'I know I should. I always feel better after a game. It's just that time seems to be taken up with so many other things. Poor excuse, though.'

'You work too bloody hard, you know that Robert? You tire yourself out.' Mike shook his head. 'We aren't young anymore and stress can be a killer.'

'Thanks very much. I needed cheering up.'

'Come on, I'm bloody hungry,' Mike rubbed his hands together. 'Bacon sandwiches! I can smell them from here.'

They walked over the short grass, striped by the weak sun's rays, heading towards a small hut with wooden benches set out in front of it. Someone on the committee had thought up this bright idea of a 'pit stop', as it had come to be called, just off the twelfth. Coffee and hot food served for two hours midday. They put in their order then sat down next to each other, stretching their legs, looking out over the fairway.

'This is the life,' said Mike. 'I bet not much has changed since my dad played here. Except he used to wear plus fours! Don't see many of those nowadays!'

He chattered on and Robert didn't need to reply or talk at all. He took off his glove and smoothed down his hair, which had been tangled by the wind. For the first time in weeks, he stopped trying to solve all the problems that he was sure only he could sort out – just breathed in the cool air and gazed out over the familiar contours of grass and bunkers and raised tees. If anyone had asked him what he was thinking at that moment, he'd have replied, 'Nothing.' It was never true, of course. But right now it was good to just appreciate the moment, no decisions to make, no demands.

With a start, he realised Mike had asked him a question.

'Sorry, wasn't listening.'

'I said how was Holly. Last week.'

Robert stirred himself as the young cook brought out the bacon sandwiches, wrapped in thin, greased paper, and placed them on the table. Nothing like that smell in the outdoors, Robert thought. They turned round to eat and he didn't answer until they'd both taken their first mouthful.

'Better than I'd hoped, really,' he said. 'Quiet at first, but we took walks round the lake every day and climbed a bit – she seemed to get her appetite back – and started telling me about her friends and her plans. Which was good. She looked a lot better by the time I took her home.'

'Kids worry you to death and then manage instant recovery while you're going grey. I should know. She'll be fine.' Mike took two enormous bites, finished his sandwich and balled up his paper, aiming it at the bin.

'Paula's met someone.' The words came out before Robert could stop them.

Mike's eyebrows shot up and he opened his mouth to speak, but shut it again. Then managed to say, 'Really?'

'Yes, really.'

'After all this time!' Mike seemed to be having trouble believing it. 'Well, that's good, isn't it? I mean, you want her to have a life, to be happy, and at least if she's with someone else...' He stopped. 'Robert, it lets you off the hook. You can stop feeling so bloody guilty. Can't you?'

'That's one way of looking at it.'

'When did she tell you?'

'It was before Holly and I went to Malham. I'd just gone to buy Amy's birthday present on the Wednesday night and I'd spent quite a lot on it and... oh, I don't know... perhaps my conscience suddenly got the better of me...'

'Nothing new there! You've been beating yourself up for years.'

'It's odd, you know? It was obvious she had something to tell me, took me to one side, looked serious - and that was the last thing I expected.' He shrugged his shoulders. 'Certainly took me by surprise. But I wasn't to mention it to Holly; she made out it wasn't that serious yet.'

'And...?'

'I just hope she knows what she's doing. She's not the best at making the right decisions. Well, she *wasn't*.' He gave a short, mirthless laugh. 'And this'll sound ludicrous ... I felt as though I should have been consulted.'

'Christ, never mind "sounds", it *is* ludicrous.' Mike blew out his cheeks and pulled a face. 'It was inevitable she'd find someone eventually and she's mature enough to choose sensibly. Isn't she?

She's hardly naive and impressionable.'

Robert stared ahead.

Mike waited. 'Oh, come on. You're being a dog in the manger. You've got everything *you* wanted. You don't know how lucky you are – Amy's wonderful and you have Harry. You can't have the best of both worlds – you knew that when you left.'

'Of course I did. But if this relationship, or whatever it is, goes further, it'll affect the children and I don't want anything to give Holly any more worries at the moment.' He could see Mike looking at him in disbelief and tried to appear diffident instead of embarrassed. 'Oh, I don't need you to tell me I'm being absolutely selfish. Paula's every right to do what she wants. But... I don't want things to change and I suppose I'm thrown by the fact that they will.'

'You've just got to get used to the idea. But I can't believe you didn't think this would happen. Sometime.'

'No. I never thought about it. She was never comfortable socially, was she? New people. She hated all that. Ok with a few close friends, but entertaining and business dinners – she'd much rather stay at home and watch television.'

'Well, she's made an effort to get out there and good for her.' Mike slapped him on the shoulder, which Robert felt wasn't quite as much good-natured as a rebuke. 'You're making a meal of this when there's no need. Come on, let's play some golf.' And he got up and caught the handle of his trolley, striding off to the next hole.

Robert wished he'd said nothing. He didn't know why he'd needed to tell him, but Mike was his oldest friend and full of good sense – and he'd been a good listener before – a sounding board ten years ago when life had been such an unholy mess. A mess he'd made all by himself, Robert thought; he couldn't blame Amy. Or Paula, for that matter. And everything Mike had said now was absolutely fair. Not judgemental, just fair.

As they walked on, he went over that Wednesday evening, trying to remember what it was about Paula that had seemed different. She'd looked as though she'd taken more care of her appearance, her face less anxious, softer, somehow. And she'd sounded more confident as though she was taking charge, rather than defer to him. It seemed out of character.

Reaching the twelfth tee, he took a wood out of his bag and forced himself to just get on with the game. After all, this was his day off and he was damned if he was going to let hypothetical questions and baseless worries cloud his mind.

By one o'clock, they'd finished the round and were walking down to the club house, which lay in the dip below the eighteenth. The setting was certainly spectacular. When you approached it from the road, you drove down a long drive, which crossed a bridge over the river Mersey and wound down to a car park edged with huge oak trees. The building itself was tall and wide, painted white, with an imposing entrance way, two pillars standing either side of a doorway twenty feet high and crenelated walls along the flat roof like a castle. Trellises covered the exterior and four huge arched windows were situated across the frontage. Robert had always thought the architect must have had delusions of grandeur. And the finishing touch was a flagpole adding to its air of importance. Presumably sending the message - don't bother coming here unless you can pay the fees, and then some.

They sat for a few minutes on the wooden steps leading to the locker rooms, Mike scraping the wet leaves and mud off the studs that had stuck to his shoes, and talking away as though he'd forgotten Robert's earlier concerns. But he suddenly turned and studied his friend's face.

'Surely you're not regretting anything now.' It didn't sound like a question, just a way of Mike reassuring himself of what he wanted to hear.

'No, of course not. God, I wouldn't go back and alter any of it, even if I could.' He sat, looking out over the calm, familiar scene, hearing the hollow smack of golf balls being hit along the fairway to the right of him and the sound of laughter drifting down from the clubhouse.

He didn't like change. Perhaps because he found it unnerving. You think life'll always continue the way it has done . You don't really think about it. You *expect* that there'll be constancy, keeping that sense of order – the same weekly routines, the same hobbies, going to work, home and family, seeing friends. A structure that shores you up - a recognizable world. But of all people, surely he'd learnt what a fragile edifice that was! Look what he'd done ten years ago. Thrown everything up in the air. Although he could honestly say, he hadn't seen it coming.

Meeting Amy all that time ago hadn't heralded any impending catastrophe. It hadn't initially disturbed his organised way of life or shaken his innate belief in his own stability. He was a man who'd followed a conventional path - sound education, a steady climb up the professional and social ladder, acquiring a nice wife, producing the requisite number of children. Money and a sense of entitlement had helped to smooth the way, of course, and his family's approval bolstered his integral sense of worth. So there wasn't anything he had ever considered that could throw him so off-balance or change the course of his life dramatically. He was satisfied with the way things were – if his marriage wasn't filled with fun and excitement, that was the same for most marriages of most of his friends and acquaintances, from what he could see. There were always compromises.

So that morning when he first saw Amy, his mind had been on the day ahead. She'd been waiting, in the panelled reception area, where the receptionist was taking calls. When Robert came out of his office to greet her, she'd been sitting upright in her chair, watching through an open door the secretaries and accounts clerks busying themselves with seemingly urgent tasks. Robert thought she looked quirky – dressed like a student in clothes that didn't seem to match, a military-style jacket over a white t-shirt and mud-coloured trousers – not his idea of an office type. But he had to admit she was pretty, yes, and she had an alert manner, her expression and posture full of quickness and curiosity.

He led her into the quiet sanctuary of his room and ordered coffee over the intercom for them both. He'd contacted the paper about the firm's involvement in a charity day, getting together a team to tidy up a local centre but hadn't given many details; so he thought she'd begin by asking questions. But as she sat down, and didn't speak, he remembered looking at her with a more discerning eye. She looked far too young to be a reporter, fresh-faced, smooth pale skin, wide eyes – couldn't be more than nineteen. Yet there was no doubt about her self-composure. She didn't look as though much would faze her.

His first reaction when he'd taken all this in was annoyance. Why hadn't the paper sent someone more suitable, older, more experienced? She could mess this up and it was too important for that.

After the coffee had been brought in by Sue, his secretary, and poured, the girl pulled a notebook and pen from a battered leather bag.

'So,' Robert placed his elbows on the desk and gave her what he hoped was an encouraging smile, but his face felt too tight and he sensed she knew he was judging her. 'Where do we start?'

She took her time, eyeing him steadily, holding his gaze. 'I thought we should concentrate on two aspects – the activity itself on the day – the painting of the hall and the cleaning up the surrounding grounds at the centre. And then concentrate on some human story – what it all means to one individual who'll benefit from this project – that'll show the readers how much this kind of help means to that community.'

Robert nodded, briskly. She was bit too sure of herself, he thought, and he was suddenly determined to have the last say about all the arrangements. It was his firm that was putting up the money, after all. 'Yes, fine. But our name needs to be prominent in the text and in a photo – we've made a banner that can be held up by the staff who've volunteered to do the work, with the firm's name on it. That's got to be seen.'

She seemed to be weighing him up. 'I know this is a promotion exercise for your company, Mr. Wilson, but if you want to be seen by the local community as caring and altruistic, you have to play down the publicity side. I can write you a good feature, if you let me show how creating a pleasant environment at this centre enhances the lives of the people using it.'

Robert took his elbows off the desk and sat back, his coffee untouched. That's me told, he thought, not sure whether to be irritated or amused. And she was right about how to handle the project, he supposed. She'd taken him by surprise. Young, maybe, but bright. He just wasn't used to someone telling him how to handle things.

'Miss Middleton...' he began.

'It's Amy.' And now at least she was smiling. A warm smile that reached her eyes and took away any offence he might have taken from her tone. 'Look,' she put down her notebook with nothing written on it. 'I'll talk to your team, the ones who're going to do the work, then I'll go down to the centre and get what I can from the warden. It'll take me a couple of days to put it together – then you can go over the article – see whether you approve or not. We'll do the photo you want on the day. How will that do?' She put out her hand to shake his and waited for him to say 'Fine' before standing up and heading for the door.

He felt he'd been steam-rollered.

Looking back now, he realised he hadn't stood a chance. Like being blown off course by a headwind, he'd lost control long before he knew it. He was so used to having the upper hand – he wasn't prepared for someone like her - strong willed, forthright, intelligent; she was exhilarating and frightening. She challenged him. He remembered thinking after she'd left that first time – Damn, a mere girl, half my age! What next? It was the beginning of the end to his ordered, predictable life.

But over the last ten years, he'd regained his equilibrium, settled into his marriage with Amy, enjoying his young son, the familiarity of it all reassuring. He'd become used to this way of life, compartmentalised perhaps, but at least the two families had been a constant in his daily routine for a long time now.

And Paula's announcement had shifted the balance again.

Robert shook his head and pulled himself up off the steps. 'Come on Mike. That pint's calling me. I'll even pay for yours.'

Mike slapped his knee in mock surprise. 'Wonders never cease.'

And there was nothing else either wanted to say about the matter.

Chapter 21

Jake stood in his kitchen and filled the kettle, eyeing the three empty wine bottles on the work surface. He was getting through one a night and it was becoming a habit. Not counting the odd whiskey. How many units did all that add up to? No idea, he thought, but it was time for a bit of control. He'd have just one tonight. Slow it down. How odd it was that through your twenties, you think, whatever your lifestyle, you'll last forever. But get to thirty and you start believing in all the health scares. Reading all the new studies published in the newspapers about what alcohol does to your liver, your heart, your brain, you imagine your whole body disintegrating. He'd never get to fifty at this rate.

He'd rung his mother half an hour ago, and she'd sounded quite cheery. She would though, and he wasn't sure she was telling him everything the doctors said in their check-ups. She was good at asking questions and not so good at answering them. And he knew she'd wave his dad off in the same breezy manner. He needed to go back home at the weekend and see for himself.

He made a cup of tea and sat down with the morning paper he'd pinched from the Media table at school, turning to the Education section. It was peaceful sitting in the kitchen, just the sound of a dripping tap he hadn't mended and the faint whoosh of a car going past in the street outside. He decided he really liked his own company. No pretending to be interested in conversations that bored you, no faking amusement at people's tasteless jokes, no wasted effort being sociable. I'm becoming misanthropic, he thought, smiling to himself. Catherine's probably right when she says I'm really a loner. I can live with that.

He read Michael Rosen's column – how clever that man was with words – and turned the page to see whether he could work out the political cartoonist's take on the latest news. He knew he should start on the Gatsby essays - typically, Matthew, so full of it in lessons, hadn't handed his in, offering a lame excuse about the computer's printer playing up (how often had he heard *that* one) – and there was the mock exam he needed to plan for the year elevens, but he didn't want to move. He didn't even want to get up off his chair to pull the blind down and shut out the night sky.

The peal of the doorbell, sudden and loud in the quiet house, made him jump and tear a sheet of the newspaper. 'Christ, not tonight,' he closed his eyes, weary at the idea of any intrusion. 'Let's hope it's only the church warden coming for his monthly five quid. Anyone else can sod off.' He wondered when talking to himself had become another habit.

He walked slowly up the hall and could feel his mood sinking as he opened the door.

At first, he couldn't quite make out the figure on the doorstep. Short grey woollen coat, fur-lined hood hugging the face, the dim light from the kitchen making it hard for him to focus. He screwed up his eyes, then opened them wide in astonishment.

'Amy! I... what are you doing here?' He hadn't time to think of anything more welcoming to say.

'Can I come in?' She was already stepping quickly through the doorway.

He stepped back for her to pass; the closeness of her shocked him, making it difficult for him gather his wits. 'Course you can. It's great to see you.' Then, walking ahead of her down the passageway to the kitchen, he couldn't help thinking how ironic it was that this should be happening after Catherine's visit the week before. Both unexpected, neither invited. But Christ, what a difference in the way he was feeling. His heart was beating so fast he thought she could probably hear it, an adrenaline rush flooding through him, making his legs suddenly weak. He tried to recover from the shock by talking quickly but not making much sense. 'I was just having a cup of tea, reading the paper, you know, doing nothing really, so I'm glad of the company. Come and sit down in the kitchen. It's warm in here. Let me take your coat...' Where were the right words when everything you've ever wanted lands at your feet? Jake couldn't believe she was actually sitting at his kitchen table, shaking her arms out of her sleeves, then rubbing her cold hands together and clasping them under her chin. Her cheeks were flushed and strands of her hair were corkscrewing into the air.

'How on earth did you find me?' he asked when he'd put the tea in front of her and yanked the biscuit tin from the cupboard. She didn't touch either, but he could see her shoulders relaxing and the corners of her mouth went down in an apologetic smile. 'Investigative journalism. That's what I'm good at.'

He laughed. Delighted. He was on a high. 'Am I glad about that!'

He sat next to her and it took all his willpower not to reach out and put his arm round her. But he hesitated, not sure what the score was. She'd have to take the lead. If she didn't, there was a chance he'd ruin it all. And he couldn't risk that.

There was an uneasy moment when they just looked at each other.

'I needed to see you,' she said, her words coming slowly, her eyes serious. 'This evening seemed a good opportunity – Robert's in London and Harry, he's with my sister, so I thought we'd have time to clear something up...'

'Ok,' he said.

She began to fiddle with the bracelet of her watch. 'The night we were at the pub, listening to the jazz, you know... I feel you might have got the wrong impression.' She threw him a quick look then concentrated on the biscuit tin in front of her. 'I should have made it clear that it would never... that we... I let my guard down a bit and I'm sorry if I led you to think...' She paused.

'Think what?' he spoke quietly, his expression giving nothing away.

'That there's going to be some sort of... Oh, Jake, look, I'd be lying if I said I didn't find you attractive. Of course I do. But this is going nowhere. And it's scaring me. To be honest it's giving me real heartache. I can't stop thinking...'

'Amy.' He couldn't listen to any more. He took hold of both her hands and felt her fingers tremble and tighten round his. 'You don't need to say anything, explain anything. There's something here that I don't understand either. And all the words in the world won't make any sense of it. It's happening, that's all I know.'

'But it shouldn't, Jake. It really shouldn't.'

All he could think about was how beautiful she was this close to him, the curve of her cheek, the perfect mouth, those wide eyes meeting his, intense and sad. He drew her to her feet and pulled her gently towards him, wrapping his arms round her waist until their bodies were so close, he could smell the scent of soap on her skin. He wanted her so much, he ached.

'I've never felt this way about anyone. Ever.' His voice was a murmur, full of anguish. 'It's burning me up.'

Her gaze was steady, as though she was still trying to hold on to some remnant of control. But when she spoke, it was faltering and became a confession. 'I haven't been able to eat. It's as though I'm ill.'

He lifted one hand and stroked her hair, tucking the wayward strands smooth against her head, as though he was trying to soothe her, take away the hurt, make up for any pain she might be feeling. He couldn't stop sensing how fragile this situation was; he couldn't go on and he couldn't break away. It was as though he was in limbo. Just like, when as a child, he'd built a tower of playing cards on the kitchen table, placing them so carefully in position one by one, and knowing that the slightest tremor would bring them tumbling down.

The dripping tap beat a soft, slow tempo, accentuating the quiet space surrounding them, their world shrunk to a circle of two.

'I'm in love with you,' he said. 'I have been since the moment I saw you.'

'You don't know me, Jake.' She shook her head and pulled slightly away from him. 'I'm not what you think you see. I'm selfish and destructive and I never stick to anything. I'm bad news. I create problems I can't solve and then other people suffer...'

'Amy, you have no idea what I see.' He touched her cheek and held her fast, not understanding or questioning where his courage was coming from. 'Sometimes, you just know about someone. I saw you at the airport all those months ago and I knew. From the way you smiled, how you moved, the expression on your face. It was like connecting with something you've been waiting for your whole life. I didn't need to be told that you're warm and funny and bright and full of life. It was written all over you. I meet people every day – have done, year in, year out - and I've never before thought to myself, in that instant – wow!'

She smiled, then and pulled a face. 'Oh, Jake.'

'There's no logic to it.' He didn't know if he was making any sense, but he carried on saying what he'd wanted to say for months. 'Something unexpected like that hits you out of the blue and you're not just going to walk away. Because of the rules. Who makes them anyway? Fuck the rules!'

And he stopped talking and kissed her, slowly and with all the pent-up feelings he'd had over the long days and nights she'd haunted his dreams and waking hours and working weeks. He pulled her body tight against his and felt the heat of her skin against him. Then he drew away and looked at her, a moment of understanding passing between them. No words were needed now.

He took her hand and led her up the narrow passage, up the old, steep staircase and into his bedroom. He bent down, still holding her hand, and switched on the bedside lamp which sent shadows round the uneven walls and onto the low ceiling. Going over to the window that looked onto the street, he drew the curtains and turned back to her. The look on her face was solemn, half-bemused – and she seemed to him lovelier than he'd ever seen her. He couldn't wait any longer.

'I don't want us to regret anything, Amy,' he said. 'I couldn't bear it if you were ever sorry.'

'I won't be sorry. I promise.'

Then she smiled - a smile that took the last doubt away. It was a memory he'd conjure up over and over again and for as long as he drew breath. And he had a sudden strange foreboding – was it intuition or just plain fear at defying some long-established ethical code - that he was sealing his fate – in a way that he could never have imagined. A moment in time which could never be eradicated or retrieved, even when the tide had turned.

*

It was loud. Very loud. A hammering on the door which seemed to shake the whole house, and then the clang of the letter box as it was pushed open from the outside. It clattered closed, then opened again.

A voice was shouting his name. 'Jake, open the door. Please, open the door. I can see the light. I know you're there.'

He had sat bolt upright on the bed, at the sound of the first bang – why hadn't she rang the doorbell? – and he knew immediately how disastrous this situation was. Catherine was trying to catch him out. She'd said enough lately about how distracted he'd been, put two and two together and come up with... what? How could she know anything? Well, serve him right – he should have seen how anxious she'd been lately, worried that he was going to leave her. He should have finished it before it got to this state. God, what was he going to do?

Amy was pulling the sheet over her and looking up at him in horror, the quick intake of breath, eyes full of alarm. 'It's her, isn't it? The girlfriend who doesn't want it to end.'

Another rattle of the letter box. 'Please, Jake. Just let me know you're all right. Open the door and I'll just go home. I just want to see you. For a minute.'

Amy was shaking. 'She'll wake the whole street.'

'Christ! Bloody woman. What on earth's the time?'

'Never mind the time, you idiot. Go and open the door and talk to her.'

'Open the door?' Jake stifled a laugh, something like hysteria rising in his throat. 'And what are *you* going to do? Hide under the bed?'

Amy was struggling between fright and laughter. 'She's not going to search the place, is she?'

'I don't bloody know. Probably.'

Two more thumps on the door had Jake with his head in his hands. 'I can pretend I had my headphones on... or I was in the bath.' An unreasoning wave of fury swept over him. 'What a farce!'

'Jake, go down. She needs a few comforting words and she'll go away. For heaven's sake, do something.'

He nodded, grabbing for his pyjamas under the pillow and pulling them on, catching his foot in the seam and cursing. 'Christ! How to end a wonderful evening.' He looked at Amy with a rueful expression and leant over and kissed her. 'I love you. Remember that when you hear I've been slaughtered at my own front door.' And with that, he almost slid down the steep staircase into the hallway.

He had no idea of the time, so he'd have to wing it - he'd been tired, decided to go to bed early and read his book. Anything to keep Catherine at bay. He had a twinge of guilt that was soon overcome by his fear that Amy would be discovered. She had everything to lose. He had to keep her safe.

He pulled open the door, trying to look bleary eyed and half asleep.

Catherine stood on the doorstep, looking dishevelled with her coat hanging open and her hair falling limply round her shoulders. She looked tearful.

'Why didn't you answer the door, Jake? I was worried.'

'I was asleep, Catherine. I wasn't expecting anyone. What time is it?' Even to him, his voice sounded shaky.

'It's not late. Nine thirty. You never go to bed this early.'

They were still standing on the doorstep and Catherine was peering over his shoulder into the house. Could she see Amy's coat on the back of the kitchen chair? What if she pushed her way in? This wasn't the calm, even-tempered woman he thought he knew. He'd never seen her so insistent, demanding – well, not quite like this. She hadn't taken it well when he'd left her behind on his trips to Leeds - but he'd been too preoccupied, of course he had, and not taken enough notice. He could see she was going to make a big thing of it.

'Look,' he said, and smiled the best he could. 'I was tired. I went to bed early. I'm sorry I didn't hear you knocking, but...' He shrugged. 'I didn't.' What could he say to make sure she'd leave. 'I'll see you tomorrow and we'll go somewhere special. I'll book a meal at the Forester's Arms for Saturday night. You haven't been there. It's nice...'

She hesitated, 'I think your doorbell's bust.'

'I don't think so,' he said, knowing she wanted to prolong the conversation and desperately thinking of a way to curtail it. 'I need to go back to bed, Catherine. I'm knackered. You're getting upset about nothing. Go and get some sleep yourself.' And pecking her on the cheek, he closed the door on her worried, pinched face.

Bloody coward, that's what I am, he said to himself as he took the stairs two at a time. Why can't I be honest and tell her it's not ever going to work? Was never going to work from the start. But he knew why – he was too aware of the precarious situation both Amy and he had nearly found themselves in. He should have realised where that might lead. Catherine, he could see now, was capable of blowing the whistle on them. She would keep going till she'd found the truth of it all, and she'd make sure someone suffered for it. And the 'someone' would be Amy. He couldn't allow that to happen.

He climbed back into bed, cold and jittery, and didn't look at Amy as he pulled the duvet over them both. But she sat up, leaning on her elbow, waiting .

'How did that go?'

'Ok, I think. I said I'd gone to bed 'cos I was tired. I think she was all right.' He saw from Amy's doubtful expression that she wanted more reassurance than that. 'Don't worry. It's just... well... she's been saying I've changed lately – not paying her enough attention. Which is right – she's dead right - I've been thinking of you.' He stroked her bare shoulder and she shivered.

'Your hands are cold.'

'Sorry. All I can say is, it's a bloody good job I didn't let her have a key. That'd have been fun.'

'Oh, Jake, you've got to feel sorry for her. She's obviously fond of you and doesn't want to lose you.' She sounded exasperated with him. 'How long have you been together?'

'We're not *together.*' He felt he had to justify himself. But it was a sham. He knew he was being unkind, and only half-truthful, and didn't like himself much for it. 'It's tricky, Amy. We've gone out for quite a while but not with any talk of a future. She's thinking it's going somewhere when it isn't. And never has been.' He stopped and couldn't help feeling annoyed that Catherine had broken the spell with her knocking and shouting. 'Forget about her.'

'That's not so easy.'

'Look, Amy. I can't pretend to feel for someone what I don't feel. I know I'm being selfish, but you're all I care about. I love *you*. There it is. And I don't even want it to be any different.' She had a thoughtful expression on her face as though she was working something out in her mind, but he didn't want to ask what it was. 'Come on. Leave it. We don't know how long it'll be before we can have time like this again. It's too precious to waste.'

And as she lay with her head on his shoulder, Jake prayed to a God he didn't believe in, and hoped for what he knew was beyond his reach, that one day, time would be all theirs.

Chapter 22

The curtains were drawn, lamps turned on and an open fire sent out a comforting heat into the living room of the old house. The night outside was cold and the forecast had threatened snow, but the four women had now shed their coats and scarves and gloves and seemed intent on just getting warm again; certainly in no hurry to get down to business and discuss the chosen book. Two sat on the sofa, while Amy and the host, Jackie, sank back into the cushions of huge armchairs, hands wrapped round coffee mugs, paperbacks thrown carelessly onto the table in front of them. The fifth member of the group, Harriet, the one Amy had joined with and the one who always brought humour and insight to the discussions, hadn't managed to find a babysitter, only letting Jackie know at the last minute. Jackie wasn't pleased.

The conversation had already turned to the latest news about the Arts Centre. Council cuts meant it was due to be closed in the New Year. They listened and gave murmurs of encouragement, as Nancy, her long face etched with disapproval, brought them up to date on the petition that was going the rounds.

'We've got the backing of most of the companies in Stockport and even some of the Councillors, and what's more important - thousands of signatures from the on-line site. So we stand a good chance of reversing the decision. The council's got to listen.'

'Don't you bet on it.' Jackie, who always seemed to have friends in high places and knew everything, was almost sneering in her contempt. 'They're going to pull that beautiful eighteenth century building down and sell the land. That'll make way for two hundred and fifty houses. Profit's behind all this.'

Olivia, gentle and willowy, arty in her floating outfits and hand-crafted necklaces, and at sixty-five, always beautifully made-up and emitting some exotic fragrance, looked alarmed. 'Surely not. It has so many wonderful activities. What about the music nights and art gallery and the children's theatre? Where will they all go?'

'Out the window,' said Jackie, a harsh edge to her voice. 'No-one cares anymore about *culture*, Olivia. Sorry to upset you, but it'll be the libraries next to close. And then the subsidies for the orchestra cut. You wait and see.'

Amy felt as though she was watching all this from a distance, the voices heard but what was said, barely registering in her mind. She was already wondering how on earth she'd get through the evening, but she nodded in the right places, her expression giving a semblance of interest, and drank her coffee. For the last few days, her whole being had been taut with nerves, even when she was alone, and now, her calm exterior belied an agitation that she was finding increasingly difficult to hide. She could hardly sit still.

She'd forgotten, until this afternoon, that it was the monthly Book Club night. What was it she was meant to have read? It took her some minutes to remember. Of course, that was it – 'The Go Between'. She'd studied it at school and when Jackie, whose turn it was to choose, had suggested it, she'd genuinely looked forward to reading it again. It was one of those novels that stayed with you and at least she wouldn't be bored, slogging through something that didn't interest her at all. She'd had enough of the last few – Nathaniel Hawthorne with that scarlet woman, and Donna Tartt's long, rambling effort - and she wanted something she could relate to.

Well, she hadn't reread the book. Of course she hadn't. It had been the last thing on her mind. She just hoped she could remember enough to offer at least some relevant comments, even if she couldn't fill in the details. She'd found her old copy in the bookstand and leafed through it, thankful that there were notes in the margins and some passages coloured in with marker pen.

She'd left Harry, ready for bed, Robert helping him build a Lego car. Calling out over her shoulder that she wouldn't be late, she'd closed the front door behind her, standing on the step for a moment to let out a long breath. Trying to relieve the tightness in her chest. It was no good now being contrite, wishing... what? That she'd exercised some damned control, that she'd behaved differently? Too late to be sorry. She'd allowed it to happen and she couldn't start making excuses for herself. Everything she valued was being put in jeopardy and common sense had deserted her. That was the truth. It wasn't as though she was twenty any more. For God's sake, hadn't the past taught her anything?

She drove slowly, not wanting to be the first to arrive. Really, not wanting to go at all. But the routines of last week and the week before and the week before that had to be maintained – life couldn't just change course after last Tuesday, not outwardly anyway.

But changed it had.

She'd arrived back home that night at eleven. When she'd put her key in the lock, she'd heard Jasper give one sharp bark and felt sorry she'd shut him in the kitchen. But on a few occasions when he'd been left on his own with the run of the house, he'd created havoc, knocking over tables and digging up carpets. When he saw her, he leapt up to full height and she hugged him, glad to be able to give an instinctive response. Dogs always welcomed you, no matter what.

She'd opened the back door and let him out into the garden, then paused to look up at the clear night sky. It was pinpricked with stars, the sliver of a moon sharp above the trees. She needed some time to think about the whole evening; and she wanted to be honest about it all, not paint some romantic picture, as though she was a teenager with a head full of pipe dreams. That'd be fooling herself, anyway. Real life was so much more complicated. Even this evening, when she'd been carried away by an impulse that seemed uncontrollable, there were moments of absolute clarity; when, however much she was attracted to Jake, she'd been acutely aware of the newness of it all, of an awkwardness between them – hesitant whispered questions, two bodies searching for some sort of accord, and more prosaically, the clatter of the alarm clock falling off the bedside table. Inevitable, between two people who didn't know each other well.

And what had once seemed light-hearted and fun was serious now. It was all frightening and strange. But, slowly, they'd relaxed, trusting themselves, losing themselves, free from all restraints in the final moments. She supposed it was Jake, patient and tender, and so sure for the two of them, who'd made it seem – what? – as though no matter what the circumstances might have been, they'd have found each other. They'd have been drawn towards each other by some force so fundamental that it couldn't be resisted.

'I never realised,' he said, as she was leaving, 'I've been waiting for you all my life. However corny that sounds, it's true. I've never known what I wanted, till now.'

And she'd joked. 'That sounds like a song lyric!'

'Well, if it is,' he'd smiled, his face close to hers, dark eyes amused, 'someone knew what they were talking about.' And he'd kissed her forehead. 'I'm in love with you, Amy.'

She hadn't been able to answer, to give him any words that would commit her further. She'd been certain once before and made promises she'd meant to keep – and, at the time, even though it had caused terrible upset and outrage, she'd been so sure. She'd turned lives upside down and been damned on all sides. And here she was again, knowing that someone would get hurt, knowing she'd be the cause of it, acutely aware her behaviour was beyond the pale. Even when Catherine had hammered on the door, she hadn't felt any real compassion for the girl; she'd been more concerned about her own situation and fear of being caught. I'm morally corrupt, she thought, that's what I am. Someone who's aware of the consequences and never takes any responsibility for them.

So there were no words she could find for Jake. No words that carried any meaning. They'd been used up long ago.

She'd watched Jasper exploring the night-smells round the garden, nose tracking some scent across the grass, and wished her life was simpler. Like other people's lives or what they seemed to be. Did *she* just complicate everything? Or does everyone struggle behind a front they put up to the world. Are others covering up just as she was doing?

'Amy, you're miles away,' Nancy's voice, rather shrill, brought her back to the moment. Three pairs of eyes were fixed on her – two impatient, and Olivia's, kindly and questioning - and she realised she'd let her book close on her lap. She made a grab for it before it slid onto the carpet. Nancy had waited long enough. 'Come on, it's not like you to drift off. Aren't you getting enough sleep?'

She blushed. 'No, no, I'm fine. Sorry, where are we up to?'

'Structure,' Jackie said weightily. 'Does the Prologue work - having the old man finding the box and the diary before going back in time to when he was a boy? Or does it make for obscurity?'

God, thought Amy, *who talks like that?*

She did her best but grew tired of the arguments, the harshness of the voices, the tortuous analyses. It was such a good story, such a moving story, leave it at that, she thought. Just enjoy it. Not exactly the attitude to adopt at a Book Club evening, though! She tried to get in the right frame of mind, scolding herself. Offer an opinion, for heaven's sake, take part. Then just as her thoughts were ready to wander again, Olivia was delving into the question of who, among the characters, was the victim. As though it was as simple as that and there was only one.

'Ted's the victim, surely,' said Olivia, her voice quavering slightly, as though not sure she should be taking the lead. She smiled, apologetically, at Jackie. 'Well, he shot himself, poor man. Doesn't that prove he really loved Marian and felt bereft? And he never knew he had a son.'

Jackie looked at her with a solemn expression and said firmly, 'Leo's the victim. An impressionable, out of his depth. What happens to you when you're a child lives with you forever. I should know.' She looked round, her expression full of meaning. 'He never recovers from being the go-between, does he, when he's too young to work out what's going on. Look how devoted he is to Marian and she destroys him.'

'That's a bit strong,' muttered Amy but no-one was listening. Olivia looked at her and bowed her head, fiddling with her necklace of blue beads.

Nancy sighed. She had a habit of always arguing against whatever anyone else had suggested and Amy knew she'd do it now. 'Lord Trimingham. Don't forget him. He marries her after all, fully aware she's had an affair with Ted and he knows the child isn't his.'

Suddenly, Amy had the urge to play Devil's Advocate and stir things up a bit. It was all too serious and high minded and *certain,* with everyone thinking their opinion was the correct one. The only one. Doesn't interpretation mean you can see other possibilities, consider different points of view? But here they were, with all the answers, dissecting lives – OK, fictional lives – as if their take on it wasn't to be challenged.

'I don't think it's that simple,' she said. 'Surely, you have to consider the time they're living in – aren't they *all* victims, even Marian...'

'Oh, Amy, honestly, she's a manipulative, selfish madam.' Nancy had gone quite pink.

'Hold on, just let me finish. I say she's a victim as well, because she's stuck in a class system that hems her in. She's *expected* to marry well, so Lord Trimingham fits the bill, even though he's not right for her. She loves Ted, but he's only a farmer, so not good enough. And that mother's going to make sure she does her duty, marries the rich war hero and then all the family benefit by association...'

'But, Amy, what about how she uses Leo?' This from Olivia.

'He takes messages. She doesn't know he's going to be infatuated with her for the rest of his life, does she? She isn't aware she's doing any damage to him. She's managing the situation as best she can...'

'Oh, Amy, for goodness sake.' With a flap of her hand, Jackie dismissed the whole idea. 'She had a choice.'

'No, she didn't. None of them had, really. They were caught up in a difficult situation, trapped in a way, and all of them suffered in the end.'

'Some more than others,' Jackie sat forward in her chair. 'And you could say that about any tragedy – come up with 'mitigating circumstances' – but in the end, this book deals with moral obligation. Marian ruins the boy's life.'

Amy felt a rush of anger. 'But she's not doing it for...'

Jackie got up, bringing any more discussion to an end. 'Come on, it's time for a cup of tea. And I've made a coffee cake, especially. We need to make a decision about our next book, and we'll have to do that without Harriet.' She made it sound as though Harriet had missed the meeting on purpose. 'I suggest we pick a modern book for next time. One none of us has read before.' And she swept out to the kitchen, annoyed, Amy could see, that things hadn't gone quite according to plan and someone in the group had dared to disagree with her.

When Amy, with Nancy and Olivia, was shown out into the street and the door had closed, they stood briefly under the porch light, ready to go their different ways home. Nancy was the first to set off, hunching her shoulders against the night air. And as Amy turned to say goodbye to Olivia, she was suddenly and unexpectedly, pulled into a hug.

'We forgot to wish you happy birthday. I've just remembered!' Olivia said, her voice muffled against Amy's shoulder. 'Dear girl, you worried me tonight. What is it?'

'Nothing. Nothing at all.' Amy drew back, uncomfortable at the sudden intimacy.

But Olivia held onto her hand, her expression warm and sad. She wasn't going to be put off. 'You have so much, Amy – you're young, you have beauty, intelligence, a lovely family. But something's making you unhappy and I don't like to see it.' She gave an embarrassed laugh. 'Forgive me, I'm speaking out of turn, but there are times when you need to look after yourself. And I'm sure Jackie didn't mean to be so… forceful. Believe me, she isn't worth getting upset over. '

Amy took a deep breath, embarrassed and a little alarmed. But she was also touched. 'Olivia, I really appreciate your concern but you don't have to worry about me. I've just got too much on at the moment. And Jackie? Yes, she irritates me at times. I just don't have your good-nature, that's all. You can't change people, can you.'

'You certainly can't,' she smiled, and lifted up her book in a farewell gesture. 'Just look after yourself.' She turned to go, clamping a hand over her long skirts as a gust of wind sent leaves and dust off the pavement swirling round her legs.

Amy watched her walk away. So strange when you discover how

others see you, not at all how you see yourself. Olivia's words had unnerved her - the last thing she wanted now was for someone to start analysing her mental state, however kindly it was meant. She'd have to be more careful or she'd give the game away. What a curious expression, she thought - this was anything *but* a game. Too deadly serious for that.

Chapter 23

It had been over a week at least since she'd been round to see her father and she knew the kind of reception she'd get. Resentful and accusing, the same old treatment she'd experienced time and time again. Anticipating it never failed to make her less anxious. Even when you've left home, she thought, it's amazing how parents can still have a hold on you. She wished she could put off going at all.

Her steps were deliberately slow as she headed for the house, knowing by the time she got there, her dad and brother would be well into the evening's TV viewing. She'd probably be interrupting a football match or a reality show, beer and crisps within easy reach of their chairs and not much to talk to her about. Other than questions and the odd criticism. When had it all got this bad? Her mother had kept a balance of sorts – but even she was always trying to keep the peace – 'he's your father' she'd say - even now, those words echoing like a mantra in Catherine's head – 'just do as you're told' and that's how it was. The boys were treated differently. They had a given status. She saw there was a divide – an unjust one because she was a girl – and this festered like a wound, beneath the compliancy and mute anger.

Her mother had looked peaceful when she'd died, sitting in the armchair for a brief rest before washing the kitchen floor. A brain aneurism at fifty-two. It was the school holidays and Catherine had come in from the garden and sensed the stillness in the room. No movement, except for the sunlight flickering on the patterned carpet and on her mother's slippers. After a few paralysing moments of shock, Catherine knelt down and touched her mother's hand, saying over and over, 'Wake up, please, wake up,' knowing it was useless and in the end, thinking - she's escaped, got out the only way she could. She stared at her mother's body, head a little on one side, mouth half open. So relaxed. And she felt angry and frightened. For herself.

No one to care for her now.

She had a good idea how things were going to be.

But, in fact, it was worse. There was no-one to stop the unfairness of it all or moderate her father's tempers, the mood swings, the rantings. There were no quiet moments, no respite. His voice had bellowed through that house, loud and demanding for as long as she could remember. Always angry. Always fault-finding. *Can't you tidy yourself up... Don't be having any fancy ideas... Get that washing up done.* On and on, until all she wanted was to go to bed as early as she could and pull the covers over her ears – anything to escape the sound of that voice.

On the day of the funeral, he'd stood in the crematorium, stony-faced, his hands held stiffly at his sides, while she and her brothers tried to stifle their tears and many in the congregation had wept openly. When the chords of the last hymn were dying away, she'd risked a brief look at him and could only see the blankness in his eyes and the hard lines round his mouth. If he's feeling anything, she'd thought, then, it's nothing like what I'm going through.

And yet... two weeks later, she'd been allowed to go to the cinema with a girlfriend. 'Be in by ten – at the latest,' her father had barked at her as she was leaving the house. The film hadn't finished till nine forty-five, and although she'd caught the bus just in time and run all the way home, she was still going to be thirty minutes late. She'd turned her key in the front door as quietly as she could and made it down the hallway. But as she put one foot on the bottom stair, a muffled sound from the kitchen made her pause. She held her breath and listened. Someone was crying, she was sure of it. The kitchen door was half open and she moved with all the stealth she could manage in her nervous state, towards it. There sat her father, his back hunched over the table, sobbing as though he'd never stop, his shoulders heaving and buckling as if a weight was pressing down on him. A whiskey bottle and half-filled glass were by his left hand, a cigarette smouldered in the ashtray. And through the terrible crying, Catherine could hear him saying, over and over again. 'Oh, Annie, Annie.'

Perhaps he'd loved her after all, Catherine thought. She backed away, holding her breath, and climbed the stairs, tip-toeing past the boys' room. She didn't turn on her light or wash her face or take off her clothes. She lay down on her bed, staring into the darkness, frightened by the outpouring of emotion she'd witnessed, so out of character, so *unnatural*. Yet something, at least, she could understand.

And if she'd seen, in all those years since then, a glimmer of that sorrow, that humanity, she would have found some compassion for him, some way of dealing with the harshness of him. But never again did he display anything remotely tender or caring.

And it was all too late now to expect it.

The house fronted the street and she could hear the television even before she'd sorted through her key ring and pushed open the door.

'Hi Dad,' her voice louder than she'd meant it to be, as though preparing for battle before it had even begun. She took off her coat and hung it over the bannister, immediately recognising Bill's black jacket – when he wasn't at work, he spent more time at their dad's than in his own flat. They seemed to get on in a way she could never hope to do.

As she pulled a chair round and joined them in front of the television, they turned their heads slightly and mumbled what passed for a greeting, then fixed their gaze on the screen.

'Who's playing then?' she asked.

'Newcastle versus Man. United,' said Bill, leaning forward. 'Just started.'

'There's beer in the fridge.' Her father waved his hand towards the kitchen. 'Get yourself one.'

And when you counted up the conversational exchanges through the evening, they didn't amount to much. It was a relief to make an excuse as the match was ending and head for home. She'd promised to cook the Sunday dinner for them this weekend and do the washing, but at least that wasn't for a few days. As she set off for home, she hurried although there was no need, conscious of the heaviness in her chest – a solid weight that wouldn't shift. She felt weary. Not out of tiredness. Out of despair.

'This will never end.' The words kept repeating in her head. Nothing was as she wanted it. Any hope for her own future, for an escape, for having a life with Jake, was drifting away from her.

Unless she could do something. She didn't know what, yet, but she'd find a way.

*

Saturday came and it had been difficult from the start. Tricky. As though she was walking on eggshells.

They'd seen each other at school but never alone; there were always other people coming and going, in the staff room, in the English office and she began to wonder whether Jake wanted it that way. In case she asked questions he wasn't going to answer. But in the end, he'd done as he'd promised and booked a table at the Forester's Arms in Lymm for Saturday evening.

She'd put on the navy dress with the high collar and black lace-up boots (they always reminded her of the times she'd gone to the skating rink as a child), a solid silver bangle and earrings and she'd used the curling tongs so that her hair hung in waves to her shoulders. She wasn't sure whether the style suited her, but it was too late now. She only had five minutes till he picked her up and she wanted to be ready. She stood at the window in the front room looking down the street, coat on, clutch bag in her hand, nervous. Not how it should be, she thought to herself. It was just a meal, another evening together...but that was the trouble, it wasn't. She couldn't rid herself of this sense of foreboding.

When she opened the door to him, he looked surprised, eyebrows raised, an embarrassed smile on his face. 'You look different... your hair,' he stopped and pursed his lips together. 'Sorry, Catherine, that was... it looks very nice.' But the moment was awkward, too formal, as though they weren't used to one another. As though it was a first date. 'Have you got everything?'

There was little conversation as Jake drove them through the town onto the motorway, then turning off onto winding lanes, heading for Lymm. By the time the pub sign came into view round another bend in the road, nearly three-quarters of an hour had gone by. Jake pulled in. Set back from the road, it was old and established, with cobbled parking bays and lamps placed at intervals, leading up to the entrance. The building was low with an overhanging roof and mullioned windows. A thick oak beam served as a lintel over the door, so Jake had to duck his head slightly to walk under it. It was a village pub and the bar area to the left was crowded with locals, already gathered in noisy groups and shoving their way through the throng with full glasses held above people's heads and shouting friendly insults to anyone they knew.

Jake steered Catherine through to the right, where the meals were served and a fire was burning in the hearth. When he'd sorted out the reservation and ordered drinks, they sat at a table, their backs against the wall, facing out into the room.

'Good job I booked,' he said, looking round. 'Gets crowded any night, but Saturdays are usually packed.'

'Have you been here often, then?'

'Used to, a few years back.'

We sound like strangers, she thought. And why hadn't he brought her here in the year *they'd* been together?

'With Hannah?' The words were out of her mouth before she could stop herself.

He pulled the menu towards him and began studying it. 'With lots of people. Hannah, yes, other friends...'

'Lots of people?' she inclined her head, pushing her hair outside her collar and fiddling with an earring. 'But... not with me.'

She could hear her tone – petulant, needling, but the other night had shaken her, out in the street banging on his door; he must have heard the first time she'd knocked. Why had he taken so long to answer? The whole frustrating episode had filled her head with ideas and images that wouldn't go away. There was someone else. No matter how many times she told herself this was nonsense, she couldn't let it go. Or perhaps, *it,* the whole horror of betrayal again, wouldn't let *her* go.

The tension between them now was almost palpable – his refusal to look at her, deliberate, face set; her backbone hurting as she sat straight against the wooden bench, her hands curled in her lap. Fear was making her foolish, saying all the wrong things and yet, she couldn't help it. She needed answers. He couldn't just ignore her feelings.

'Why not with me?' she repeated, slowly, a question now, her voice flat and quiet because she was struggling to keep her emotions under control.

He put down the menu with an exasperated sigh. 'Because I never thought the food they serve here would be what you'd want to eat.

You like sushi and Caesar salads and health drinks, for heaven's sake. Here, it's pub food and... well, a bit stodgy - *you'd* think so, anyway. I don't know...' He broke off and splayed his fingers, as though trying to find the words. As though he was making *excuses* and he knew it wasn't quite the truth. He looked at her at last. '*You* like that Continental place in Stockport with the plain wooden tables and fancy lighting, crab salad and sparkling water. Not like here - always crowded and a fight to reach the bar...' He shrugged. 'I don't know why I'm having to justify this. Just choose something plain to eat and enjoy it. Can you do that?'

She could hear the sting in his tone and flushed. She put out her hand to touch his, but drew back, afraid at even the *thought* of rejection. 'I'm sorry. Jake, really, I am. I've been —well - upset since the other night. When I couldn't get you to come to the door. At first, I thought you were ill.'

'Really?'

'At first I did.' She hesitated. 'But then it seemed very odd.'

Jake said nothing.

'I'm bound to be thinking all sorts of things.'

He looked up then. 'Like what?'

At least, she'd got his attention; at least, perhaps, he cared enough to want to put it right. Explain himself so she could believe him. But before either of them could speak, the waitress sidled between the tables, pad in hand, to take their order.

'Can you give us a minute,' Jake said. 'We haven't quite made up our minds.' And the girl retreated, saying nothing but Catherine could tell she wasn't going to hurry back.

'What d'you mean – thinking what?' he frowned, looking at her keenly, his eyes seeming to bore into her.

She took a deep breath and lowered her voice, aware that the woman at the next table had stopped eating and might be able to overhear their conversation. She leaned closer to him. 'Oh, it's not just the other night. Somehow that was the final straw.' He was watching her intently now and she felt, at last, they could talk about what really mattered – she was sure he'd understand and once she'd told him how unhappy she'd been, what she'd feared, they'd find a way back to being comfortable with each other again. *Like* each other again. Surely, as long as there was no one else, they could do that.

'All I know is things have changed, Jake, you're just not the same. If it's something I've done, then please tell me. But if...'she forced herself to go on. 'If you've met someone, or you've gone back to Hannah...'

He stared at her. 'Catherine, Hannah left Stepping Hill two years ago; she went to work in a hospital in Preston. It's hardly likely – one, that I'd start that relationship up again after all this time, and two, she's bloody miles away. It's not just improbable, it's laughable.'

She could feel tears stinging her eyes and quickly pulled out a tissue from her bag and blew her nose.

'And you promise me there's no-one else?'

'There's no-one else.'

Of course, she was imagining things, silly things; she was being paranoid and he was getting annoyed, she could see. He pushed the menu towards her.

'Come on, choose a starter at least – that girl's heading this way again. What do you fancy?'

Catherine looked down the list and chose baked brie and then fish cakes, thinking that the menu suited her quite well. Jake ordered and tried to persuade her to have some wine -'You're not driving' - but she felt wobbly enough without alcohol making things even worse.

They sat, waiting.

'Can I at least ask one more question?'

'Of course,' he said.

'Is everything all right between us now? Are we still okay?'

He took a second too long to answer and she sensed it. Just a second too long to put her mind at rest. 'Catherine, you're worrying about nothing. We're fine.'

But it didn't feel fine. And although the evening passed in talk about school and families and places to go, there was a moment at the end of the evening, when she began to feel it all slipping away again.

He was helping her on with her coat, the bar was relatively quiet and she could at last just hear the background music, a haunting song that sounded vaguely familiar, but sad, she thought, so sad.

'Food was good,' she said, over her shoulder. 'But why can't the music be a bit more cheerful.'

And when she turned round, the expression on his face was strange - bemused, irritated, full of disbelief. 'Catherine, that's Ella Fitzgerald – *Every Time We Say Goodbye*'. It's one of the greatest love songs ever written.'

And driving home, when he'd barely spoken a word, she sat puzzling over how a throwaway comment about music could open up such a gulf between them, so wide she couldn't breach it. Her mouth began to feel dry and her head ached. She was on the brink of tears but she knew crying would make the whole situation worse. She'd been too wound up this evening – that was the trouble. When she got home, she'd find those pills in the back of the drawer and calm herself down. This was just like last time, the same feeling of dread, the nausea, the headache that blurred her vision. She felt she was holding on by her fingertips.

But holding on she was determined to do.

She wasn't going to let go.

Chapter 24

Robert sat in the kitchen, watching Amy prepare dinner. It wasn't often he was home in time to sit and do nothing but now he relaxed, a glass of martini in his hand. The comforting sound of Classic FM was playing on the radio and there was an hour to wind down and chat about the day's happenings – inconsequential, unexciting, maybe, but to him, it was what made up the very fabric of their life together.

There hadn't been enough of these moments, lately, when Harry had gone to bed and they had some time on their own. He knew he'd been spending too much time at work, but still, that surely benefitted both of them, didn't it? And these days, you had to be one-up on the competition, however well-established the firm was. He'd always spent long hours at work – that was the nature of accountancy: monthly deadlines, projects, new computer systems that took ages to bed-in, auditors constantly checking and making demands. That's just how it was. And he was sure Amy understood that – after all, she'd met him in the middle of a merger.

He wondered sometimes is she was happy. At times, he sensed she was bored, especially when the paper hadn't given her an assignment for a couple of weeks. He didn't *want* her to work – especially for a weekly newspaper that was only mediocre at best – but he'd come to realise she needed some outside interest. She needed something to occupy her mind, other than Harry and the house. She wasn't like Paula, who'd always been content to stay at home. No, Amy was different. Being young was part of it, he supposed. And the very fact that she was outgoing and sociable was what had attracted him to her in the first place. He couldn't have it both ways. But he sometimes found her difficult to fathom. You grow up as an only child in a household where very little is talked about and, yes, you learn to be independent and strong-minded but you don't always learn how to read others. .

But tonight, she seemed to be making a special effort. Almost too bright, too talkative. Up-beat as Ben would say. He sat, watching her, with a lazy pleasure, looking forward to the evening ahead.

He twirled the ice round in his glass and sauntered into the dining room to get a refill. Coming back into the kitchen he sat down, loosened his tie and stretched against the hard-backed chair. Funny how some rooms in a house seem to be at its centre and this one was like that for him – the big round pine table, spice racks, chopping boards and coffee canisters on the work surfaces, Harry's paintings stuck on the wall by the window and the warmth and light from the oven adding to the homeliness of it all. Jasper lay in his basket, head and droopy ears hanging over the side, snoring. The sound was soft and rhythmic and somehow soothing, even to Robert this evening, who often found the dog's behaviour and odd habits irritating.

Tonight, he'd been in time to put Harry to bed, read him a story and now the evening was theirs – just him and Amy and he wished he didn't have a difficult subject to brooch. But after the phone call, there was no way he could delay it. Not for long, anyway.

At least they could eat first.

Amy was concentrating on making the lasagne, carefully placing the layers of pasta sheets and sauces into an oblong dish, then grating the cheese and adding the seasoning. He sat there, not uttering a word, just sipping his drink and when he didn't speak, she looked up for a brief moment, and smiled.

'Don't give me any hints on what I'm doing wrong!' She held her hands up in the air, fingers spread. 'I know I'm a sloppy cook, but it'll taste good.'

'When do I criticise your efforts?'

'There you go – 'efforts'. That doesn't give me much confidence.' She raised her eyebrows in mock annoyance. 'Just because you're a perfectionist – looking through endless recipe books, all the preparations done three hours early and everything weighed *exactly...*'

'My meals are good though, aren't they?'

She laughed as she went to the sink and washed her hands. 'Ok. I'll give you that. But I improvise. I like that feeling of surprise when it all turns out well. Every meal an adventure.'

'Now that's certainly true.'

He should have showered and changed into some casual clothes after he'd read to Harry, but he'd felt tired tonight and now he didn't want to leave the kitchen. He picked up the day's letters from the kitchen table and started to look through them, charity appeals, a political circular, a letter from his old university. And a bill, forwarded from Paula, for Ben's drum lessons. Why on earth couldn't the boy play the piano or the saxophone? He'd drive the neighbours mad.

'What?' Amy was looking at him.

'Nothing.' He flipped the bill towards her. 'Ben – drum lessons. What next! Could you imagine living next door to that sort of racket?'

'It's a detached house, Robert. And anyway, it'll be a phase. He'll outgrow it and move on to smoking cannabis.'

'Very funny.' Robert took another swig of his drink. 'I just wish Paula would say 'no' sometimes. They can't be allowed to have everything they want.'

Amy didn't answer.

'Did I tell you,' he coughed slightly, suddenly embarrassed that he hadn't said anything before. Days ago. 'Paula's met someone. Going out on dates, I think that's the stage it's at.'

Amy's face lit up. 'Good. That's really good. She's been on her own for so long and I'm glad for her.' Suddenly, her expression became clouded. 'What a nerve I have, saying that. When I'm the cause of all her pain.'

'Don't be silly, Amy.' Robert had no intention of allowing her to open up old wounds again. 'Anyway, this new... relationship... it might not even come to anything, but I suppose she felt she should tell me...'

'She'd no need to, though, had she? I mean, for heaven's sake, after all these years, her life's her own. She doesn't have to explain to you what she's doing.'

'Well, she does in a way. The children...'

'Oh, Robert, how old fashioned is that! They must know by now how the world works – if their father's got a new partner, then why not their mother?'

He was acutely aware, at that moment, of being from a different generation, with different attitudes and values. You didn't just move on when a marriage ended. Not when you had children. There still had to be commitment and, well, a sense of duty, of care for their well-being on every level. It might be 'old fashioned', but he'd been brought up to live by traditional principles, of marriage being for life and the responsibilities that go with it. No wonder his own defection had been such a body-blow to his parents – he'd transgressed in a manner abhorrent to them, only lately forgiven by his mother. Never by his father who had died the same year Harry was born. Yes, he hadn't *stayed* with Paula and the children, but he had – and would - look after them financially and support them in every other way. It was the very least he could do.

His relaxed mood was ebbing away and the kitchen suddenly seemed over-warm. Amy didn't understand at all. Not at all. He wished he hadn't brought any of it up when there were more testing things to discuss after dinner. So much for peace and harmony. Blast!

He sat, silently berating himself for a moment. 'Don't you want a drink?'

'I'll have one when we eat. There's a bottle of Chianti already opened – we can finish that.'

Seven o'clock and the lasagne and salad had been eaten, the wine bottle nearly empty, and Amy was clearing away the plates.

It was Time, Robert knew, to tell her.

'I had a phone call today from Mother,' he said.

'She rang the office?'

'Well, she only rings here when she knows we're at home.' Even to Robert's ears, this sounded weak.

Amy stopped what she was doing and sat down opposite him, her eyes narrowed slightly, head to one side. Ready to pounce, he thought and immediately recognised how unkind that was.

'And?'

'Amy, you know why she rang! She expects us to go down for Christmas. She's made plans – a get-together on Boxing Day with George and my cousins – Christmas is a big thing for her – and she's had Harry's room decorated. So she's trying...' (wrong choice of word, he thought too late) 'and she sees very little of her grandchildren...'

'Mostly because she never comes north. How many times have we invited her here? She came once and complained all the time how cold and wet it was. As though we lived in the Outer Hebrides!' Amy closed her eyes for a second. 'We've been to Windsor for the last four years and Harry won't have anyone to play with. No-one his age. And I haven't had one Christmas with *my* family for ages, and with Sarah pregnant, I'd like to have it here...'

'I know you would,' Robert made an effort to sound patient, to keep the tone of his voice from becoming strident. 'But she sees nothing of Harry and your family see him all the time...'

Amy stared at him. 'You've agreed, haven't you?'

'Yes, I have. She's old and lonely and I'm not going to upset her. It won't kill you to go for a week and be pleasant. Surely you can do that!'

'Yes, I can do that,' Amy snapped. She stood up, walked stiffly past the kitchen table, looking straight ahead as though he wasn't there and out of the room, closing the door behind her. He knew that was the end of any chance of a pleasant evening when he heard her climb the stairs and run the bath water. She was obviously making a point.

Robert sighed, not in relief at having told her, but in a fit of resentment at the way she reacted. He could see why she was reluctant to go, of course he could, but sometimes you had to do what was right. And Amy could never just give in with good grace. Particularly lately. In the early days, she'd been keen to meet his family and made a great deal of effort to please them, on the rare occasions when they journeyed south. And more than that, she'd seemed happy to be part of his world, even the formal dinners and golf days and charity functions. She'd take hours getting dressed up, excited at meeting new people, slipping her arm through his as they entered the venue, and listening with genuine interest to what he had to say.

It wasn't the first time the thought had crossed his mind that he'd expected too much of her. However sociable and at ease with yourself you might be, when you're twenty-two, there's still a lot to learn. A lot of growing up to do. When he was that age, he'd just left university to start work in one of the biggest auditors in Manchester and was studying for his Chartered at the same time. All he'd done was work.

For years. He was nearly thirty when he'd met Paula in a coffee shop off Deansgate and by that time, he was fairly certain he was ready for marriage and ready for a family. And Paula was gentle and kind, with no ambitions of her own, dependent on him, he supposed, and the relationship was comfortable. Comfortable rather than exciting, he had to admit. But it had suited them both for a long time.

Until he met Amy.

And, just at this moment, he didn't want to think about that, how infatuated he'd been, the madness of the affair and the headiness of it all. 'Completely out of character' he'd heard one colleague say and his father kept muttering about a mid-life crisis, as though it were some disease he'd caught and would recover from. Difficult to explain unless you're caught up in something so unexpected and so damned wonderful...

Well, not much point in going over all that again

He poured the last of the wine into his glass.

He'd been in the middle of a meeting when his secretary gestured to him through the glass door, mouthing words he couldn't decipher and miming, extravagantly, holding an imaginary phone to her ear. He excused himself and left the room.

'What is it, Sue?'

'Your mother's on the phone.'

'Couldn't it wait?'

'Well,' Sue looked embarrassed. 'She insisted on talking to you. Now. And I didn't know whether it was urgent, so...'

'Ok.' Robert nodded. He knew how insistent his mother could be. 'Give me a minute then put it through to my office.'

He excused himself from the meeting and went into his room, sitting on the edge of his desk to pick up the receiver. 'Mother, it's Robert.'

'That took you long enough.' She always spoke slowly, her voice deep and each syllable articulated with precision. 'Now, I'm making arrangements for Christmas and need to know when you'll be arriving. George and his boys are coming – you haven't seen them for a long time, so that'll be nice for you all – a family reunion.'

He wished his mother wouldn't always refer to his cousins as 'boys' when they were fifty, at least. 'Well, I haven't thought about Christmas yet, Mother.' He could feel the tightness round his collar. 'I haven't had the chance to talk to Amy...'

'Surely that's not a problem.' Robert could hear the finality in her voice. She wasn't going to be put off on any count. As if he didn't know.

'Well, we couldn't be there before Christmas Eve. I have to work...'

'That's fine. As long as you don't expect a hot meal when you arrive. Mrs. Daniels has enough to do with so many on Christmas Day.'

'Yes, of course.' What choice had she given him? 'Just don't go buying expensive presents for everyone...'

'No, Robert, I won't. Traipsing round the shops at my age isn't something I look forward to. I'm putting money in envelopes as I did last year.'

'That'll be fine.' He always had the strange feeling, when talking to his mother, that she still saw him as a twelve year old boy, tucked away in his boarding school, who must be reminded of his lowly place in the family hierarchy.

Before she'd hung up, she'd made a point of telling him about Harry's bedroom, about the cost of the Christmas lights which would decorate the garden and how no-one had been to visit in two months. When he put the phone down, he searched in his desk drawer for a Migraleve to ward off the headache that was threatening.

He needed to get back to the meeting, but he was having trouble remembering the figures they'd been in the process of discussing. He could have done with a few minutes to himself so that he could function effectively again.

And now, sitting alone with the dirty dishes still on the table, he wished that Amy would just come through the kitchen door with an apologetic smile on her face, shrug her shoulders and tell him it would all be fine, Christmas would be fine, life together would be fine.

Well, there wasn't much chance of that.

Chapter 25

Newspaper day in the school had been tricky - much trickier than he'd thought it would be. His young team of journalists and photographers hadn't been the problem – so many volunteering that he'd had to pick names out of a hat – and they'd worked hard, writing up school events, sports fixtures, human interest stories. The ones who could draw had done illustrations and a couple of cartoons. One girl had even composed an editorial on a local issue – 'Litter in the streets of Stockport – a public disgrace.' Matthew, full of himself as ever, had got in on the act, writing his piece on 'New Rules in the Sixth Form Common Room'; which to be fair was pretty good. He'd sat at his computer wearing a green eyeshade (where did he get *that* from?) and telling everyone his Coca Cola was Bourbon.

'You've seen too many films, Matthew,' Jake told him.

'Just getting in the mood, Mr. Harper. You wanted it to be authentic...'

No, the problem hadn't been with the students.

The problem had been with the whole damned idea of mixing two worlds that should have been kept separate.

From the start, the day had been filled with nerve-wracking moments with Amy arriving, vibrant in a bright red coat, hair piled up on her head and that innate confidence she had that made people turn and look – you just had to notice her, Jake thought, it isn't just me. So she became a topic of conversation and a focus of attention that he could have done without. Why hadn't he thought it through?

As the hours went by, he became more and more tense. It was as though she'd brought her own torment with her.

Tim, enjoying his role overseeing the project, had put his arm round her in a proprietary gesture as he ushered her into his office and Jake had to grit his teeth in a flash of jealousy; later, Brandon, a boy from year eight had suddenly looked at them working with their heads together and asked, in a voice uncomfortably loud, 'Is she your girlfriend, sir?'; as Jake had passed a folder to her, their fingers touched, making him jerk his hand away as though he'd been burned. Worst of all, as they ate sandwiches in the staff room at lunch time, Catherine had hovered near the coffee machine, pretending to study the notice board, her whole body tense, Jake could see, in the expectation of what? Joining them? Jenny had already plumped herself down in the chair next to Amy and was talking non-stop and Andy couldn't help himself from stopping as he passed and making a lame joke, slopping his tea over his shoe as he did so. In the end, Jake felt he had no choice but to wave Catherine over and hope for the best.

Christ, it was already like the Mad Hatter's Tea Party!

Jake concentrated on Jenny, the safest bet, as she rattled away about an article on film she was helping with, asking Amy questions about lineage and column inches and not taking any notice of the answers. Thank God for Jenny!

Catherine sat opposite him, carefully unwrapping her sandwiches, but leaving them untouched on her lap. She sat very still and watched them all with an unwavering gaze, then looked at Jake, eyes unsmiling. She hadn't joined in, just listened intently and Jake felt that every word, every intonation, was being weighed and analysed. Don't read anything into this, he begged silently. Don't you dare read anything into this. His conversation became as stilted as though he were in an amateur production of an Alan Ayckbourn farce. Why had he thought this was such a good idea? It was a bloody strain.

By the end of the day, he'd been exhausted. Yes, the day had gone well, Tim was delighted, the students were buzzing with excitement, but Jake harboured a growing sense of unease. He was acutely aware, now, of the danger, the hidden threat lying just beneath the surface, which was sure to drag him down. And with him, of course, Amy. And he mustn't let that happen.

For perhaps the first time, he realised how serious the consequences would be. One mistake... that's all it might take. And everything would change.

*

It was eight o'clock he walked hand in hand with Amy along the cobbled walkway by the Mersey, spots of rain and a misty spray from the grey waters touching their faces. It had grown dark and wintry, but Jake was hardly aware of the raw air that surrounded them. He was just happy. To be here, to be alive. To be at peace with himself, for once. If only you could keep hold of moments like these, he thought, preserve them to stave off all the days that were dull and wasted, all the weeks that were second-rate and utterly forgettable. He'd trade them all for this.

The path leading from Albert Dock was deserted; they met no-one. All around was a monochrome landscape: the darkness of the smudged sky blending with the darkness of the water, a buoy only just visible tossing to and fro; black bollards and a chain link fence bordering the river, and the rough stones shadowy and uneven beneath their feet.

Jake stopped and pulled her towards him. They stood close, looking at one another. He couldn't quite believe she was here, that this was actually happening. Whatever he'd imagined, wished for, it hadn't taken him this far.

'God, I'm so glad I found you.' He cupped her face in his hands.

Her expression was solemn. 'Where were you ten years ago?'

'In the wrong place. That's my defence. I was in the wrong place.'

A gust of cold wind made them shiver.

When Jake spoke, his voice was low and unsteady. 'Was it difficult to get away? I didn't give you much notice.'

'Don't ask. I'm here.'

He nodded. There were some things off limits. He accepted that. 'I've found us a place, a café off down a side street that looks quiet and a bit old-fashioned. The sort of place no-one would go to unless they'd spent an hour searching for it. But it does pizza and paninis, stuff like that.'

'Sounds fine.'

He was relieved to see her smile. He'd spent two hours searching for somewhere warm for them to spend the few hours they had together. He'd wandered along streets lined with towering brick buildings only to reach a dead-end, then suddenly, heading down an alley, he was in a brightly lit mall, with no chance of finding a suitable place there. He wasn't familiar enough with the city to know what was in the vicinity – he'd tapped into the app on his mobile, but it hadn't proved helpful - and then he'd had another worry - that they wouldn't find each other, never meet up at all, even though he'd chosen a landmark no one could mistake.

He was just thankful, now, to have her by his side.

'Come on.' She pulled at the scarf round his neck. 'Don't look so worried. I'm hungry and I bet they play jazz to go with the expresso. That really would make your day.'

Jake put his arm round her as they set off along the path. 'I'm beginning to think, even if we were lost among eighty thousand people, we'd end up on the same street.'

She tucked herself against his body, keeping in step. 'Fate works in mysterious ways.'

'That's not an accurate quote, Amy. But who cares! I'll settle for it.'

They began to pick up a faster pace as the shower grew heavier, drops of water glistening on their hair and winter coats. He turned to kiss the rain off her nose and her eyelids; he had so much in his head that he wanted to say to her, yet he couldn't speak because words were never going to be enough. You can't explain feelings in language, he thought. It has a language of its own. Primal, instinctive. Coming from God knows where.

They were breathless when they reached The Baker's House, opening the door on wooden tables and dim lighting, the smell of ground coffee and the low murmur of conversation. The café wasn't even half full, just a few couples huddled together out of the wintry weather, absorbed in each other, mostly, and showing no interest in anyone around them. *Good. Let's just be anonymous, no curious eyes, cut the risks.* He'd been uneasy about meeting in a city so close to home, but he'd have been uneasy wherever he'd picked.

You just never know, he thought. One summer holiday, he'd bumped into a pupil outside his hotel in Sorrento and how was *that* for a coincidence!

He followed Amy into the back of the café, drawing some comfort from the poor lighting of the interior and the rain on the windows sealing them off from the street outside. Safe here, he hoped. He wanted to think of this whole thing as something special, magical, not as a shabby way to behave, but he couldn't quite do it. He imagined his mother looking at him over her glasses and shaking her head, disapproving. Disappointed.

Watching Amy now, sipping a cappuccino and looking at him with an expectant expression on her face, he thought, damn it, it's all worth it. Just to sit opposite her and feel this good. If it's selfish, then that's the way it is.

They placed their order with the young waitress for coffee and mozzarella cheese and sun-dried tomato paninis. Jake rolled his shoulders, feeling the muscles loosen and his body relax. Amy pushed her coat over the back of the chair. 'I dreamt of you the other night,' she said.

He put his elbows on the table and clasped his hands together. 'It was a bit of a nightmare, then.'

When was the last time he was this happy, he thought, just living for the minute and that minute being enough? A memory flashed into his mind from a long time ago – he was a child, running over the sands with his brothers on a family holiday, the smell of seaweed in the air and salt stinging their faces, laughing, just the pure joy of being there. When you're young you never question that it could all end.

'It was strange.' Amy was screwing up her eyes, remembering. 'I don't usually remember dreams. I was looking for you in this tower, a sort of lighthouse, climbing a spiral staircase and you were just in front of me but I could never catch you up.'

'Well, plenty of symbolism there,' he smiled, glad to listen. He wanted to share everything with her.

'Isn't it odd how, even though you're asleep, your mind retains just enough for you to recognise what's going on?'

'Well, have a go at analysing this,' Jake said. 'I have a recurring dream that I'm driving a bus down a mountain road, going fast and I can't steer it. Passengers are clinging on like mad, and I can't do a thing because I've no brakes. I'm on the edge of panic, just hoping I can turn the wheel in time for the next bend.'

'So what happens?'

'I never find out. I wake up!'

'Well, obviously, it means you feel out of control... your life is running away with you...'

'Oh, great!' He laughed. 'That's good to hear, doctor. Really makes me feel better.'

'Don't you think I'm right, though? *Do* you know where you're heading?'

He sighed, the question difficult to shrug off. 'Of course I don't. Does anyone? Since I met you, anyway, I'm flying by the seat of my pants. It's doing wonders for my heart rate! I probably won't make forty.'

Her expression was suddenly serious. 'Don't say that. Even as a joke.'

The waitress brought them their food and they concentrated on eating.

Then, Jake glanced up and a shock ran through him, a frightening rush of fear, which seemed to freeze his brain. A man was coming through the café door, head lowered, shaking his wet hair, and although Jake couldn't make out his face clearly, there was something familiar about him. The coat. Dark blue with a big collar. Didn't Jenny's boyfriend wear a coat like that? He'd often come to the pub after parents' evenings and end-of-term dos and always had the look and build of a lumberjack. Just like this bloke. It couldn't be him, surely. Then, as the man stepped forward, his face caught the light and Jake sank down in his chair in relief. A complete stranger.

'What on earth's the matter?' Amy was looking at him in alarm. 'You've gone really pale.'

'Ashen. I've gone ashen.' He sank back in his seat, annoyed at his reaction. Way over the top. 'I thought that bloke who just came in was... well, someone I knew. But...' he raised his eyebrows.

'Obviously, I'm becoming paranoid.'

'Well, you're making me damned nervous.'

The mood had changed. Not light-hearted now. He could kick himself for being such an idiot. 'I'm sorry.' He wanted to talk, really talk – about what was happening to them, the bloody elephant in the room, but he knew that would darken things even further. Yet they couldn't ignore what was obvious. This situation wasn't normal. Hopeless trying to brush it all under the carpet and pretend there weren't complications.

He'd have to try. 'Look, Amy, half of me is glad to be here, so glad, and the other is waiting for the sword to drop. I'm putting you in a bloody difficult position and I know it. Even here, hidden away in a corner, there's always a risk.'

She looked at him, sombre now.

He tried again. 'Doesn't the whole thing scare you?'

She frowned and pushed her chair back slightly, making a scraping noise on the tiled floor. 'Of course it does. I'm not an idiot.' She looked down into her coffee cup, wiping some froth away with her finger, fiddling with the paper napkin beside her plate. When she looked up again, Jake could see she was holding back tears.

He sighed. 'Of course you're not.'

She spread her fingers flat on the table, in a gesture of exasperation. 'We can hardly go back now. Can we? Don't you think I know I should have stopped it - and I could have once...' She hesitated, shaking her head wearily. 'If *you're* torn in two, what d'you think I am? I look at Harry, six years old, trusting and loving – I'm his whole life – how can I do anything that would hurt him? If I wasn't such a self-centred bitch...'

'Amy, stop.'

'No, you wanted to open this up, so let's talk about it.' She lifted her chin. 'I know that whatever this is, it isn't a casual thing. It's all too late, but you're perfect for me. It's like... like finding the one person who understands you even before you speak. And you just know. Even after a few minutes, however crazy that sounds, you know.' She held his gaze and he guessed there was more that he didn't want to hear. ' But, Jake, there's one thing I'm certain of. I could never leave my child under any circumstances. If it came to it, you'd be sacrificed.'

'Amy, I'm not asking...'

'You are. You're asking me to put you first, to say...' she stopped.

'To say what?' He held her gaze, silently begging her – *say it, Amy*.

'Jake, you don't need me to spell it out for you.' She spoke so quietly, he had to lean forward to catch the words.

'Perhaps I do, Amy. More than anything.'

She sighed. 'Words don't mean a great deal. They really don't. I've said them all before and look where I ended up. I've always been so sure of what I wanted – and usually *got* what I wanted - and now? Christ I haven't any idea what love is anymore – between a man and a woman, anyway.' She made a sound in her throat that sounded almost like a sob. 'Yes, love for Harry, for my sister, for my daft dog. That I totally understand because it's constant. It's not going to change.'

Jake nodded, unsure of where this was heading.

'You go through all the sexual attraction bit, the emotional upheaval, believing this will last forever and you can be so wrong. The words you want to hear are like old currency. At this moment, they might be true. But I can't guarantee they'll be true in six months' time. I know myself and I'm not reliable. I'm really not.'

Jake sat back and was frightened in a way he couldn't explain. He wanted her to make something up, something comforting. But Amy wasn't going to do that.

She reached out and put her hand over his.

'Listen. With you, everything's easy, I can be myself, I'm never bored. That's something, isn't it?'

He couldn't even smile at that.

'Oh, Amy.' He could hear the catch in his voice and he hated the sound of it. 'I understand everything you're saying, but that's not me. I've never felt like this before - like a bloody teenager needing reassurance - and it's painful. For me, it's serious. I'm in this up to my neck and if it isn't the same for you, then you're risking too much for something that's just a passing phase.'

'For heaven's sake, I didn't say that!' She folded her arms, defensive and irritated now. 'Don't you see, I was convinced Robert was 'the one' for me, I destroyed his family to get what I thought I wanted, and now... now, I'm ashamed to say I don't want it anymore.' She was crying suddenly, tears running down her face.

He let out a long breath. 'Oh, Amy. Don't cry, please don't cry. I shouldn't have started this. I've ruined the evening and I'm sorry for being such a shit. I should have left it alone.'

She pulled a tissue out of her bag and wiped her face. 'No. We're not going to kid ourselves about any of this. However painful it gets. Are we?'

'No we're not going to kid ourselves. I promise.'

The coffee had gone cold and the café was emptying, but they kept sitting there, Jake hoping he could lift the mood before they had to leave and go their separate ways home. He'd so wanted the night to go well and he'd made a hash of it, worried now because he had no idea when they'd see each other again.

He rummaged in his jacket pocket and brought out a blue paper bag with a silver logo on the outside. 'I bought you a Christmas present. Spur of the moment thing when I was walking round the shops. Looking for a café.'

He sounded like a stuttering kid who'd no idea how to cope with an emotional situation. It was how he felt.

Amy's smile was watery and her face flushed, but she reached out and slid the bag towards her across the table. She pulled it open and began folding back the tissue paper, giving a little laugh when she saw what it was – a furry rabbit sitting upright, perhaps twice the size of a Christmas ornament, with gold glasses on his nose, a green scarf wrapped round his neck and holding a small bell in his hand.

'It's lovely, Jake. Not exactly what I was expecting.' She laughed again. 'What a funny man you are.'

'I'll take that as a compliment.' He was relieved the mood had lightened up. 'I don't know what made me buy it.'

'I love it.'

'I just wanted to give you something. It's not much of a present, really.'

'Well, it is to me. I'll treasure it. Thank you.'

The look she gave him was warm, even tender, he thought, but it didn't quite check the fear that a few moments before had threatened to swallow him up. The fear that he was going to lose her, perhaps not now, or next week but in the end, he would reach out and there would be nothing to hold on to.

He was on borrowed time and he knew it.

Chapter 26

The tyres crunched on the long drive, which curved through fields covered in a light frost. Welcome to the stately home, Amy thought, as the house came into view. A beautiful house, sprawling and dignified, cream stone with white painted window frames, it always reminded her of something out of a Jane Austen novel. There were two wings either side of the main building with huge bay windows, an arched entrance way, tall chimneys rising at each end of the gabled roof, even a balustrade, and twelve rectangular windows evenly spaced along both storeys. She'd been told its history before she'd even seen it (Robert, preparing her for that first visit) - originally a rich landowner's dwelling, with hundreds of acres, outbuildings and stables, but the farmlands had been sold off years ago and it now stood, a handsome structure with no other purpose than to accommodate one person, plus a few 'retainers' to keep it from falling into disrepair.

Today the house looked anything but empty, with five cars, one a sleek red sports car, parked on the forecourt and lamps from the downstairs windows throwing some light into the dusky afternoon.

But it didn't make Amy feel any more hopeful that the next few days would be enjoyable. More like an ordeal. She pulled her jacket around her, already imagining the cold inside when she entered the hallway. Robert's mother never managed to keep the place warm and its high ceilings and tiled passageways always chilled her to the bone. And she knew the reception she'd get. That would be even chillier.

She twisted in her seat to look at Harry, wedged between carrier bags and boxes of Christmas presents in the back; he was sleeping peacefully, mouth open and snoring gently. He always fell asleep in the car and it made no difference that it was only four o'clock and Christmas Eve. She'd have to wake him up properly now so that he didn't greet his grandmother with yawns and mutters. She was glad Jasper was in kennels back home because he'd have caused trouble just panting doggy breaths, never mind muddy prints on the carpets. One thing less to worry about. Poor dog hated being left but it couldn't be helped.

Robert gave her an encouraging smile as they drew up and he pulled on the handbrake. 'Not as much traffic as I'd thought,' he said. 'Let's leave the stuff in the car till we've had something to eat. It'll take me ages to get everything out of the boot.' He sat for a moment looking at the house. 'It always seems bigger than I remember.'

'Well, it's grand by anyone's standards.' Amy unbuckled her seat belt. 'I remember when you first brought me here, I thought I should have dressed in a long skirt and a hat with a veil. It's from another era.'

'Yes, it is.'

Amy climbed out and lifted Harry from the back seat. He was half-awake and had started crying in an irritable, distracted way because he'd caught his foot in one of the bags.

'Come on, Harry, don't whinge. You're here now and Grandma's waiting.' She could hear how short she sounded. *I'm already uptight before I've even gone up the front steps. God, don't let me be a grump – it's only three days.* But she felt her heart beating faster, ready to defend herself before she'd entered the fray.

When she'd told Sarah, as they were heading down Market Street on a shopping trip, that she was not going to be with them all at

Christmas, her sister had been angry. 'For heaven's sake, Amy, it must be our turn. You go there every year. Charlotte'll be really disappointed. Can't you persuade Robert to go at New Year instead?'

'No, I can't. She phoned and he'd already told her we were going. As always. And this year, as an added treat, we've got Uncle George, who spends the whole time telling long-winded stories then knocking back the wine till he nods off. And his sons! Who are *so* successful, who didn't disgrace the family by moving north, who talk about houses they've bought and cruises they've been on and leave me desperate to go to bed. Oh yes, and the wives ... they'll be in fox furs or leopard skin shoes (and you know how I *hate* people wearing fur) - only Irene doesn't mention them because she only rates the men in the family, the heirs.' She gave a sarcastic smile. 'One bright spot, then - at least Harry's doted on.'

'Blimey, where did all that come from?' Sarah looked at her in astonishment, as they pushed their way past a tram queue which was taking up the whole pavement. When they drew side by side again, Sarah was shaking her head. 'I'd no idea it was *that* bad. I know your mother-in-law can be difficult, but you sound... well, murderous!'

Amy sighed and slipped her arm through her sister's. 'I do, don't I! I'm exaggerating, of course I am, and it isn't really *so* awful. Forget it. Let's buy this baby of yours something to welcome her into the world. I thought you'd wait to find out what it was, but in a way it's rather nice to know.'

'Yes, it is. I like thinking she's just here, waiting to join us. Puts paid to all the daft worries we had. Somehow you manage, whatever trouble you think you're in. Don't you think?'

Amy had never loved her sister more. She wanted to hug her and tell her so. But theirs wasn't the sort of family for demonstrative shows of affection, certainly not in public. So she just squeezed her arm.

'Yes. Somehow you manage.'

They turned into the Arndale Centre, which, after the cold on the street, was too warm and the artificial lighting made them both blink. They found a children's-wear shop and Amy bought a tiny sleeping bag and a dress with old-fashioned smocking. She watched the assistant carefully folding them up. How quickly you forget the smallness of new-born babies, she thought. I can't remember Harry being so little. Only six years ago, but it seemed longer.

'They're lovely and thank you,' said Sarah. 'But that's enough. It's months before she's here and it'll be summer, so let's wait. Come on, we need to catch the 2 o'clock if you're to be back to pick up Harry.'

They shoved their parcels under their feet as the train gathered speed out of Piccadilly and as they settled in their seats, Sarah turned to Amy, a stern look on her face. 'OK, what's up? Something's not right. What is it?'

Amy couldn't tell her. Not honestly, anyway, so she stalled. 'I'm fine. Really. It'll pass. I'm just going through...I don't know what I'm going through, but I'll work it out.' She paused. 'I'm never satisfied and that's an awful thing to have to admit. You hear about all the dreadful tragedies happening in the world, the bombings and the refugees and you know your life is perfectly *nice* and yet...'

'And yet?'

'Sometimes you feel at a loss - as though there should be more.'

'Oh, Amy, d'you know what this reminds me of?' Sarah folded her arms. 'That doll's house you got when you were about ten. You mithered and mithered for it, and after a few weeks, barely played with it again.'

'Well, what does that say about me? Perhaps I've never grown up.'

'Still,' Sarah sounded sad. 'You'd have added to our Christmas.'

They sat in silence as the train clicked over the rails, Amy lost in thoughts she couldn't share. However much she wanted to.

But Grandma was waiting now and thinking of home wasn't going to help, so she set Harry on his feet, smoothed down the front of his hair and straightened his jumper, which only made matters worse.

'Stop it!' he said, loudly, twisting away. 'I'm all right.'

The front door opened slowly and Robert's mother stood waiting for them to climb up the steps to greet her. She held her body very still, eyelids lowered, her mouth a straight line.

'I thought you were going to get here before dark.'

Robert reached her first and bent down to kiss her on the cheek. 'It's hardly dark yet, Mother. I said we'd be here in time for tea and we are.'

At least when they reached the main sitting room, it was more cheerful, with the family assembled and chatting away to each other. There was a fire burning in the hearth and a Christmas tree stood in one corner – a real one, smelling of pine and the outdoors - tastefully decorated in silver and blue. Everyone got to their feet to greet them as they were ushered in. Perfunctory pecks on the cheeks and hand shaking, lots of 'Lovely to see you', 'It's been too long', and 'Hasn't Harry grown?' made up for the initial awkwardness and Amy tried to show some Christmas spirit and look happy.

After a few minutes, Irene held up her hand, like a Victorian headmistress indicating she was about to speak; the murmuring died and they all looked at her expectantly. Funny, Amy thought, how some people have a way of commanding attention just by the expression in their eyes or the smallest gesture. You really wouldn't want to cross her. When her husband was alive, what a formidable pair they were. Amy vividly remembered first meeting them - and how difficult had *those* circumstances been - but back then, just married and knowing how tormented Robert was by the situation they'd got themselves into, she'd have done anything to ease things for him. But it had been very clear - this was not what was expected of their son. Irene, particularly, had let it be known how suitable Paula had been as a daughter-in-law. And how this twenty-two year old who'd turned Robert's head was not just unsuitable, but downright disagreeable to her.

And who could blame her, really! Amy looked at her now, standing before them all with that air of innate authority, a woman from a society and generation she would never fully understand; there might always be a chasm dividing them, but let's be fair about it, she thought, I have to accept some responsibility for the hurt I've caused the whole family.

In the end, it was Harry who'd saved the day. Just by being born. He'd been a blessing in more ways than one.

Irene waited until the guests stood obediently, quiet at last, the only sound in the room a log shifting in the grate.

'We'll eat at five thirty, so you have time to go to your rooms and freshen up.' It sounded just like it was - an order. 'Mrs. Daniels has laid out a buffet in the dining room. Do be prompt.' She turned to Harry and held out her hand.

He hesitated until Amy pushed him gently forward. 'Grandma wants to show you how she's done up your room. I'll come with you while Daddy unpacks the car.'

They set off, climbing the wide staircase and although Harry was unnaturally quiet on the way, he brightened up when he saw his room. One wall was hung with pictures of Disney characters and a bright blue duvet covered a new single bed. Best of all, standing against the wall, was an old school desk, the genuine article, with a sloping top and an inkwell. Harry was fascinated, immediately sitting down on the worn wooden seat.

'Look, Mummy. The lid lifts up! And there are pencils and books in there.' He was searching through the contents and turned a beaming face to Amy.

'I thought you'd like that,' Irene said, going over to him and straightening the books he'd disturbed. 'A proper desk for a big boy. It was your father's, and his father's before him. Goodness knows how old it is.' She came to stand behind him and patted his head. 'When you're nine or ten, you must come and stay on your own, Harry. So that I could see much more of you than I do at present. It would do us both good.'

He nodded but raised his eyes to look up at Amy with a puzzled expression and she half-smiled to reassure him. But she couldn't find anything appropriate to say. The thought of the family Wilson trying to take over the child's future, dictating a life in some archaic tradition, frightened her. And annoyed her. What was it with rich people? Were they just too used to having control that they assumed a preordained right?

Or was she over-reacting? In a treacherous moment, she longed for the comfort of Jake, of seeing him smile, the warmth of his hand in hers. It made her feel weak. She had to stop thinking like this. Stop thinking, full stop. They'd made an agreement - no contact over Christmas, or over New Year, those were the rules and she'd stick to them. But it was hard. She didn't belong here, she didn't belong in the family, she was merely tolerated and this year, she felt it more keenly than ever.

In the end, it was a rush to make it down to the dining room with barely two minutes to go. Amy almost expected a gong to be struck to summon them from their quarters, like in an Agatha Christie story where the family is gathered together the evening before someone is murdered. In a giddy moment, she fought back inappropriate laughter, not daring to share the thought with Robert. He didn't look in the mood to find it funny.

Harry skipped ahead as they entered the dining room with Robert a few steps behind. He touched the boy's shoulder. 'Best behaviour, mind.' He waited until Amy caught up and put his arm round her waist, guiding her to where the others were standing. The long table was laden with a wonderful array of food – good for Mrs. Daniels, thought Amy, she'd done a buffet worthy of a royal garden party - beef en croute, glazed ham, new potatoes, salads, home-made bread and a chocolate and strawberry gateau on a silver cake stand.

Under Irene's watchful gaze, they filled their plates and sat down on sofas and armchairs round the room (Robert taking charge of Harry and helping him choose food he wouldn't drop all over the carpet) and Fiona, the wife of Monty, the older cousin, came to sit by Amy. Probably under orders. She had a lined and kindly face, which creased into folds when she smiled. Smoothing down her skirt she placed her glass of wine on the side table and laid a napkin carefully on her lap before speaking.

'Such a good little boy, Amy. A credit to you both. How old is he now?'

'Six- and a half. Not always good though. He can be a bit hyper at times.'

'Hyper?'

'You know, all energy and not much self-control. But he loves school and generally, he's a happy kid.'

Fiona paused, a forkful of ham halfway to her mouth, and looked at Amy with a soulful expression in her watery eyes. 'You hang on to that, my dear. They grow up far too quickly and then they're out there and you've lost them to the world.' She looked down at her plate. 'What a sad thing to say on Christmas Eve! Forgive me.'

'No.' Amy wanted to put out her hand, to show she understood, but it seemed patronising. So she just nodded. 'I think this is such a precious time and you're right, it won't last long enough. I suppose as a parent, you just hope you've managed to create a strong enough bond that won't break. One that'll last when they've grown up.'

'Yes,' Fiona said. 'You certainly hope that.' Then she braced her shoulders, and stared across the room at Monty who was relating some story, with great enthusiasm, to Robert. Like a dagger, that look, thought Amy.

The conversation hung in the air for a moment, suspended in what wasn't said, before moving on to safer ground. When a few of the others grouped round them, the talk turned to shopping in Knightsbridge and golf handicaps and holidays in Sardinia. Words and more words, showing off, one-upmanship, no meaning behind them.

After they'd eaten, they trooped into the sitting room, where Irene brought out two decks of cards, insisting everyone must play whist, or at least learn and Amy decided it was a good time to take Harry up to bed.

'Can't I stay up?' he asked plaintively, as they climbed the stairs. 'It's Christmas Eve.'

'Stay up?' Amy pretended amazement. 'And Father Christmas would find an empty bed so he'd leave no presents! That'd be dreadful. Wouldn't it?'

He grinned. 'He'd leave them by the chimney. Well, perhaps not the bike, but he'd leave the others.'

'And how do you know you're going to *get* the bike? You have to wait and see.'

'I think I'll get it,' he said with such certainty it made Amy smile.

It didn't surprise her how quickly he fell asleep, he was dog-tired, and she lingered in his bedroom for a while, happier to stay there than join the others downstairs. Coward, she told herself. For God's sake, get down there, for Robert's sake at least. It's three days, that's all.

And in the end, the evening passed pleasantly enough, a bit of reminiscing about childhood (Robert happily remembering incidents with his cousins that Amy had never heard about before), a bit of half-hearted banter and teasing, mistakes over the cards, some attempts at humour she didn't find amusing, but the evening passed. Until one remark. Not intended to upset her, but there you go.

You can't get away from the past.

The red wine and punch had been flowing and perhaps everyone became less guarded. Perhaps they just forgot she was there. Amy wasn't sure. It was Monty who suddenly looked over at Robert and said, 'So what are the children doing this year? Staying at home?'

There was a still moment, a trembling silence for a second, time to consider the question. The children – Robert's real family, thought Amy. The children, who by rights should be here. And, of course, Paula.

Someone coughed and Robert responded in a voice that wasn't quite natural. And from the look of discomfort in his eyes, Amy knew he was trying to save her from any embarrassment; he was trying to protect her.

'Paula's parents are travelling down from Edinburgh on Christmas Eve, I believe. So there'll have plenty of company and I'm taking them all out for a meal after New Year...' He tailed off and Amy felt a sympathy for him she hadn't experienced for quite a while. He might be reserved, he might appear distant at times, but underneath was a kind man.

At bedtime, Robert brought all the presents in from the car, tiptoeing into Harry's room and standing like a statue when the boy stirred. 'Mustn't waken him,' he whispered too loudly to Amy with his finger to his lips. He placed all the presents in a bulging pillowcase at the foot of the bed.

All except for the bike.

It stood by the bedroom door, shiny handlebars and green paint catching a glimmer of light from the curtained window, for Harry to find in the morning.

*

You think Christmas is going to follow the same pattern, with its familiar traditions and rituals, year after year, Amy thought later. Always with the expectation that things aren't going to change. You're not ready for the unpredictable and it makes you careless of dangers. Off guard.

On that Christmas morning in Windsor, Amy had no sense that anything would be different. It began with breakfast - porridge, hot rolls and coffee at the kitchen table; then, presents opened by the fire in the sitting room, followed by a glass of sherry and mince pies around eleven thirty; the Christmas dinner late because the turkey always took longer to cook than anticipated ('Mrs. Daniels always lets it rest for thirty minutes,' pronounced Irene 'otherwise it'll be tough. There's no point in hurrying her.'); and then, afterwards, the time when everyone could relax and Harry could spend time playing with his new toys.

The afternoon had settled down into a calm, after-lunch quiet. Robert was reading yesterday's paper, Amy had gone upstairs to put on a sweater over her dress, so she'd be warm enough to take Harry out on his new bike. Later, going over the day many times, she blamed herself for not seeing what was so obvious – it should have been - but when someone drinks, it's hard to recognise how out of control they really are, how clever they are at deceiving everyone, even those close to them - not a tremor, a slurred word, an unsteady walk.

Fiona had covered it up well.

Throughout the morning, she had become so taken with Harry that she spent more time with him than the rest of them. Amy had looked on, glad to see the little boy engrossed in playing (with no other child there, he could have been at a loss, even though they'd tried hard to keep him amused). But Fiona had been a godsend, helping him create an army from model soldiers, reading to him, listening to his endless prattle. She hadn't seemed to drink more than a glass of Prosecco with lunch... or perhaps two.

It was soon obvious that wasn't so.

In the upstairs bedroom, Amy heard the crash and caught her breath in shock as an awful screaming rose to such a pitch it seemed to pierce the walls. Something dreadful had happened to Harry - he was hurt and hurt badly. She flew down the stairs, two at a time, through the side door and onto the terrace as the others followed, tripping over each other in the rush.

Harry's crumpled body lay at the bottom of a flight of steep stone steps, his bike overturned on top of him. And there was Fiona, looking down also, aghast, hand over her mouth, immobile.

The child was sobbing loudly now, his legs tucked under him, arm at an odd angle, and blood on his forehead from landing on the gravel. Robert leapt down the steps and picked him up, holding him gently against his body. Reaching the terrace, he gave Fiona a look of fury as he strode past her; she tottered and stumbled as he brushed against her, ignoring her frantic gasps of, 'I'm so sorry! So sorry! Shouldn't have let him...'

'No, you shouldn't.' Irene towered above her, face white, hands shaking. 'You're not fit to look after yourself, never mind a child.' She turned to Robert. 'Get him in the car. St. Thomas's is only fifteen minutes away. Hurry.'

So Christmas Day ended in the hospital, waiting for the doctor to put Harry's arm in plaster. Amy clasped Robert's hand tightly as they sat beside each other on plastic chairs in the corridor. They stared ahead in silence, listening for the swish of the swing doors and for footsteps coming from the operating theatre, with news of how it had gone.

'It could have been much worse,' said Robert, almost talking to himself. 'Arms mend. And the bang on the head is nothing, considering how steep the steps were.' He rubbed his eyes, in a frustrated gesture. 'But why the hell didn't someone tell us about Fiona? They must have all known she'd become a drinker, for God's sake. Mother certainly did.'

Amy shrugged, too tired to stay angry. 'It's Christmas. I suppose everyone wanted it to be pleasant.'

'Yeah. Well it's bloody *un*pleasant now.' He squeezed her hand. 'I'm so sorry, Amy.'

'Don't be silly. You're not to blame.'

They stood up as the doctor strode towards them. Smiling. 'You can go and see him now. He's drowsy, but nothing to worry about. I'll give you some notes to take to your local hospital when you get home.'

Amy said a silent prayer of thanks and thought about all the times she'd imagined the kinds of accidents he might have and how she'd have prevented them. Trouble was, you could never anticipate the ones that do.

Chapter 27

Catherine always thought Boxing Day was a bit of an anti-climax. Nothing much happened and the evening never came quickly enough. She'd had a friend at school, who every year, went to the pantomime at the Palace on Boxing Day and she'd been so envious. Envious of someone who had a treat to look forward to, when she had nothing but empty hours to fill. She'd imagined the magic of Oxford Street as the evening closed in, the lights on the theatre promising such fun - a world of colour, the dame in a silly costume and huge wig, the audience booing the bad fairy, the silly jokes, the fairy-tale ending. She'd watch the one on television on Christmas Day but it wasn't the same as *being* there. Not the same at all.

She sat down on the narrow bed and felt tired and listless. What was the point of thinking about Jake. He wasn't here, that was the beginning and end of it. He hadn't chosen to be with her. Even though things had been so much better, there were still doubts and questions that didn't seem to have answers. And the one person who could put her mind completely at rest was miles away.

She looked out of the window at the street, listening to the muffled sound of music with a vibrating base coming from a few doors up. A party perhaps. Downstairs she could hear the drone of the television. Indistinct voices. Canned laughter. She'd managed to escape for a few minutes to her old bedroom for a bit of peace.

There were still posters on the walls of Olympic running stars and high jumpers – she could barely remember their names now - and one of a young George Michael with Andrew Ridgely in Wham! – floppy hair and smiling eyes staring out at her. She'd been such a fan.

It all seemed a long time ago.

This had always been a dark house, she thought. Even in summer, the trees in the narrow street too close and blocking out the light. On grey days in winter it was even worse, with the overhanging branches, black and leafless, giving the whole house a gloomy aspect. Or was it that Catherine always thought of it that way? More so after her mother died. At least when she was alive, there'd been some sense of life and enjoyment in the household. Not now, with this dreadful, depressing atmosphere filling every corner.

*

She felt weighed down by it all. She had so hoped that Jake would take her with him this holiday. To a Christmas surrounded by a real family, people who cared about each other. Surely she was entitled to be included – she'd been his partner for a year! Well, hadn't she? And even though nothing had been said, she'd convinced herself she'd be invited. She'd even bought presents for his brothers and his parents – OK, small gifts but she'd spent quite a while choosing them. But no, other plans had already been made. They'd all got together and agreed their mother was tired, she'd done enough over the years and it was time someone else did all the work. They were all going to Nick's house for the holiday.

And nothing had been said. Nothing. Catherine hadn't found out until well into December. And it had sent her reeling.

She'd gone to Jake's room in the break to check the date of a party they'd been invited to, and had to wait till he'd finished discussing an essay with a girl from his A level class, the one who always wore provocative clothing and far too much make up. She was arguing that she'd spent ages on the work and couldn't understand why it hadn't deserved a higher grade.

Jake's tone was measured and deliberate, as though trying to keep his patience. 'It's careless. You don't follow up on your quotes and beside that, there was far more material you needed to cover. We'll go over the question in the lesson. Tomorrow. You can have another go at it.'

'Are you kidding?' the girl almost snatched the papers out of his hand. 'Don't ask me to do it again. It took me ages.'

'Well, you'll only get better grades if you put the work in. Now go!'

The girl looked up, saw Catherine waiting and pushed past her at the door, face flushed and mouth trembling.

'Someone's not happy,' she said.

Jake shrugged. 'Tough. She wants everything too easy.'

Catherine hesitated. There were times, like now, when he didn't seem approachable; he'd half turned away from her, almost dismissing her as though she was another disappointing student. 'I just came to ask if Ted's engagement party was this Friday. We said we'd go, didn't we, ages ago, but I didn't write down the day?'

'It's Saturday. Starts in the Cross Keys and then back to his house.'

'And Christmas... we haven't discussed...'

He shot her a look that silenced her and rubbed his hand down his face as though forcing out the words. 'Really sorry, Catherine. I only found out myself last week. The family's going to Nick's this year, giving Mum a rest, and I'm only staying for a couple of days, so this time, I'll go on my own.' His face took on the look of a guilty child. 'I'll be back by New Year and then we can go somewhere...'

He trailed off, unable to meet her eyes.

He's rambling, making excuses, she thought, he's known about this for a while. He never intended me going. A tightness was spreading across her chest.

'Why couldn't I go with you to Nick's? One more person won't make much difference, surely. Why couldn't I do that?'

He sighed, closing a book on his desk, and getting up. 'It's a small house. You've seen it. And I couldn't suggest it now...'

'But it's the middle of December. I've bought presents, I just thought...'

'I'm really sorry. I've been so wrapped up with school work and organising the poetry magazine, I forgot to tell you. I should have done...'

'Yes,' embarrassment and shame lost itself in anger. 'You bloody well should have.' She saw the shock in his eyes that she'd sworn, something she never did. And sworn at him. But she wanted to strike him. How could he let her down like this? What was she meant to do now? Go cap in hand to her father and ask to go there, when she'd made it clear that was the last thing she wanted?

She felt sick. This was just too much. After the months of worrying, the nights lying awake, too often alone in her own bed, the sense of ... what... betrayal? Yes. That was exactly the word. How could he?

She tried to fight back the tears, but it was beyond her. She was finding it hard to breathe and something in her seemed to snap, releasing all the frustration and despair she'd suffered in the past months. All the thoughts tumbling out, impossible to keep inside.

'I know what's going on here.' Her teeth were gritted so hard it was difficult to speak. 'I'm not stupid. There's someone else, isn't there? You're seeing someone else. Behind my back.' Then, she was shouting. 'You're trying to get rid of me, shake me off, as though I'm nothing, but you're a coward, you haven't the guts to tell me to my face...'

Jake reached out and pushed the door to, grabbing her hard by the shoulder. 'Lower your voice, for God's sake. This is crazy. You'll have the whole school in here.'

'I don't care. I don't care who hears me.' She put her hands on his forearms and brought her face close to his. The tears were hot on her cheeks and the words wouldn't stop, the words that would make things worse. Somewhere in the back of her mind she acknowledged that, but things had gone too far to hold back. 'It's Jenny, isn't it? You two always seem to be huddled together, talking away, laughing at jokes. Such good friends. Or, wait... worse than that - one of your sixth formers! They're always in here asking for advice, needing 'help'... is that it?' He opened his mouth to protest, but she didn't give him time to speak. 'No, you wouldn't take a risk like that... not you.'

'This is just ridiculous. Catherine, stop it!' Jake was backing away, caught off balance as he knocked against the filing cabinet, but she held onto his arms, her nails digging into the fabric of his jacket. She clutched him to her so closely, her breath made him blink his eyes.

'What about that reporter, the blond girl, all smiles and fancy clothes? You seem fascinated by her. You get on *really* well with her. She's just the sort you *would* fall for. Sure of herself and pretty and seems to know everything...'

She stopped.

There was a look of horror on Jake's face, his mouth half open as though about to say something, but unable to, eyes so dark and accusing they seemed to stab her. It frightened her.

They stared at one another.

'Is that it?' she said, trying to read his expression. Had she hit a nerve?

Jake shook himself free and pushed her away. But calmly. The lines on his face gradually softened and his fury had changed to something else. She tried to make it out — worried, yes, and thoughtful. She felt better about that look. It meant he cared. Cared for how he'd hurt her.

But she had to know. 'Is it her?' she said again.

He caught both of her hands in his. 'Of course not. I barely know her. She's married, anyway. I don't know where all this is coming from. It's all nonsense.' She could feel him trembling. 'Catherine, you're bloody scaring me – I've never seen you like this and I don't understand what's going on in your head. For God's sake, if Christmas is that important, I'll just stay here... I'll stay here.'

'No, no, I don't want you to do that.' She began crying again, but softly now. Of course she wanted that, to be together wherever it was, but she couldn't bring herself to say it. He'd resent her, blame her later and things would be worse. She sniffed and bowed her head. 'Of course you can't do that. It would upset your mother and I'd feel awful. No, you must go. I'm being selfish. I'm sorry. But I was so scared I was losing you...'

The bell rang. Time's up, she thought. He'll go to Leeds on his own and I'll have to live with it. Nothing I can do.

'Look,' Jake said. 'It's me who should apologise. I've been thoughtless. Come and stay after the party – stay for the weekend. We'll go shopping on Sunday and you can pick your Christmas present. How's that?'

It was some sort of consolation, thought Catherine. She'd have to settle for that. And be grateful. At least they'd made up and she could stop tormenting herself.

But now that Christmas had come and nearly gone, she wasn't so sure. She was finding it hard to stay positive, unable to stop going over and over the same worries. The old fear that blind panic was going to consume her again kept returning and it was more than she could bear. She remembered only too well the dreadful long months it had taken to get over it last time – the exhaustion, no fight left in her and those terrifying moments of utter despair.

She kept telling herself there was no real reason to feel this wretched. Although she had feared the worst, Christmas with her father and brother hadn't been as bad as she'd expected. The dinner she'd cooked had been appreciated, really appreciated and they'd been thoughtful in their choice of presents for her - a writing case and trainers and headphones. It made up for a lot, she thought, wishing she'd spent as much time choosing theirs.

But time spent with them was just going through the motions - they were separate from her other life, the one that held such importance for her. She sat, now, in her old bedroom, thinking about Ted and Angie's party. It had started well. Jake had been in such a good mood, she'd wondered whether he'd already had a few drinks - anyway, he'd been quite attentive, including her, putting his arm round her when they were in a group. More *concerned* about her. People could see they were a twosome again. It had been almost like old times.

They'd booked a taxi for midnight to take them back to Jake's and it was after one before they closed the front door and took off their coats. The house was so cold, they moved quickly into the kitchen, and Jake turned the stove on to warm them up. The last two whiskeys at the party had made him mellow and talkative, and Catherine was grateful to see him relaxed.

He's glad to be with me, she thought. *It's going to be all right.*

But that feeling didn't last long. Looking back at that weekend and examining every detail, she began to question it all again. Something wasn't right. It was as though Jake was making too much of an effort to keep her happy. He'd talk just a little too loudly, humouring her, suggesting possible things to do or places to go. On the Saturday morning, he'd brought her the newspaper and sat down beside her, smiling. 'So, what would you like to do today? See if the Christmas markets are on? And then go to the Tapas Bar on King Street this evening?'

And the lovemaking in that dark little bedroom she'd so wanted to make less masculine when she'd first stayed over, had been hurried and clinical, somehow. It wasn't lovemaking really – it was just sex. Or had it been so long since they'd been together that she couldn't seem to get much pleasure from it? She realised, of course, it wasn't going to be the same as when they'd first met. Common sense told her it never could be. But even so...

That night, she'd found comfort in the very fact he was there, lying beside her. Hers again. But looking back, now, she couldn't quite believe in him. Somehow, things were different.

And, yes, he'd come to the concert at the youth club a week later. He'd arrived early, sitting in the second row, and seemed happy enough talking to one of the parents he knew in the audience. He hadn't come up to the stage area, just lifted his hand and nodded to her and she'd understood - the whole thing was about to start. She'd needed all her concentration to work through the list of acts again with Tony and check that Lucas was ready with all the changes in the lighting and accompaniments. Most of the performers had managed to line up in the right order, back stage, although one boy, dressed as a rapper, had already lurched into the flimsy backcloth and nearly brought it over on their heads.

It might well be a shambles, she thought, with fifteen minutes to go. She glanced across to where Jake was sitting and saw that he was staring into space now, as though there was nothing going on around him, no noise, no people. He looked as though he was in another world. *Oh dear, he's going to be so bored.* Possibly, she'd have understood if he'd stayed away – amateur shows were only really appreciated by parents and friends and she knew it wasn't going to be particularly polished, not like the one at school; these weren't the same kind of kids.

But in the end, the first half was good. She let Tony do the introductions for each act, and it was obvious there'd been some serious practising going on. You could see from Peter doing his Michael Jackson routine and a girl called Kerry miming to Adele's 'Turning Tables' to a couple of lads telling rather lame jokes. They were doing their best. And at least Beth hadn't managed to train her dog to do tricks well enough to be included, so that was one act that Catherine didn't have to fret about.

It had been decided not to have an interval, so the evening was virtually over by nine. Everyone gathered round the stage, plenty of laughter and congratulations, the whole hall filled with good humour and shouts and smiling faces.

'Well done. You really pulled if off!' Tony turned away from the clamour and put his hand on her shoulder. 'Shows what you can do, girl!' And Catherine felt a surge of relief, grateful for his approval and glad he'd said so when parents were around to hear him.

She began searching for Jake, and caught sight of him, standing a bit apart, waiting for the hall to clear. She went over and slipped her arm through his. This was her night and she wanted him to be part of it.

'Come and say hello to Tony,' she said. 'And meet Lucas, my main helper. He's been such a godsend. He did most of the stage managing with very little direction from me.'

She led him over to the stage area. Tony turned and smiled, shaking Jake's hand rather formally. 'Catherine's worked so hard on this,' he said, as though speaking to some official who had no idea the amount of effort she'd put into it. 'They're not easy kids.'

'No,' Jake nodded in agreement. 'She's done a great job.'

Catherine gently pushed Lucas forward, keen to have his contribution acknowledged. 'And this is Lucas, who's been such a help. The lighting, the sound, the tickets. I couldn't have done it without him… this is Mr. Harper. He teaches at Forest Green.'

'I know.' Lucas kept just enough distance from Jake to avoid a handshake and turned to Catherine. 'If you give me the key, I'll put the equipment in the storage cupboard in the office.' He turned his gaze back on Jake, pale eyelids flickering slightly. 'Nice to see you again, Mr. Harper.' And he turned away in that slow, measured way he had, leaving Catherine staring after him.

She looked up at Jake, puzzled. 'He doesn't know you, does he?'

'I wouldn't have thought so,' Jake frowned and shrugged his shoulders. 'He didn't attend our school, I'm sure of that. Perhaps he's mates with some of our lads.'

Tony gave an awkward laugh. 'He's an odd one, is Lucas. Doesn't mix very well. When he comes to the club, he's like a spectator most of the time. But Catherine has the knack of getting him to help and that brings out the best in him.' The place had emptied and, looking round, he realised he'd spoken too loudly. 'Anyway, let's get home. We can tidy up on Wednesday – last one until after the New Year.'

And on the way home, walking beside Jake out of the park onto the street, Catherine's buoyant mood had slowly dissipated. She wanted to talk about everything that had happened throughout the evening, but he seemed in a sombre mood and she soon gave up trying. There were just too many silences, too much distance. She sensed it, not something she could put her finger on, just a feeling of separateness. Two people walking side by side. They could have been strangers.

*

A shout came from the bottom of the stairs, Tom calling her name, then again, impatiently.

A programme on the television she'd wanted to watch. Just starting.

She pulled herself up off the bed and walked slowly down into the living room that was now too warm and smelt of cigarettes. The TV was turned up to nearly full volume. Just one more evening, she thought, then I can go home.

The only time her father spoke was in the commercial break.

'How about another beer? By the fridge,' he said, not taking his eyes off the screen. 'If you're quick, Catherine, you won't miss anything.'

She got up without a word and brought in a bottle, putting it on the table beside him. She knew he'd already had far too many but what was the point of saying anything. He picked it up and took a long swallow and without looking at her, he began chuckling. 'See, if you'd played your cards right, you'd be doing this for your young man.'

Catherine looked at him sharply. Where was this going?

He kept his eyes on the television screen and took quick gulps of his beer. 'He's done a runner, though, hasn't he? I knew he wouldn't stick. I'll bet he's heard what you did to that other fella in Sheffield and he's had a frightener! Word gets out, you know, people love to talk. Specially in this town. I'll bet he's heard and run for the hills...'

Catherine straightened up and stood stock still.

Even Tom turned his head, looking embarrassed.

But the old man was pleased with himself, swigging his beer and still laughing to himself. It seemed to have made his day.

Chapter 28

'Of course I'm angry. I've every right to be.' Robert still had the same horrible sensation in his chest when he thought about the accident, when he thought about Fiona and how negligent she'd been. Amy, following him down the stairs from Harry's room, had just said the wrong thing. That he needed to be calm in front of the boy. That he couldn't go on being so angry about it. After all, it was two weeks ago now. But his shoulders ached, his whole body tense from looking at his son's tiny frame, his small thin arm cased in plaster. The boy was struggling to get comfortable, so he'd propped him up with a pillow and smoothed some Vaseline on the skin where the cuff of the cast was rubbing.

'Shout if you need anything,' he'd said. 'And don't get out of bed on your own. You'll fall over.'

Harry had given a weak smile. 'No I won't. Mummy says I'm fine.'

Amy leant down and kissed him. 'The light's on, Harry. We won't turn it off till we come to bed.'

Robert felt physically drained. He could hear Amy sighing behind him and knew it was no good going on about it all. He blamed Fiona, he blamed his mother for not warning him; and he blamed himself. He should have been more… what?… well, more observant anyway. You can't trust people who aren't used to kids, who have no sense of what *might* happen. Damn the bloody bike! He wished he'd never bought it.

He'd been glad to get home and leave all the apologies and recriminations and noise behind him. As soon as Harry had been allowed to leave hospital, an alarmingly short two days in his opinion, he'd insisted on packing up - far too hurriedly for his mother – and felt a desperate need to get away - leave the whole episode behind him. As he'd piled the last bag into the car, he looked back at the house, its ivy-covered walls, its huge dark windows and shuddered slightly. He could hardly think of it with any warmth anymore.

The moment of leaving had become strained, with the family standing on the steps at the front door, not knowing quite how to behave or what to say. There was no sign of Fiona, which didn't surprise him.

His mother had moved towards the car as Amy was tucking a rug round Harry in the back seat.

'Stay until the boy's a bit more settled,' she'd said. Tactlessly, he thought. 'I'm sure he won't be comfortable in the back seat of a car.'

Robert closed his eyes briefly to make it clear he was irritated. 'Mother, I have to get back to work. And anyway, we need to get him to the hospital in Stockport, arrange for him to see the doctor there.'

She held out her hand, eyes full of tears. 'My dear boy, I'm so very sorry...'

'Yes, I know,' he said. Then, more kindly. 'This wasn't your fault. These things happen. It's just...'

She sniffed and tilted her head in the direction of the group waiting behind her. 'Knowing the circumstances, I should have been vigilant. I wanted it to go so well, the first time the family had all been together for years... I wanted it to go so well.'

'I know.'

She was more upset than he'd ever seen her and however exasperated he felt, it needed hiding. He couldn't allow his mother to believe it was all her fault. That would be too cruel. So he said, more kindly, 'I'll ring you when we get home and keep you posted on Harry's progress. Take care of yourself.' And he bent down to give her a dutiful kiss. The best he could do. Then he climbed into the car and breathed a relieved sigh. They'd be home before dark.

'Have you got my bike in?' Harry had asked as soon as the car door slammed.

Robert and Amy looked at each other, both trying to suppress smiles that they knew would be misinterpreted by the family waving them off. And as the car swung round the forecourt and up the driveway, Amy twisted round in her seat.

'Of course,' she'd said. 'That wasn't broken. As soon as your arm's fixed, we'll practise in the garden. No steps.'

He laughed. 'No steps.'

They'd journeyed north through the day, only stopping at a motorway café for a toilet break and a quick sandwich. Amy was uncharacteristically silent and Robert didn't feel the need to talk either. He was emotionally spent. So much for a Christmas in the bosom of your family. It had turned out to be pretty awful. And they'd made light of it to Amy's parents when they'd phoned, so giving them all the details of what really happened was another thing they'd have to deal with.

Of course, they'd cancelled their plans to attend the New Year's Eve dance at the golf club. It had meant letting down Mike and Sophie, but that couldn't be helped. He wasn't going to leave Harry in the care of a baby sitter and go out enjoying himself. They'd made the most of the night by opening a bottle of Sancerre, and he'd cooked steaks, and they'd toasted the New Year in by watching the celebrations on TV, lifting their glasses as Big Ben struck midnight.

But Robert's spirits still didn't lift and he couldn't explain why. Days passed and instead of comfortably settling into his usual routine, he felt out of sorts. 'Out of kilter' his father would have said. It was as though life was conspiring to make him lose confidence in all he had been so certain of. As though a benign god had decided he'd had enough good luck for the time being and needed to balance things up.

He'd made arrangements long before Christmas to take Holly, Ruth and Ben out for a New Year's treat – a meal at their favourite place, The Blacksmith's in Disley. There was a favourite table in an alcove where they always sat and they'd settled themselves on the upholstered bench seats and pulled off their gloves and winter coats, Ben snatching up the four menu cards to read aloud what was on offer.

'Hand them out, Ben. We can all read,' Robert said, taking them off him as a young lad came to take their drinks order.

Ruth, looking much older than fifteen, her father thought, with her hair piled high on her head, was fiddling with the holly and mistletoe sprigs arranged in a pewter jar in the centre of the table. 'You know the story about Achilles and how he died because the only bit of his body that was vulnerable, was his heel?' She'd looked round at them expectantly. 'Well, in one book I read, it wasn't a poisoned arrow that finished him off. It was a branch of mistletoe that struck him. There was even a picture showing it landing on his heel... and he's screaming out in pain as it strikes him...'

Ben screwed up his face, puzzled. 'Why did he die from that? Doesn't make sense.'

Ruth loved coming out with anything that needed a long explanation. Especially if it baffled Ben. 'It does,' she said. Robert and Holly studied their menus, knowing this could go on and on. 'You see, his parents, who were gods, wanted to protect him from death – someone had said he'd die young – so they dipped him in this special liquid, but held him by his heel, so that was the only bit that wasn't dipped, so of course, he wasn't protected *all* over...'

'Ruth, just look at the menu for the minute and decide what you want to eat,' said Robert. 'Otherwise, it'll be midnight before we're served.'

'Why didn't they throw him in,' said Ben, 'then he'd have been all right.'

Holly was smiling, 'It's a myth, Ben. Made up. Probably as a sort of warning that you can't change destiny.' Robert was thankful that she was looking so much healthier than a few months ago. She still had shadows under her eyes, but her face had lost that pinched look that had so frightened him.

'What's destiny?' Ben wasn't going to give up.

Robert had glared at him. 'If you don't choose what you want to eat, son, I'll get you a packet of crisps and that can be your dinner. Now, what's it going to be?'

They'd ordered at last and chattered on about the presents they'd received, ones they'd liked and ones that were 'totally minging' according to Ruth, about the Father Christmas who'd ridden round the streets in a motorised 'sledge', the pantomime at Buxton and the church carol singers carrying lanterns who'd filed into their hall and given them a most peculiar version of 'When Shepherds Watched'. The wrong tune, according to Ruth.

Robert watched their faces as they told their stories, imagining it all.

'And, on Christmas Day,' said Ben, 'Grandpa Joe snored all the way through the Bruce Willis film. Grandma kept nudging him, but it was no good.'

'And we had a party on Boxing Day,' Ruth stopped eating, putting her fork down as she got ready to give her father all the details before the others could chip in. 'We had salmon and quiches and fancy potatoes and Mum had made a chocolate gateau thing...'

Robert looked up, eyebrows raised. Paula had never liked entertaining.

'Not a real party,' Holly had flushed and shot her sister a warning glance.

'Well, not a *big* one,' Ruth admitted, seemingly unaware of any attempt to slow her down. 'About ten people. Next door came and old Mrs. Havers from across the road, and Grandma and Grandpa and Bradley, Mum's friend, and we'd made punch in a big bowl, and we played '*Articulate*' which is *such* a good game...'

She stopped to jab some scampi with her fork. 'And I wanted to go to a dance in Stockport...'

Robert interrupted her. 'This Bradley, Mum's friend, – has he just moved into the neighbourhood?'

It didn't sound like the right question, even to him.

'Don't know, but he's nice,' said Ruth. 'Mum's been to the theatre with him and he was on his own over the holidays, so she thought it'd be nice if we let him join us.'

'He even got me out of the washing up,' Ben added. 'And he was brilliant at Jenga!'

Robert noticed Holly said nothing, and he didn't feel he could ask anything else.

He'd driven them home and dropped them off at the gate, without going into the house. The porch light was on, which seemed to him like a welcoming beacon in the dark. He'd looked on as the two girls walked quickly up the drive, with Ben following, hopping from one leg to the other as he went.

When Amy asked how the meal had gone, he didn't know quite how to reply. He settled for saying that the children had enjoyed it.

January had begun cold and dank, a mist heavy with rain shrouding everything, day after bleak day. The evenings descended at four o'clock in the afternoon and he'd sit in his office, under the harsh strip lighting surrounded by clients' accounts and Self-Assessment forms, aware that it was still two hours before he could go home.

It hadn't helped that his mother had rung for the tenth time since Christmas, wanting to take charge of everything from a distance, insisting that she be given the name of the doctor who was looking after Harry - was he a specialist – had they found the physiotherapist the boy would need (and she would pay). And then, when she'd already interrupted Robert in the middle of a particularly complicated task with all her ideas of how she could 'help', she muttered something then stopped abruptly.

Robert waited. 'Mother, are you still there?'

'Of course I am,' she said. 'I was going to say this when you came on Christmas Eve, but thought it might wait for a better time. But there never is a better time, is there?' Another pause. 'You look tired, Robert. Rather drawn. And you're putting on weight. Don't let yourself go. You need to take more care of yourself. I say this because I'm only thinking of you, with a young family...'

'Thank you, Mother. I'll bear it in mind.'

Just what I needed, thought Robert, *a real morale booster. She was always good at that. As if I haven't enough to worry about.*

But he knew she was right. He *did* look tired and he'd noticed his trousers and shirt collars were just a bit tight these days. He'd always prided himself on being fit, on *looking* fit, and had taken it for granted. His mother might be tactless, but he had to admit she could be unnervingly honest. Well, part of the problem was he'd stopped playing squash on any regular basis since he hadn't found a new partner who played at his level. A round of golf just wasn't enough.

It was still on his mind the next evening when Amy returned from covering a memorial service for a local sportsman.

'Did Harry get straight off to sleep?' she asked, her coat still on and her face flushed from the cold outside. Sometimes, at quite unexpected moments, Robert was struck by how very young she was, her movements always quick, her eyes wide, as though she had so many thoughts swirling in her head, she couldn't express them fast enough. And the way she seemed to have no fear, facing things head on, trusting there were answers to everything.

'Yes. He was ready for bed. Going back to school's been the answer. And he's getting used to his arm in plaster. Must be heavy for him, though, even in a sling.'

She poured the coffee and cut both of them a wedge of cake.

'Not for me,' he said.

She pulled a face. 'You always eat my lemon cake!'

'I'm starting on a health kick. Mother says I'm beginning to look worn down and overweight.'

Amy let out a disbelieving laugh. 'Well, that was kind of her!' But she could see that he was taking this seriously and put her hand over his. 'Rubbish. You're fine. You might have put on a few pounds and sometimes you *do* look tired when you're working too hard. But it's January - the worst time of the year. Everyone looks a bit jaded. Forget it.'

Somehow, her words didn't sound all that comforting. There were times lately when that age gap, that twenty years, which hadn't seemed so important eight years ago, struck him with an unnerving jolt. He wondered whether Amy thought about it. Really thought about it. Did she see him now with a bit more clarity and notice what others must have been aware of from the start? That he was too old for her. Perhaps ok when you're forty, but approaching fifty?

So the words 'Don't let yourself go' had played on his mind and sent him back, ten days later, to the squash club. It was a Sunday night, quiet on Heaton Moor Road as he pulled into the car park. He looked round to see if Nick's car was there and was relieved to see it wasn't. He'd had one text, an apology of sorts, just after the night in the pub, and he hadn't answered it. So that was that, surely, but he'd avoided going anywhere near places where he might meet him. The last thing he wanted was another embarrassing scene.

And he was lucky. No Nick.

But on his second visit to the club, his luck ran out.

He'd found a partner, the son of one of the regulars, back from university, keen to take him on, and after putting all his energy into an easy win, he went for a shower feeling better about himself. It was what he'd needed, a fast game against someone competitive who really wanted to play, not waste time talking.

He was coming out of the changing rooms and there was Nick with his back to him. Fully dressed and about to leave the club at the same time he was. Blast! He hadn't seen his car. Too late now. Anyway, couldn't expect to shy away from this for ever. They were both yearly members, and Nick obviously hadn't gone completely to the wall as he'd so desperately predicted – he hadn't resigned from the club, anyway.

They reached the outer door almost at the same moment, Robert following and hoping Nick wouldn't turn and see him. But it was inevitable.

'Ah!' Nick bent his body in a mock bow. 'If it isn't the Man who has Everything!'

Robert sighed. He knew it was no good trying to push past him. 'Hello, Nick.' He wasn't going to ask how he was.

'I thought you might have answered my text,' Nick shook his head. 'I did apologise.'

'Yes, I know you did. Sorry we ended on such a bad note.' Robert hesitated, wondering whether he dare say more. Curiosity got the better of him. 'Did everything get sorted out?'

Nick gave a short, harsh laugh. 'Well, no thanks to you, chum.'

'You went to the police?'

'Are you kidding? There was no way I was taking *your* advice!' Nick nodded to himself, as though confirming he'd made the right decision. 'I managed to get my hands on the money. Don't ask how.' He pulled on his gloves. 'But I can tell you it was hell for a time. I was damned close to the edge. But,' he wagged a finger in Robert's face. 'So far, you'll be glad to hear, she hasn't been back for more. All's well. I'm clear and free.'

Robert didn't know what to say, so he muttered, 'Good,' and was about to move onto the street, when Nick caught his arm, almost knocking him off balance. He could sense the menace in the man. It was all so uncivilised, so distasteful. Robert wrenched himself free, but Nick wasn't ready to let him go that easily.

'The whole business has taught me a lesson, Robert. And I'll pass it on to you. Don't trust a woman. Even one you think you know. They can turn on a sixpence when it suits them.' He gave a mean smile. 'Especially when they're young. And beautiful. How *is* Amy, by the way?'

And with a look of satisfaction on his face, he left, with Robert staring after him, astonished that, even now, Nick wanted some sort of revenge. He took a deep breath and stood for a moment, nonplussed by the malice in the man.

This whole thing is so distasteful, he thought to himself. *Forty-odd years old and behaving like a miserable youth.*

But it unsettled him. The past few *weeks* had unsettled him and he could have done without this latest broadside from someone who had no idea what decent behaviour was.

Damn him. Forget it. He's just trying to get under your skin. 'The Man who has Everything' indeed!

But the whole nastiness of the encounter had just that effect, however much he tried to dismiss it from his mind.

Chapter 29

Jake had retreated to the English office, pretending he had an urgent report to write, but now he sat, door closed firmly behind him, staring at the wall. He'd found it impossible to sit in the staff room and hold a normal conversation with anyone. It wasn't just on this particular Thursday. The whole week back at school had been like that and he couldn't pull himself together.

No good going over it for the umpteenth time, but it was all he could think about. She didn't mean it, surely she didn't mean it! But it was twelve days now, and the phone call had ended on such a final note. He felt as though something was broken inside him and nothing would ease the pain. Nothing, except hearing her voice, hearing her say she couldn't let him go. That she couldn't end it. But that seemed a forlorn hope now.

He let his chin rest on his clenched fingers and went through all he could remember of the conversation again in his head.

It had been eight o'clock. He'd been listening to Chet Baker sing in that haunting way of his and deciding he couldn't be bothered washing up tonight. It'd wait till the morning. Then his mobile rang.

He snatched it up as soon as he read the caller ID.

'God, it's good to hear from you.' He'd been so elated, so damned glad to know she'd been thinking about him.

'Hi.' She sounded quiet. Too quiet. Even in that one word, he sensed something was wrong.

'Are you all right?'

'Not really.'

He waited. 'What's happened?'

'We have to end this, Jake,' she was rushing now. 'We can't… well *I* can't do it anymore. I have a family and I can't just push them to one side…'

'Hold on.' He was having trouble breathing. 'I'm not asking you to…'

'No, I know. But that's what's happening. I'm forgetting to…to take care of them. I've had a horrible shock and I've come to my senses. About time, I keep telling myself.'

'Amy, slow down. Tell me what's happened. Because something has.'

'We were down south – you know, Christmas with Robert's mother - and Harry had this accident, went down a flight of stone stairs on his new bike. He broke his arm, I can still hear the screams and… of course it could have been much worse but at the time it was so frightening.' The words died away and he thought she'd gone. He rubbed his forehead. He felt he was in limbo, wanting her to speak but afraid what she would say.

'Are you still there?'

'When I thought about it afterwards, it seemed like some sort of punishment. As though I deserved to be punished for us, for how I've behaved.' She made an odd sound and Jake thought she might be crying but he couldn't be sure.

'I don't know what to say, Amy.' A spasm of fear ran through his body. How selfish we are, he thought later, knowing the fear was for himself. 'Of course you're upset and I can understand that. Is he all right?'

'His arm's in plaster, but, yes, he's ok now. Well, getting there.'

Silence.

Jake didn't want to go any further. He'd wished this conversation had never started and dreaded where it was going next. He took a deep breath and waited.

'So it has to end, Jake.' She sounded more in control now and he heard determination in her voice. 'I'm sorry, so very sorry. I know I've hurt you and, believe me, that's the last thing I wanted.' Another pause. 'But we were heading for disaster. You know we were. And it isn't worth it.'

'If that's what you want.' How reasonable he sounded, when inside he was choked with an anguish he could barely contain. 'But Amy...'

'Yes?'

'I'll be here. Always.' He couldn't say goodbye. 'If ever you need me...'

'I'm sorry.' she was whispering now. He could only just hear her. But then, louder, as though someone had just come into the room. 'You take care.'

It sounded like the farewell you'd say to an old acquaintance.

And now? Too many dreadful days later? Well he couldn't phone her. He had to accept it. And he couldn't go on drinking a bottle of wine a night and feeling this bloody hungover. Mourning what he knew he hadn't a hope of holding on to in the first place.

Funny, he thought, you'd think I'd have known better, prepared myself for the inevitable, but common sense doesn't stand a chance in the end. There's something far stronger that takes over – call it what you like – but once it's got you, you might as well give up. Doesn't matter what you do, it's all a waste of time. You're fucked.

The worst of it was, he couldn't afford to let it show. Not at work, not to Catherine, not to anyone. He had to suffer in silence. And it served him right.

A knock on the door made him sit up and pull some papers in front of him.

'Come in,' he managed to make his voice sound almost normal.

It was Eleanor, a wispy little girl from year 8, with a note for him. Someone needed a talking to on G corridor for swearing at a prefect and he was meant to be one of the teachers on break duty. Damn. It'd gone out of his mind, but at least it shook him out of his inane self-absorbed ramblings.

'Are you ill?' Catherine had asked a number of times over the past week.

He looked ill, he thought. Might as well go with that. 'Yes, I think I am. Having trouble sleeping and feel sick when I try to eat.'

At least that was the truth.

She persisted, as she always did these days. 'Is it your mother you're worrying about, do you think?'

'Perhaps.' He felt ashamed to be using her as his excuse. Although she'd looked a bit frail over Christmas, she'd joined in with everything and seemed to enjoy being looked after. It had all been fairly quiet for once, as his brother's house wasn't close enough to where his parents lived to gather the usual crowd of exuberant neighbours. Close family only and, this year, he liked that better. He didn't have to be sociable and fend off questions about how he was doing. He couldn't even answer that himself.

*

A school at the end of a day always seems uncommonly hushed and still. No babble of voices or shouted laughter, no shuffling of shoes along corridors, no banging doors or piercing whistles. Just the cleaners working away, moving from classroom to classroom, emptying bins and sweeping floors.

Jake sat in the Quiet Room, marking books, no one else around. It was peaceful and he did his best to concentrate. The window blinds hadn't been pulled down, but there was little to see beyond the reflecting glass. Just a sky so dark and heavy, it seemed as though night had already fallen. He felt enclosed in a world that was separate from every other human being – as though he couldn't be heard or seen. And he felt glad of it - he'd lost the ability to engage in everyday routines, anyway; he wasn't willing to smile and utter platitudes. He had removed himself from it all.

Of course, he was deluding himself because just as he was indulging in another meandering reverie, Andy stuck his head round the Quiet Room door.

'Found you! Are you playing Five-a-Side tomorrow? You have to put your name down if you are.'

Jake put his pen beside the pile of books. 'No. Not in the mood. Might do next week.'

Andy came further into the room and stood in front of him, looking down with a frown on his face. 'Christ, you're a misery these days. What on earth's wrong with you? Takes you all your time to speak, let alone laugh.'

Jake rubbed the back of his neck, wearily, unable to summon up any words that would send Andy away. Leave him to his misery. It was all just too much. All of it. He'd only himself to blame for the whole mess, he knew that; he wasn't an immature kid with no experience of what life was all about. He'd gone into this with his eyes open. He was getting what he deserved. Bloody heartache. But no amount of reasoning made him feel any better. He could only think of Amy and that phone call. Losing her was eating away at him like something corrosive in his gut.

He was aware minutes had passed and Andy was staring at him.

Andy, always so laid back about everything, a concerned expression on his face, eyes wide, anticipating sharing some dreadful secret. 'Come on. What is it? Have you hit some kid? Set the wrong exam paper? We've all made mistakes that turn out to be nothing terrible in the end.'

All Jake's resolve to keep his problems hidden was swept away, sure if he kept it to himself much longer, he'd break.

'Close the door,' he managed to say.

Andy did so and sat down opposite him. Waiting... the only sound, the fluorescent ceiling lights buzzing intermittently above their heads.

'Look, we haven't been friends for all this time that you can't come out and say it. Whatever it is.'

'If you ever tell anyone about this, I'll have to kill you.'

'Ok, I won't tell anyone then.'

Andy's efforts to find some quirky humour in his misery made Jake shake his head impatiently. What was the point, anyway? Talking wasn't going to help. And trying to make light of it *certainly* wasn't going to help.

Andy pulled an apologetic face. 'I'm listening. Honestly. If I can do anything, I will.'

Jake took a deep breath. 'How do I put this? I'm a bloody mess because... I'm having an affair. What a cliché. Ok. I'm involved with a married woman.' He gave a rasping, embarrassed laugh. 'And I'm desperate because she's just finished it.'

'Blimey. That *does* sound serious.'

'It is. I love her, Andy. I've never felt like this about anyone before. It's so corny and predictable. Pathetic, really. And it's so unlike me. But it's knocked me for six.' He was struggling to explain it now he'd started, but in a way it was a relief to let it all out. 'D'you know when you meet someone who's just perfect for you...?'

'No. It's never happened. There's always something irritating after a bit.'

'Well, not with Amy. She's everything I've ever wanted and it's bloody hopeless because she's married and she's got a child. And she's not going to ever be with me, is she?'

Andy looked thoughtful. 'If it's over, she's already made the choice for both of you. So there's not a lot you can do. Isn't that better than being found out? That'd be a real train wreck.'

'I know. I know. But I can't believe she really meant it.'

'She's not a teacher, is she?'

Jake shook his head. 'She's not in our crowd at all.'

'Ah!' Andy suddenly leaned forward. 'It isn't that newspaper girl, is it? The one who came in that day to work with the kids? I thought you two were a bit cosy...'

'Christ, I hope no one else thought so.' Jake groaned. 'I was walking on eggshells the whole day. It was a hell of a strain.'

They stared at each other.

'What about Catherine? Does she have any idea?'

'She's beginning to think there's someone – I'm not exactly behaving normally – but other than a few wild guesses, no. I've tried to smooth things over.'

'Why? I never thought you were suited anyway. Life'd be less complicated if you finished it.'

'I tried. But she sort of freaked out and I can't risk her guessing right and blowing everything up in the air.'

'Doesn't sound like her. She always seems so... passive.'

'There's another side to her, believe me – bloody scary!'

A discreet knock at the door and Maggie, the cleaner, looked in.

'Is it all right if I do in here, Mr. Harper? I've only got this room left and it's half past five.'

*

Jake cycled home, wishing he'd put on his waterproof coat to keep the wind from cutting into his arms and throat, and cursing any motorist who came within an inch of his pedals. The oncoming lights blinded him sporadically and he cursed those too.

He was in a foul mood.

As he skirted the pavement into his street, he had a horrible feeling that Catherine might be waiting for him at his door, and slowed the bike down to walking pace. He strained his eyes, looking for her car parked against the kerb, but that wasn't always a clue, because she sometimes walked. God, this was ridiculous. He couldn't even find peace in his own house.

For a moment, he thought he saw a figure at his gate, but whoever it was moved off and apart from a white van coming towards him, there was no movement in the street. Just the trees blowing and the wind stirring up dead leaves.

He shoved his bike into the hallway, made a hurried cheese sandwich, drank a glass of water – no time to make a cup of tea – and went back out again to his car. He had to go somewhere. To escape. The night stretched ahead of him in all its hopelessness and he couldn't face even one hour of it indoors.

He knew where he was going really. It was better than home. A place where he'd been on the edge of something so intense, so wonderful, an evening that was stamped on his mind like an indelible handprint. An evening he would never be able to forget. Even if he lived to be a hundred.

The bar at the Green Dragon wasn't crowded. It was early and the jazz upstairs wouldn't get started for some time. Still over an hour to go and he couldn't drink more than one pint if he was driving, so he stepped back into the alley and made his way to the shopping precinct. He'd feel better walking, keeping himself going. His whole body was tense; it wouldn't allow him to sit still, with nothing to do.

The town was quiet too. The shop windows were lit, brightness flooding out into the darkness, but it only made the streets look more deserted. It was cold and bleak and people with any sense had gone home for dinner, home to their families, to some peace after the working day.

But for him there was no peace. His thoughts wouldn't allow him that. So he tormented himself with questions he couldn't answer. He had no real idea of what her life was like, what she did with her little boy, who her friends were, how she was with her husband. He was on the periphery of her existence. While, to him, she had become his whole world.

School, now, was a way of getting through the day, not something he took real pleasure in. Colleagues who wanted to talk, he got rid of as soon as possible. He lived, like some besotted teenager, in a state of make-believe, one step removed from all the practical aspects of every day. It was like an illness he had no control over.

He'd read about this. Never thought it could happen to him.

Well. Now you know.

The clock in the square struck seven thirty, so he went back to the pub, bought a beer and took it up to the first floor. The musicians were warming up. Lovely sound – that discordant blend of notes, before they made a special kind of harmony – particularly the tenor sax. Jake had always promised himself he'd learn to play it one day.

He'd put his mobile on silent, but he felt it vibrate in his pocket and fumbled to pull it out, only one thought in his head. But it was too much to ask for.

Catherine's ID showed on the screen.

He looked down at the phone lying in the palm of his hand and, with slow deliberation, pushed it back into his pocket. He couldn't bear the sound of the thing, the feel of it, offering him hope and then irritation, pain and more pain. He downed what was left of his pint and walked over to the bar in the corner.

Sod it! He needed a real drink.

He took his time to choose, surveying the bottles of spirits standing in a row like toy soldiers against the rear glass, shades of amber and red reflected in a double image. The idea of drinking himself into a haze was comforting. He needed something to blur his mind. And a double Jack Daniels would certainly do that.

In the end, he didn't leave the stool by the bar. He listened to what seemed to him like distant music. Ah, yes, *That Old Feeling, Pennies from Heaven* and – how ironic, he thought, on his fourth drink – *You Go to My Head.* When the band members took their break and sauntered over to where he sat, he listened to them talk, nodding sagely, as though he was part of their world.

What a brilliant night, he told himself at the end of the session, making his way, unsteadily down the stairs and then into the cold night air. Which hit him with the force of a slap, and he stood for a moment in the alley, trying to focus, trying to remember which way he needed to go to reach his car. He managed to leave St. Peter's Square in the right direction and there it was, parked on the roadside, just where he'd left it. It took him by surprise. He pulled the fob out of his jacket pocket, tearing the lining with the prongs of his door key which was attached, and fumbled with it, hands cold and useless. He stared down at the gadget and pressed hopefully. No answering click of the door opening. Perhaps this wasn't his car.

A hand clapped him on the shoulder, firm and hard, pulling him off balance. And although he managed to stagger back up, he was too dazed to turn.

'Don't do it, pal. You're not in a fit state. You'll kill someone.' To Jake, remembering it later, the voice seemed to come from the sky, from some benign being sent to watch over him. Whoever it was pushed him gently down the road. 'There's a taxi rank just up there to your right. Get yourself home.' And by the time he managed to turn his head, the street was empty.

He carefully placed one foot in front of the other and made progress – slow and difficult, but he was moving. His head buzzed and his legs felt heavy, shoes catching on pavement slabs, so keeping upright required all his concentration. Street lamps danced and car headlights dazzled him, so he screwed up his eyes to help him focus. He'd passed the taxi rank before he'd realised it and he found he was heading out of the town, away from the lights, when his mobile vibrated again. He'd put it in his inside breast pocket and it took him a while before he worked out what it was.

Another call from Catherine. Another call he wasn't going to answer. *Go away, for God's sake. Just leave me alone. We're done.*

How he found his way home, he never knew, but some instinct sent him down unfamiliar roads and across junctions and into the home stretch, where he at last recognised street names and pubs and shops and his brain began to start up again, like a car engine that had been flooded and could now function.

At three o'clock in the morning he reached his door and clambered upstairs, lying fully clothed on the bed, his body exhausted yet feeling oddly lucid in his thoughts, determined that something just had to be done. He pulled out his phone and rang Catherine's number. Of course he knew she wouldn't answer – not at this hour of the morning, but what he had to say couldn't wait till daylight. He stared up at the dark ceiling, until the ringing turned to answer mode; then, closing his eyes all the time he was speaking, as though his voice alone would take all the responsibility, he left his message: 'I'm sorry, Catherine, really sorry, but it's no good anymore. I can't go on with this. I know you'll be upset but we're never going to make it. Find someone else, someone who... well, anyway.'

He dropped the phone onto the duvet and promptly fell asleep.

*

He woke with a start, his back stiff and his mouth dry, his mind coming to much more quickly than his body. The bedside clock read 8.30 and it was a school day. That was bad enough. But he knew there was trouble brewing much worse than being late for work. Something he'd done.

His hand knocked against the mobile lying on the bed and then it all came back to him The phone message he'd left for Catherine in the early hours of the morning. She'd have listened to it by now and there was nothing he could do about it. No good telling himself that, anyway, he'd meant every word, that he should have finished it months ago, that it was always going to end one way or another. But, God, to leave a phone message like that after a year with someone! That was crass. No, it was cruel.

He sat up and put his head in his hands. What a screw-up he'd made of it all. One thing leading to another and all going downhill. Like a row of dominoes falling, one crashing into the next and then the next in a horrifying chain reaction, the consequences – dire and irreversible - as inevitable as the pull of gravity.

And there was nothing, now, that he could do about it.

Chapter 30

It was a relief to sit in the warm familiar kitchen, an escape from the bitter wind and frosted ground outside. Amy sat with her elbows on the table, nursing a cup of tea in cold hands, with Harry, opposite her, munching away on chocolate cake, cut into squares, managing to eat with his good hand. Jasper sprawled at her feet, stretching his long legs under the chair. She felt more peaceful here. The family home. Being looked after, as though all those years of growing up, becoming an adult, hadn't made any difference. You could allow yourself to be treated like a child again.

'Your mum won't be long.' Her dad was putting the cake tin away and finding a Bonio for the dog and making them all feel welcome. 'She'll be back from the hairdresser's by eleven and we can have lunch. Cheese and ham toasties, eh, Harry?'

'Got to eat my cake first.'

'That'd be lovely, Dad,' said Amy, watching him. Such a kind face, she'd always thought, but somehow today, she found that kindness, so basic in his character, that consideration for others, touching. He could take offence, flare up at times, be obstinate, but immediately any slight would be forgotten. He'd been a father who was rock solid, she thought, loving them through all the ups and downs – and she hadn't always made things easy for him – but now, she felt an appreciation for the steadiness she'd taken for granted. He'd spared the time to take her and Sarah to the woods 'bird-nesting' (they never found anything remotely interesting), for a day out in Blackpool (and he hated fun fairs); he'd attended awful school concerts and bumped up their pocket money for some special trip and gone out in his car for them when they'd been stranded after missing the last bus home. How lucky she'd been. It was only lately she'd realised it. And he'd be embarrassed if she put that into words. It wasn't that sort of relationship.

She watched him as he ruffled Harry's hair. 'The panto was good then?'

Harry smiled as he ate, chocolate crumbs smeared on his cheek. 'It was Peter Pan – and he flew right over our heads. Mummy couldn't see any wires holding him up. And Captain Hook had a real steel hand.'

'Sorry we couldn't come with you. Visiting your great aunt Rene wasn't much fun. In fact, I fell asleep the whole bloomin' weekend.'

'Grandad. That was rude,' said Harry laughing.

'I know. But she never stopped talking. *And* I missed the football.' He turned to Amy. 'You spoken to your sister this week?'

'Yes. Seems fine. Much happier with it all now, isn't she? Just took some getting used to.'

'Don't know why she was so upset. However broke you think you are, you can always find ways to get by.' He sat down, watching Harry thoughtfully. 'Like this young man - he'll soon mend – young bones do. And he's not worried by it, is he? Just a nasty tumble.'

Amy sighed. 'They're an odd lot down there, Dad. Different in every way. No one's really interested in what anyone else does. Money's what counts. Robert fits in because he's done well and he's in a profession they think's admirable – but I don't speak about the newspaper, ever, because they see that as a bit sleazy – a weekly rag. Not *The Telegraph*. I'm a hack writing either trivial local stuff or making things up. The whole set up... well, it's not relaxing. You're on tenterhooks all the time. It's hard work.'

Her dad didn't say anything for a while. 'In-laws can be tricky. You're fortunate if you can fit in.'

'But what if you can't?' Amy sighed and shook her head. 'You always think, growing up, that everyone has the same home life as you – the same habits, the same relationships. You think that's the norm. But you soon learn how different we all are. And my God, the Wilsons are another species!'

Harry, bored with the conversation, rolled onto the floor to stroke Jasper, who lay on his back with his legs in the air to have his stomach scratched.

'Listen, they live miles away – you don't have to spend a lot of time with them. It's not a big deal unless you make it one.'

'No, you're right.' Amy made an effort to sound more positive. She didn't want her dad to see how oppressive it had all become for her. No good upsetting anyone else. 'I know Robert's mum's lonely, living in that big house with no one around – I should be kinder. Well, I try when I'm there, but she expects ...I don't know, she expects Harry to be Robert, or a version of him, anyway, and I don't want Harry to be... *tramlined*. She'd like to take over and mould him into a little robot.'

'You're fretting about something that may never happen, Amy.' He paused and scratched his head, leaving his white hair standing on end. 'Just live for today is what I do. You never know what's coming, so worrying about it is a waste of energy.' He took Harry's plate to the sink. 'Get on with life instead of analysing all the time. You'll learn when you're older and look back - you regret the time you didn't just live for today. And that time - you'll never get it back.'

It was as though a shadow had passed across his face and Amy wondered for the first time what it was he might regret, even now.

Perhaps everyone has a sense of missed chances and unrealised dreams that still linger, even when they seem to others to be settled, contented.

Amy had trouble swallowing. Suddenly, without warning, she felt a terrible sorrow for what she'd lost, what she'd thrown away. That last phone call and his words, 'If ever you need me...' Well, she needed him now. It was as though the longing was physical, a hollowness in her chest, one long ache.

She sat very still, staring at the kitchen notice board, with its array of postcards stuck haphazardly on to its surface. She was acutely aware of everything around her, but her mind was elsewhere, consumed by one thought. Just one thought. She looked across at her father and made an effort to control her breathing and appear calm. But what she had to do was so clear, so inevitable, somehow. Perhaps she'd known it all along.

One thing was certain, she thought, this time there was no turning back.

'Dad, I need a favour. I can ask Sarah, but it's rather short notice.'

'Go on.'

'Could you look after Harry and Jasper on Saturday? Robert's at a head office meeting tomorrow and won't be back till late Saturday evening and the paper wanted me to do an interview with this bloke who's moved to Kirby Lonsdale, so it means it'll take a bit of time. I could get it done in a day...' Even as she said it, she knew it sounded made-up on the spur of the moment. If her father knew it too, he showed no sign.

'Course, that's fine. You go. Why don't you let Harry stay the night? And you pick him up Sunday and stay for lunch.' They both heard the front door open and looked up. 'Your mother's here. We'll tell her what we've arranged. It'll give her a lift.'

'God, I'm such a shit! When did I get so good at lying?' The deceit in the

face of such decency settled on her like a dead weight – so much worse lying to a father who loved her. No questions asked. But there it was. A pull that was impossible to fight and not something she could begin to understand. All she knew was that she had to see Jake and she couldn't wait. She had to see him.

*

It was two o'clock when she drew up outside his house and quickly slipped the note through his door. There, it was done. If he could make it to the meeting place on the Saturday morning, then he'd be there. She barely considered whether he'd have anything else planned. It was as though nothing would stand in their way – no other plans or other people or responsibilities.

It just had to be.

*

She pulled into the car park, wheels crunching on the icy ground and turned off the engine, which hummed slightly as it died. An early morning mist clung to the trees on the far side by the fence, the branches pale and spidery with frost, untouched, as yet, by the slow-rising sun. It was as though the whole scene had been painted to create a backdrop, ethereal and ghostly, which added to the heightened sense of drama. She shivered.

Surely he would come.

She was conscious of each breath, each beat of her pulse as she waited.

Ten long minutes and no Jake.

All around her was still, the only sound a pheasant squawking as it flew over the country road she'd just left behind her. Nothing else. And just as it occurred to her, for the first time, that he might be angry with her and not want to start all the subterfuge and upheaval again, she heard a car slow down and turn in, pulling up alongside hers.

She got out and watched him come towards her, navy overcoat unbuttoned and scarf loose round his neck. His eyes – it always surprised her how dark and intense they were – never left her face. He didn't speak, just put his arms around her and pulled her close, his cheek cold against hers. Amy hugged him tighter and felt she never wanted to let go. *Just remember this,* she thought, *just remember how happy I am at this moment.* And yet, the voice of reason wasn't far behind, letting her know the craziness of it all, how unrealistic it was. How hopeless!

'I'd have understood if you hadn't come,' she said.

He cupped his hands round the back of her head and kissed her. 'Amy, I couldn't stay away if I tried.' She could hear the tremor in his voice, but then he smiled and pulled a face, his expression the diffident, amused look he nearly always wore. 'I have to say your instructions weren't too clear. D'you know how many turn-offs there are on this road? All leading to little square spaces where you could park? Four. I turned into four.'

She smiled back. 'Good job you found me then.'

'I'd always find you.' He held her to him and kissed her hair. 'Don't you know I'll always be close, waiting for you. That'll never change. You're part of me now, Amy. What I feel for you only happens once. I'm sure of that.'

Amy suddenly felt a terrible sadness for him – not thinking of herself for once. She wanted to reassure him, say something that would match his certainty, offer some commitment, but she couldn't. It was more than she could honestly give. So she hugged him again so that he wouldn't see the hesitation in her eyes, that awful sense she already had of betrayal. She wanted them to have a good day – one that was fun, that was light-hearted, without worrying about what was coming next or how wrong it was. What had her dad said? Live for today. Well, she was going to do just that.

She turned towards her car. 'I've brought coffee and toast in case we get hungry on the way...'

'To where? Where are we going?'

'The Lake District. We used to go there as kids and I've always loved it.' They climbed into Amy's car and she started the engine. 'Every June, we'd stay in a bed and breakfast place and explore different bits of it. Ambleside, Hawkshead. My favourite was Ullswater, because you could get the ferry back after you'd walked for what seemed to us like miles. We'll do that and have lunch in a pub, and talk. Does that sound ok to you?'

'It sounds wonderful. Let's go before we freeze to death.'

As she turned the wheel to navigate the car park entrance, she had the sense of an adventure stretching before them, not just a day out, something more, exciting and risky. Was that the attraction, she wondered? The old cliché of what's forbidden...?

The roads were empty as they sped across country, the view as they dipped into the first valley almost magical – snow on the hills, black ribbons of water running down the rocky escarpments, sheep scattered through the heather. She didn't want to spoil the atmosphere with small talk and Jake seemed comfortable enough sitting beside her, so she barely spoke.

She remembered it later as one of those days that's as near perfect as you can get. They walked on the rough, stony path round the dark expanse of water, ice at its edges, skirting the marshy ground and boulders, until they found a wooden bench, with a tiny plaque dedicated to someone long passed away. Amy took out the flask from her backpack and spread out the toast on a paper bag beside them.

'This is the only way to have breakfast,' Jake laughed. 'It beats bacon and egg in a warm kitchen any day.'

'I'll share it with you if there are no more wise cracks,' Amy said. 'Look, you've even got apricot jam on the toast.'

'A feast. You're a wonder! Just a pity you didn't tell me in advance where we were going and I'd have worn waterproof shoes. As it is, I now have webbed feet.'

'Stop complaining. Think how lucky you are to be here, with this view, no people around and the whole day ahead of us.'

Jake held up his metal coffee cup in a mock salute, his breath visible in the cold air. Then he reached out and covered her hand in his, so that she turned her head to look into his eyes, serious now and filled with emotion.

'I know how lucky I am,' he said. 'I found you. You don't get much luckier than that.' He leant forward and kissed her, so gently, she felt her whole body trembling. And they sat staring at each other, the only sounds distant, of branches creaking and birds calling as they circled over the water. There was nothing else except the two of them and any sense of time or reality had no bearing on who they were now. It was as though nothing else existed.

So this is how it should be, thought Amy.

They made their way along the shoreline, pulling on gloves and muffled up with scarves, wrapping their arms around each other, only letting go when the path became too narrow or they met a group of walkers. At times, they paused to look out over the mist that was now shrouding the hills and spreading a veil across the lake

Amy suddenly stopped She was narrowing her eyes and peering out over the water. Two swans were circling and dipping their heads below the surface, then performing slow balletic turns.

'Do you see that?' She pulled Jake over to look.

'Swans.'

'Yes, but do you see how one of them keeps lifting its head, then trying to loosen something hanging from its beak.'

Jake looked harder. 'No. I see two swans happily swimming in circles, enjoying life.'

'But look closer. That one has a long dark strip of something trailing down its neck. It's obviously caught in some sort of fishing line. Then it struggles with it underwater, but it's still there when it lifts it head up. It needs help. We can't just leave it like that.'

'Amy, how good is your eyesight?'

'Well, I'm wearing my lenses.'

'You need a stronger prescription then.' He laughed. 'Your swan is digging up food from the bottom of the lake and the thing trailing from its beak is pondweed, not a fishing line. So if you're going to call the RSPCA, I'll be long gone.'

'You're sure?

'Come on. They're having more fun than we are and I'm hungry.'

They trudged on, the path leading to a winding minor road, which was easier to walk on, sheep on the heather to their right and a few isolated stone shelters higher up on the hills, the tops hidden in clouds.

'There's something about this place,' said Amy. 'Even in the rain. It's so beautiful. Don't you think?'

Jake nodded. 'Yes, it is.'

Joining a rough pebbled path again, they began to feel the cold and quickened their steps as they neared the pub. It stood, surrounded by thin trees at the end of the lake, old and oddly shaped, its gables dark against the clouded sky. It looked as though it had been there forever.

They pushed open the heavy oak door into the heat and condensation of the bar; walkers crowded the whole room, jostling for a few inches of space, stripping off their waterproofs and damp coats, stamping their boots free of mud and talking over each other. To add to the noise, orders were being shouted for beer and beef sandwiches and chips, and trays passed from one to another over heads and around shoulders - there didn't look to be a square inch to stand, never mind sit down.

Amy looked at Jake. 'Even if we have to wait an hour for something to eat. I'm not leaving.'

They shoved their way through the crowd until they reached the back of the room, where a log fire was blazing in a huge old-fashioned grate, old ski shoes and poles hanging from the beams above it.

They smiled at each other, grateful for the warmth.

Jake went to the bar and ordered two glasses of mulled wine and sandwiches. There'd be a wait, the barman said, so he carried two bags of crisps back to where Amy had found half a bench free. He squeezed in beside her and looked around the room, his face ruddy and still wet from the droplets that had fallen off the trees. His expression seemed to reflect his surroundings - the good-natured atmosphere, the high spirits of the walkers. He looked content.

'What are you thinking?' asked Amy.

He didn't answer for a moment. Then he glanced away from the crowd and met her gaze. She would remember that look for a very long time. Bright and optimistic, as if a promise had been given. And when he spoke, he seemed to be measuring his words.

'I don't think anyone could be as happy as we are now.'

She had no answer. So she touched his cheek with the back of her hand and nodded.

He went back to the bar to collect their lunch and Amy pulled off her jacket and scarf, rubbing her hands together to warm them. She'd lost sight of him in the crush of people and began to wonder what was taking him so long. She sat, unable to think beyond the moment. Let what happens, happen, she thought. You have to live when you get the chance. Who says what's right or wrong, anyway? When he edged back to their bench, balancing a little tray with the glasses of warm red wine and sandwiches on it, he was smiling. As though he had a secret.

Amy took a sip of the wine. 'I'm driving. I can't have any more of this.'

'I'm staying,' said Jake. 'I've got a room for the night. Ok, a cubby hole, but still, it's a room. I'm not going back tonight.'

Amy looked at him. 'You know I can't stay. I have to be home by seven at the latest.'

'Well, we have four hours then.' He lifted his glass of wine. 'Cheers. To us!'

'You're a devious one, d'you know that?'

'Yes, and you're welcome to come and share my bed? If you want.'

She laughed, bemused. 'How will you get back?'

'I'll get a train tomorrow and Andy'll pick me up.'

She shook her head. 'Won't you be missed?'

'Who by? It'd only be Catherine. And to be honest, I don't want to be in the house right now. It's finished but she won't accept it. It's getting a bit much. Worrying, really.' Amy looked sceptical. 'You've no idea. She tries to corner me at school, rings me, knocks on my door, leaves notes, all the stuff that makes me want to run. So I'm staying here out of the way.'

'Poor girl,' said Amy. 'She's in love with you.'

'I can't do it, Amy. I can't pretend any more. Not even...' he didn't finish. 'Anyway, I get my room key at one o'clock. If you want to come up and inspect my accommodation, you're welcome.' And he sat back and munched his sandwich and grinned at her. 'Eat your lunch.'

*

It was a box room, tiny, the bed so narrow it looked like a child's cot, the ceiling low and slanted down to a leaded window, which barely let in any light. But it was theirs for the afternoon. They could hear the hubbub of voices and laughter from the bar below but as they shut the door behind them, the little room seemed like a sanctuary. No one could harm them here.

They fell on the bed, limbs entwined and began to undress each other, slowly at first, then with a hunger that couldn't be satisfied, until both were naked, warm skin against warm skin, enfolded in the curves of each other's body. Like coming home, thought Amy. So different this time, they were equals, her desire matching his, the release of every inhibition, losing thought. Somehow sensing, without knowing, how to move, to give, to feel. They came together as one. Amazing.

Afterwards, they lay on their backs, arms wrapped round each other, Amy's head on his shoulder. She shifted on the pillow, pulled her plait from under her neck, and lifted herself onto her elbow to look into his eyes.

'Jake, you're lovely, do you know that?' she said.

He raised his eyebrows, amused at the idea. 'Men aren't lovely.'

'Well, you are.' She kissed him. 'You really are.'

A chill had settled on the room, so they pulled the eiderdown over themselves and drifted, close and comfortable. The only sound their slow breathing. It was like being cocooned, Amy thought, held in a protective shell that no one could breach.

Time must have passed because when she was wakened by a clock striking five in the pub below, the room had grown dark. They dressed hurriedly and went down the stairs into the bar, where the fire had died down and the room had emptied, apart from two old men playing cribbage. The steamer had left an hour ago, they discovered, so Jake phoned for a taxi to take her back to her car.

It was strange, sitting, waiting, knowing that in minutes, she had to go, leave what she thought of, now, as their safe haven. They didn't speak, just held hands, until they heard the car horn and went outside. She gave him a brief kiss and climbed into the back seat of the taxi, which took off before she had time to put on her seat belt.

As the car threaded its way back along the lakeside road, Amy looked out at the shadowy blackness of the countryside, not wanting to go. She closed her eyes, listening to the wind picking up as it blew through the valley and the swoosh of the tyres on the country road. Then they rounded the lake and came to the village with its street lights and stone houses and closed shops, a few people hurrying along, muffled up against the cold.

How on earth am I going to act as though nothing has changed, as though I'm the same person I always was, as though this deceit is something easy to pull off? Unless I'm very careful, I'm going to damage everyone around me and I'm afraid. And I've a right to be.

But when she entered the house, and had turned on all the downstairs lights and poured herself a gin and tonic, she vowed not to worry about consequences anymore.

She was home now.

And this, however difficult it had become, was the real world.

Chapter 31

At seven o'clock in the morning, Catherine took shelter under two large trees which lined the road. The same spot she'd found last night. Almost opposite his house but enough of a safe distance to see and not be seen. It would be another three quarters of an hour before it got light and lifted the traces of fog which hovered close to the ground, blurring the edges of the buildings and gateways; there was no way she'd be noticed in the gloom. But, just as she'd done last night, she'd put on a navy raincoat and a navy woollen hat, not only to keep warm, but as a kind of camouflage. She knew if she told anyone what she was doing – certainly if she told Rosie – they would say this was going too far. But at least she wasn't sitting in her room crying about it, taking it lying down; at least she was *doing* something, taking the first step to finding out what was going on. And she was determined to get to the truth. He hadn't been honest with her, *that* she knew. There was more to this than he was saying.

When she'd woken up to hear that phone message, those awful words, so cruel and spoken without a hint of apology *'I can't go on with this',* she'd had a panic attack. Fighting for breath and feeling her chest caving in, she'd resorted to scrabbling in her bedside drawer to find her pills, tearing open the packet and choking one down without water. And it was a school day. She'd have to go in and teach. She couldn't do it. But she must see Jake. She'd listened again to the voicemail on her mobile and tried to work out when it had been sent. Obviously after she'd gone to bed. Perhaps he'd been drunk and regretted it. Perhaps he'd be feeling sorry now.

Or perhaps he wouldn't.

She strained her eyes to focus more clearly on the house. It stood dark and empty, as it had last night. She could see the curtains hadn't been drawn and there was an empty space at the gate where he usually parked his car. So he hadn't returned at all.

She was fairly certain he hadn't gone home to Leeds.

She felt bile rising in her throat and swallowed. The last two weeks had been hard enough, but this was too much. The last straw. Everyone at school would soon find out; gossip spread like wildfire in the staffroom. They'd pity her. They'd know what had happened and realise what a fool she'd been, thinking it was serious when that wasn't how Jake had seen it. And her father...she found she was whimpering and caught her breath.

A car door shut and headlights lit the street, so she moved further back against the hedge. She mustn't be seen. She felt humiliated. And desperate. He couldn't just ditch her like this. She hadn't given him any reason. All she'd ever done was care for him, be the sort of girlfriend he wanted, willing to fit in with his life, his friends.

So what had changed him?

She gritted her teeth against the cold. There was someone else, there had to be.

So she watched. And waited. The damp seeping through the soles of her thin boots and her shoulders aching, but she had to stay. Her nerves may be on edge and her mind whirling round with frightening thoughts, but she was determined, now, determined to find out the truth.

She wasn't going to give him up without a fight. She loved him.

It was Sunday, so there was no early morning traffic on its way to work. The street was quiet, just a paper boy on a bike, stopping at a few houses before he disappeared round the first corner. Catherine couldn't decide how long she should wait. He might not come back till late and she couldn't spend the whole day, standing under a tree in the damp. Someone was bound to notice her. She felt anger building up inside her, sudden, all-consuming anger. He'd put her in this impossible situation. She'd a right to be furious. Then, a moment later, all that anger was swept away and she wanted to weep and weep... and reach out to him, do anything to make him realise the mistake he was making.

That morning, after hearing his phone message, she'd got into school early, aware she was driving too fast as she pulled through the school gates, but anxious to be there, ready for when he arrived. But what could she say? She had to make him explain, but in private, not in the staff room where everyone would hear their conversation and pretend not to.

Trying to look busy, she'd gone to her pigeon hole to collect any messages, then sat down to read them. Or try to. She'd concentrated on the door, her heart beating fast and her hands making the slips of paper that she holding, damp.

Eight forty five and no Jake. He'd arrived late, looking dishevelled and stood, his back to the wall, through the last items in the breakfast briefing. It was only when the bell rang for lessons and they were all trooping out the door that she'd managed to catch up with him.

'I need to talk to you, Jake,' she'd whispered and saw him half turn away, so she rushed on. 'I'll come to your office at break.'

He'd nodded and given a weak smile. *He's ashamed*, thought Catherine. *He was drunk and he's ashamed of what he said. That's something, anyway.*

And she'd felt easier in her mind as she went down to the PE department.

272

*

The morning after that fateful voicemail, they'd sat in his office facing each other, the space left between the desk and the bookshelves so confined that their knees were almost touching. He'd looked shattered, she thought. He hadn't shaved and he had circles under his eyes. Well, he should have thought about what *she'd* been through since she'd got that phone message. She wasn't going to feel any sympathy for *his* suffering.

The moments stretched out into a silence – uncomfortable. Almost tangible. She had to break it.

'Were you drunk when you rang me last night?'

He'd rubbed one eye in a tired gesture. 'Yes, I was, but that's no excuse for leaving you that message. To tell the truth, I barely remember doing it.' He held up his hand to stop her interrupting him. 'But I meant it, Catherine. I'm just sorry I didn't tell you face to face. It wasn't kind. It wasn't a kind thing to do.'

She'd put out her hand to his, but he pulled back and shook his head slightly.

'It's not like you, Jake. You aren't cruel. I couldn't believe that you'd...'

'Catherine. I know you're hurt, but I can't go on pretending it's all right or that this relationship is going anywhere. I don't feel enough for you and you deserve better...'

'What on earth does that mean?'

She'd watched in panic at he looked away and started fiddling with a pencil on the desk. Her breath came in short bursts and a band was tightening round her chest. Fury came frighteningly fast.

How dare he! It sounds as though he's rehearsed it all.

'What a cliché!' Her voice rose in anger. 'Is that all you can say after a year... a year when we've been happy and almost *living* together? *I deserve better.* I really do!'

'We haven't been almost living together. We've dated, we've spent the odd weekend with each other, but it's petered out...'

'Petered out?' She stood up, heart pumping, her face red and pinched as she spat out the words. 'And what if I was pregnant...?'

He looked stricken and she was glad. Let him think about *that* possibility.

'Catherine, you're not. You can't be.' He'd gone white, his whole face drained of everything but horror. He was paying attention now. Well, good.

'I was sick last week. If you'd been around, you'd have noticed.'

He seemed to be searching for words, but none came. He just sat there, staring at her, obviously trying to comprehend what this would mean to their *relationship*. Well, let him take it in. It'd make him think before he just walked away.

He'd closed his eyes, then, after what seemed to her a long time, opened them and almost whispered, 'I don't know what to say. I really don't.'

She'd looked down at his bowed head, the dark curly hair, the hands she knew so well and she couldn't bear to see him in pain. She wanted to hold him close and comfort him, knowing all the time that *she* was the cause of this anguish. She'd wanted to hurt him and now she couldn't bear it.

She took a deep breath. 'No,' she said, finally. 'I'm not pregnant. I wish I was. I dearly wish I was.'

And she saw what she thought was gratitude on his face, an expression of old she recognised as fondness. His whole body relaxed. And whatever he might say, she was sure he still cared for her. He was just frightened – of being too involved, of tying himself down. She could understand that.

'I'm so sorry, Catherine. I wish things could be different.'

But she wasn't going to listen. She could change his mind, she was sure of that. He just needed some time.

A knock came at the door, startling them both. They looked at each other, almost guiltily, Jake's expression like a man about to be hanged. She gave him a watery smile.

'It'll all turn out ok,' she said, quickly. 'You'll see. We'll be all right.'

*

But however much she'd wanted to believe it, they weren't 'all right'. Jake avoided being alone with her at school and when she'd gone round to his house on the following Saturday morning, he'd been kind, but firm. It was over. She'd rather he'd been angry or impatient with her, but he just seemed tired, as though he could barely summon up enough energy to talk, let alone have an argument.

She'd gone to quite a lot of trouble to look her best, curled her hair the way he said he'd liked it, put on a pale blue jumper with a collar, black skinnies and her favourite body warmer – no running gear or headbands – she'd even found some perfume that she'd always thought of as a bit heady.

It had taken her some courage to knock at his door. He wasn't expecting her, and she wasn't sure of the kind of reception she'd get. But although she couldn't tell what mood he was in when he saw her, he'd nodded and led her down the passage way. They sat at his kitchen table, drinking coffee like they'd done so many times before. But she knew this was different. The atmosphere was different. She was a visitor.

She drank slowly and made small talk, about school, about a girl they both knew, anything to prolong the moment when she'd have to leave without anything really being said. Anything to give her hope that there was still a chance.

She searched his face for some sign, some indication of what he was thinking. But his expression was blank. Finally, she couldn't hold back any longer. 'I've sent you four texts and you didn't answer any of them.'

He sighed, then. 'I didn't know what to say, Catherine. Other than what I'd said already.'

'But you could have told me you'd got them.'

He stood up. 'This is pointless. We could go over every conversation, every day from the time we met, but it wouldn't make any difference.' His voice was unsteady, she thought. But his expression was set - cold, uncaring. 'I can't pretend to feel what I don't feel. I'm sorry you're hurt. I wish...well... that it could have worked out. But it hasn't. And it won't.'

She could feel the tears welling up and allowed them to fall, looking up at him the whole time. *See what you're doing to me. You should have some pity, be ashamed. At least show some emotion.* Laying her head down on her arms, she gave way to sobs that wracked her whole body.

'I don't want to live without you,' she managed to say between gulping breaths.

'Oh Catherine, don't be silly. You'll meet someone else. I'm certainly not worth all this.' He stood rigid behind his chair, not even leaning forward to comfort her. 'Please stop crying. Don't do this to yourself.'

And so it had been useless. She'd had to leave. Pleading had got her nowhere.

That week dragged on. She managed to get through the lessons but she knew she looked ill. Pretending she was getting flu had to be her excuse. It was January, so no one thought anything about it. But, how slow the days were. She could turn to no one. She had always pretended to Rosie that the relationship was solid and anyway, she could guess what the advice would be – *better now than later, 'good riddance', you're better off without him.* Glib remarks that she couldn't bear to hear. She'd always been so private about her and Jake. But she needed comfort from somewhere. She wanted someone to talk to, someone who'd understand and she couldn't think of anyone other than Tony. He'd always shown her nothing but kindness. He'd be there for her.

So on Wednesday night she found herself in the only place where she felt really at home. The Youth Club — loud, dysfunctional, demanding. But where she was wanted, sure of a welcome. And she needed that now.

It was fifteen minutes into the evening session when she arrived. Moving through the groups of youngsters, she tried to put on a cheery face for the ones who turned towards her, but it was a struggle and she looked to see if Tony was in the office. Not yet. He was setting up a darts game and didn't see her come in. But Lucas was there by the office door, standing separate as usual, in his own world, a still figure in a room full of animated vibrant bodies. He watched her as she crossed the room, leaning against the wall as he often did, shoulders hunched, eyes hooded, surveying all before him. When she was about to pass, he met her gaze and nodded his head very slightly. As though to say, 'I've been waiting.' She wished he'd go away. She knew it was silly but he unnerved her, this evening of all evenings, when she was feeling so down and already off kilter. She didn't want to talk to anyone but Tony. But there the boy stood, those eyes too intense somehow — pale, staring, blinking so slowly it looked unnatural. Like a chameleon she'd seen once in a nature programme.

She nodded back to him and he smiled. *Really,* she thought, *what's the matter with me? I should know enough about kids not to judge by appearances. He's a kind, unhappy boy who's probably as lonely as I am. Ok, perhaps he's on something to keep his head above water, well, join the club. That makes two of us.*

She side-stepped past him into the office, switched on the kettle and hoped Tony wouldn't be long. She could tell him all about the whole sorry affair. He'd always seemed to understand her. He was used to dealing with trouble. And she was in trouble.

He came blustering through the door and stopped as soon as she turned towards him. 'What on earth's the matter?' he sounded horrified. Good, she thought, someone who realises how desperate I am. She let the tears fill her eyes and Tony put his hand on her arm, gentle, concerned. 'You look... you look dreadful.'

'Oh, Tony. I *feel* dreadful. I shouldn't have come but I didn't know where else to go. It's such a terrible mess. Everything's fallen apart.'

He put out his arms and she was grateful to be hugged, grateful there was someone who cared enough to comfort her. The relief of sharing it all made her let go and cry. There was no one else who'd bother, she thought bitterly. He kicked the door to close it behind him and held her for a few moments, then stood back to look her in the eye.

'So?'

She sobbed, unable for a moment to get her breath. 'It's all over.'

Tony sighed and shook his head. 'He's finished with you, hasn't he?' He sounded half weary, half angry. 'I knew he would. Catherine, he's never cared for you the way you cared for him. I could see that. When you kept saying everything was fine, it wasn't, was it?'

'No,' she wiped her tears away with the palm of her hand. 'I so wanted it to work out. And for a long time, I thought it was... you know... going ok. Not perfect, nothing ever is, is it? We weren't really talking much. Just a patch, I thought, just being too used to one another. But the last few months, oh, Tony... it's been so difficult.' She sniffed and looked away. 'I... I think he's met someone else. And I've no idea who. But there's somebody, I'm sure.'

Tony hesitated, his expression full of concern. 'And what's he said?'

'Nothing, except it's over. It wasn't working out. Telling me to find someone else. He sent me a text – that's how he finished with me... A text... I can't believe he'd be that cruel.'

'What a bastard!'

'I think everyone on the staff must know. I can barely get up the courage to go to work. It's a nightmare.'

'I'll bet it is.' Tony shook his head and hugged her again. 'He never deserved you, Catherine – always had that arrogant air about him, as though doing anything for you was an effort. Condescending shit! Well, you might not think so now, but you're better off without him, believe me. You've got to forget him...'

'Oh, that's so easy to say.' She drew away from him and sat down on the only chair in the room. She didn't want to hear platitudes, meaningless advice that wasn't really advice she had any intention of following. 'I love him, Tony. And some of this is my fault. I should have tried harder. Been more... I don't know... more keen on things he liked. And I was too slow, when we started to drift apart, to realise there might be someone else. Why didn't I face things? Have it out with him? Even when I went round to his house one night before Christmas – it was getting late and I knocked on his door – and it was odd. He wouldn't let me in. Said he was sleeping and hadn't heard me. Which wasn't true! He *must* have heard me. And he sent me away. He could have been with her that night. I'm certain, now, he was.'

'Who is she, then? Haven't you any idea?'

'No, I haven't. Not someone at school, I'm fairly sure of that.'

Tony shook his head. 'I don't suppose it matters who it is, Catherine. If it's over, there's not much you can do. Take comfort in the fact that you're not married, no kids involved, you can make a clean break. Go to a different school if that's what you want, but he's the past. You feel awful now, but it's a lucky escape...'

'Oh, Tony, who wants a lucky escape?'

He seemed to have run out of things to say. And she knew there was no help coming. How can you explain to someone else the pain, the pit of despair that you feel when you know there's no going back? When there's no way forward either. She felt horribly alone.

There was a banging on the door. Tony was needed. He had to go.

Catherine made her way out into the main hall. She felt unable to stay. She couldn't act normally, as though nothing was troubling her. Enough of pretending. Her mind full of her own sorrow, she took no notice of Lucas, standing close to the office door, head down, apparently concentrating on a picture on his mobile.

Neither did she notice how his eyes followed her across the room, eyes that gave away nothing.

*

Troubles never come singly, she thought, as more problems arose at school adding to her misery.

She'd made a mistake on some department paperwork that the office had picked up on. Something she could have corrected, but Mrs. Partington had already taken the offending sheets to the head. Tim had called her in. 'You need to concentrate, Catherine,' he'd said, his tone quite stern for him. 'You mustn't let your private life impinge on your job.'

She blushed and bit her lip. This was embarrassing, humiliating. So even *he* had heard what was going on. Of course, everyone knew.

He picked up a folder as though he'd finished and wasn't going to say anymore, but he stopped and looked at her knowingly. 'You've got this Cordon Hall trip in a couple of weeks' time, Catherine. And there can't afford to be any... slip-ups. Are you sure you feel up to it?' She was shocked he'd asked and didn't have time to reply before he went on. 'Is it all organised?'

She lifted up her head and set her jaw. 'Yes, of course. The parents' evening is set for next Tuesday and all the transport and accommodation was booked in November.'

'Good. But if you're not feeling up to it, Heather could go in your place.' He drummed his fingers on the desk. 'I know the staff there do all the instructing, but... well, with activities like abseiling and kayaking, you've got to be particularly vigilant.'

'Of course. I always am.' She forced herself to smile. 'I'm fine, Tim, really. Just had a bit of flu. But I'm fine now.'

But as she walked out of his room, she realised she hadn't sent out the consent forms or checked on the bus company. She'd do it before the end of the day.

No more mistakes.

She stood, now, in the cold morning air, chilled and disheartened, watching. The silence in the street seemed to flood her eardrums. Unnatural. No sound of voices or traffic to break the covenant of isolation.

She turned away, down the street, already planning her next move.

She was on her own. So be it.

Chapter 32

'Have you found it, Robert?'

Amy was calling up the stairs as he rummaged in the bedroom drawers. What a time to break the cord on his phone charger. It wasn't like him to be careless. He'd been trying to carry three things at once and dropped his mobile, the weight of it breaking the attached cable and losing the one function it was needed for. And he was due to leave at eight for a two-day conference in London.

So where was the spare? Tucked away so long ago, he couldn't remember for the life of him where it could be now. He had fifteen minutes before the taxi arrived to take him to Piccadilly and it was time to be methodical. He'd start with the drawer in the small table on the landing, then work through all the ones in the main bedroom. Amy was sure there was nowhere else they'd have put it.

After four precious minutes, he'd been through all the drawers except for the small pine cupboard on Amy's side of the bed, and in what he considered to be a last hopeless effort, he'd kneeled down and pulled open the hinged door, pulling out everything inside – old newspaper cuttings, tubes of cream, contact lens boxes, some nail files and... a mobile connector and cable. What a relief! He sank back on his heels and looked at the bedside clock. He had seven minutes before the taxi came.

It was as he was pushing the clutter back into the cupboard that he saw it - tucked away in the back corner, a blue paper bag with a silver logo and printed on the side, Liverpool ONE. He took it out and held it in his hand, not sure whether he should open it. But curiosity got the better of him and he lifted it out and began separating the layers of tissue paper, pale blue, flimsy under his fingertips, until he uncovered a small toy rabbit dressed as a little old man, even down to glasses on its nose. Like a Christmas decoration, but too big to hang on the tree. Was it a present? Surely not suitable for Sarah's baby. And when had Amy gone to Liverpool? Certainly not recently, to his knowledge.

He was wasting time. He quickly put it back where he'd found it. He'd mention it later. Odd, though, that it was tucked right at the back of the cupboard behind all the other stuff.

He shoved everything back as best he could, picked up the cable and got to his feet. And as he made his way down the stairs, he heard the impatient beep of the taxi.

Amy came into the hall, with Harry darting close behind. 'Did you find it?'

'Yes, eventually. In amongst a load of odds and ends.' He kissed her cheek and snatched up his coat and overnight bag.

'I'll ring tonight. Might be late.'

'Ok.'

Turning to Harry, he bent down and stroked his head. 'Be good.'

As he climbed into the taxi, he looked back at the two of them standing in the doorway. A strange feeling that he couldn't quite explain made him keep them in sight until the very last moment. He felt he should have said something else before he left. Something more meaningful. He was never good at expressing his feelings - in business, fine, but not in an intimate way - and he was aware of what was lacking now. A few perfunctory words as he hurried off were not enough. There was a sense of a missed opportunity

But as the car sped down the road, he shrugged it off. Ridiculous. He was regressing into a needy adolescent and he found it distasteful. He'd always been self-sufficient and if his confidence was having a wobble, he couldn't think of a good reason why. What he was comfortable with were facts, numbers, solutions, not intangible thoughts that threw you off balance. He was the first to admit that he had always shied away from emotional closeness. Not so much with the children – it was easier with them. You had a responsibility for their well-being. But with Amy? With Paula? He'd fallen short in their eyes, he knew that. He could never think of what he should say. Even in the closest moments, he didn't know what they wanted to hear. And if he managed to come out with words that he thought would be tender, they sounded false – as though he was making something up to fill the moment. Which he probably was.

But then, so much is learned behaviour that's difficult to undo. Growing up as an only child in a house that required discipline and duty, above all else – there certainly hadn't been much laughter and family fun – he'd missed out on the love and warmth he'd seen in Amy's family. Where everyone seemed to live easily together, shared the same memories and understood each other without analysing how it all held together. Without much effort. It had all seemed a bit chaotic when he first met them, but it made him aware of what he'd never had the chance of experiencing.

It was when Amy had finally persuaded him to meet the whole family ('In one fell swoop' was how she'd put it) that he'd realised how pervasive was the influence of one's childhood. She'd been so sure, now they'd got this far – he'd separated from Paula by then - that they'd accept him. 'Once you see how they are, you can stop worrying.' And he *had* worried. He was so much older than her, his divorce hadn't come through and he was hardly what they would be expecting. Were his intentions honourable? However old-fashioned that sounded, he imagined that thought would be running through her parents' minds. So that first meal with the Middletons was an eye-opener, in more ways than one.

'It'll just be a barbecue. Not a bit formal,' Amy had said, her arm through his as they walked through Manchester on a warm day in June. They'd been to the travel agents to decide on their first holiday together and she was excited about the whole novelty of it. Crete in August. Robert had protested that they'd be fried alive at that time of the year, but Amy had fallen in love with a hotel in Agios Nikolaos and wouldn't let anything put her off.

'You must meet them all before we go away,' she'd insisted.

'All?' Robert could hear his voice rising at the prospect of being thrown in at the deep end. Before he was quite ready.

'Well, my parents and my sister and her family. And perhaps Freda, my mother's friend, who always seems to be invited to everything that's going at our house.' She bowed her head. 'For me. Do it for me.'

'Oh, Amy, I think we've been through enough over the past few months. Couldn't it wait?'

'Please, Robert.' She smiled up at him, eyes wide, expectant. She was irresistible, he had thought then. Even though he knew he was being manipulated, he wasn't capable of denying her anything. 'My mother will find you as charming as I do. There's no need to be nervous.'

'Amy, I'm not nervous. I'm trying to manage all this with some... decorum.'

'I know. But we're not going to tell the local paper. Who'll know? Just us.'

And, of course, he'd gone. Stepping over the threshold of the Middleton house with mixed feelings – a sense of betrayal to the past twenty or so years of his life, and a sense of commitment to the new one. He wanted to make Amy happy and he knew how much her family meant to her. They had to welcome him in, even though they might not actually approve of the situation.

Her mother had come out of the kitchen and hugged Amy, then held out her hand to Robert. 'Really good to meet you at last,' she'd said, deciding suddenly that this wasn't good enough and putting her arm round him, shepherded him into the lounge. 'We've only just lit the barbecue and it takes ages to get going. So you've time to have a drink and meet everyone. They're in the garden and luckily it's not raining, although the forecast wasn't good.'

Robert realised after a few minutes that everyone was more apprehensive than he was, but as the drinks flowed and the steaks were cooking, the atmosphere relaxed. It helped that a small child and a toddler diverted attention away from him and, listening to Amy's father and Dan discussing cricket, they could have been any group of people, long familiar with each other, with no undercurrent to bely the genial mood. It turned out to be much easier than he'd thought. No one mentioned the circumstances –at least out loud - or the difficulties their relationship had caused and - he had to admit - was still causing. He was taken into the fold with the in-jokes he didn't understand, the banter that brought good-humoured laughs and the kindness of them all.

Or so, he thought.

There was one moment which unsettled him. He wasn't meant to have overheard the comment, but that didn't make it any more palatable. He had come through the French windows from the garden to pick up some glasses, and was looking round for a tray to carry them on. He heard someone speaking quietly in the hall and realised it was Sarah, Amy's sister, who'd gone into the house to wash the baby's hands. Of course, it was about him and as she spoke, he couldn't move away.

'Well, he's charming, I agree, but he's… oh I don't know, kiddo… he's sort of aloof – detached somehow. I hope you know what you're doing 'cos he's very different from you.'

'It's the first time he's met you all, Sarah. It's a bit of an ordeal considering what's happened. You're expecting too much.'

And he picked up as many glasses he could get a grip on and moved quickly out of the lounge before Amy came through the door and realised he'd heard.

But it shook him.

As they were leaving and Amy was going round the group, slightly drunk, kissing everyone, her mother gave him a hug and looked at him in a way that meant some advice was coming. 'You'll get used to us, Robert. The thing is we're almost too close. If one of us is in trouble, we all feel it. And we don't want this to go wrong after… well, after what you've both had to face already.' She took a breath. 'I don't think you're a man to take anything lightly, so leaving your family to be with Amy must have been a huge decision. But what I need to know is that you'll look after her. She's just, well… very young.'

He didn't know what to say, so he just smiled and nodded and, in his embarrassment, wanted to escape. They were a wonderful family, but he wasn't used to this sort of openness. He remembered wondering, when he was alone with Amy that evening, how things would work out. They *were* so different, Sarah had been right about that. And he could see how much Amy was an extension of them all, a part of a closed network he could never wholly belong to.

He was brought back to the present with a jolt, as the taxi suddenly jerked to a stop at a zebra crossing, throwing him forward, and banging his head against the side of the cab.

'For heaven's sake, drive more carefully,' he shouted.

'Sorry, sir. That old man suddenly decided to cross. One minute he was walking along, the next on the zebra. Sorry about that.' The taxi driver didn't sound at all apologetic, just flippant, Robert thought.

He didn't want to go to this conference. He felt a sudden weariness that he'd have to shake off if he was going to make any impact with the presentation he'd been asked to deliver. Life seemed to be wearing him down. Couldn't be a middle-aged crisis, could it? He'd never believed in such things. But he was certainly losing some of the confidence of his youth – something he'd always taken for granted.

*

The call from his secretary came just as he'd closed the door to his hotel room, glad to be on his own at last after a day of talk and more talk, hand shaking and manoeuvring. Needing to make an impression. Or that's what it had felt like. One more day to go. It was five o'clock and he'd been thinking about opening up the mini bar and downing that miniature bottle of whiskey before the evening meal. At least *that* would be less formal, thank goodness, than the day's proceedings. And the complementary wine helped. Everyone was more relaxed and forgot to be constantly on guard.

But the unfamiliar burring sound of the hotel phone stopped him short.

'It's Sue,' she sounded breathless. 'Sorry to ring you this late, but you weren't answering your mobile.'

'No. I'd put it on silent. What's the problem?'

'Lattimers have been on and John says you were dealing with it, so I thought I'd better get in touch before tomorrow.'

'Couldn't this have waited till I got back?' He couldn't keep the irritation out of his voice. 'Go on.'

'They aren't happy with the audit, Robert. In fact, they're quite upset...'

He didn't want to hear any of this. 'Look. Tell them I'm back in the office on Thursday and book some time for them to come in. I'll sort it out then. I can't do anything over the phone. That'll have to satisfy them.'

And he put the phone down before she could answer. Before he lost all patience and said what he really felt. God, was he sick of all the weight falling on his shoulders. Sick of worrying about everything. He needed a drink.

He opened the mini bar, emptied the whiskey into a plastic cup he found in the bathroom and downed it in one. He pulled off his jacket and hooked it over an armchair that had seen better days. Nothing helped to lift his mood. Amy hadn't even picked up the call he'd made earlier in the tea break; it'd had just gone to voicemail and he hated talking to a machine. It didn't help that the room was like a cell, situated on the eighth floor of a tower block – square, beige and functionary. It had the smell of something closed off from the air for too long – musty and dry, with dust particles floating in the artificial light. A television screen dominated one wall and the windows looked out onto the walls of another concrete building. There was no way to open them, even if you'd wanted to.

He lay down on the bed and stretched, not even bothering to take off his shoes, and closed his eyes. He needed to sleep, just for half an hour.

He wasn't aware he'd drifted off until he woke with a start, and, confused for a brief moment, he couldn't think where he was. But seeing the time on the bedside clock, he realised he had only ten minutes to shower, dress and get downstairs for the dinner at seven thirty.

He could hear the buzz of conversation as he walked towards the private dining room on the second floor, and hoped he wasn't too obviously late. Taking a cocktail from the tray by the door, he made his way in and stood, sipping his drink, with no desire to join the small groups that had gathered near the long dining table. He just hoped he'd struck lucky and they'd seated him next to someone undemanding, someone who wasn't going to play one-upmanship or, worse, slurp their soup.

In fact he found himself next to a smartly dressed woman in her forties, who leaned over and held out her hand, a warm smile reaching her eyes and deepening the lines round her mouth. She was certainly someone you'd notice, he thought, as he settled into his seat. Dark brown hair cut short, with strands curling onto his forehead and at the nape of her neck, bright green earrings that dangled and caught the light. Not what he'd expected.

'Hello,' she stressed the last syllable, which made him think they must be renewing their acquaintance. But he couldn't remember seeing her through the day. 'Robert, isn't it?'

'Yes. Have we met earlier?' He was sure he'd have remembered.

'Not actually met. No, but I was in the audience this morning. I'm so glad I've got the chance to tell you how impressed I was with your lecture.' She nodded her head to emphasise her words. 'It was the only analysis that made sense all day. So thank you for that.'

Robert flushed and busied himself with his napkin. 'I thought I'd bored everyone to death,' he said, half laughing. 'Good to know *someone* understood what I was on about.'

'*I* certainly did.' She touched the name tag pinned to her collar. 'I'm Abi, by the way. From Hale and Gamble in Bristol. I usually try and get out of these conferences - they can be an awful waste of time. Well, sometimes.' She took a sip from her glass of water. 'But occasionally, someone lights the place up. You're from the north, aren't you? I think they mentioned that in your introduction.'

'Manchester – well, Cheshire really. Have a medium-sized office there.'

'A pity.' She gave a rueful smile. 'That came out all wrong. What I meant was, a pity you aren't further south. We could do with someone like you round our way.'

And for the first time, in a long while, Robert felt happy. Pleased that he'd made an impression, that he'd done something that was appreciated. It lifted his spirits more than it should have done, he thought later, but at least the evening might turn out to be enjoyable after all.

As they waited for the wine orders to be taken, they chatted about the deficiencies of British Rail, the choice of venue, their past visits to London. He barely noticed the man to his right. Abi seemed to demand all his attention. He found he was telling her about how he'd started with one of the big accountancy firms when he was studying for his Chartered. And how he'd doubted at one point whether he'd succeed.

'Well, you must be one of a rare breed,' she said. 'When I started in auditing, the whole profession seemed to be full of over-confident young men who were good at bull-shitting. When I met anyone new, I'd never admit what I did for a living. I didn't want to be associated with that type of swaggering egotism. But then you learn a bit about human nature and realise no-one's really *that* sure of themselves.' She gave him a quizzical look. 'Although I thought perhaps you were.'

Robert raised his eyebrows, surprised at how direct she was. But he liked her for it. 'No. I put on a good front. The older I get, the less certain I am. Particularly about people. I used to think I was a good judge of character.' He shrugged his shoulders. 'Now...'

'Now... what?' She cupped her chin in her hand and held his gaze.

He paused. 'Just a feeling. That you never really know anyone. Not totally.'

She didn't reply. Just nodded her head slightly and looked away. It was unlike Robert to question whether he'd said too much, he usually said too little - about personal feelings, anyway – and he wanted to get things back on a more formal footing. So he started to ask her opinion on how the latest government measures might affect investments and the indicators for a downturn in the markets.

All safe stuff. And earlier, it had been the sort of conversation he'd been hoping to avoid.

The service was surprisingly slow and there was an atmosphere around the table of restlessness as the first course hadn't arrived. Most had had a few drinks already and were not prepared to wait too long before complaining. Voices grew louder. The man who'd organised the event stood and left the room to find out what could be causing the delay.

Abi, impatient as everyone else, pushed back slightly from the table and leaned towards him. 'Let's take a bet on the meal,' she said in a conspiratorial tone. 'My guess it'll be smoked salmon and prawns, chicken in a sauce no one could possibly recognise, followed by sticky toffee pudding. What are you going for?'

She was so close, her cheek almost brushed his shoulder and he wasn't sure how to respond. How to take her at all. One minute earnestly discussing serious issues, objective and focussed... the next, creating a sense of intimacy between them based on fifteen minutes of meeting. What had seemed like a pleasant chat between colleagues had suddenly turned into something else. And he wasn't sure what. He was glad that, at least, the wine had been poured and resorted to emptying half his glass, just as the young waiter was putting a plate of asparagus and parma ham in front of him.

'There, you see,' Abi sighed. 'Wrong again.'

There was an ironic cheer from the diners as they were served at last, which Robert considered bad taste, and he said little as the next course was brought in. He filled up their glasses from the bottle of Merlot closest to them and the evening began to take on a more relaxed, congenial mood, as he felt tiredness creeping through his whole body.

Abi talked and he was a good listener. He learned about her college days, her parents' expectations, the neighbourhood where she lived now, her passion for tennis and the films she'd seen. Suddenly, she stopped and looked at him closely.

'Here I am chattering away and you've told me nothing about yourself.'

'Well,' he said. 'What do you want to know?'

'Anything,' she smiled to encourage him. 'You're married. Do you have children?'

He twisted the wedding ring round on his finger. 'Yes to both.'

'How many?'

He hesitated for a fraction of a second. No point going into all the intricacies of his complicated life at this point. 'Four. I have four children.'

'Well, make sure you don't push them too hard. They'll end up doing something they don't really enjoy. I'd have loved to have gone to art school. But that wasn't *academic* enough.'

'I suppose we're all under one sort of pressure or another. Money, expectations, what we feel we have to live up to. But what's more worrying... the eldest girl, Holly, she's seventeen and studying for her A levels - she doesn't need me to push her – she seems to be doing that all by herself. To the point where it's wearing her out.'

'Yes, it's a difficult age. They need plenty of support and sensitive handling in their teens. Good for you for caring. I'm sure just showing some understanding'll be enough.' Then she laughed. 'I sound like a guidance counsellor, don't I? It's all fake.'

Robert waited for more questions, but none came and they drifted into a companionable silence. It was good to talk to someone who didn't know anything about him, not really, who saw him in a completely different light. And liked him. That wasn't what he was used to. Disapproval seemed to have followed him around for too long – from his mother to Paula, to Amy and even at work.

Someone banged on the table with a spoon to announce the speaker, who stood with an air of importance and a promise that he wouldn't talk for too long. Robert nodded his head. He'd heard that before. He was finding it hard to concentrate and hoped they'd hurry up with the coffee so he could stay awake.

When it came time to leave the dining room, they walked out together and stood at the bottom of the stairs. There was a moment of hesitation. A sense of unfinished business hung in the air.

Abi gave him a tentative smile, moving aside to let a woman pass. 'Do you want to go to the bar for a final drink? It's not so late.'

Robert didn't immediately reply. He shuffled his feet, looking past her to the groups filing out of the dining room and wondered how to answer without seeming boorish. 'I'm sorry, Abi, but I need sleep. I'm tired out and, believe me, I've had enough wine for one night.' He knew it sounded abrupt. 'I don't mean to be rude...'

She laughed, a gentle, kindly laugh and he was glad he hadn't offended her.

'You're not rude at all,' she said and leaned up to kiss him on the cheek. 'Anything but. You're just a really nice man. And you know something? Your wife's a very fortunate woman. I hope she knows that.'

And with that, she left him.

Back in his room he lay on top of the bedcovers, the sound of the television coming through the wall from next door. Funny, he thought, eyes closing and a headache starting, Abi had liked him for what she believed he was. How could she know all the entanglements that made up his life, that the woman she'd referred to as 'fortunate' was not his first wife, that he'd abandoned three of his children, that he wasn't the kind, thoughtful man she'd assumed he was.

Perhaps he'd been right earlier in the evening. Just a throwaway remark, but close to the truth. *You never really know anyone.* You might think you do, but… we all only show what we want others to see. There's always something to hide.

But he'd drunk too much to be kept awake for long. In minutes, he was fast asleep, snoring peacefully.

Chapter 33

The door, slamming shut behind them, echoed through the house. The hallway was dark, but Jake didn't switch the light on till he'd reached the kitchen. The heating had gone off at nine, so there was a chill in the room but neither of them noticed.

'He knew, Jake. He knew.'

'You're reading too much into this, Amy. I could have been anyone – a friend, another reporter on the way to covering a story. A councillor from that meeting. Christ, someone you'd just bumped into.'

She had reason to be upset. He'd been shaken, too, but one of them needed to stay steady and think. He watched, helplessly now as she paced round the small kitchen, knocking into one of the chairs and shaking her head as she walked. She stopped suddenly, hands clenched, rocking slightly, her eyes fearful as she looked at him.

'I've only seen him once or twice. Picking Robert up from the squash club... I should never have asked you to meet me tonight. Why on earth did we go into that bloody M & S food place? It was crazy! This was bound to happen...'

'Jesus, Amy. Calm down.' He tried to put his arms round her, but she stood, her body rigid and unresponsive, her fingers covering her mouth, her eyes never leaving his. She looked so pale, so fragile. So unlike her. He had no idea what to say to comfort her, but he tried anyway.

'Listen, he knows nothing. What could he have seen? We were just buying some groceries. We might have just met in the shop. By chance...'

'We had one basket. Between us.' She glared at him. 'Wine, French bread and cheese. What would that tell him?'

'God knows. Nothing, probably. He's not clairvoyant. He can't *know* anything...'

She tossed her head in annoyance. 'Oh, come on, Jake. He made a point of coming right up to me. Close. That questioning look when he said my name. Introducing himself as though he was a long lost friend. And then that smirk on his face when he said it was *so* nice to have seen me.' She was talking fast and all Jake could do was let her vent her anger on *him*. 'He could have been there for a few minutes. Overheard everything we said. I wouldn't have noticed.' The anguish in her voice cut through him. 'What did we say in that bloody shop?' She broke away from him and started pacing again. 'Oh, God! What an idiot I've been. How did I think no one would ever see us.'

She sat down at last, elbows on the table, staring in front of her.

Jake tried again. 'Amy, whatever he thought, or heard, why would he say anything? What would be the point? People aren't that malicious.'

But she wasn't listening.

*

They'd arranged to meet on the street outside the council buildings at seven, when Amy's stint was over covering the latest Housing Committee Meeting. Jake's car was being serviced so he'd caught the bus into Stockport and was now waiting impatiently near the main entrance, shuffling his feet to keep warm. The time ticked on and it was half an hour before she came down the steps, fastening the ties on her coat and trying to get past some council members, who were carrying on the discussion from inside.

As soon as she joined him, and they'd turned down a side street, she slipped her arm through his and laid her head briefly on his shoulder before heading for the car park. He was ridiculously happy to have her beside him again, chatting away, walking along like any ordinary couple. Except they weren't. It had seemed a long time since the Lake District. Ten days *was* a long time when everything depended on hearing her voice, listening to her news. Knowing she still felt the same. Phone calls weren't as frequent as he'd have liked, but, well, her life was more complicated than his.

He stopped himself from expecting too much.

What made them pull in at that roadside convenience store as they drove through Hazel Grove, he'd never know. But Amy was hungry and he knew there was nothing to eat in the house that she'd fancy.

'Just stop here,' he told her, as he spotted the lights. 'This place is always open. I'll get some bread and cheese and some crisps. Would that do?'

'Perfect.' And as he opened the car door, she unclipped her seat belt and joined him on the pavement.

'You'll buy the wrong sort of cheese,' she smiled. 'I'll guide you.'

'How much choice do you think you'll get in a shop like this?'

'Well, you never know!'

And they'd walked in together, one basket, a walk down one aisle and up another. Deciding which cheese to buy, surveying the shelves of wine... Jake didn't notice the man until he crossed over and stood in front of them. In front of Amy, with a puzzled frown and a tilt of his head. As though trying to work something out.

'It's Amy, isn't it?' A smile on his face. A question that wasn't really a question.

Jake tensed, feeling his stomach turn over. Who the hell was this?

Amy said nothing. Just stared at him.

'Nick.' The man kept smiling. 'We met a couple of times outside the squash club. When you came to pick your husband up.'

'Yes, of course,' Amy nodded.

'Well, nice to see you again. Give my regards to Robert. We seem to have lost touch.' But he didn't move. Kept standing there for too long, looking at them both, as though making up his own scenario, Jake thought. Making two and two add up.

When he'd moved on, Jake could hear Amy breathing fast and shallow as they moved to the check-out. She was trying to walk as slowly as she could, but left Jake to pay for the food and wine and went out to her car standing by the pavement. He didn't know quite how to avoid further problems, but decided it would look worse if he didn't join her.

'Just get in and drive away,' he said. 'He can think what he likes, but he'll have a job to make anything of it.'

So they opened the car doors without looking back, waited for a gap in the stream of traffic, and drove slowly away.

*

The bread and cheese lay unopened on the kitchen table. The wine still in its paper wrapper. There was an uneasy quiet throughout the house. Jake and Amy sat on the sofa in the front room, the only light coming from the kitchen, which filtered down the hall and spread faint patterns on the carpet. He'd drawn the curtains and they sat, arms round each other, lost in their own thoughts. Jake didn't know what else to say. Any attempts at reassurance just made her angry and he could understand why.

She turned her head towards him. 'I shouldn't have taken it out on you. I'm sorry.'

He hugged her closer. '''Love is never having to say... '''

He sensed her smile in the darkness. 'What a load of crap! And the film was crap too.'

'Made a lot of money!'

'Ah. Well!'

They drifted into a more comfortable silence, her body warm against his and he was thankful that she hadn't just dashed home in a panic and left him alone, unable to share the worry. Far greater for her than him, he was well aware of that

He stroked her hair and kissed her forehead.

He was responsible for all this. He found himself thinking about the first time he'd seen her – this lovely girl in her high heels, off on holiday, looking forward to... well, a life she'd chosen anyway. So bright and confident, so full of fun. She'd been happy, at least. And he'd made the first move at the Marathon, and the second, outside the church hall. And on and on, bringing her down to this unholy mess. Perhaps the moment he'd first seen her, he'd envied her in a way. She'd seemed so certain of herself. She hadn't been drifting like him. And he'd filled what was empty in his existence with her. How selfish that was he could see now. Too late, of course. Too late for guilt to make any difference. He'd shifted the ground under her feet, upset the status quo and this was the outcome. Had he wanted happiness for her as well as for himself? No, he hadn't thought anything through. He'd just obeyed his instincts and damned them both.

It was a sobering thought.

'We've never danced,' Amy said, her voice quiet and sad in the darkness.

'No, we haven't. But I can certainly fix that.'

He pulled himself up and went into the kitchen, finding what he wanted – the second track on the John Coltrane CD –*'You don't know what love is'* – and when he got back to the room, Amy was standing, waiting. They held each other, circling slowly, not really dancing at all, barely moving their feet, just keeping time with their bodies, with the haunting notes of the music, slow and melancholy. It was as though they were shutting everything out, Jake thought, closing themselves off from the world beyond these walls. A forlorn hope, so sad, because they knew it couldn't be kept at bay. It never could be. A line from Gatsby came into his mind, the moment when everything is lost... *And only the dead dream fought on as the afternoon slipped away.*

Oh, for heaven's sake! He closed his eyes, irritated. *I've read too many books.*

So Nick, the man in the shop could be the reason this would end. It was always the small things that scuppered you, however hard you tried to avoid them. Circumstance. Being in the wrong place. At the wrong time. The trouble with life, he thought, it was too full of practicalities. They didn't just get in the way. They could come from anywhere and floor you. You never knew where or when they were lurking. He seemed to have learned nothing from thirty-odd years of living.

He held her tenderly, the rhythm swaying their bodies and keeping them close. Amy rested her head on his shoulder and he felt a weight of responsibility towards her. He was causing her such distress, in fact, putting her in danger. You couldn't be careless about that.

He must let her go, even though it would break him. He swallowed and tried to speak but he couldn't bring himself to hear the sound of the words. He felt sick at heart, not wanting the music to end, not wanting to face what he had to do – say what he knew he must – words that would lose him the one person he'd remember the whole of his life...

The CD began playing the third track and Jake pulled back and gently took her arm. He led her into the kitchen and turned the music off. He needed a clear head and the light on.

'Sit down, Amy. I need to say something.' He pushed the forgotten groceries to one side and took both her hands in his. She stared at him, eyes unblinking, ready for bad news.

'I think,' he began, 'for your sake, we should end this. You're risking too much and it's not worth all the worry and the... pain. I pushed my way into your life – didn't think about you or your family, your little boy... just thought about myself. Now it's time...'

She put her hand up to his mouth. 'Stop it, Jake. I'm just as much to blame as you. I could have pulled out at any time, and I didn't. No, it isn't a decision you can make alone. We're in this together.'

'Ok.' He nodded, slowly.

'Are you regretting this?'

'Hell, no. That's the last thing...'

'Then, be honest. What do you *really* want?'

He rubbed the back of his neck and narrowed his eyes. 'Me?' *Not so easy to be completely honest.* 'I want you to be happy and you're not. You're scared and I don't blame you. If I thought you'd leave Robert and come to me, I'd fight like a... well I'd do anything to have you with me. But that's not on the cards. Is it?'

She looked down. 'No.'

A siren wailed in the distance as a police car chased through the streets. Then it was silent again. He was trying so hard to say the right thing, for her, for himself, but he wasn't sure what that was. So he said nothing. Just looked at her as she sat at his kitchen table - sorrow in her wide eyes, the downturn of her mouth, the slight frown. Despite all the noble words, he willed her to want him enough to carry on.

She steepled her fingers under her chin. 'I think I over-reacted tonight... I panicked and that's not like me, I know.' It was almost as though she was talking to herself. Working it all out. 'He might have meant nothing by it. Just recognised me and what...? Said hello. Naturally. Anyway, whatever he thinks he's seen, he's hardly going to say anything to Robert about seeing me in a shop. And if he did, I can explain it away. I was buying food, for heaven's sake. It's not as though we were in a bar.' She leant across the table and put her hand over his. 'I'll stop worrying.'

He wanted to say something as reassuring but he couldn't pretend the same confidence now. It was as though their earlier reaction to the situation had been reversed.

She stood up. 'I must go. You made me leave the car so many side streets away, it'll take me five minutes to find it.'

He smiled. 'I was being cautious. A bit late, I know. It's called shutting the stable door...!'

'Listen. I'm all right.' She straightened her shoulders as she walked along the passageway, pulling her coat off the hook as she went. Jake wondered whether she was acting brave for his sake and loved her all the more for it.

As he let her out of the front door into the cold night air, he couldn't help feeling he'd had a reprieve - a sort of stay of execution - that there was still a future he could hold on to. But for how long? What was the likelihood that some other chance meeting might bring everything crashing down on their heads?

Chance was so damned precarious.

*

Morning briefings had become more and more difficult. It was the one time in the day when Jake couldn't just sit in his office and escape. He had to join everyone else in the staff room and that meant Catherine seemed to be watching his every move. She sat far enough away from him with another girl from PE, but there was no doubt her gaze constantly sought him out with an intensity that he found unnerving. Even worse, she looked ill. Her face had become gaunt and her naturally small frame, angular and bone-sharp. It was as if an accusing finger was pointed in his direction, righteous and unwavering.

He was thankful that Jenny, dizzy and talkative as ever, kept him up-to-date with English department news and gossip, whenever Tim paused in his announcements. She, at least, didn't seem to notice any discomfort, or she was wise enough to ignore it. He'd noticed before that she'd never had much time for Catherine, who'd always been hanging around waiting for Jake to finish talking business. And Andy behaved as he always did, casual and good humoured. Jake was grateful for them both.

'Catherine, you wanted to make an announcement.' Tim was waving some papers at her, encouraging her to stand up. Jake was suddenly awake.

She stood, always nervous when she had to address a large group. 'Could you remind all the pupils in your tutor group who are going on the Cordon Hall course next week that we have a meeting in the hall at twelve forty today. I'll be checking consent forms from parents, so it's really important that they attend. If anyone is absent, could you let me know. Thank you.'

'It'll be a good experience for them, Catherine and I appreciate that a number of you are giving up four days of your half term holiday to do this. I'm sure it'll be well worth it.'

She sat down, blushing at Tim's praise and Jake breathed again. What on earth did he think she'd been going to say? He was getting so bound up in himself that he didn't seem to be noticing ordinary, everyday happenings. He'd even forgotten his father's birthday last week, and couldn't remember the last time he'd sat down and discussed sport or the latest films with Andy. Or anything important. He was like a teenager, everything revolving round himself. Bloody sad at his age.

'And just one more thing.' Tim was winding up with a minute to go before the bell. 'You've got this week before we break up. Keep them on their toes till last thing on Friday.'

'Meaning...' Andy said in his ear as they herded out of the staff room,' keep *us* on our toes. No slacking off.'

Jake grinned. 'Quite right. Some of us are a bit distracted.'

'You can say that again.' Andy stopped at the bottom of the stairs. 'Are you OK?'

'I'm OK. Really. Things are good. Let's hope it lasts.'

'Just watch out for yourself.' Andy frowned and shook his head, then turned down the corridor towards his classroom. Jake looked after him, wishing now he hadn't bared his soul to anyone, even a good friend. He didn't want to see this whole story through another's eyes. There would always be judgement, clear sightedness; when you're emotionally involved, it does away with all that. No wonder they say Cupid's blind. You just love. Full stop.

Jake liked it better that way.

At break time, he made his way to his office, with the usual encounters as he passed through the building, taking a poem from a hopeful pupil for the magazine, admiring 2nd year Beverley's new glasses, confiscating a mobile phone. Something comforting and normal about being part of school life, a cog in the wheel. And his sense of well-being lasted only as long as it took him to open the door and reach his desk, where he saw the letter. Placed on top of his papers. His name written neatly on the envelope. In Catherine's handwriting.

God, what next! This is never going to end.

He sat, not wanting to pick it up. But he knew he'd have to read it. Better knowing what was going on in her head, than guessing what was coming next.

The envelope contained a blank sheet of A4; behind it was another sheet with a blurred photograph printed on it, obviously taken in near darkness because it was difficult, at first, to make out the details. But Jake, in a horrible moment of realisation, saw that it was the front of his house, the front door, his car parked to the left of the gate, the streetlight nearby.

'Christ, I'm being watched. I'm being bloody *stalked*!' He couldn't take his eyes off the photograph. He looked carefully at the windows, one light in a bedroom but the curtains were drawn. Nothing to see. Just this awful, hazy, camera-gaze picture in the night, predatory and terrifying.

One thing was certain, Catherine wasn't giving up. She wasn't giving *him* up. But what on earth did she hope to gain from this? His everlasting love? It was crazy, absolutely crazy. Should he pretend he'd never seen it, shove it in the bin and forget about it? But that didn't solve anything. He had to deal with Catherine face-to-face, tell her to stop before... then another thought struck him. Had she taken other photographs? Ones which would cause much more trouble, photographs which would be a disaster for Amy? He could hardly breathe. What a bloody nightmare!

How he got through the afternoon, he didn't know, but he managed to finish the last lesson and be out of the building by 3.45, even before the buses were loaded. Something he never did. He wrenched his bike from the sheds and cycled towards the school gates, feeling exhausted with the sheer effort of pushing down on the pedals. All he wanted was to get away from the deluded mind responsible for sending him that photograph, from the malevolence that was closing in on him.

He manoeuvred gingerly round a few people standing in his way at the entrance, a mother with a push chair, a hooded, pale-faced teenager, an overweight grandad in a long overcoat who stood stubbornly in his way, making him brake. He heard a shout behind him, and not even caring whether it was someone calling his name, he picked up speed and rode as fast as he could until he could hear nothing but the wind in his ears and his breath coming in short, gasping pants.

But even home wasn't a safe place anymore.

Chapter 34

Amy didn't expect it. Even when she heard the thud of the car door closing and the key in the latch, she wasn't ready for the anger in Robert's voice as he called her name. He hardly ever came home at lunchtime. Driving into Manchester and back once a day was bad enough. So the shock was instant.

She came down the stairs, keeping her pace steady and her face expressionless. What on earth...? But he didn't wait for her to say anything.

'Why would you be so stupid?'

He was brandishing a newspaper – her newspaper – and glowering at her, his face carved in grim lines and his eyes furious.

'This article. With your by-line. Supporting Marie Wallace. All that guff that she's been spouting for the last year. And you're backing her up with the same arguments, the same pie-eyed logic and false accusations... and you've made sure your name's on it.' He threw the paper on to the floor. 'It's not even well-written.'

Amy was trying to catch her breath and work out why he was so angry. They'd had a few disagreements before over some of the topics she'd written about, but civilised discussions. Nothing like this. She walked down the last two stairs and picked up the paper. It was folded already at what was obviously the offending page, and she stared at the headline.

ARTS CENTRE TO BE SOLD FOR HOUSING.

She shook her head. 'I wrote this months ago. They wanted an opinion piece and I thought this was important. They'd already made plans to close the library... This isn't something I wrote this week, Robert.'

'What the hell does it matter *when* you wrote it.' He seemed to tower above her and she instinctively shrank back. 'Your name is on it.'

The way he was acting put her immediately on the defensive. She was damned if she was going to be shouted at when she couldn't work out what all this was about. There was more to it than he'd said already, obviously. 'Yes, exactly. *My* name.'

'And it's not the same as mine?' he said, sarcastically. 'For heaven's sake, Amy. This looks as though I support that left-wing do-gooder, whose sole aim is to disrupt everything the council tries to do – when they put in more stringent methods to save money, when they cut any services that aren't needed...' He stopped and snatched the paper from her hands, the inside pages falling to the floor. 'She hasn't even been elected by anyone. She's a self-promoting loud mouth who likes publicity. Just because she was once a two-bit actress...' He was looking at her for some explanation, which Amy wasn't going to give. Not in a way that would satisfy him, anyway.

Then she found herself nodding slowly, at last beginning to work things out. 'And this is so important because...?'

'You know damn well why!' He glared at her. 'How many of my clients – and many come from round here, from this neighbourhood - will read this and draw the wrong conclusions about where I stand? How many of our *acquaintances...?*'

'*Your* acquaintances, Robert. *Your* well-heeled social circle. Let's be honest here.'

The expression on his face should have silenced her. But she was angry now – angry enough to fight back, never mind the consequences. She knew the rows they'd had in the past, although not many, always left an underlying distrust of one other, a questioning of where they stood, not just in their relationship, but where they stood out there, in the whole moral spectrum. And it set in a wariness, a drawing back from confronting the fault line that would widen if examined too closely. Better to step round it and pretend.

But Amy had gone beyond reason. She could feel her face growing hot and her heart beating faster; only her voice was steady. 'It matters more what people *think* than anything else, doesn't it, Robert? Fitting in, having those traditional views that mustn't be challenged, not upsetting this comfortable world by saying anything controversial. Because then, we'd lose influence, we'd lose money...'

He cut in. 'Well, I know who'd be bloody upset by that! Amy, my dear, if ever there was someone who liked what money buys, it's you. Oh, yes, you talk a lot about social justice, supporting causes, caring about the underdog, but what do you do about it? Nothing. You sit there and write your pieces from the comfort of this house, the luxury of financial security...'

She laughed, hearing the harshness in it. 'Christ, we're coming to that, are we? I now have to be grateful for being kept in this prosperous way of life by my husband. The only thing is - I must stay silent. My opinions may embarrass him. Not sure what you call that way of thinking?' She sniffed. 'Victorian comes to mind.'

Robert dropped his head. 'You know I didn't mean that.'

'Well, that's what it sounded like.' Amy pushed past him to make her way to the kitchen. 'Must get on with the cleaning and the cooking. Don't want to upset the master any more than I have already.'

It was a few moments before she heard him leave and had time to regret some of the things she'd let fly. But she'd meant them. And it was too late to take them back, even though there'd be tension for days unless she made the effort to show some remorse. At this moment, that wasn't what she had any inclination to do.

She stood at the kitchen window, willing herself to calm down, Jasper pushing his large head against her thigh, sensing something was wrong. She stroked his ragged, silky ears and spoke quietly to him. But she couldn't shake off the feeling that she'd reached some sort of watershed moment. It was as though she'd gone too far, as though there was no turning back. She passed some minutes, staring out at the garden, the bleak scene with its bare branches, the flattened grass and wintry sky matching her mood.

And she thought about Jake.

*

The afternoon had been long. She'd managed to put her energies into typing up a brief news story and sending it in to the Sub Desk, immediately turning off the computer in case there were any amendments they wanted her to make.

And she'd arrived too early at the school gates.

But as soon as Harry came running towards her, his reading book swinging from his hand in its plastic case, she'd only been able to think of him, his wide smile when he saw her, the unquestioning love he surrounded her with. How could she think of messing up his world?

So they'd shut the front door against the cold and Amy had managed for a while to shut out what she didn't want to worry about any more.

She put another log on the wood burning stove, even though the room was too warm already, finding it comforting to see the flames flickering behind the glass door. There was something about a real fire that took her back to her own childhood – Monopoly played in the front room on winter Sunday afternoons, with her father reluctantly drawn into a game he hated, complaining every time that it always went on too long.

She settled back into the double chair, pushing Harry's legs over and lowering her shoulder so that he could nestle his head there. They were watching 'The Incredibles' – they had seen this so many times, Amy could repeat most of the dialogue, but it was Harry's favourite and he never seemed to tire of it. Now he watched, totally focussed on the screen, as though it was all new.

Amy loved this time of day in the winter. School over, just the two of them, such easy company, speaking in a sort of shorthand only they could fully understand, the same afternoon routine as yesterday. And the day before. *Is it because he's so young and so part of me,* she thought, *that it's as close as I'll ever be to another human being?*

The curtains were drawn against the darkening afternoon and it would be two hours before Robert got home, so it felt as though this air of lazy enjoyment would go on and on. But she was being self-indulgent. Harry had already brought home a problem she had tried to make light of.

He'd been eating his boiled egg and toast fingers when he'd stopped and looked up at her with a serious face. 'Today...'he took a swig of his juice.

'Yes?'

'Today, I got something wrong.'

'Ok. I do that often. What did you get wrong?'

'Well, we were playing this game... and we MIME...' He'd spoken slowly as though trying to remember exactly what happened. 'You do this with your hands when you're telling the class something. Or you show them by doing it.'

Amy tried to follow. 'Show them what?'

Harry screwed up his face. 'I'm telling you what.'

'Start at the beginning. Did Mrs. Baker ask you to do something?'

'Yes. On Tuesdays, we do NOUNS. They name things.'

She nodded.

'So I thought of a NOUN. And she told me to go to the front and show everyone.'

'And you chose...?'

'Sitting. I chose Sitting. I MIMED it and Bryn said CHAIR and Harriet said KNEES and no one got it.' He looked at her, bewildered. 'When I told Mrs. Baker it was SITTING she told me that was wrong. It was a VERB... But, Mummy, it's a name of something, isn't it?'

He'd stopped eating and Amy looked at his small, unhappy face and could have cried. What a stupid idea to teach 6 year olds this list of rules that wouldn't mean anything to them until they could at least read properly. What use was that? It wasn't like learning tables. It seemed to Amy as though it was destroying any enjoyment in words before the kid had left the infants. Christ, it got her so annoyed.

She took a breath. 'Yes, Harry, it *is* a naming word in a way. But it's also a DOING word.' She pushed back his hair. 'Eat your tea. Don't worry about it. We'll read that new book you got at Christmas at the weekend and work it all out from there.'

He smiled again and she wanted to keep him smiling, so she pulled *The Incredibles* from the shelf under the TV and put it in the player. 'Dash does loads of things wrong and it always turns out all right. Doesn't it?'

And he'd forgotten about it, she could see, as soon as he became absorbed in the story playing out in front of him. She wouldn't tell Robert about it. It was hardly the right time. Anyway, he'd probably think Mrs. Baker was quite right and the rules had to be followed, no matter what. Whoever made them up!

*

They'd parked their cars in the long, narrow lane that wound its way down to the river, driving past the Norman church with its crumbling walls and overgrown foliage, past the small cemetery, along the rutted dirt road, right to where the track ran out. Three o'clock on a dank February afternoon, deserted as Amy knew it would be.

She'd rung his mobile, something she didn't like doing, two days after the row with Robert. She wasn't going to tell Jake about any of it, but just being with him would steady her, make her feel less alone.

He didn't ask many questions, listened mostly. He was happy to hear from her, she could tell, as though he'd been waiting for that call all day. Yes, he could meet her. Yes, he'd find the place.

Not that there was much time. She had just over an hour while Harry was at a birthday party, but it would have to do. They'd arrived almost at the same time. She'd pulled into the lane and saw his car moving slowly in front of hers. *He never lets me down,* she thought. *Never. And I don't deserve it, this...constancy.*

Jake climbed out of the car, pulling up the collar of his anorak and opened her door. 'Perfect timing!' He reached over and kissed her. 'God, it's good to see you. Even if it's only for ten minutes.'

'Well, we've got a bit longer than that.' For a moment she thought she was going to cry. Understandable really, she thought. After the last tense few days, any sign of affection would have been enough to make her unravel. She straightened up, as though bracing herself. 'Come on, let's get going.'

They clambered slowly up the bank onto the towpath, the river swirling below them in furious eddies, stripping the coarse brush from the banks as it swept along. Heavy rain clouds, dense and low, darkened the hedges and the wind was bitingly cold.

Jake laughed as he stumbled over some rough ground. 'Only you would pick a place like this in a storm. I should never listen to you, Amy.'

Amy stretched out her hand and pulled him up onto the bank. 'Think of the good it's doing you. Better than sitting watching another box set and becoming a lounge-lizard.'

'Ha! Who says!'

They trudged along the path, hanging on to one another as the earth became slippery and treacherous in parts, lowering their heads as the weather worsened. The rain came horizontally now, biting into their faces, and even though they were almost shouting, their words strung between gasps, the strong gusts tore them away.

'Good thing I left Jasper at home.' Amy pushed wet strands of hair off her face. 'He's such an idiot, he'd be in that river and we'd end up drowned, trying to get him out.'

'Well, I couldn't cope with you *and* the dog. He sounds as crazy as his owner.'

'Believe me, he's far worse!'

They struggled on for a few minutes longer, barely able to stand upright now against the force of the wind, and Amy was thinking of turning back, when she spotted some splintered wooden boards, standing on lower ground, the remains of an old shack. It was tucked against the hedge, no more than a lean-to, and it was certainly doing that, but it offered some protection from the weather. They half fell down the bank and huddled, gratefully, in its shelter, slowing their breathing and smiling at one another, as though on some adventure.

'We're mad,' said Jake, shaking the rain from his hair. 'We should have stayed in the car.'

'I know. But it's nicer here.'

'Be better in the summer – sun shining, sitting on the river bank...' Jake coughed and shifted his weight, pressing his back against the struts. 'God, I wish I'd never smoked. It's telling on me.'

'I didn't know you had.'

'As a teenager, to look cool. Then gave up when I started teaching. Couldn't afford to do both.'

'When I was sixteen, I went to Creamfields - you know, the pop festival – and smoked cannabis. Felt *so* adult. My dad would have killed me if he'd found out. We do some silly things when we're young.'

He said nothing for a while. 'There's so much we don't know about each other.'

'It's perhaps just as well. You might change your mind about me. Sometimes, I look back and cringe. I certainly don't deserve to be happy.'

'I don't think it's anything to do with deserving. Most of the time you're shuffling along, not even aware what being happy is. Then you find out and it's so unexpected it knocks you off your feet and you realise how, for years you've only been half-living. You get the measure of it and everything else pales in comparison.'

'God, that's deep!'

'Sorry,' he was smiling. 'A bit of a philosopher these days.'

The thought left them with nothing else to say, but Amy found comfort in his willingness to share what was in his mind - not something practical - something considered, something insightful. She felt close to him that had nothing to do with being physically near. They seemed to have found an affinity which she would never have believed possible. Such a rare thing.

But perhaps she stayed quiet for too long.

'Come on, Amy. Something's happened.' He put his arms round her, the wetness of his coat slick and cold against her cheek. 'You didn't ring me like that for no reason. What is it?'

She tried to think of what to say. Some things just couldn't be solved, however much talking you did. Some things were better not said. For a moment, she felt a lot older than him.

He sighed in a way that showed his impatience. He wasn't going to give up. 'Amy, come on. You can't keep everything bottled up.'

'It's not like that, Jake.' This was so hard - she was not going into some detailed account that would leave them both ragged - separated by their different existences. 'It's... I come with a load of baggage. Hardly need to say that, do I?' It wasn't meant as a question, of course, but she was floundering, trying to stall, to keep her two worlds apart before a collision ruined both. *You can't live a double life and hope to please everyone*, she thought. A bit late to realise that. She tried to focus, find the words that would give her reasoning some sort of coherence. 'Whatever problems I have to face, well, they're mine. Of my own making, if I'm honest. And... it's different for you. You're not married.'

She could feel his body go still.

'No, I'm not,' he said. 'But I'm not an insensitive clod, either. I might just understand.'

'Oh, Jake, I didn't mean it like that.'

But it was as though she'd purposely hurt him. And he wasn't going to let it go.

For a brief moment, they seemed at odds, on opposite sides. Cold, through and through, wary, on edge.

She sensed, the second before he spoke, that he was going to ask the one question that she couldn't answer. His expression was so forlorn and so expectant at the same time, she wanted to stop him. But it was too late.

'Do you love him, Amy?'

Her reaction was too slow. Too slow.

She shrugged. Spits of rain were driving through the slats of broken timber and landing on her eyelashes, making her blink.

'Believe me, I've often asked myself that lately. And the truth is… I don't know.'

He was watching her face as though waiting for the hammer blow.

'Jake, I've been married for eight years. We have a son together. A life together. You can't just dismiss that. So…' she took a breath. 'I suppose I do. But it's not what I feel for you.'

He closed his eyes and rested his head against hers.

'I just wish we'd met before, years ago. Then there'd only be us.' She could hear the break in his voice. 'I'd have made you happy.'

'I'm sure you would.' She stroked his wet hair, trying to comfort him, knowing she'd said what he didn't want to hear. 'But you can't go back. How many people get what they really want? Not many, believe me.'

They held each other close, arms encircled, Amy wishing she could lie, be kind. Fool both of them. But it was as though the tumult around them, the battering of the rain on the flimsy wooden boards, the rush of the wind, would drown out any comforting clichés she might come up with. It was all too difficult. She stopped trying.

She pulled away far enough to look into his eyes, dark and soulful, his face shadowed in the half light. 'I'm here, Jake. With you. In this ridiculous little hut. In the rain. And I wouldn't want to be anywhere else. Isn't that enough?'

Even to her own ears, this sounded a poor substitute. But he managed a smile. 'Not quite. But it'll do for now.'

She realised time was running out. 'Come on. Let's go. I daren't be late.'

She led the way through the downpour to the cars and as they reached the track, she turned. 'We'll work something out for next week. Promise.'

Making a tight turn, wheels skidding in the loose earth, she set off, glancing in the rear view mirror for a last glimpse of him. But he was already just a dark outline, indistinguishable from the overgrown hedgerows and trees surrounding him.

Chapter 35

The four days at Cordon Hall should have been just what Catherine needed – a change of environment, children to supervise, activities to occupy her. And she would have company - Murray who taught football and basketball in the PE department, and young Will, who was in his first year, keen and easy going. They wouldn't make too many demands on her. She'd feel better, she was sure, being among people who wouldn't ask questions or make her tell lies.

But it hadn't turned out that way. Of course, it was inevitable that she'd have been anxious organising any trip of this kind, but it was so much more than that. Even as she counted the children onto the bus and reassured the parents, she could hear her voice getting shrill and sharp, every nerve in her body drawn, like a tightly strung wire.

'Wayne's asthma pump.' A mother was thrusting a package into her hand. 'He won't need it unless he overdoes it.'

Great, she thought, *another thing to worry about!* But she gave a tight smile and told the bus driver to go.

Catherine occupied herself on the journey, checking through the paperwork, passing round details of what was on offer to the children, quietening the singing which had got louder and louder until the driver complained, answering questions from Will. But she couldn't help taking out her mobile every half hour to check there were no texts from Jake. Was she really expecting any? Perhaps not expecting, but hoping. It felt almost like a physical pain in her chest when she thought of him. He must have seen the photo she'd left on Friday. If he was angry... well, he knew now she wasn't just going to fade away. She was waiting for him and he'd realise at some point, that she was the one who really cared for him. Even if it took him a while to acknowledge what he was throwing away.

And she should have found the four days a welcome break from all the heartache, the stress of the last few months, but she couldn't lift her mood. It was as though her mind was in lock-down, unable to rid itself of thoughts that wouldn't go away. She did find more energy and interest in the daytime, when she could concentrate on physical exercise, taking part in the kayaking or climbing the wall. She tried to be patient with the children, although that took all her effort - some of the 2nd years were demanding and constantly asked questions, even when the instructors had told them what to do. In the evening, though, when she sat with Murray and Will in the small staff dining room, the conversation bored her – it was either endless replaying of football matches, or of managers who didn't deserve their job, of TV comedies they'd watched or Murray, endlessly showing photos on his phone of his two daughters, of his dog, of his garden. She couldn't join in and didn't want to, slipping more and more into a lonely place, wrapped up in her own misery.

She managed to escape to her single room by 9.30 each night, after checking on the children and at least then, relieved to be alone, she didn't have to pretend. She lay on the single bed, shoes kicked off but fully dressed, and pieced everything together again and again, as though this would help her understand. Give her some answers. But, of course, it didn't.

She thought back to when she used to long for a Saturday night to come so she could hurry to his house, and he'd cook, they'd have a glass of wine, listen to music; she'd lie beside him all night, and sometimes in the early morning, she'd be awake before him and just look at his sleeping face, the crease on his cheek, his hair on end, and put her arm round him, feeling contented that she belonged to someone at last. And going to restaurants, to the cinema, to friends' parties; and the day he'd cheered her on at the marathon. We were fine then, I know we were. You can't tell me we weren't. He loved me. That doesn't just disappear.

Sleeping was difficult and she was tired, weary in fact, ready for the whole trip to end. By the time she arrived back at the school car park and had dispatched all the children and rung Tim to tell him all was well, she was glad to be home. OK, everything had gone smoothly, no major mishaps, but that didn't seem to help. She was still worn down and fractious (one of her father's words, she realised). Well, she was certainly that. It was when she saw herself in the bathroom mirror, she realised how thin she'd become, how her face, once rounded and almost pretty, seemed too long and her eyes had a haunted look. There was an ugliness in what she saw. She turned away. *It's his bloody fault!* She felt a familiar rage building up again and swallowed to calm herself. Then it was as though an answer came to her that would explain everything. Make sense of the past few months and why he'd pushed her away. It all added up. *He's ill and doesn't want to tell me. Perhaps he's having a breakdown. That would explain things – his odd behaviour, his refusal to answer messages. He doesn't look well either. Perhaps something's happened that he can't talk about.*

There was a way to find out. She would ring his home. His mother would answer and she could pretend to be a friend worried about him, hadn't seen him for a few days and was he in Leeds with them. It would reassure her to know, she'd say. As long as he's all right. Good to talk to you, Mrs. Harper. They'd only met once. She wouldn't remember a voice from a year ago. Yes, that would do it. And if... if... he wasn't at home...? Then he wasn't ill – he was with her, whoever she was. He was two-timing her and she wasn't going to forgive him for that.

She began to doubt now whether sending him that photo of his house had been a good idea. She'd wanted him to know she was there, close, and she would always be there, waiting for him to come back.

She couldn't bear for it all to happen again. Surely this wasn't like last time, when she'd spent weeks hoping against hope that it wasn't the end. And then finding out on that disastrous evening, finding out...

No one really understands the sense of loss when you're betrayed, (because that's what it had been – a betrayal) when you've loved someone, when you've seen your whole future with them, and they pretend it was nothing, just something casual. That's what he'd said. Nothing serious. And the aftermath had been devastating. A backlash she'd never expected. *She'd* been painted as the villain and *he'd* been the victim. She'd been the one to suffer, everyone turning on her because she'd acted in the only way that seemed fair and just. So much for the student counselling, for the welfare service - a lot of good those were! They wouldn't listen to her side of the story. Just looked at her with unbelieving eyes. And looking back, perhaps she did go too far. But she'd been *heart-broken*... she'd been...

Catherine took a deep breath and made herself sit down. She must keep steady. She must be careful.

She didn't want to make such a mess of it this time.

She looked in her diary for the Leeds number. It was tea time so someone would be home. She practiced what she would say then dialled.

'Hello.'

It was his mother's voice.

'Hi there, Mrs. Harper. Sorry to bother you, but I'm a friend of Jake's and I've been trying to contact him. I was wondering whether he was there with you, as it's half term. I haven't seen him for a few days and thought he might have gone home.'

There was a hesitation. 'No, he's not here. He rang on Monday, so I'm sure he's all right. Are you worried about him? I can give you his address if you want that.'

'No, no, I'm sure he's ok. He just wasn't answering his mobile, that's all. Don't worry, I'll chase him down.'

'Who shall I say rang if he asks?'

'Er,' her mind went blank for a moment. She hadn't thought this through. 'It's Jenny. Don't worry. Thanks, Mrs. Harper.'

Catherine dropped the phone and gripped the table. Her hands were shaking and her head ached. What had she learned? Nothing, one way or the other – he hadn't gone home. But, if he *was* ill, perhaps he wouldn't want his family to know. Or... perhaps he'd spent the week with his new girlfriend, this mystery woman who'd never been seen. Which was more likely.

Please God, it was driving her mad. She felt exhausted. Going round and round in circles, gnawing at her, making her ill; she began to think that unless she knew something for definite, she'd lose control, do something crazy and then, Jake would be gone forever. He'd never forgive her. Never understand.

She foraged in the bedside cabinet and, under the hair conditioner and moisturiser, found the box of pills. She needed to calm down. Then at least, she could think straight. Could work out what to do over the next three days, three long days before school started again. She must sort this out before she had to sit in that first breakfast briefing and have to watch Jake from a distance, as though he were a stranger. She couldn't bear the thought of that any more.

And she'd made such a stupid error. She should never have let him see that photo. Why didn't she ever learn?

First light on Friday morning had found her wide awake and shaking, in spite of the pills. Or because of them. She'd taken more than she should have the night before and lay, exhausted, sheets wrapped round her in a stranglehold, body wet with sweat. She stared at the curtained window, the darkness outside seeming to shut her in. So she got out of bed, showered and dressed. She needed to get out of the house, so she took the car, filled up with petrol at the local garage, finding herself the only one on the empty forecourt.

She drove back through the quiet narrow streets, and slowed as she reached the one road she couldn't just pass by. The street lights were still on, although the gloom of the early morning was lifting and she could see long before she reached Jake's house that his car was outside. All was in darkness. Anger left a bitter taste in her mouth, anger that she wasn't there with him, as she should have been. As she passed, she had a brief moment of madness – wanting to turn the car round and let his tyres down, scrape the paintwork, give him grief. Do anything to hurt him. But the fury gave way to such sadness, such pain, that she had to force herself to focus on the road ahead as tears streamed down her face.

After a couple of turns, she'd pulled over and sat for a while. Empty hours lay ahead of her and time seemed to go so slowly. Another long day. After a while, she'd looked at her watch. Seven thirty. She'd go to the shop at Heaton Moor and get some paracetamol for her head, and perhaps buy some groceries. There was nothing to eat at home. And she must eat something. She returned to her car with a few necessary items, flinging the bag onto the front seat and sitting down heavily behind the wheel.

Blast. She'd forgotten to do her father's shopping like she'd promised a week ago. It had gone completely out of her mind. The thought of seeing him of all people made her feel physically sick but if she didn't call, he'd be on the phone leaving messages; she wasn't going to spend the whole day psyching herself up. She'd have to get it over with and the earlier the better. She was in the wrong frame of mind, she knew that, but she was determined to put on a good face and bluff it out. Leave as fast as possible, telling him she'd a lot on.

She parked outside his gate and fumbled in the shopping bag. She'd got bread buns and lamp chops and vegetables for herself – well, he could have those to be going on with. She took a deep breath, and although the thought of dealing with him made her stomach churn, (he'd been annoyed when she'd told him she was away for a few days), she felt a sense of duty towards him. He didn't deserve it and she couldn't explain it. Misguided, perhaps, but there it was.

She hoped he'd be out of bed and dressed. But no. He'd been in his dressing gown. And bad-tempered.

Funny, she thought, once something's been said, it won't go away. What had she expected? What could possibly change after all these years? Nothing. He could always be cruel, could always reach her at her most vulnerable. It was as though he enjoyed it - the taunting, the belittling. And for the rest of the day, however hard she tried not to, she heard her father's words, even the tone of his voice, echoing in her mind.

From the moment, she entered the house, with its smell of cigarette smoke and old vegetables, the onslaught on her senses seemed merciless. *Took your time, didn't you? Barely a thing to eat, while you go off, doing God knows what! I haven't had a hot meal all week.* And then, when he saw her face. *You do look a poor thing.* And even though she'd spent four days outdoors and exercising, she was reduced to just that – a poor thing.

But the worst was when, with a crooked smile, he guessed what had happened and couldn't help gloating. *He's finally gone then.* He didn't wait for any response. *Well you've only yourself to blame. He'll have heard about the last one and the fuss you made over that. You don't seem to ever learn.'* He shook his head. *Only met him once but it was obvious. He didn't think that much of you. You could see it.* She should have had an answer. Should have given something back, but she buckled under his contempt, as she always did. Yes, she could usually think of something to say afterwards, when it was too late. But facing that familiar, bullying voice whittling away at her, she remained silent. *Hope you're not thinking of coming back here, girl. Because that won't be happening.* And he lifted his mug and drank his tea, never taking his eyes off her. Wanting the reaction he knew he'd get and satisfied then.

She turned away from his whiskered face and his cruel mouth and his scorn and fled - out of the door, up the street, crying as she sat in the early morning traffic. And when she'd closed her own front door, she sank down behind it, and sat, clasping her knees up to her chest, and closed her eyes. Oh, how she wished her mother was still alive, she thought. It would have made all the difference in the world.

Eventually, she got to her feet and had a shower for the second time that morning, turning the temperature dial so high, the water stung her body. But at least she felt clean.

It was still so early - only nine o'clock.

The way to get through the day, she decided, was to do something practical. She'd clean the downstairs, wash the bedclothes, mend the broken door catch to the larder, cook a meal. At last, she felt angry, rather than upset. She wouldn't go back till the miserable old man had learned his lesson – if he was relying on his lazy sons to be at his beck and call, keep the cupboards stocked, then he'd be a long time waiting.

It was as she sat down at lunch that she allowed herself to take out her mobile and check it. Nothing. But the screensaver always comforted her. A photo taken many months ago of her and Jake, cheek to cheek in a selfie. They were smiling. How it should be.

She ate her sandwich slowly, feeling as alone as it was possible to feel.

Everything was falling apart.

*

She should have asked Rosie to go with her but she'd left it too late and she needed to run. It was dark and wintry on the streets, but if she stuck to the main roads, she'd be safe enough. This was when she felt good, pacing herself, heart pumping, legs stretched and her mind on nothing but moving forward. A rhythm her body understood.

She'd been restless all afternoon and the only answer was to get outside and run. Dark now at only five o'clock, but it was good to speed past the stationary cars in the traffic jams and have the freedom to just go, flying along the pavements, crossing at the lights, heading towards the road which ran alongside the park.

She could see the lamps by the gates as she turned the corner and was easing back, breathing evenly, ready to go past.. But as she slowed to go round a woman with a pushchair, she caught sight of someone sitting in the bus shelter by the park entrance. He was too distinctive to miss – the pale hair falling over his face, white under the street lighting, the baggy clothes he always wore, the heavy boots. Lucas. He sat, shoulders hunched, elbows on his knees, staring at the ground. He certainly wasn't waiting for a bus.

She stopped in front of him. 'Lucas.'

He barely looked up.

'Hey, are you all right?'

He shuffled his feet and mumbled something she couldn't catch.

'Sorry, what was that?' She bent down. 'You don't live near here, do you?'

He bowed his head lower and Catherine hesitated, unsure of what to do or say.

At last, he shifted his seat and sat back, leaning against the metal bar behind him. 'No.' His eyes finally met hers. 'But I sometimes spend time around here. The park's peaceful. And the club's over there, so...'

'But you're not in the park.' She was saying the wrong things, intrusive and not getting through to him. What on earth was he doing there? But as he turned his head, she could see now that his cheekbone was red and the skin puffy round that side of his face.

'You haven't been in a fight, have you?'

He gave a short laugh. 'Not exactly.'

She sat down next to him on the dirty bench. He probably wouldn't confide in her, but she could at least try to find out what was wrong. What had happened to cause that injury to his face. She couldn't just leave him and anyway, she'd grown fond of him. He was a tough kid with a rotten home life and no friends. He always seemed to be alone and that wasn't right for a fifteen year old. It wasn't right for anyone, she thought ruefully.

'So, what's happened? I promise you I won't tell anyone, if you want to keep this just between you and me, but I might be able to help.'

He was silent.

'Ok.' She got up. 'Perhaps I'll see you at club on Wednesday then.'

But he looked up at her with such a woeful expression that she sat down again.

'There was a row,' he began, speaking slowly, not exactly talking to her, but into the space over her shoulder. She had to concentrate to catch what he was saying. 'There's always rows, have been for years, but this one... it turned crazy. My dad was sacked a few weeks ago and today... he went ballistic, just lost it. He started on my mum, she'd spent some money on a coat. It hadn't even cost much. She shouted back at him - big mistake - and he hit her... hard... she was on the floor and I got in the way, I suppose. P'raps I meant to. I don't know what I wanted to do.'

He took a breath which sounded rasping and angry. 'But then... Mum told him she was leaving him, she'd had enough. And Dad left the house in a worse temper... nearly took the door off its hinges.'

'And what happened then?'

'She was... upset, said, that was it. He'd blown it. When he came back, she'd be gone, just like my brother. She'd find a flat, move away.' He looked at her then. 'It'd be just me and him in the house. A bloody nightmare that'd be.'

Again a pause. Just the sound of cars passing and a group of schoolkids on the opposite pavement, shouting and laughing.

'D'you think she meant it?' He wanted answers and Catherine knew she didn't have any.

She sighed. 'People say things when they're in a state when they're angry. Even if she meant it at the time, she probably won't feel the same once things have calmed down.' She put her hand on his shoulder. 'And Lucas, if your mum does leave for a few days, your dad might start thinking that, maybe, he can't live without her. He'll be sorry for what he's done. Sometimes,' she sighed, as much for herself as for him, 'people who hurt others need a shock to bring them to their senses. Then they appreciate the damage they've done.'

He sniffed and finally nodded.

'Yes. I see.' And then he raised his head and fixed those ice blue eyes on her, steady, unblinking. 'That makes a lot of sense. Thanks, Catherine.'

She was taken aback by the way he said her name. It was too familiar, somehow and she withdrew her hand.

'Well, I just hope things improve.' She knew she sounded nervous. 'I must get going now. Look after yourself, Lucas. See you in the week.'

And she left him in the bus shelter, confused about the whole episode, not knowing whether she'd said the right thing, and uneasy about him in more ways than one.

He was a very strange boy.

Chapter 36

He sat on the sofa with papers on his lap, but he wasn't really concentrating. At the other side of the room, Amy was working on her laptop, her face lit by the light of the screen. She didn't look up. The atmosphere since the row over the newspaper column had been uncomfortable – distant and guarded – both of them defensive and not prepared to make the first move.

Perhaps he'd been too harsh, but she didn't seem to understand - or to be more accurate, she didn't *want* to understand – how the world of business worked. How there was basic, common sense behaviour to adhere to if you wanted to survive. You knew who the people were you couldn't afford to upset. No-one got far without some restraint, some sense of how the game was played. He'd learned that at school. And if he was too much of a conformist, well, it had worked out well. He was successful, he earned good money, very good money, and he provided for his family.

But now, he was beginning to doubt whether that was enough. It didn't seem so for Amy. She wanted him to be a different sort of man. It wasn't the first time over the last few months that he thought with some disquiet about the age gap. In the beginning, there'd been bigger worries. It had mattered far more that he was married and with children than those twenty years between them. He'd even believed that 'opposites attract' had some truth, created a healthy balance. His formality and reserve challenged by her forthright, lively personality. A good mix. Now he wasn't so sure.

'D'you want coffee?' he asked, to break the silence. He'd rather have had a whiskey.

'I'm fine. Shall I make you one?' Her eyes never left the screen.

'No. I'll get one when I've finished this.'

He sat back and tried again to read the figures on the sheet in front of him. But he wanted this rift to be over. He couldn't just let it go on and on. It must be making Amy as unhappy as he was. Did it matter whose fault it was?

The memory of those first days in this house - those warm, wonderful days, Amy pregnant with Harry, he amazed at his good fortune - came into his mind with a sense of nostalgia and regret. One evening when they lay on this sofa, her head on his shoulder, she'd place her hands either side of his face and kissed him - 'I can't believe we've made it,' she'd said. 'It doesn't matter what anyone else thinks, does it? As long as we're all right.'

Well, we're not all right.

A slow feeling of fear spread through his body. What if, after all, she was going to leave him? Everything he lived for, everything he'd worked for, would be worthless. All that upheaval, all for nothing. And there was Harry. He would never allow another child of his to grow up without him. He'd done enough harm in the past, three children left without a father, however much he liked to fool himself that he was 'there for them.' He'd gone. That was the truth of it. No, that wouldn't happen again.

He gave himself a mental shake. He was getting this out of proportion. It was up to him to make the first move.

'Amy, will you stop that a minute? We need to talk.'

She looked up, no expression on her face. But she came over and sat opposite him. She was giving him no encouragement to start and he saw this wasn't going to be a two-way transaction.

He leant forward, elbows on his knees. 'I apologise for coming at you too hard. I was upset and I said things I shouldn't. So I'm sorry. I was thinking of the business. I was thinking of our livelihood. But I could have handled it better.'

She nodded, thoughtfully. 'I didn't realise I was treading on anyone's toes. Well, not yours, anyway.' She shrugged and shrank back a little and he could see she wasn't going to see things from his point of view. But he didn't want this to drag on, become something bigger than it was. He wanted peace. It was hard enough battling with problems at work. Home needed to be some sort of sanctuary, and it was hardly that now.

Jasper wandered over and sat at Amy's feet. He flopped down, lay his head on his paws and whimpered. Robert didn't know how to go on.

'See, even the dog's on your side,' he said, hoping a joke would lessen the tension.

Amy didn't smile. 'It's not about sides, Robert. It's just that we're from different...'

'What? Generations?'

'That's not what I was going to say. We're from different backgrounds, we've had our own experiences. They've shaped us. That doesn't mean we have to fight. We just have to give each other room.'

'What does that mean?'

'Be tolerant, accept that we can't agree on everything.' She hesitated and put out her hand and touched his knee. 'I'm not Paula...'

'I've never compared you to her.' He was stung by the suggestion.

'I know. Not openly. But I'm a challenge, and she wasn't. She's a much nicer person than I am, from what I gather. And when you married, you were starting out and she was happy to fit in with your ambitions and...'

He could feel anger building up. 'You don't know what it was like, Amy. Don't try and tell me how things were.'

'Ok.' She sat back. 'But that's part of the problem. We've never really discussed a lot of things. You don't find that easy.'

He couldn't follow how her mind was working. What was she trying to say?

'I thought we'd covered everything that was important,' he said. 'We certainly did at the beginning. How many times did we go over my leaving, the hurt I was inflicting on the children, the bloody awful dilemma I was facing? We talked then.'

He thought she looked as closed up as she could be. Holding back.

'Let's forget it,' she said quietly. 'We're both over-reacting. It's not such a big deal. I should have thought more and you were too quick to judge. Just let's leave it at that.'

She got up and went back to working on her laptop at the far side of the room.

Robert couldn't think of a way to reach out to her. Everything he said lately seemed to be wrong or provoke an argument. Was he becoming old and predictable and boring? Someone so rigid and unsympathetic that it made her dismiss his opinions as barely worthy of consideration?

He certainly hadn't felt that way with Holly a week ago, when he'd taken her on an Open Day to Newcastle University. It had been a day of easy companionship, one he'd remember for a long time. He'd felt pleased – no, more than pleased - that she'd asked him, and made plans to pick her up early so that traffic hold-ups wouldn't make them late. He could tell she was excited because she chatted more than usual, filling him in on the plan of the day, studying a map of the buildings and working out where they could go for lunch. As though she was in charge, which was exactly what he wanted for her. Nearly eighteen and ready to go out into the world.

They arrived in plenty of time and entered the reception hall, full of anticipation, parents and teenagers alike. It was catching, this buzz of excitement - Robert had the feeling he'd like to be starting all over again and hoped Holly was as enthusiastic as he was. The morning went by quickly, a packed agenda with a lot to take in, and it was no time at all before they were sitting in a little café off Market Street, drinking tea from large, heavy mugs and eating toasties. Not exactly what Robert had envisaged for lunch, but it was Holly's choice. They'd had time to take a brief wander round the city centre and this place looked warm and inviting, so they'd quickly found a table and sat down next to a misted-up window that looked out onto the shoppers passing by.

Robert looked round, conscious of being out of place in his dark suit. 'I'd have taken you somewhere for a decent lunch, Holly,' he said.

'I know, but this is the sort of place real students go – cheap and cheerful. Don't you think?'

He'd laughed in agreement. 'Well, you have a point. It feels authentic.'

She'd tucked into her sandwich and started going over all that had happened in the morning. She'd thought the lecture was a bit over her head, but she'd soon learn. And there were so many clubs and societies she could join, there'd barely be time to study. It was just the sort of place she wanted to be and it had to be her first choice now.

Robert watched her and listened, so grateful to see her brimming with ideas and regaining a confidence she'd seemed to have lost.

'What about the course? I thought you liked the one in Birmingham.'

'Well, I did,' she said, brushing crumbs from her scarf. 'But this town is... well, it's alive, isn't it? So much going on. The theatre, the music clubs, the bars. And The Baltic, which is famous, you know.'

'I know.' He decided he couldn't drink the tea, which was an odd shade of brown. 'I was most impressed with the sports facilities. It'd cost you the earth to join a gym like that.'

Holly was watching the door as the café filled up. 'And I'm not too far away that I couldn't come home some weekends.'

'And we could come up here.'

She didn't follow up on that one. Very wise, Robert thought. A new start and if she's optimistic about this first step of independence, then he would be too.

'I'll miss everyone, of course, but this is what I've wanted for two years. And now Mum seems happy, I won't worry about leaving her.' She flushed. 'You know what I mean. She's got company now.'

What a thoughtful girl she'd become, he realised, and sensed she wanted his approval for the changes that were being made without his sanction. 'Yes,' he said. 'I'm pleased about that.'

'Are you?'

'Of course. Sometimes… you have to just move on. No good going backwards. Life's hard enough.'

There was a moment when he thought she was going to leave the whole subject behind, but she wiped her mouth and put down the paper napkin. 'One day, I'd like to meet Harry and Amy. Would that ever be possible?'

He was taken totally by surprise. Had this been on her mind for a while, or had it come to her suddenly. He put out his hand to cover hers. 'Of course, Holly. Not perhaps just yet, but later on. As long as your mother doesn't mind.'

Her eyes filled with tears. 'Thank you.'

'Now,' he said, determined to lift the mood. 'What shall we do this afternoon?

She spent the next fifteen minutes looking up *What to do in Newcastle* on her mobile, then they set off like explorers to cover as much of the sights in the city as they could before it got dark. And when he dropped her off at home, she'd hugged him and thanked him for a lovely day.

He didn't know when he'd enjoyed one so much...

But that wasn't how he was feeling now.

The room had grown darker, with only the reading lamp behind Robert's head and the pool of light over Amy's computer creating separate circles in the gloom. There was a stillness that he found unsettling, a quiet where the smallest sound seemed magnified – the faint rustle of paper, the dog's nails scratching the skirting board. It was like the hour before the storm, he thought. He hated how unpredictable their relationship seemed at the moment, the not-knowing what was coming next. He liked order, however mundane that might seem. It was how he could function. And this atmosphere was making him uncomfortable, unable to settle; he'd had enough of it.

'Amy,' his voice sounded loud and harsh. He hadn't meant it to be.

She looked up.

'I've upset you and I'm sorry about that. But at least let's come to some sort of...'

'Robert, stop. Please stop.'

She crossed the room and knelt on the carpet in front of him, her hands resting on the sides of the armchair. 'I'm thoughtless. Impetuous. I don't think ahead and it's not fair that you're hurt because of what I do.' She bit her lip and he was about to speak, but she hurried on. 'I apologise - for being a pain, for being a selfish cow. But I've always been that way and you know it. I'm a lost cause.' He could tell by her voice that she was near to tears. He put out his arms and pulled her to him, holding her against him to ease the rawness of it all, the fear ebbing away but leaving him shaken. He didn't want to let go. He had a feeling that there were things to be said, but this wasn't the time. And perhaps there never would be a time when they could be completely honest with each other. Perhaps there were too many differences, too painful to be examined closely.

They held each other close for a few minutes.

'I'll make us some coffee.' Amy said, sounding like her old self. 'And I made a carrot cake. D'you fancy some?'

Before he had time to reply, Harry was shouting from his bedroom, loud and demanding. Unusual for him to wake up once he'd gone to bed. Amy hurried up the stairs to his room, and Robert followed more slowly. The night light was on, and the little boy was sitting bolt upright in bed, arm out pointing towards the opposite wall.

'What is it Harry? Why were you shouting?' Amy sat on the edge of the bed.

'Take him out,' he was still pointing. 'Take him out.'

'Who, Harry? There's nobody here.' Robert looked round trying to understand what was going on.

Harry was staring fixedly at the bookcase at the far side of the room. On the top sat three of his favourite toys, a teddy bear, a floppy-eared donkey and a life-like wooden puppet, dressed in a sailor suit and slumped over to one side.

'Take him out.'

Amy looked across at the toys. 'You want me to take out Teddy?'

'No.' Harry's voice quivered. 'The sailor man. He watches me. Take him out.'

Robert moved across and picked up the puppet.

'He can't watch you, Harry,' he said. 'He's made of wood. He's not real.'

'His eyes move.'

'Well, he's gone now,' said Amy, taking the puppet and throwing it out onto the landing. 'He won't stay in your room any more. So you've nothing to worry about. He's not coming back. Is that better? Now, come on, let's get you back under the covers.'

But it took half an hour before he was settled and they were able to go downstairs.

'Isn't it funny what you imagine when you're little,' said Amy. 'I used to look under the bed every night before I climbed in. What on earth did I think I'd find under there?'

'Well, you'd have scared a burglar! *My* only worry was whether I could read under the covers without my father finding out.' Robert shook his head and exchanged a knowing look with Amy. 'Never mind the coffee. I'm having a vodka tonic! D'you want one?'

Amy smiled. 'Make it a large one.'

Robert poured the drinks and sat down beside her. He turned on the television and they sat taking in all the depressing news of the day, political mayhem, floods, killings. After some minutes, he turned down the sound. He wanted some sort of commitment on Amy's part, some assurance that they'd moved on to firmer ground.

'I'd like us to take a holiday – somewhere warm, by the sea – Harry would like that. Spend some time all together. I think we need it.' He found he was studying her face, waiting for the reaction he was hoping for and worried he might see something else – a shadow of uncertainty, a fleeting moment of dissent.

He went on before she could brush him aside. 'Not now – May or June when I can get away from work and it'll be warmer. Perhaps Menorca or Greece...'

She nodded and turned towards him. 'Yes, it's a good idea. We've plenty of time to think about it.' She put down her drink, half-finished and yawned. 'I'm not going to do any more tonight on that story. I think I'll go to bed once I've let Jasper into the garden.'

He gathered up the papers he'd been working on and put them in his briefcase, then took the glasses into the kitchen and rinsed them. Amy was giving the dog his nightly Bonio as she let him back in and was drying his paws, talking to him as though he understood. Robert could never understand how she could give this dog nearly as much attention as she did Harry and in some illogical way, it irritated him. But tonight he wasn't about to spoil the mood by showing any sign of disapproval.

He checked his mobile before plugging it in to recharge in the kitchen and saw there'd been two calls. He'd made it a habit to turn it onto silent in the evening, because after eight hours at the office, he'd had enough of work problems. He saw that one was from his mother. Why she didn't ring the house phone was beyond him. Well, too late to return the call now. He'd ring her tomorrow. And, Christ, he had to look again to make sure - one from Nick. Bloody nuisance! What on earth could he be calling for after all this time? And it had gone to voicemail. Why didn't the man give up? Easy enough to block the number, though, before he tried to reach him again. And delete the message.

It could wait till the morning.

He climbed the stairs, feeling to some extent relieved. At least the row wasn't hanging over them anymore, that awful tension that poisoned the atmosphere and made him question the very nature of their relationship. When there was probably no need. Robert liked order in his life and he wanted that restored. And it would be. They just needed time together. Time to enjoy each other's company. And if they could get away for a week or two, be a family with nothing disastrous happening, no broken arms or misunderstandings that would wreck the whole thing, then they'd be back to normal.

Chapter 37

Jake hadn't meant to go out. The evening was cold and snow was forecast overnight. Heavy cloud hung over the houses, making the street lamps hazy and the trees mere shadows against the sky. The sort of night that made you glad to be in the warm, watching a video and going to bed early.

But then Andy had rung, sounding cheerful and talked him into meeting up at the pub, which stood halfway between their two houses. Just for a 'quick one'. Of course, it hadn't turned out that way.

'Meet us at the Crown, have a few bevies and a laugh. It's what you need, you miserable old sod.'

'Andy, it's freezing outside and it's a twenty minute walk to the Crown. Make it another night.'

'No, I'm not being put off again. You're becoming a hermit, for God's sake.' Jake could hear from his voice that he wasn't going to give up. 'I'll give you half an hour to get down there.' And the call ended before Jake could protest further.

In a way, he was glad to be doing something. Nights when he knew there'd be no Amy were just a matter of waiting out the hours until he'd be with her again. Even when he tried to occupy himself with all the familiar rituals of his previous life, reading, planning lessons, listening to the radio, he found himself drifting.

Remembering her face, the texture of her hair, the warmth of her hand in his, how he felt when he was with her. Just wonderful. What a romantic idiot he'd become!

So he pulled on his shoes and coat, grabbed his old university scarf and set off walking towards town, but not before, as he'd pulled his gate shut, looking across the road just checking no one was there. Not that he could see anyone in the dimness. But he couldn't get over the oddness of that photo Catherine had taken, and the idea that someone could be watching at this very moment.

The good thing about the Crown, he thought, was that it was always warm, the landlord cheery and welcoming, and the beer was good. Andy was already there, standing under the Specials Board, holding a pint, half empty, the other one balanced on a nearby ledge. He was already one drink ahead of him, or perhaps two, Jake could tell by the expansive gestures and wide smile, but that was fine; he was glad of some company and the usual arguments about football and politics and films. It'd take him out of himself.

He certainly didn't want to discuss anything personal; he had no desire to continue the conversation they'd had in the staff room. He'd said enough.

But, to begin with, there was no fear of touching on that. Andy had his own agenda. 'Now listen, my friend.' He waited till Jake had taken a swallow of his drink. 'We're not to mention anything about school. I've not had the best week - a mother came in and said I'd been sarcastic to her Damian. Well, hell, of course I was. You need some line of defence against the little dears.' He raised his glass. 'Let's drink to retirement. Can't be that far off, can it?'

They moved away from the small dining area to sit on stools at the bar and set about analysing last week's football results, the merits of 'Narcos' and deciding 'The Wire' was the best thing that had ever been on TV. It was good to be doing something normal after the upheaval of the last months. Good to be just sitting there, distracted by what was around him - two girls laughing hysterically at something one of them had said, a group of lads playing darts and cheering, making so much noise the barman had to give them a warning.

'Remember when we were young and daft like that?' said Andy, turning back to the bar. 'Seems a long time ago.' He sighed. 'Don't know whether I'd want to be eighteen again, though. Too much angst. All for nothing.' He put down his glass and looked at Jake. 'I get the idea that it's curtains between you and Catherine. She spends a lot of time giving you the evil eye.'

Jake shrugged his shoulders. 'Well, it is as far as I'm concerned. She seems to think I'll change my mind, and I'm sorry about that... but you know when it's not working out. It's not pleasant, though, to see someone getting hurt... But, yes. It's over.'

'And...?' Andy tilted his head.

Jake smiled. 'I'm fine, Andy. Don't you worry about me. I know what I'm doing.'

'You *think* you do, mate. But you're deep into something that could turn nasty if you're found out. For God's sake, be careful.'

Jake nodded. He knew he wasn't listening, not really. The advice was way too late. The whole thing was too big, too all-consuming to think of stopping now. It was like riding a gigantic wave – the ones you see surfers crest and fall – and it had a power and will of its own. He just had to hang on and pray he could keep upright. And hope his instincts would see him through.

At ten o'clock, he was on his way home, tired and at peace with himself. Not often he felt like that these days, but tonight life was ok. Helped, of course, by a few pints and the thought of a warm bed and no hassle from anyone. As he walked through the night, not always steadily, his thoughts were pleasant ones. They were of Amy, of course - odd moments of their time together, conversations they'd had, remembering places they'd been to, everything so clear, as though printed on his brain. It seemed extraordinary to him that they'd found each other.

He swung through his gate, forgetting to shut it behind him and fumbled with his keys, realising now he'd drunk more than he should. The last time he'd overdone it was that awful night when he thought he'd lost Amy for ever, that it was the end, and he'd sent a final, half-witted text to Catherine. Not one of his better moments.

Well, the past was exactly that – no way to change it now.

And lying in bed in the dark, drowsy and unable to put off sleep any longer, he wrapped his arms round his pillow and drifted off...

It was the clank of the letter box that woke him. The room was in total darkness and the sound confused him. He sat up on one elbow and listened for something to follow – a knock, a voice calling (hadn't Catherine done just that a couple of months ago?) but there was nothing. He rubbed his eyes and checked the bedside clock. A few minutes past midnight.

All was quiet. He lay back, his head still fuzzy and soon he was asleep again, dreaming of driving a truck with no brakes through town streets, desperately trying to steer round obstacles in his way.

The second time he woke was with a start.

He was glad to be out of the dream and lying in his bed, but his heart was pounding as though it had been real. Too much imagination, that was his trouble.

But now his senses were alert. He could hear a hushed flurry of movement. Surely someone wasn't in the house! Surely not.

Well, something was outside his bedroom on the landing, something making sounds that he struggled to identify. A strange rustling and cracking, not loud but constant, a swishing, whirring... what on earth was it?

He leapt out of bed and wrenched opened the bedroom door.

A mere second of utter surprise.

Then a force hit him with incredible power, pummelling his chest and sucking the air from his lungs, suffocating him, throwing him backwards onto the floor

no time,

no mercy,

no chance.

*

Amy sat impatiently, waiting in a line of traffic for the lights to change. Of all the times for Ellie to choose to brief her on a story, the tail end of morning rush hour wasn't the best. Ten past nine already so she wouldn't make it for nine fifteen. She'd woken with a sore throat and a headache, so things hadn't started well. And now she was going to be late. Why couldn't she have been given the details over the phone? A new exhibition opening later in the morning of a well-known local artist – she'd done enough research already to do a decent interview. But Ellie had known him personally and wanted a thorough job.

A horn sounded and someone was revving their engine. Mornings were always busy heading into Stockport and she should have given herself more time after dropping Harry off at school. Well, she couldn't do much about the traffic, so if Ellie kicked off, too bad. She tapped her fingers on the steering wheel, praying the car in front would get a move on before the lights changed again.

She found a parking spot and put coins in the meter, the cold making her fingers numb and her eyes water. Thank heavens the office was warm, she thought as she ran up the stairs to the news room. She waved hello to Sam and Peter, who were preoccupied at their desks, and went to the glass door of the editor's office. Ellie beckoned her in impatiently.

'At last!' she said. 'There's not that much time before the opening and we need photographs to go with the article. Just a few pointers...' and she waited for Amy to get out her notebook and pen.

'Well,' said Ellie, when she'd finished, sitting back in her chair, 'how are things with you?'

'Good.' Amy wondered what was coming next.

'We'd like you to do some more features, at least up until the summer. Can you cope with more work?'

'Yes, as long as it fits in with school hours and I can usually do evenings, if that's necessary.'

'That's what I wanted to hear. Ok, then. Go and interview Picasso!'

Amy went back into the main room, smiling to herself, pleased that her recent efforts had obviously been appreciated. She was about to tell Sam as she passed his desk, but he was on the phone, listening intently and frowning. She paused.

'Where? Anything official yet? Do they suspect arson?'

She never knew why she didn't just walk on. Why she began taking notice of this story as it unfolded from a one-sided conversation, but she did, waiting till he put the phone down.

'What is it?'

'A house fire,' he said. 'In Crosby Street. That was just my contact, no police announcement yet.'

She felt a stab of fear, her mouth dry. 'Is anyone hurt?'

'Don't know. But the fire took hold bloody fast, apparently. Fire brigade were there pretty quick, but it was too late to do much.'

She tried to stay calm, be reasonable. There were at least eighty houses in Crosby Street. Why would it be his? Before she could ask anything else, Sam's phone rang again.

'Is that all you have?' he said and she had trouble breathing. 'Christ!'

Still holding the phone to his ear, he looked at her with an odd expression on his face. Something in his eyes that seemed like a warning. 'OK. Keep me posted.' And then he turned to her. 'Remember the teacher you did that school press piece with, Amy? They're saying it's his house. I don't...'

But she didn't wait for him to finish. She ran through the door, down the stairs, feet hammering the treads, her pulse pounding. She couldn't get to her car fast enough for pedestrians blocking the pavement, frustratingly slow, two abreast, looking in shop windows. *Move, for Christ's sake, get out of my way.* She pulled out of the tight parking spot, grinding into first gear, and picked up too much speed as she headed out of town. All the time not daring to either hope or dread what she had to face next.

She skidded to a stop close to Jake's house and got out of the car. She could see neighbours standing round in silent groups, on the opposite pavement and in the middle of the road, just staring at the burnt-out house, blackened bricks, window frames buckled, a jagged piece of roofing black against the sky.

Specks of ash still floated in the air.

The front door was lying on the charred grass.

Amy stared at the burnt outline with utter disbelief. It was something out of a nightmare. In the perfectly neat row of terraces, with their neat little gardens, it looked incongruous, ugly and frightening. She covered her mouth with her hand but she couldn't hold back a choking, despairing sound, which made one of the women look round.

'Terrible, isn't it?' the woman said, turning her gaze back to the blackened shell. 'Happened in the middle of the night. The fire just took hold. He'd no chance, poor man. They're saying someone stuffed burning rags through the door. Who would do something like that? Makes you wonder about people, doesn't it?'

Amy was fighting to breathe, her chest so tight she wondered how she could still be standing there, upright, in the street. It was as though the air was thin and the space around her, huge and isolating, the ground far away beneath her feet. She was going to faint, a dizziness behind her eyes and the sensation of falling. *Hold on. Breathe.* It took all her willpower to stay upright.

Another woman, wrapped in a navy blanket, was crying. 'He was my neighbour - lived right next door - such a nice young man. The fire never spread otherwise I'd have had it, too.' She wiped her eyes with her coat sleeve. 'I can't believe it could happen here. Arson. That's what it was - I heard the copper talking to the big-wig from the fire station, this morning. Looks like it was deliberate, he said.'

Amy heard the words but refused to believe them, refused to believe they hadn't saved him. These were just rumours, these women didn't know anything – he'd got out, he was in hospital... He *couldn't* be dead. *Oh, please, he couldn't be dead. Not Jake.* How could she lose him like this?

She saw the first woman looking at her. 'Did you know him, love?'

Amy managed to gain control of herself and found her voice. 'I worked with him sometimes.'

'Ah, so sad. His poor family. You can't imagine being told something like that'd happened to your son. Such a waste. I'll bet it was some toe-rag from the school he taught at – wanting revenge or something.' She shook her head. 'Kids don't know consequences, do they? And then it all goes too far.'

A hush fell over the watchers, as though they'd run out of things to say that might possibly sum up the awfulness of it all. The sort of hush that stills people when they hear the wail of an ambulance as it rushes by – *There but for the Grace of God...*

Amy slipped away without anyone noticing, and walked on unsteady feet back to her car. She sat behind the wheel, her hands shaking, a film of sweat cold on her face. She was too shocked to even cry, it was beyond tears. Her whole body was wracked with a grief she'd never experienced before. He wasn't in the world anymore and the loss of him was terrible. And then she felt anger at the cruelty of it all. Anger at the person who'd wreaked such devastation. How could anyone have wanted to harm him like this? Surely not a pupil! Surely not Catherine in a fit of pique! Perhaps it was some horrible mistake – the wrong house targeted, the wrong man.

And she couldn't stop thinking about the way he must have died, terrified, struggling for breath and realising there was no escape.

Please God, let him not have known what was happening.

We always pray at the wrong time, she thought, always too late and when we don't even believe. Because, in our despair, there's nowhere else to turn. Nothing to give us comfort except a cherished hope that some greater being will listen and come to our aid.

She leant back against the headrest. Just wanting to close her eyes and go to sleep, blot out the pain and the horror and the finality of it. But there was no saving her from all that.

*

Robert sat in his usual chair by the fireside, whiskey glass within reach on the coffee table, reading the morning's Guardian as he did every night about this time. It had been dark since four thirty, the afternoon had been non-stop, and after their meal, he appreciated the quiet in the room, no television news, just the sound of the wind blowing outside and, every so often, Amy turning the pages of her book.

But when he came to the shorter news stories on the inner pages, as soon as he saw the headline, he folded the paper in half to read it more closely. SCHOOL IN MOURNING FOR POPULAR TEACHER.

Two days earlier, the TV regional news channel had given the first details of the fire, a reporter standing in front of the blackened house, speculation whether it was a gas explosion or arson, the fire chief's brief statement, comments from shocked neighbours. He'd been watching the news with Amy and he'd thought she'd been as detached as he was as the details were broadcast. Just another sad happening, more so because it was local, close at hand. That's how it had seemed to him, anyway. He'd taken little notice of Amy's reaction. She'd suddenly got up and gone into the kitchen to rescue a cake that was burning in the oven. He hadn't thought anything of it. Events like these were upsetting, yes, tragic for the victims and their families, but when you're not personally involved, they're a news story that won't be remembered in a few weeks.

But yesterday evening, it was back on the news. The national news this time. The investigation had escalated to a murder inquiry. More details were emerging - a 33 year-old man had died in the blast, a teacher at the local school, Forest Green Academy and more speculation about how the fire had started. Arson was suspected.

He pulled himself forward to concentrate on the TV, unaware that Amy had come down the stairs into the living room and was standing behind his chair. Only a vague sense that she was there made him turn round and look, absently at first, then with concern. It was the expression in her eyes that alarmed him most – a hollowness and dread as she stared at the screen. And her face was so pale, he thought she was going to faint.

Looking at Amy now, Robert realised this wasn't just a story for Amy. As soon as the name of the school was mentioned, he remembered. She'd worked there some months ago, had probably met this man. It was more personal than he'd thought. He got up and put both his arms round her, feeling like an thoughtless fool.

'It's the school where you did that project, isn't it? Forest Green Academy.' He hugged her, but she held her body rigid, her arms loose by her sides. 'Oh, Amy, I'm so sorry. Did you know the man who died? Come on, sit down. You look as though you're about to fall over.'

She sat, her colour gradually returning. 'I'm all right,' she said. 'It's all so horrible. A horrible way to...' She stopped.

'Did you know him, this teacher?'

She didn't look at him, kept staring at the TV, even though other news of a bus strike and a store closing in the High Street was now on the screen. 'Yes, I knew him.' Another pause. When she spoke again, Robert had to bend forward to hear her. 'He was the English teacher. We worked together on the school newspaper... with others, of course. Quite a few of the staff, but yes... I knew him.'

'They're saying it's arson,' said Robert. 'So someone must have had it in for him. Unbelievable. Have you heard anything from the *Mercury*?'

She shook her head. 'I haven't been there. Not since it happened.'

'I thought you were doing an interview with an artist.'

'No. It was cancelled.' She turned her head and pushed her hair, which was hanging loose, off her face. 'I'm ok. Really, Robert. It's just upsetting. When you've known someone and he was so young...'

He didn't know what else to say and she didn't seem to want to talk any more – shock, he supposed - so he made her a cup of tea and watched her drink it. Hoping she'd soon look a bit more like her old self. He wasn't always good at saying the right things so rather than blunder on, he stayed silent. And through the evening, she was so quiet, so removed from him, he felt fearful. Of what he wasn't sure, but then, he hadn't known of anyone who'd died in such a horrific way. She was bound to be shaken by it all. It was only natural.

So now, as he read the headline, above the latest on the story, he glanced across at Amy and didn't know whether to ask if she'd seen it.

Better not, he thought, it'd only upset her again to talk about it. So he moved on to the sub-heading – *Suspected Arson Attack* - and learned that the house was in Crosby Street, the Emergency Services had been called to the property just before 3am. Launching a murder inquiry, officers identified the dead man as Jake Harper, a teacher of English at the local comprehensive school. *'At the terraced home yesterday afternoon, scenes of crime officers and fire investigators could be seen sifting through the wreckage, in what is usually a quiet residential street. The only part of the roof remaining was a brick gable end, while every window on the upper floor had been shattered. One neighbour, who had dialled 999 said, 'We just couldn't believe how quickly it spread.' A police spokesman confirmed they were treating this as a murder investigation and the questioning of a number of individuals was ongoing.'* Then a statement from the head teacher, Tim O'Neill. *'We have lost a dedicated, much-loved teacher who will be sadly missed. The students and staff are receiving counselling. That's all I can say at this time, as the police are dealing with a number of matters which I am not at liberty to discuss.'*

Robert looked over at Amy. She was listless, not really present and although he understood that she'd be upset by the loss of someone's life – someone she'd known, however briefly – this seemed... what?.... too extreme? It was beyond his experience, so who was he to judge? He noticed in the evenings as they followed some serial on Netflix that she stared ahead of her, barely seeming to concentrate, stroking Jasper's head like an automaton; and twice, finishing their meal, she'd seemed lost in thought, answering Harry's questions, but with no real interest. He'd have to think of something that would cheer her up, bring her back to her old self, bring her back to him. That might be selfish, he considered that, but living with someone who is absent... yes, that was exactly it... was disconcerting.

A week later, he left work early and found himself at Mike and Sophie's door. His pretence was that the golf times needed registering on the club notice board for Sunday, but he knew that wasn't the real reason he called. They were a touchstone in his life and he needed that more than anything at the moment. He could hardly go round to see Paula and expect her to listen to his problems. How ironic would that be?

The door was opened almost as soon as Robert had finished ringing the bell and Mike hustled him into the kitchen, where a pan of curry was bubbling on the stove.

'At a critical point, my man, so can't leave it. Take a seat while I stir. Sophie'll get you a drink when she comes down.'

Robert sat. 'No, nothing to drink. I was on my way home and wondered if you'd put our names down. We won't get a decent tee-time if we're not pretty quick.'

'It's done. Nine o'clock, so we won't have to be up at dawn.' Mike turned to look at him. 'You should have phoned me. Save you going out of your way.'

Robert said nothing. Just nodded.

Sophie gave him an affectionate tap on his shoulder as she joined them. 'Stay for supper, Robert. Mike's trying a new recipe and I don't want to have food poisoning on my own.'

'Very funny!' Mike brandished his wooden spoon. 'How's Amy?'

Robert wondered how much he should say. 'A bit down, actually, Mike. Well more than a bit. You know that house that burnt down and killed the teacher? She'd done some work with him on a school project – remember, we talked about it the night you came for dinner – and it's really upset her.'

'I'm not surprised,' said Sophie. 'What a dreadful thing – poor man. They haven't caught who did it yet, either.'

'Not that I've heard.'

Mike nodded his head. 'Sick bastards, whoever they are. Sometimes you're frightened to turn on the news.'

'I've been thinking of booking a holiday for us, early, say Easter. Amy loves the sea and it'd be good to go away as a family. The Canary Islands.'

'Lovely idea,' said Sophie, sitting down opposite him and putting her hand over his. 'It'll do you all good. You've looked worn out lately, Robert. You need a break as well.'

'Thing is, she hates putting the dog in kennels and her parents both work or they'd have him. I don't like to ask, but...'

'Say no more. You want us to have the dog for a week. That mad thing that never does as it's told?' Sophie was pulling a face and smiling at the same time. 'Of course we will. Go ahead, book the holiday.'

And for the first time in a while, Robert felt he was coming out from under a cloud. It wasn't just the idea of a holiday. He was making a decision that would put things right, that would somehow make amends for all the difficulties, the wrong turnings, the things unsaid... all the treacherous undertow that hits every marriage at some stage.

It'd be like making a fresh start.

*

'I know we've asked some of these questions before, Catherine, but we need to go over some points again.' DI Stevens sat at the desk in the small, airless room and shuffled his papers that lay in front of him. He regarded her steadily and waited while she tried to compose herself. The woman officer sitting beside him maintained a blank expression on her face, giving nothing away.

Catherine wept silently, tears running down her cheeks, both hands clutching a sodden handkerchief. Bereft. She was beyond caring what they thought. This was all a nightmare that would never end. Jake was gone and she'd loved him so and life would never be the same again.

'Catherine. Would you like a glass of water?'

She nodded her head but couldn't look up. A chair scraped against the floor and a moment later, a glass was put into her hand. She took a sip and could barely swallow.

DI Stevens tried again. 'Catherine, just tell me about your relationship with Jake Harper. You were his girlfriend, you've already told us that. And yet you hadn't seen much of him over the weeks before the fire. Why was that?'

Catherine blinked hard to stop the tears, but nothing worked. Yet she had to find her voice, explain the situation, get this over with. 'We were having a break from each other. Temporary. That was... that was what he wanted. But we were in touch, texting, that sort of thing...' more tears, a sob and a gulping breath... 'Of course, I saw him every day. You work in the same school and you see a lot of each other...'

'His colleague has told us that this *break* was more permanent than that.'

She looked up angrily. 'That'd be Andy Pierce. He didn't know how things were between us. How could he? Jake was a private person. He wouldn't talk about us to anyone else. I don't think I'd pay any attention to what Andy Pierce has told you.'

'All right.' He had been listening intently, seeming to weigh her every word. 'But you were upset that Jake had decided to, let's say, break off the relationship, even though this was temporary.'

'Yes. Yes, upset. At first I thought he might be seeing someone else, but that was just... it was just me being silly.' She rubbed her forehead and took a deep breath. 'We'd been together for at least a year. I'd spend most weekends at his house...'

She stopped. 'These questions! You've asked me the same things before and I've given you the same answers.' She could hear her voice becoming harsh and loud. 'Why are we going over it all again? Unless you think *I* wanted to hurt him.' She stood up, leaning against the table and towering over the policeman. He didn't flinch, just stared at her. 'You really think *I* could do something as awful as this? The man I love is dead and you're accusing me...!'

'No-one is accusing you, Catherine. If that was the case, you'd have legal representation and you'd be under caution.' DI Stevens stood also. 'I'm sorry if this line of questioning seems insensitive to you. All we're trying to establish is what happened and why. And you were the one person who can help with this.' His voice softened. 'Please sit down and we can get this over with as soon as possible.'

Catherine sat, shaking with fury, tears streaming down her face.

'We have no idea whether this arson attack was a vengeful action that went horribly wrong, whether it was a random act or what the motivation was,' he continued. 'No-one was meant to die, in all probability. Putting oily rags through a door isn't uncommon and it doesn't often end in tragedy. But sometimes it does. There are many possibilities. A pupil at the school, an ex-pupil, an enemy he might have had. Is there anyone you can think of who would want to harm him? You were close to him, so you more than anyone would know.'

Catherine felt some relief that he'd decided to change tack. He was doing his job, she thought, wearily and I'm too heartbroken to think logically. She just wanted to leave, stop all this *dissecting* of her personal life, go home and grieve. Shut herself away.

It wasn't even midday, she realised. She had no idea how long they'd keep her here, how many more questions they were going to torture her with.

It'd gone too far. She'd lost him. Nothing could make up for that.

'Anyone who had a grudge against him?' DI Stevens prompted.

She sighed. 'There's no one I can think of. There really isn't. Everyone liked him. He was a good man, a good teacher... fond of his family. You'll have heard the same things from them...'

'Yes. We've talked to his family. But they're in Leeds and you're here. So you'd know...'

'There is no one who'd want to harm him.' Catherine felt a stab of fear as he stared at her, his gaze penetrating as though he could see into her mind. Did he know about the photograph she'd taken of the house? That she'd been keeping watch? Had someone seen her and told the police?

She took a drink of water, waiting for the next question.

'You've said you thought he might be seeing someone else.'

She looked over at the woman constable who had yet to utter a word. 'It was just me being a bit jealous.' As soon as she said it, she knew they'd take it the wrong way. 'Not really jealous, just puzzled that it was taking so long for us to get back together. I was looking for a reason...'

'So you had no proof of this other person.'

'No. I was... anxious, I suppose. Naturally.' She gave a nervous laugh. All wrong again, but it felt as though her nerves were taut wires that were about to snap. She wanted more than anything to get out of here, away from this horrid little cell-like room and this horrid little man. God, what did he want from her? There was something he wasn't saying, something behind all these questions that she'd answered once, something lurking and dangerous that he was withholding till... what?

'You've told us you helped to run a youth club with Tony Parr.'

'Yes, every Wednesday in term time. But Jake had nothing to do with that. He only went once to a talent concert we'd organised. Why do you ask about that?'

DI Stevens tapped his pencil on the table. He looked thoughtful for what seemed to Catherine a long moment. 'I have someone in the next room, Catherine, who has suggested that you know more about this than you're saying. Do you know who that might be?'

She stared at him, mouth open in astonishment, unable to find her voice. There was ringing in her head and in her ears and she could feel her heart pounding in her chest. This couldn't be happening, it couldn't be true, this hateful man was making it all up. To scare her.

He repeated the question. 'Do you know who that might be?'

'I have no idea.' Her hands gripped the table. 'I haven't done anything. I don't know what or who you're talking about.' She was clenching her jaw so tightly, her teeth hurt. 'Whoever it is, is a malicious liar.'

'His name is Lucas Hetherington.'

She stared at him.

'I believe you and he met a week ago, at a bus stop. You were out running. You had quite a long conversation. Is that true?'

She couldn't speak.

'He remembers virtually every word you said to him that night. About how people sometimes needed to be taught a lesson. I quote: "those who hurt others need a shock to bring them to their senses then they realise the damage they've done." Is that near enough?'

'Yes, but I didn't mean...'

'Perhaps you didn't. But Lucas believed you did. Impressionable, see. He's a mixed up boy. A troublesome family life and a loner. He seems to have thought a lot about you in one way or another. The only one who was kind to him, those are his words. And he'd heard how upset you were when your boyfriend left you. So, in his mind, he thought he was doing you some sort of favour.' DI Stevens sighed and gestured the futility of it all with his hand. 'He didn't mean to kill Jake Harper, of course. He wanted to "teach him a lesson". But things like this can get out of control and you get consequences you hadn't thought of. Certainly, *he* hadn't thought of them. All he kept saying was. "I did it for her".'

Catherine closed her eyes and lowered her head. 'Oh, my God.'

She wanted, more than anything, to go back in time and stop the clock ticking. Change the course of events, behave differently and save a life.

But one unguarded moment, one instinctive reaction can cause a ripple, like a pebble thrown into a stream, which spreads out and beyond, its path irrevocable, touching those it was not intended to reach.

That's the truth of it. And the sadness of it all.

ABOUT THE AUTHOR

The author has spent her working life in journalism and education. Originally from Manchester, she now lives in a small village in County Durham with her husband, two dogs and two horses. She has an MA in Creative Writing.

Printed in Great Britain
by Amazon